25

Stories
Unsuitable
for Children

Edward Hulton

Peahen
Publishing

To Caroline, Ned and Johnny

One day I left my car at the Forum car park in Cirencester. On my return I was surprised to find a hardback book of ghost stories on the car bonnet. After a moment's thought, I put the book on a low wall nearby and drove off.

When I told a friend of mine about this later, he said I should have accepted the book – it had been intended for me. This was one reason for writing these stories. If you enjoy reading them, then you are lucky. And if you're unlucky?

You will have nightmares...

First published in the UK in 2021 by Peahen Publishing
www.peahenpublishing.com

Copyright © 2021 Edward Hulton

Designed by Nicola Moore
Illustrations by Darran Holmes

ISBN: 978-1-9161282-9-3

A CIP catalogue record for this book
is available from the British Library

Printed and bound in the UK

www.25stories.co.uk

Peahen
Publishing
Bringing your stories to life

25

Stories Unsuitable for Children

Edward Hulton

∿ Contents ∾

ONE

Chufty-Pufty

Chufty-Pufty was a very old engine. He was a steam engine, with a fire in his boiler lit by coal. Two men needed to work him - a driver, and also a fireman, who shovelled the coal. The manager of the railway had decided to replace him. Instead they were going to have a diesel, which has a motor like in a lorry or bus.

"I can't afford to be sentimental," said the manager, "after all, this is a business."

He was right, in a way. First you had to light Chufty-Pufty's fire in the morning with straw, waiting ages while he was raising steam to get enough strength to pull his train. And sometimes you had to put his fire out and empty all the ash out of his boiler, like cleaning out the grate at home. Also, unlike with a diesel, they had to pay two men to operate him. His driver, George, was quite old and about to retire, but his fireman, Stan, was a young man. He had already been on a training course to drive diesels.

"Much cleaner and more efficient, the diesels," he'd say. "You just turn the key and you're off. None of that smoke

9

and soot, and no more shovelling!"

"Yes, but nothing beats a fried egg on a hot shovel," George would reply.

Chufty-Pufty was going into a museum, and George was to help them put him on display. He'd have a few feet of rails fixed to the museum floor and a sign saying what 'Class' of engine he was, and where and when he was built. He had already been scheduled to finish work, but the new diesel hadn't yet arrived. He was being shipped from Germany and there had been some trouble at the docks. So, Chufty-Pufty was being kept on to do 'light duties'.

One day, George came out of the manager's office with a piece of paper in his hand. He showed it to Stan, who had just finished building up Chufty-Pufty's fire.

"This is our route map," he said. "We've got to go to this siding right out in the country with some old trucks to be scrapped."

They steamed off and reached the line of trucks – four coal waggons, a tank truck, and a wooden box van that smelt of cattle. Stan got down and coupled them on. They were hard to budge, as if they knew they were going to the scrap heap.

"Come on, Chufty!" said George.

With a spurt of effort and brown smoke shooting from his funnel, he got the trucks rolling with a jolt. Their rusty wheels grinding and graunching, they made their way onto the main line. It was a fine day, quite windy, and they were making a good speed over the smooth shiny rails. Chufty-Pufty wondered what life would be like inside the museum, with no steam in his boiler, being stared at by people all day.

When they got to the junction, the signalman, who was an old friend of George, waved and switched them onto the branch line. This went to Bigglestone-on-Sea, and years ago, Chufty-Pufty would pull trains there full of children and holidaymakers. After some time, George turned off steam, put on the brakes, and stopped the train.

"This must be Eversley Junction," he said, looking at the piece of paper. "We get off the branch line here."

There was no signal box, so Stan got down and moved the point lever. As they went off down the line, Chufty-Pufty couldn't actually remember ever going down there before. After a few miles they came to another junction. As George leant out of the cab, the piece of paper blew out of his hand. He quickly put on the brakes and jumped down but the paper was already flying away across the fields.

"Where to now?" asked Stan. There were three tracks to choose from, the third one a few yards further on.

"I'm sure it's this one," said George, pointing to the left-hand track. They reached the next set of points.

"Now where?" said Stan.

"If only we hadn't lost the map," said George bitterly.

"No trackside telephone," muttered Stan. "Stupid… should have brought my mobile. We could have rung up the manager's office for directions."

"I'm pretty sure it's the right-hand one," said George.

"You're guessing," said Stan, "and that's unprofessional."

"Well, if we're wrong we'll just have to back up again

11

down the line," said George.

"I hope you know what you're doing," said Stan as he got down from the cab to pull the point lever. It was stiff and he had to put his back into it. The points moved with a clunk.

"Can't have been changed for years," he said.

The train moved slowly down the rusty lines. The track was covered with weeds, and sometimes you couldn't even see the rails. And somehow Chufty-Pufty knew they had made the wrong choice. On and on they went, at half speed. The countryside seemed to get strange and lonely.

"This can't be right," said Stan, "we should stop and back up to the points."

"No, we're fine," said George. "I had a good look at the map when I left the office. I'm sure it was left then right after Eversley Junction."

Stan looked worried. "We're getting low on coal. Water not too good either."

"We'll be able to fill up when we get to the siding," said George confidently.

Ahead there were some gates closed across the line. It was a level crossing. They stopped and Stan got down to open them. Their rusty hinges creaked.

"I'm not getting on again!" he shouted up, "this is crazy. We're lost, aren't we? And soon we'll be out of steam too."

"There's a job to be done and I'm going to finish it," said George firmly.

"It's all right for you, you're retiring soon," said Stan, "but I've got a whole career ahead of me. I'm off. I'm going to catch a bus or hitch a lift back to the depot."

"Just you and me now, Chufty," said George as they passed over the crossing. He looked back. Stan had closed the gates again and was walking down the road.

They carried on, now going through some woods.

"We must be getting there soon," thought George. Chufty-Pufty was beginning to feel tired. George took a look at the steam pressure gauge. It was getting lower. He let some more water into the boiler and looked in the tender. There was almost no coal left.

"Got to do two jobs at once now," he muttered, as he stoked up the fire.

After the woods there was a cutting, then a tunnel.

"Nothing about this on the map," said George to himself.

It was pitch black inside, and smoke and cinders from the funnel blew into George's eyes. Then Chufty-Pufty started slowing down. George looked at the gauge. The steam pressure was really low. The tunnel widened out and there was now another track alongside them.

By now Chufty-Pufty felt really weak.

"Come on, Chufty,'" said George, "try your hardest." But they were running out of steam.

"We're not going to make it," he realized, "I should have listened to Stan. We're going to get stuck in the tunnel."

Then George had an idea. He jumped down and disconnected the trucks. That made it easier for Chufty-Pufty and they steamed off again. But soon the tiredness came back. The pressure gauges showed one degree above zero. Chufty-Pufty was now so weak he could only manage to go at walking speed.

Then he heard some voices. On the next door track was a long line of engines, buffer to buffer. Some of them Chufty-Pufty could recognize – he'd missed them at the depot and wondered what had become of them.

"It's no good, Chufty," said one of the engines. "You'll never get out of here."

"Don't you see? It was a trick," said another. "It wasn't the trucks they were going to scrap, it was you."

Chufty-Pufty looked round. What was once a mighty gleaming express engine was now a rusty derelict wreck.

"What's the point in struggling? You know they don't need you anymore. Come and join us. We can talk about old times."

For a moment Chufty-Pufty was tempted to do what they said and give up. Then he thought, "However boring it might be in that museum, at least I'll be seeing people and children. Better than spending the rest of my days rotting away in this gloomy graveyard."

He summoned his very last ounce of strength. With his pistons and connecting rods aching with tiredness he inched forward.

"Chufty! Don't leave us! We need you," begged the engines. "Please stay!"

But George had collected the few remaining bits of coal dust in the tender and put them on the fire.

"Come on, Chufty," he urged, "one final effort."

With his very last breath of steam Chufty-Pufty pulled away. Then there was a chink of light shining through the darkness. It got bigger and bigger. It was daylight showing through cracks in a wooden door.

"Don't stop now, Chufty," said George.

Chufty-Pufty rammed it with his buffers. There was a crash of splintering wood and they were out in the open again.

"Phew!" exclaimed George, rubbing his eyes.

Now the line sloped downhill and they could coast to the bottom. Though exhausted and quite out of steam, Chufty-Pufty was relieved to have got away from that awful place.

"Maybe something to do with the War," thought George. They rolled to a stop.

"What now, Chufty?" he asked, as he looked at the fire. It was a dull, dark red glow and going out. Leaning out of the cab George smelt something. Sausages. There was a little hut by the track and smoke was billowing out from the tin chimney. He jumped down and knocked on the door.

"Come in," said a thin old voice. George opened the door and went in. An old man in dark blue overalls and a railway cap was sitting by a stove.

"Like a cup of tea? Have some sausages – just cooked them," he said, looking up.

"Thank you," said George. After all he'd been through, he felt quite hungry.

He told the old man everything that had happened.

"Oh, no one ever comes here nowadays. Been no train here for years. I'm the Track Superintendent, you know.

Don't know why they still employ me. No – no trains here anymore."

George told him they were stuck.

"Out of coal, eh? Ooh no, that won't do, will it?" said the old man putting his kettle on the stove. "Nearest coaling station Bigglestone Junction."

George asked him how far that was.

"Three and a half miles," replied the old man.

"Well, I'll have to walk it, I suppose," said George.

"Wait a minute," said the old man, "have another cup of tea." He got up and shuffled through a door at the end of the hut. A moment later he returned with an old sack.

"Prime coal, this. You can cook well with it," he chuckled, "never know when it might come in handy. And you can use that water butt outside."

George thanked him, got up onto Chufty-Pufty, and poured the sack of coal into his fire. Then he filled some buckets from the water butt and emptied them into the tender. The steam gauge started to move up.

"One more thing," said the Superintendent. He went over to an old signal, by the hut, set at 'danger'. He pulled a lever and with a clunk it dropped to 'go'.

With brown smoke coming from his funnel Chufty-Pufty steamed off, and George waved goodbye. After some time they were on smooth shiny rails again, and soon reached the terminus at Bigglestone-on-Sea. George got down and used the Stationmaster's phone to report to the Manager.

"Call in at the office when you get back," he said.

On arrival at the yard George said goodnight to Chufty-Pufty and knocked at the office door.

"How on earth did you end up at Bigglestone?" asked the Manager. "You just had to uncouple the trucks at the scrap yard, then at the next points, reverse past them on the loop line and return here through Eversley Junction."

"I didn't see any scrap yard or loop line," said George, "only a straight track ahead."

He then told him about the tunnel, the derelict engines and the old superintendent in his hut. The Manager gave him a strange look.

"George," he said, "after the scrap yard it's the end of the line. Just sidings and buffers."

He knew the old engine driver was close to retirement and wondered if he had gone a bit potty and was starting to imagine things. But at home that evening he consulted his book on the history of the railway. The track had orignally continued on through a tunnel. In World War II the tunnel was used as a shelter for locomotives, then it was heavily bombed in an air raid. It caved in and all the railwaymen in it were killed and the engines destroyed. After the War the rails were taken up a short distance past the level crossing.

That was the end of Chufty-Pufty's adventure. Well, not quite. The Manager was so impressed that he had some special track laid running out of the end of the museum, to join up with the railway. So now, once a year, George and Chufty-Pufty take an excursion train full of children to Bigglestone-on-Sea.

TWO

The Barometer

We've always lived in London, though actually I'm only half English. My mother, who is Swiss, met my father while he was in Switzerland climbing mountains. That's what I'd like to do when I grow up. I've read lots of books about things like Whimper and the Matterhorn.

I like collecting things, especially if they're scientific.

I've got a compass, a brass sextant, and a thermometer that records maximum and minimum temperatures. So when my Aunt, who lives in Geneva, asked me what I wanted for Christmas, I said a barometer.

One day a parcel arrived with Swiss stamps on it. It was a small square cardboard box. When I opened it on Christmas day, and had got rid of all the paper padding inside, I found a little chalet.

"Oh! It's a musical box!" I said. A friend of mine has got one. You wind it up, open the roof, and a little dancer twirls round and round to a tinkling tune, called 'The Blue Danube'.

But no, in fact it was a barometer, though not the usual kind with a dial and a pointer. The upper floor of the chalet was like a normal house, with two windows, but the ground floor was an empty square hole, with a pillar in the middle.

"I don't see how it works," I said.

"Let's put it in the kitchen, on the windowledge," said my mother.

"Keep the box," said Dad.

I looked at the instructions. There was also a guarantee. And a warning from the makers, Huber A.G., Solothurn: *Dismantling of the product voids the warranty.*

Next day it was rather cloudy, then it started raining. I took a look at the chalet. A man had come out of the ground floor. He was holding an umbrella. I showed this to Susie (she's my little sister).

"Perhaps he's got a wife," she said.

A day later the man had gone. Then the sun started shining. A lady came out, with a parasol.

I became more and more fascinated by the chalet. Every morning, at breakfast, I would go into the kitchen to look at it. You'd never know which person you'd see, and sometimes there'd be nobody.

I started to keep a log.

'R' meant rain (the man), 'F' stood for fair (the lady), and 'N' was for nobody (or neutral weather).

"Why can't the man and the lady come out at the same time?" asked Susie.

What a stupid question! How can it be both good and bad weather? Girls have got no logic! And no knowledge of engineering either. The man and the lady stood on a wooden bar, which was obviously on a pivot behind the central pillar. To see both of them together you'd have to break into the chalet. Which I'd never dream of doing (unlike some of my friends, who always end up wrecking their toys).

I began to know the barometer quite well. The man wore a hat, a red waistcoat, brown knee breeches and green stockings. He had a black umbrella. The lady wore a blue dress over a white blouse, with a pink apron, and carried a yellow parasol.

I also noted the details of the chalet itself. There was a chimney and also stones on the roof. (In Switzerland many chalets have wooden roof tiles, and the stones are there to stop the wind blowing them off). There was a front garden with flowers growing, and on one side a woodpile with an axe lying on top.

The first floor had a balcony, and two windows. Between the lace curtains you could just see a man's head in one, and a woman's in the other.

The trouble was that Susie also began to take an interest in the barometer. She started picking at the stones on the roof.

"Leave it alone! It's mine!" I shouted.

Then one morning I came down to inspect the barometer and record the reading. Something looked different. The axe wasn't there any more.

"Susie! You've been touching my barometer!" I screamed. Then I saw the axe lying on the kitchen floor. Well, luckily it wasn't lost (it could have easily ended up in the vacuum cleaner). As I was already late for school I picked it up and left it in the front garden of the chalet. I was going to buy some model makers' glue and stick it back onto the woodpile when I got home. But for some reason I put off doing it for a while.

It was summer now and it was getting warmer. Although it had been raining recently, it started to get drier. The man went back into the chalet, and I expected the lady to come out soon. Next day it was really sunny. But there was no sign of the lady. The weather forecast talked of a heatwave. But still no one appeared in the chalet.

I realized that something was wrong. I turned on Susie.

"You've broken it! You knocked it off the windowledge, didn't you?"

"No, I didn't," she said.

"Liar!" I shouted. She started crying.

Well, perhaps Susie was telling the truth. But what was wrong with the barometer? The pivot must be jammed. I resisted the idea of prising out one of the figures with a blunt knife and squirted a few drops of oil behind the central pillar.

"You should wait a day or two for the oil to penetrate the mechanism," said Dad.

Next day it was very hot, but no sign of the lady - proof that the barometer really was broken. The weather was very close, and in the evening we heard thunder in the distance. That night there was a violent thunderstorm. The whole house shook, and we thought we might have been struck (luckily we've got a lightning conductor). Through my bedroom curtains you could see forked lightning.

Next morning when I had my usual look at the chalet to record the log, the man was back. So at least half of the barometer worked.

On my way back from school I remembered to stop at Humberts Model Shop. It's full of electric trains, model aeroplanes, and armies of toy soldiers. I bought a tube of plastic cement.

After tea I went over to the chalet to glue the axe back onto the woodpile. But it wasn't in the front garden, where I'd left it.

"Susie!" I screamed.

"Nothing to do with me," she said pertly.

Mum came into the kitchen. "How dare you shout at her like that!" she said.

I told her I suspected Susie had picked the axe off the woodpile. Now that I'd got the glue it was really frustrating it was lost.

"Well, perhaps it fell on the floor," suggested Mum.

So I spent half an hour on my hands and knees looking under the kitchen table and chairs, and behind the curtains. Or maybe Tinkerbelle, the kitten Susie got for Christmas, had been playing with the axe and had dropped it somewhere.

"Anyway, you shouldn't have left it loose like that," said Mum, "it would have been safer in the kitchen drawer."

So I would either have to do without the axe or make another one. This would be a fiddly job – I'd have to get some balsa wood from Humberts, cut it to shape, paint it and glue it back on. I went to bed in a really bad mood.

When I woke up the next morning the sun was pouring through my bedroom curtains. After breakfast I had a look at the barometer. Lo and behold! The lady was back.

"Mum!" I shouted, "it's working again! The barometer! Do you remember how only the man would come out?"

"Oh yes," said Mum, spreading some marmalade on her toast.

"Well, now the lady's here again."

Susie was eating her cornflakes and stroking Tinkerbelle.

"It's not the same lady," she said suddenly.

"What do you mean?" I asked in surprise. Susie really was crazy.

"Her clothes are different."

To be honest, I couldn't remember much about them. But Susie said that the blue dress on *this* lady had tiny white spots on it, and also her apron was orange.

First I put this down to Susie's imagination. But she *did* have a collection of dolls and was always changing their clothes. So she must have been interested in this kind of thing.

Next day it was cloudy, and the man came out.

"What about *him*?" I asked.

"He's the same."

I didn't think much about the barometer for the next few

days, except to write the morning log. But one day I didn't have school and I sat in the kitchen and took a careful look at it. The lady had come out that day. I thought of what Susie had said. Of course she was pulling my leg, in revenge for my accusing her about the axe.

Or *was* she joking? Two silly thoughts came into my mind: Either the lady really *had* changed her clothes – but how could a wooden toy do this? Or...it was another lady.

I had another look at the chalet. The first floor balcony had holes cut into it in the shape of hearts. In the left-hand window was a man's head. But in the right-hand one there was nothing.

Mum came into the kitchen.

"Why don't you do your homework now?"

"Aw Mum!" I protested.

But actually she was right. We had been given loads of homework. Mr Robbins, our maths teacher, was ill at the moment but he'd still been emailing it to us. "And don't think that because I'm in hospital you'll get away with it."

When I went to bed that evening I couldn't stop thinking about the barometer. Though I couldn't put my finger on it, something wasn't quite right. I woke up in the middle of the night. I was dead sure that something dreadful had happened in the chalet. I sat up in the darkness and put all the facts together. The lady was different. Had she been replaced by the one in the upstairs window? Anything to do with the man? And what about the axe?

I took the torch out of my bedside table and crept

downstairs. I got my model makers' screwdriver and went into the kitchen. I was going to solve the mystery and open up the chalet.

I had just picked it up when something furry jumped at my face. Tinkerbelle! I dropped the chalet and it crashed onto the kitchen floor.

The door opened and the light went on. It was Mum.

"What on earth are you doing? Get back to bed at once! You've got school tomorrow."

When I came down to breakfast the next morning there was nothing on the windowledge.

"The barometer!" I screamed, "where is it?"

"Oh, Dad's taken it to the Post Office on his way to work," said Mum, "to go back to Switzerland. We can get a new one under the guarantee."

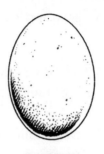

THREE

Elsie

Elsie lived in a village in Southern Germany called Schwemmingen. Her parents had a small farm. As he could not afford to employ any help, her father did all the work himself. Her mother kept chickens, and they made some extra money selling the eggs.

One Sunday, Elsie's mother told her to collect up the eggs and take them to the market.

"Don't break any, and make sure you get the right money for them," she said, wagging her finger.

The market was in Obersdorf, a town across the river. The river was a raging torrent, as there had been a lot of rain recently. The bridge was in bad condition and Elsie was nervous of crossing it.

When she got back to Schwemmingen, Elsie took a short cut through the village field. It was next to the Rathaus (the Town Hall). There were plans to cut down all the trees and bushes in it and make it into a municipal park.

Elsie climbed over the fence, something she would not have done if her basket had been full of eggs. But now it just contained the money. She was almost over the fence when her dirndl got caught, and she fell head over heels. When she picked herself up she found the basket on its side. All the money had rolled out.

"Mother will be furious," she said to herself.

Elsie got onto her hands and knees and carefully looked for the coins through the long grass. When she counted them she found there was one missing. Crawling around to look for it she came to a small bush. Under it was something large, white and shiny.

At first Elsie thought it was a mushroom, but getting closer she saw it was an egg. An enormous egg, the biggest she had ever seen! No hen could have laid an egg that huge. And it wasn't a duck's or even a goose's egg. Elsie knew, because once some Canada geese had landed on the village field and laid some eggs.

Though she knew you shouldn't ever disturb birds' eggs, Elsie picked it up. It was surprisingly heavy. Then she put it to her ear, tapped it a bit and shook it. Suddenly there was a clap of thunder. A huge giant was flying through the sky, and landed next to her. In sheer terror she nearly dropped the egg.

"Take great care of that – my heart is in there," said the giant, pointing to the egg.

His deep voice boomed. Elsie, trembling, stared at him in disbelief.

"Don't be frightened, little girl," he said. "I'll do anything for you as long as you look after my heart."

Elsie drew back a bit and looked at the giant. He had

a thick brown beard and was as tall as a house. He was smiling. Elsie found that he wasn't quite as frightening as she'd first thought.

"I...I'm sorry I picked up your heart, Mr Giant," she stammered. "I thought it was an egg."

The giant slowly sat down on the grass. He told her that a witch had been very jealous of his mother and had put a spell on her baby. They discovered that its heart was not in its normal place but in an egg.

"So all my life I've had to look after it carefully," he added.

Elsie was about to offer to put the egg back under the bush when she remembered that they were soon going to clear the village field.

"You can't leave it here any longer," she said. And she and the giant wondered where it could be kept safely.

It was finally agreed that Elsie would take the egg home and look after it herself.

"If you ever need me, just tap it lightly, three times," said the giant. And in a whirlwind he was off.

Elsie stood there rubbing her eyes, thinking it was just a dream. But she still had the egg in her hand. She carefully hid it under a piece of checked cloth that lined her basket, and put all the coins in the pocket of her apron.

When she got home her mother asked why she'd been so long.

"And why's your dirndl so muddy?"

But when she saw the money from the eggs her eyes lit up. While she was busy counting it on the kitchen table,

Elsie quietly took the basket upstairs into her bedroom. She took the egg from under the checked cloth, wrapped it in one of her jumpers, and put it under her bed.

Just then she heard the front door open and the sound of heavy boots. It was her father coming in from the fields.

"I'll really have to do something about the barn. Half the roof is falling down," she heard him say to her mother.

"You'll never get round to it," she replied. She considered her husband lazy and unambitious, and would have rather married a more successful man, like Herr Müller, the landlord of the Gasthaus (the Tavern). That was where her husband spent much of his evenings drinking beer.

"I'll get Beckmann to have a look at it," he said.

He was the builder, and his son Klaus was one of Elsie's friends.

Next morning was Monday, and, as usual, Elsie got up early to go to school.

"Hurry up," said her mother, who was already in the kitchen.

Elsie finished her breakfast and picked up her satchel. She was about to go out when her mother called after her.

"I'm cleaning your room today. I hope it's tidy, with all your clothes folded up neatly and put away."

Elsie suddenly remembered the egg. She tore upstairs two steps at a time.

"What's gotten into you?" asked her mother angrily. "You'll be really late now. I don't want any more complaints from Fräulein Bullmeier."

"My project – I forgot it!" Elsie shouted down.

She took the jumper from under her bed and put it carefully in her satchel. But there wasn't quite enough room. Fearing that the egg might get squashed, she took out her French Grammar. Then she went downstairs and out of the front door.

When she got to school, class was just beginning. It was French. Monsieur Ménard was pointing to the blackboard. When no one was looking, Elsie took the jumper out of the satchel and put it in her desk.

"And today we are doing ze verbs – second conjugation," said Monsieur Ménard. "Turn to page 35 in your grammars."

He looked around the class.

"Elsie, you not have your grammar? Zen you share with Trudi."

Elsie moved her desk up to her neighbour's. Trudi was the friend of Günter, the butcher's son. He was big, strong and a bully. The next lesson was biology. When Trudi opened her desk it was still up against Elsie's, and its lid caught with hers and opened it too.

"Ooh, I like your jumper," said Trudi, "can I see it?"

Before Elsie could stop her she was tugging at the sleeve. The egg rolled out into the desk. Just then Fräulein Bullmeier came into the classroom. Elsie immediately slammed down the lid. But this attracted Fräulein Bullmeier's attention.

"What have you in there, Elsie?" she asked, coming over and opening the desk.

"An egg! Such a fine one too! From a goose? Or maybe

an ostrich?"

She took it to her desk in the front of the classroom and held it high for everyone to see.

"Quite appropriate, as today we study Reproduction," she said jubilantly.

And all Elsie could do during the lesson was to hope that she wouldn't give the egg a tap.

At the end of class Fräulein Bullmeier gave back the egg, and she wrapped it again in the jumper and put it back in the desk.

But that afternoon, after school, Elsie decided it would be safer to take the egg home with her and find another place to keep it there. On her way home, when she reached the village field, Klaus caught up with her.

"That egg was amazing!" he said, "where did you find it?"

"Over there," she replied, pointing to the bush.

"Have you got it with you?" he asked.

"Er, yes," she said meekly, then immediately regretted it.

"Can I see it?" he ventured.

"Well, it's all carefully packed up in here," said Elsie, pointing to her satchel.

"Oh, go on," he insisted. "I promise I'll be really careful."

In the village Klaus was generally considered 'mature and responsible'. Once when the church windows needed to be repaired, he had helped his father remove and replace the delicate stained glass. Elsie took out the egg and handed it to him.

"Wow!" he said, holding it up to the light. Then he slowly

moved it up and down in his hand. "It's heavy!"

"Please don't shake it," said Elsie in alarm, "and DON'T tap it!"

"Why? Is there a chick inside?" asked Klaus, smiling.

"You'd never guess," she replied.

They heard footsteps and turned round. Trudi and Günter, hand in hand, were coming towards them.

"Oh! The egg! Can we have a look?" asked Trudi.

"No," said Elsie, "not really."

"Well, Klaus is allowed to see it, so why can't we?" argued Trudi.

"I just don't want everyone handling it, that's all," said Elsie.

"Frightened we'll break it, eh?" said Günter. "Anyhow, you've got plenty more at home."

"No, this egg's different," said Elsie.

"Come on, let's get out of here," said Klaus. He was handing the egg back to Elsie when Günter cut in and grabbed it. He held it high in one hand and ran round in circles clucking.

"I've laid an egg! I've laid an egg!"

Elsie screamed.

"You give it back at once, or I'll smash your face in!" shouted Klaus, charging at him.

But Günter sidestepped. "Catch!" he said, throwing it to Trudi. "I know, it's from the goose that laid the golden egg!"

"I'm tired of this," said Trudi, "let's give them back their egg and go home."

She was about to hand it to Elsie when Günter took it again.

"A most valuable specimen," he said, holding it up and mimicking Fräulein Bullmeier. "When I tap this egg the embryo within will experience the sensation. Now: one, two, three."

Klaus grabbed him, but it was too late. There was a clap of thunder and the giant appeared in a cloud of smoke. Günter and Trudi ran away screaming.

At first Klaus was terrified, but then he saw that Elsie did not appear alarmed.

"I'm sorry, Mr Giant, I didn't mean to disturb you," said Elsie.

"It was not your fault. Those stupid children," said the giant.

Elsie quickly explained it all to Klaus.

"Is there anything I can do for you," asked the giant, "in return for looking after my heart?"

"Er, well no, not really," said Elsie.

"Are you sure?" asked the giant.

"What about your father's barn?" asked Klaus after a moment.

"Klaus!" cried Elsie.

"I'd be delighted to help with anything," said the giant, smiling.

Klaus described the terrible difficulties he and his father would have repairing it.

"No problem," said the giant, and he vanished in a cloud

of smoke.

Meanwhile Günter and Trudi had run home. They told everyone, but of course nobody believed their story.

Trudi's father was Herr Müller, the owner of the Gasthaus.

"What's all this about a giant?" asked Elsie's father as he sipped his beer that evening.

"Oh, just some childish rubbish dreamt up by Trudi," said Herr Müller, pouring some drinks at the bar.

"Günter's been going on about it too," said the butcher.

"Well, you know what children's imagination is like," said Elsie's father.

The men laughed and finished their beer.

When Elsie got home she went straight upstairs to her bedroom and hid the egg under some clothes in her chest of drawers. She was in the kitchen with her mother when her father came in.

"It's amazing!" he cried.

"What's amazing?" asked Elsie's mother. "I know, that you're late for supper again."

"No – the barn! They've finished it already! And I only told Beckmann this morning. And what workmanship!"

"Wait till you get his bill," she said, returning to the stove.

When Elsie went to school the next day she left the egg at home, as she felt it was safer there. When she got into the classroom Trudi was talking about the giant, her blond pigtails shaking with excitement. That afternoon, on the way home, Klaus told Elsie how he'd explained to his father the speedy repairs to the barn without him realizing anything. Passing by the church they saw him on a ladder halfway up the tower.

"You go home, Dad," shouted up Klaus. "I'll do a bit now."

"What a fine boy you are," said Herr Beckmann, mopping his brow. "I couldn't get by without you now. All this, and then there's the bridge to do."

The recent storms had blown the cross off the tower, and also some copper sheeting from its dome. The repairs were at least a full week's work.

Elsie arranged to meet Klaus outside the church at midnight, with the egg.

After supper she went to bed but stayed awake. At half past eleven she got dressed again, and tiptoed past her parents' bedroom. She could hear snoring. She took her key and let herself out of the front door. As she reached the churchyard the clock struck twelve. Elsie shivered, and drew her coat around her. Klaus was waiting for her. He helped her up the ladder. They tapped the egg three times and the giant appeared. Klaus showed him what needed to be done.

When the repairs to the tower were finished they thanked him, and he vanished in a cloud of smoke. But the whirlwind he'd created made one of the bells ring. A light went on in the church.

"Quick, down the ladder!" said Klaus.

They hid behind a gravestone. The parish priest came out of a side door and looked upwards.

"Work of the devil!" he muttered, shaking his head.

"Do you think he saw anything?" whispered Elsie.

"I don't know, but we'd better get home quick," said Klaus.

On her way back from school the next day Elsie noticed several men in their smart clothes, including Herr Beckmann, Herr Müller and her father, going into the Rathaus.

"It's a meeting of the Village Council," Klaus told her.

The following afternoon Elsie was leaning against a big wooden cart left outside the school when Klaus came up to her. He said that at the council meeting the Bürgermeister (the Mayor) had read out a surveyor's report on the bridge. The centre arch was in serious danger of collapse, and unless it was repaired straight away, the bridge would have to be closed.

"But my Dad just can't take on any more work," he added. "He's finding it hard enough to cope as it is." Klaus looked really worried.

"Well, perhaps we could ask the giant – just one more time," suggested Elsie.

They agreed to meet by the bridge at midnight. Elsie would also bring some hot tea in a flask, and Klaus would borrow his father's powerful torch.

As soon as they'd left, Günter's father, who had been underneath the cart checking the axles, went straight to the Gasthaus.

"It's true!" he cried, going up to the Stammtisch (the owner's table), where Herr Müller and Elsie's father sat.

"*What's* true?" asked Herr Müller, putting down his beer.

"About that giant!" said Günter's father, excitedly.

At first the two other men were sceptical. But rumours had been going around the village. Herr Beckmann just could not understand how the repairs were done so quickly. And Fräulein Bullmeier had told everyone about the remarkable egg.

"We must go and tell the Bürgermeister," said Herr Müller gravely.

That night Elsie kept herself awake reading her book. Just before midnight she slipped out of the house. When she got to the bridge there was no one there. It was frightening waiting alone in the dark, and she thought of going back home.

After some minutes she saw the beam of a torch. To her relief it was Klaus. As his parents were still downstairs talking to some people, he had had to climb out of his bedroom window.

They climbed over the parapet and went under the first arch, standing on the edge of the cliff. They could hear the rush of the torrent way below. Elsie undid her parcel, took out the egg, and tapped it three times. The giant appeared.

Suddenly searchlights went on, and the whole place was a blaze of light.

The Bürgermeister's voice rang out, loud and clear: "I claim this as the property of the township of Schwemmingen!"

Then, from behind a bush, out sprang Günter, and he snatched the egg. Dazzled, Elsie looked round, and saw all the men of the village, even the priest, who was busy crossing himself.

"That's my heart in there!" roared the giant.

As the villagers recoiled in terror, Klaus lunged at Günter, grabbed the egg from him, and handed it back to Elsie. She held it close to her.

"Give it over, you little bitch!" yelled her father.

He took her by the shoulders and shook her, while Günter prised the egg from her arms.

There was a violent struggle as Klaus laid into Günter. The egg was dropped. Elsie could only watch helplessly as it rolled over the cliff and smashed onto the rocks below. With a loud groan and an earth-shaking thud the giant fell down dead.

The Village Council had planned to embalm the body and exhibit it as a tourist attraction, but some men from the government came and carted it away. It can now be seen in the Museum of Anthropology in Munich.

FOUR

Apples

We live in a little town, my sister and I. It's quite cosy, really. Some of the streets are very steep, and have cobblestones. When it's raining they can be very slippery. Once I fell and bruised both my knees. At the top of the hill is the Town Hall and also the church, which has a very high steeple. On Sundays the bells always ring.

One day our mother and father came down to breakfast looking very smart. My mother had on a dress with flowers on it, and my father wore his suit and a hat. They had to go to an important meeting. "It's to see a lawyer," they said.

"What's that?" asked my sister. She's called Bella. Now I know what a lawyer is – I'm two years older. It's a man who sits in an office and talks about the law. He also talks to judges if you get into trouble. They wear funny wigs and long black clothes.

"David, I'm relying on you to look after your sister," said my mother. "I've left some lunch for you both in the fridge."

I felt a bit scared about this. "When are you going to be back?" I asked.

"Oh, about six o'clock," said my father. He put on his hat and my mother picked up her cardigan. Then she said, "Oh yes, we don't mind you going out on the street, but just be careful."

"Yes," said Bella and I.

"If you want to go and buy something – like sweets – we'd rather you went to a shop."

"Why?" I asked.

"Well, it's best not to buy things from people in the street."

Dad picked up his keys. The keyring has got a little Swiss penknife on it. "It's magic," he always says, "it can do anything!"

As the front door slammed I felt a bit uneasy. But why? After all, Bella and I could now do anything we wanted. Except make a mess. There's always a row if Mum comes back and finds a mess. And we're not allowed in Dad's study, upsetting his papers. Though sometimes he *does* let us go in. He'll be in there smoking his pipe. And in one drawer of his desk he keeps chocolate biscuits!

First we watched TV then played some video games. I actually had quite a lot of homework to do, but really couldn't be bothered to do it then.

"Let's go out for a walk," said Bella. So we left the house, remembering to take a key with us. It hangs on a little hook by the door.

It was fun going out, just like that, though I do walk to school every day. I took some of my pocket money with me in case we wanted to buy anything.

"Where shall we go?" asked Bella.

"Let's go up the hill," I replied.

It was a hot day, and pretty soon we started feeling thirsty.

"I want something to drink," said Bella.

Stupidly we hadn't brought any water or lemonade with us.

"Let's get some Coca-Cola," she said.

"I don't think there are any shops around here," I said.

Just then we saw an old woman standing alone, across the street.

She seemed to be smiling at us.

"Look, I think she's waving at us," said Bella.

"Perhaps she'd like us to help her cross the road," I said, noticing she had a stick. We crossed over to her. She was wearing an old brown coat with large pockets in it. Next to her was a big basket of apples.

"Wow, I'd love one of those!" I said. They were big, shiny and juicy-looking.

"Only a penny each," said the old lady.

"Let's get some," I said to Bella.

"Yes, but remember what Mum said." Bella looked worried.

"I'm sure they're all right – they look really nice." I said.

The old lady smiled. I whispered to Bella, "I think what she really meant was not to buy things, like, well, matches from funny old men with one leg."

"Yes, but do you think we really should?" asked Bella.

"You can have two for a penny," said the old lady, "one for each of you."

That seemed a really good deal! I took a penny out of my pocket.

"David!" shouted Bella. The woman gave me the apples. As I took them I thought I heard a faint whispering and a slight tinkling of bells.

I handed Bella an apple. We both sunk our teeth into them. Suddenly everything whirled and went topsy-turvy. We found ourselves in the dark, lying on something soft. Bella and I picked ourselves up. It felt odd because what we were standing on was moving slightly.

"You stupid idiot!" she said. "I told you not to buy those apples!"

"Well, I suppose Mum and Dad were right," I said, bitterly.

When my eyes had got used to the darkness I looked around. I had been right about the whispering. You could clearly hear people talking. We moved around. There was much more room than I'd first thought. In fact you could walk about easily without touching the sides of the soft stuff – was it cloth?

We followed the voices and came to a group of people. Some I recognized like Mr Travis, the baker, the postman, Mrs Williams, and some of the children from school. I saw the Mayor wringing his hands in desperation. And the Vicar. Then I heard the bells.

I turned around. The church, the Town Hall, the whole

street was there.

"Where on earth are we?" asked Bella.

I looked upwards. You couldn't really see the sky, just a dull murkiness. Then I bent down and felt the ground. It wasn't hard, like pavement. It was soft, dark brown and tweedy. Cloth.

Then the horrible truth came to me.

"You know what?" I said. "All of us - the whole town - are in that old woman's pocket."

I heard a rumbling sound and looked round. I saw a huge red and shiny thing like a giant football. It had a fruity kind of smell. It was an enormous apple. Just like the ones I'd foolishly bought, only hundreds of times bigger. Then I saw another and another.

They were rolling all around the streets, and you had to jump out of their way or you'd be run over.

We walked around. Sometimes you'd see people getting up off the ground with a dazed expression. They'd also been tricked into buying the apples.

"What are we going to do?" asked Bella. She began to cry. "What happens if Mum and Dad get back and we're not at home?"

I thought that first they'd be cross, then they'd realize that something was wrong, and would be very worried about us.

"But look," I said. "They were going away to see that lawyer, for a whole day. So perhaps they're somewhere else, and they're not caught in here in the pocket." We then saw some more people we knew, like the man who runs the sweetshop, and Mr and Mrs Herbert.

"Let's see if Mum and Dad are here," said Bella. "Mum! Dad!" we shouted. But they weren't anywhere to be seen.

I heard a loud official voice. "Can you all come over here!" It was the Town Clerk. A group of people were standing outside the Town Hall. In the middle was the Mayor.

"This is a terrible thing that has happened to us," he said, "but we must not, I repeat *not* give up hope. We've got to do our utmost to get out of this predicament."

"What does that mean?" Bella asked me.

"This mess," I answered.

"Can I have all your suggestions?" said the Mayor.

The Vicar came up to him. "We can keep on ringing the bells, in the hope that someone on the outside will hear us. If all of them are rung at once it would be louder."

That was the tinkling I'd heard before we'd eaten the apples.

"Well, with respect, I think we've already tried that," said the Mayor.

Then a policeman came up. "Why don't we all shout together at the top of our voices?"

"Good idea," said the Mayor.

Mr Herbert (he's a teacher and he runs the school choir) said, "We should all shout strictly in unison."

He got out the baton he uses to conduct the choir.

"All right...when I get to 'four', all shout as loudly as you can."

He waved the baton. "Now...one...two...three...four!"

At 'four' everybody simply yelled, and the policeman blew his whistle.

We waited. Nothing happened. Then came something as loud as thunder.

"Heh! Heh! Heh!" It was the old woman cackling. I knew then that we were well and truly caught.

Bella started crying again. "She's a witch, and she's put a spell on all of us."

Of course, I'd read all sorts of things about witches. Nasty old women who live with their cat in a cottage at the end of the village, and who ride on broomsticks at night. Or that Russian one, Baba-Yaga, whose house is on chickens' legs. But I'd thought they were just fairy stories.

"Any more ideas?" asked the Mayor.

I put my hand up. "Er, yes," I said. "Well, I'm not sure it will actually work. Perhaps it's a rather silly idea."

Everyone turned to look at me. "We'd better have it anyhow," said the Mayor nicely.

"Well you know those apples," I said, "perhaps we could use them?"

"I don't understand what the boy means," said the Town Clerk.

"Well, we're all in that old woman's pocket. And we've tried making as much noise as possible, but no one outside can hear us. That's because we're so tiny."

"Yes, yes, come on," said the Mayor impatiently.

"So what we need is something really huge like those

apples."

"I don't get it," said the Mayor.

"If we could only push one of them out of her pocket, it would fall onto the pavement, plop! Like a distress signal."

"What use would that be?" asked the Town Clerk. "First of all, no one might see it, if indeed there's anyone left at all in the outside world. And then surely the woman would just pick up the apple again."

"Yes," I said, "but if we push lots of them out, one after the other, so she's always picking one up and then another one falls out, it would distract her so much that we could all jump out of the pocket."

I was so convinced I was right that I was ready to argue.

"The idea is quite unfeasible," said the Town Clerk. "Those apples are really big and heavy. They must weigh nearly a quarter of a ton each. How on earth could we manoeuvre them up to the edge of the pocket, let alone push them out of it?" He pointed upwards. It was dark brown all the way up, except for a slit of blue sky at the top.

"Any other suggestions?" asked the Mayor, looking around. No one said anything. Some of the women began to cry.

"Wait a minute," said a man, "the lad could be right. I'm the City Engineer. Those apples must each weigh several hundredweight, so we'd need the force of at least a ton to propel them back uphill and over the lip of the pocket."

"You mean use a sort of catapult?" asked the Town Clerk.

"No – if we pushed them up to, say, the top of the church

tower, then let them roll all the way down, they might gather enough momentum to go up the cloth on the other side and out of the pocket."

"Brilliant!" said the Vicar, "but could we get the apples up the staircase? It's narrow and circular."

"Let's give it a try," said the Mayor, "we've got nothing to lose."

They divided the people into four teams. The policeman took down everyone's name into his notebook, and put A,B,C or D next to it. Bella and I were in 'B' Team. Then Colonel Scott (he's got a big grey moustache) read out the names, and everyone got into four lines. Each team went to get an apple, and pushed it slowly up to the door of the church tower.

Now it was our turn. Bit by bit we pushed, manoeuvred and pushed our apple up the tower. The staircase was narrow and cramped, and I felt giddy going round the spiral. Sometimes the apple got stuck, and we had to lever it free with a piece of wood.

After a lot of sweat and a superhuman effort, we got the apple to the top of the tower. Here there was a landing, and above that the bells. You could hear the ticking of the clock. The City Engineer put a chock of wood under each apple, to stop it rolling away.

"Line them up now," said the Colonel. "'A' Team first."

They slowly nudged their apple to the very edge of the top step of the staircase, and chocked it again. The other three teams followed.

"At the sound of the bells, push with all your might," said the Colonel. "It's our last chance." With one hand on the apple I stood and waited.

Suddenly the bells rang – it was deafening. We shoved as hard as we could. The whole tower shook like an earthquake as the four apples charged with a bumpity-bump, one after another, down the church tower.

There was a small window in the tower. I saw the apples come bouncing out of the door at the bottom, down the steps into the street, up the wall of brown cloth, and disappear over the top into the slit of blue. A huge cheer went up!

Then came the thunder again, but this time an angry cursing. Suddenly our world rocked and tilted. Bella and I grabbed a tuft of the brown material and hung on for dear life. We were jolted about violently and then flung out of the pocket. Whizzing through the air we landed on a whole pile of apples.

"Ouch!" I cried, rubbing my eyes, not used to the brightness of the outside world. "Are you all right?" I asked Bella.

"Fine," she said. "It's lucky we didn't land on the pavement."

We had landed in the basket of apples. Other people were picking themselves up. We clambered over to the edge and looked through the holes in the wicker. The apples from the church tower were all rolling down the hill and the old woman was on her hands and knees trying to catch them.

Then we saw two giants coming up the hill. One had a hat on and the other a dress with flowers.

"Mum! Dad!" we shouted.

One of the apples rolled up to Dad and he stopped it with his shoe. He picked it up and took it over to the old woman.

"Oh, thank you, sir," she said.

Mum had picked up three others.

"I'll put them back in the basket," she said. She dropped the apples in – they fell like bombs and we had to rush to the other side of the basket so as not to be crushed.

"Here, let me help you up," she said to the old woman (she's always trying to be kind!).

"Oh, thank you, thank you," said the old witch.

Dad was about to put his apple back into the basket.

"Come on, take a couple," said the old woman, "picked them only this morning." She grinned – her teeth were blackened stumps.

Dad kept the apple in his hand.

"DAD! DON'T!" screamed Bella and I. But I reckon he wouldn't have heard us however hard we'd shouted.

"Well, thank you," said Dad. To my horror he was bringing the apple towards his mouth. The old woman stayed grinning. Then with his other hand, Dad reached into his pocket and took out his keys and penknife (the magic one). He turned to Mum. "Half each, Dear?"

He sliced the apple in two. Suddenly everything went topsy-turvy, a whirlwind, clanging of bells, crashing of stones, shouting of voices – like an explosion. Bella and I found ourselves standing on the pavement near the church. And the Mayor and all the others were there too. But there was no sign of the old woman, just a few apple cores and bits of wicker in the gutter.

We ran into Mum and Dad's arms.

"Do you know what? I think it's time for tea," said Mum, and we all walked home.

***

Strangely, some time later, we were in this secondhand shop. There was a rail with coats hanging from it. One of them I thought I recognized. It was old and brown and had large pockets.

FIVE
Helicopter

The capital of Hungary is Budapest. It is a very beautiful city, and I hope you will visit it some day. But did you know that it is really *two* towns – Buda, on one side of the river Danube, and Pest on the other?

But this a story about something else made of two names – 'helicopter'. Its main rotor, above the fuselage, was called Heli and the small one on the tail was Copter. The helicopter itself was red and white. It could carry up to three passengers as well as the pilot. As it could hover, it was really useful in emergencies and could rescue people. It lived in a hangar with some aeroplanes.

It was a wonderful life. Heli and Copter usually flew in good weather. It was fun flying around the clouds, looking down at the people and houses below, as small as toys. Sometimes they swooped low over the treetops, or over the coastline, and saw the beach and the waves. People would look up and wave at the helicopter as it flew past.

There was only one thing wrong – Copter was insanely jealous of Heli. It all started when the engineer, who came to the hangar once a month, spent longer on his inspection of Heli than on Copter. He would look carefully at Heli's four long slender blades, running his fingers along them in case there were any nicks or dents. Then he would clean and polish them with a special product. Finally he would oil and adjust Heli's complex mechanism. Of course, he also made a careful inspection of Copter. But he needed less time with him, and always dealt with him second.

The trouble started in the hangar, one night.

"It's not fair," said Copter, "you get all the attention."

"Well, I *am* the main rotor, aren't I?" said Heli. "I provide all the lift for us to fly. And when I twist my blades I can also make us go backwards, forwards, sideways, or hover."

"If it wasn't for me we wouldn't be able to fly straight," said Copter.

"If I failed, we'd drop out of the sky like a stone," retorted Heli.

"Well, if anything happened to *me* we'd spin round and round like a top and crash," said Copter angrily.

"Can't you be quiet?" said the propeller on one of the aeroplanes. "We want to sleep."

But Heli and Copter continued arguing.

"Oh do shut up," said the propeller on the old biplane in the corner of the hangar. "I'm really tired." He was made of wood and was over eighty years old, and built well before the War.

The helicopter's next flight was a long one. They flew over the bay. The sun was shining and the air was calm.

Everything was fine until Copter started arguing again.

"You know, I'm just as important as you," he said.

"Well you are, in a way," replied Heli in a superior tone of voice, "but I'm still the main rotor. You see, I'm the principal lifting device that makes this aircraft fly, and I also provide most of the control."

The argument got worse when Heli said that some helicopters didn't even need a tail rotor. These were giant helicopters used by the army, and had two main rotors, one on the front and one on the back.

"That's a lie!" shouted Copter, "it's impossible. No helicopter can function without a tail rotor."

But someone had left an aircraft magazine on the hangar floor and Heli had seen the photographs.

The argument got so loud that the pilot noticed it. First he thought there was something wrong with the engine. He checked all the gauges – temperature, oil pressure, but everything was normal. The noise was like...people talking! Yes. He could even pick out the words. The rotors were talking to each other!

"I must be going mad!" he thought, "perhaps I've been working too hard and not had enough sleep."

He listened some more. But how could two rotors, which, after all, were just pieces of metal, actually know so much?

"Be quiet!" he said, "I'm trying to fly this aircraft."

"I'm sorry," said Heli, "but Copter started it."

To his astonishment the pilot found himself trying to settle the quarrel. He said that each of them played an essential part in keeping the helicopter in the air. He was grateful, and proud of them.

In fact, during the next few flights the pilot and the two rotors enjoyed their talks together. They asked him what it was like to be a human being, and told him how it felt being part of a helicopter. He never spoke to them, of course, when carrying passengers, and always made sure the radio was switched off. Otherwise people would have thought he was mad, and taken away his pilot's license!

One Saturday, it was 'Open Day' at the airfield. Lots of people, some in cars, some in coaches, came to see the aeroplanes.

A party of schoolchildren was standing around the helicopter.

"Look at the rotor blades," said one of them, admiring Heli, "aren't they long!"

"Yes," said the teacher, "and they're flexible too. When they turn round and round it makes the helicopter fly."

"What's that tiny little rotor at the back for?" asked one of the girls.

"I don't know," said the teacher.

After the children had left a furious row erupted between Heli and Copter. It lasted the rest of the afternoon.

The old biplane's propeller sighed. "Oh why can't you two be friends, like the twins?" (These were the propellers on a twin-engined aircraft, also in the hangar. They always got on harmoniously).

A few days later the helicopter had to fly on a rescue

mission. It was in the mountains. A climber had been injured and was to be airlifted to hospital.

They had a long way to go. Half an hour into the flight the arguments began.

"I may be small but I'm important," said Copter, "in fact, I'm essential."

"Yes, but I'm still the main rotor," said Heli.

"I whizz round faster than you," said Copter.

The pilot got fed up with the arguing. When he had finished speaking to Air Traffic Control he switched off the radio.

"Look, we are a team. We all have our separate parts to play in keeping this aircraft in the air. The work we do is really important, and everyone appreciates that."

They were flying over the foothills of the mountains now. There was some turbulence, and the pilot had to concentrate on keeping the aircraft level.

Copter started again. "I suppose you know it's thanks to me we can keep flying straight."

"Oh yes?" said Heli angrily, "and what about *my* part in all this? You seem to think that all I do is turn round and round. Actually my blades are constantly adjusting their pitch to keep us in trim."

"Please stop provoking him, Copter," said the pilot, "it's hard enough flying as it is."

But Copter wouldn't give up.

"OK. I'll show you," he said suddenly, "I'll stop spinning and we'll see how you can cope on your own."

"Are you out of your mind?" cried Heli in alarm.

By a crazy effort of will Copter strained and strained. There was a dreadful graunching sound, then came a hideous CLUNK! Copter had managed to stop himself and had sheared the driveshaft from the engine. The helicopter began to spin round and round, out of control.

"You fool, Copter, you've done it now!" screamed Heli, "that's the end of us!"

"Told you!" laughed Copter insanely.

"Mayday, Mayday," called the pilot on the radio, "we're going down!"

Then they crashed into the mountain.

The outcome of this disgraceful story is that the helicopter was a total wreck. It was written off and scrapped. But I'm glad to say that the pilot escaped with only minor injuries.

When the report of the accident was written, it was put down to mechanical failure.

SIX

Taxi

This is a story that happened to me a long time ago. I still think about it sometimes.

One afternoon my grandfather came to take me to the cinema. I'd been looking forward to it all week.

"There isn't much time - we'd better hail a taxi," said Grandad.

I love riding in taxis, but Mum says it's a luxury, so we normally take the bus or the Underground.

We stood and waited in the street. Each time a taxi went by Grandad waved his umbrella.

"But Grandad, it's got someone in it," I said, "the little light on the roof isn't on."

At last we saw one that was free. It pulled up with a screech of brakes.

"Where to, Guv'nor?" asked the taxi driver.

"The Odeon, Leicester Square, please," said Grandad.

Off we went. I must say, I thought the taxi was going rather fast. I could feel that Grandad was getting nervous. He tapped on the glass division with his umbrella.

"Would you mind driving a bit more slowly?"

But there was no difference. Actually I began to get a bit scared too. We hurtled round corners. I was sitting on the edge of my seat, holding onto Grandad.

"Did you see that?" I said, "I'm sure he went through a red light!"

Grandad tapped on the glass again.

"Will you please slow down!" he shouted.

That had the right effect – too much, rather. The driver slammed on the brakes and stopped dead. He turned round and opened the glass.

"What's wrong then?" he asked, facing us angrily.

"I didn't ask you to stop, only to slow down," said Grandad.

"It's my taxi, and I'll drive it the way I like."

"Look, would you kindly get going again?" said Grandad, "we don't want to be late."

But the taxi didn't move.

"First you want me to stop. Now you want me to go. Make up your bleeding mind, will you?" he said threateningly, "or get out of my cab."

"Yes, I think we will," said Grandad.

We got out onto the pavement. The driver opened his front window.

"That's ten pounds sixty on the meter," he said, leaning over towards us.

"Now look here..." said Grandad. "Not only will you get no tip, but you're getting no fare either. You have been driving most dangerously, risking both my life and that of my grandson."

"Do you mind!" shouted the driver. He leant right out of his window and grabbed Grandad by the collar.

"Let go of me at once," screamed Grandad, "or I'll have you sent to prison for assault!"

He had been a barrister, and sometimes also a judge, called a 'recorder' – then he wore a special wig.

I thought the taxi driver was going to throttle him, but he managed to wrench himself free.

"Come on," said Grandad to me.

We started walking along the pavement. I could hear the driver following us in his taxi, but was too scared to look behind.

Then we saw a bus.

"Quick! Get on!" said Grandad.

Through the bus's back window I could see the taxi still following us, with its lights flashing.

We went past a couple of stops. "Let's get off here," said Grandad suddenly, and he rang the bell.

As we got off the bus I saw the taxi behind us. It began hooting.

"Up these steps!" said Grandad.

It was his club. Just inside the entrance was a porter behind a desk. Grandad said something to him, then we went into a room full of leather armchairs, where some men were reading newspapers.

A waiter brought us some tea and biscuits. It felt really

safe and cosy there. Later, when we left the club, there was no sign of the taxi.

A long time afterwards my parents and I went to the seaside for our summer holidays. We stayed at a cottage called Spring Tide. It was just outside the town.

One day I went shopping with Mum. We usually took the bus back, but this time Mum felt tired and we had loads of heavy shopping, so she said we'd take a taxi.

There was a taxi rank near the supermarket. Three taxis were parked there, one behind the other. Mum went up to the one in front.

"Stop!" I shouted.

"Why?" she asked, surprised.

"It's the nasty taxi driver," I whispered.

"What?"

"The one I had with Grandad!"

"But that was ages ago. In London," said Mum. "Come on now, don't be silly, let's get in."

"But Mum!"

"Look, I'm tired, I want to get back to the cottage."

She went up to the driver's window.

"I'm not getting into that taxi," I said, firmly.

The taxi driver gave me a piercing look.

"Oh all right, we'll use the one behind," said Mum, really annoyed, "anything for a quiet life."

She walked up to the next taxi in the queue.

"I'm sorry, Madam, you'll have to take the cab in front," said its driver.

"I've just about had enough of this!" shouted Mum.

She dragged me up to the first taxi, pushed me inside, and threw in the shopping bags.

"Spring Tide Cottage, in West Street – just after the Esplanade."

Off we went. Although it wasn't a London taxi, just an ordinary car, there was the same bad driving. We swerved round the roundabout on the Esplanade, and nearly hit a van.

"It really *is* him," I said, under my breath.

When we got home I unloaded all the bags and Mum paid the driver. When she gave him a tip, he turned and leered at me.

Later on Dad came in and we had tea.

"David was really stupid today," said Mum, "I was *so* embarrassed."

And she told him the whole story, from her side, of course. When it was my turn, I said I was dead sure it was the same taxi driver. I had had a good look at him when he attacked Grandad.

"How do you explain a London taxi driver being here on the South Coast?" asked Dad.

"Maybe he's on holiday, like us."

"Still driving a taxi?" Dad smiled.

"Well, perhaps he's actually moved here. He got fed up with London – you know, all those fumes and traffic jams."

But Dad insisted in proving his point.

"Look. The incident was over a year ago. That's a long

time for someone of your age. And it was in a completely different part of the country. The odds are against it, both chronologically and geographically."

Dad often uses long words to win an argument.

"I know – perhaps he's got a twin brother!" said Mum, laughing.

There wasn't all that much to do on this holiday. If the weather was good we would go to the beach, and sometimes we had a picnic. But on our last week I was lucky enough to make two friends, Jerry and Mick.

One day I was walking down West Street with them when I suddenly had the urge for some sweets. The others went on while I crossed the road to the newsagents and bought some sherbert lemons. When I came out I saw Jerry and Mick pushing a car. I was about to join in and help when I noticed who was in it.

"Stop!" I shouted, "it's that taxi driver!" (I had told them all about it).

The taxi was making a funny noise

"Just one more push," pleaded the driver, "I'm sure that'll do it."

"No way!" we all said.

"Look, I've been stuck here for an hour, trying to start," he whined. Then he turned to me and his tone changed.

"I'll get even with you," he said menacingly.

And as we walked away the taxi made the funny noise again.

Two days later we went back to London, as the holidays

were nearly over. I was so busy during the Autumn term that I nearly forgot all about it.

One evening, just before Christmas, Mum and Dad had some people over for dinner. Aunt Margaret was there, and also Charles Radford. When it was time to go he offered her a lift home.

"It's really kind of you, but I wouldn't dream of accepting," said Aunt Margaret. "I live in completely the other direction."

She lived a long way past Hammersmith and insisted that we ring for a minicab. We sometimes do use minicabs. We've got a card on the pinboard in the kitchen, but this time Mum rang the number on another card that had just come through our letterbox. It said 'VALUCABS. Airport Hirings a speciality'.

After a while the doorbell rang.

"Thank you for a wonderful evening," said Aunt Margaret as she went through the front door.

She was about to get into the minicab when I saw the driver's face.

"Don't get in!" I screamed.

"Why ever not?" asked Aunt Margaret.

"It's that taxi driver!" I had already told her the story.

"Nonsense!" she said, "I can't keep this man waiting."

"I'm not letting you get in. He's a maniac!" I shouted, standing in front of the passenger door, barring the way.

"Oh, it's you, is it?" said the driver.

Mum and Dad came out.

"What's all the fuss about?" asked Dad.

"Evidently David doesn't want me to get into this cab," said Aunt Margaret, "the child's almost hysterical."

"I think the best thing would be to pay him off," suggested Mum, "we can easily call another one."

Aunt Margaret, Mum and I went back into the house.

"I'm awfully sorry about this," said Dad to the minicab driver, "can I pay you up to now, for your journey here?"

The driver got out of the car and stood on the pavement.

"No. You booked to Turnham Green, and I want my fare."

"Well, I don't think that's quite right," said Dad. He took a five pound note out of his wallet and offered it to him.

"You 'eard what I said." The driver looked quite threatening.

"Take it or leave it," said Dad. He waited for a moment, then still holding the five pounds, went back through the front door.

A minute later there was a loud knocking.

"Don't open it!" said Dad.

I crept along the hallway and looked through the peephole.

"He's still there!" I gasped.

"Oh, I do wish that man would go away, so I can get home!" said Aunt Margaret.

We all sat in the sitting room for about half an hour. Then Dad went to the front door and opened it gingerly.

"He's gone!" he announced, as he came back into the hall.

"Are you sure you won't change your mind about that lift?" asked Charles Radford, "it really isn't that much out of my way."

"Absolutely not. I'm adamant," Aunt Margaret insisted, "I'll get a black cab."

Some people are so old-fashioned!

"Well, the least I can do is go down the street and get you one," said Charles Radford.

"It's your bedtime, David," said Mum, "say goodnight to Aunt Margaret."

"Good night," I said.

"Good night, and thank you for saving me from that horrible man," she said, giving me a kiss.

Later, from my bedroom, I heard the sound of a taxi and the front door slam.

A few days later, at breakfast, Mum was reading her letters.

"Here's one from Aunt Margaret!" she said.

"Read it," said Dad.

Thank you again for a marvellous evening. The food was delicious. Dorothy, you really are such a good cook. And I got home quite safely. Such a polite young man, Charles Radford And David too!

Thank you again
With all love,
Margaret.
P.S. Oh, I almost forgot! The most extraordinary thing. When

I took that taxi home I could swear it had the same driver as the first one!

SEVEN

The Sandman

William lived with his mother and father, and Susan, his older sister, in a very modern house on the outskirts of London.

"Architect designed!" his father would often say.

"And topsy-turvy," would add his mother.

This was because the living area was on the first floor and all the bedrooms on the ground floor.

His parents' and sister's rooms were at the front of the house, facing the street, but his own was at the back. It had two large wardrobes, one of which contained some of his parents' clothes. Opposite the bed were tall French windows, which opened onto the garden. At the far end of this was a gate leading straight out onto the Common.

The French windows were always kept closed except in the summer, when they were left slightly open for ventilation. But their long blue velvet curtains, which stretched from ceiling to floor, were always drawn at night to keep out the light, as William had trouble getting to sleep.

Lack of sleep was beginning to affect his school work. He had several times been caught dozing in class. So his mother took him to the doctor.

"Childhood insomnia can lead to problems later, such as arrested growth and mental development," he said, "but I would not recommend medication until all natural remedies have first been tried."

So William had hot milk and biscuits last thing at night, and his mother told him bedtime stories. If he was still awake at the end of them, he would try things like counting sheep. Getting to sleep was always difficult.

When Susan went away to boarding school they got an au pair. She was called Claudia, and came from Italy.

"I am fat, yes. It is the pasta. In my country we have so many kinds: spaghetti and ravioli, of course, but also lasagna, macaroni, fettucine...".

Claudia had the amazing gift of sending William to sleep. Every evening she would sit on the chair next to his bed.

"I will sing to you – what do you say in English? A lullaby."

Then, in a soft, low voice she would sing songs like, "O Sole Mio" or "Arrivederci Roma". In a few minutes William would be fast asleep.

"Ecco! Now you are sleeping, Bambino," she would whisper as she tiptoed out of the bedroom.

One morning William woke up rubbing his eyes. "There are tiny bits of sand in the corners," he said.

"The Sandman did that," said his mother.

"Who's he?" asked William.

"He comes in during the night and puts sand in children's eyes, to help them get to sleep."

"I've never seen him," William replied.

"Well, he's like Father Christmas, who won't bring you your stocking if you stay awake to see him," said his mother. "The Sandman slips into your room when you're almost asleep. That's why you never see him."

"Is he good or bad?" asked William.

"Good, of course, Darling! He makes sure you get a proper night's sleep."

One day William asked Tom, his best friend, if he knew about the Sandman. He had heard of him, and thought he sounded rather scary. But he believed in Father Christmas, even though some of the older boys at school said he didn't exist.

Then William asked Claudia about him.

"The Sandman? I don't know him."

One afternoon Claudia collected both William and Tom from school. They went home a different way than usual, as she had to do some shopping. On the pavement they saw a large green plastic box, well over a metre square. It was filled with sand.

"Ooh! Can we play in it?" asked William.

"You shouldn't really," said Claudia smiling, "but OK. Try not to get your clothes too dirty."

The boys had a great time making sandcastles and digging tunnels. It was like being at the seaside. William also remembered having a sandpit in the garden when he was very small.

"I wouldn't do that if I was you," said a voice, "Council property."

It was a road sweeper who had been pushing his barrow along the road.

"We're very sorry," said William.

"That's where the Sandman keeps his sand," said the man, leaning on his broom. "Gets awful cross, he does, if anyone ever touches it."

"OK, we go now," said Claudia.

The next day William and Claudia took the same route back from school.

"Can I play in the sand again?" asked William.

"No, remember what that man said yesterday?"

"Oh please, Claudia – just for a bit!"

"OK then – but not too long."

There was no trace of the sandcastles they had made the day before – all the sand had been smoothed out. William climbed into the box and began to build an elaborate castle with a central keep and four towers, while Claudia chatted on her mobile phone. He was so absorbed in it that he failed to notice a van draw up alongside, and a man get out.

"What the bloody hell are you doing in my sand?"

A huge man in a yellow reflective jacket and big brown boots, holding a spade, towered over him. He was very angry.

"This 'ere sand is Council property, and I'm the one in charge of it. I raked it nice and smooth this morning, and now just look what you've done with it!" He was bright red in the face, and shook his spade menacingly.

"I'm very sorry," stammered William, terrified.

"Git out of there. Now!" shouted the man.

William climbed out of the box as fast as he could.

"Stop. You are frightening the child," said Claudia.

"Bloody kids. I bet it was you that messed it all up yesterday. It's a hard enough job keeping them cats out of it."

"You are the Sandman, I suppose?" said Claudia coolly.

She had her arm protectively around William, who was now white and trembling with fear.

"That's right, I'm the Sandman. Now get the bloody hell out of here, and don't disturb my sand no more. If not, there'll be trouble. Real trouble."

"Come on, let's go," said Claudia, holding William by the hand and pulling him away.

"What's more, I know where you all live!" shouted the man after them.

At school that week there was a geography lesson about the Sahara Desert. It had huge sand dunes stretching for miles and miles. If you got lost you would die of thirst. Vehicles sank up to their axles in the sand, and got hopelessly stuck. And if a sandstorm blew up it all got into your eyes, nose and mouth, and could suffocate and even bury you. Whole caravans, with strings of camels and their drivers, had disappeared in this way.

At the end of the lesson William went up to the teacher,

Miss Thompson.

"So is sand a bad thing?" he asked.

"It can be bad, but it is also very useful," she replied. "Don't forget many things are made with sand, such as glass and concrete. And in winter they put it on the pavement to stop you slipping where it's icy."

"And what about the Sandman?" asked William.

Miss Thompson smiled, but said nothing.

That evening William asked his parents more things about sand.

"Well, ostriches hide by putting their heads in the sand," said his mother, "and also there are egg timers. When all the sand has run through the narrow neck from one bubble to another, your egg is ready."

"And all locomotives have a sand box," said his father, "if the wheels start spinning they inject some sand onto the railway lincs to improve the grip."

He said that during World War II the French Resistance put sand in the axle boxes of the German goods trains. Then the bearings overheated and the wagons caught fire.

"So is sand a good thing or a bad thing?" asked William.

"Sometimes good, sometimes bad," replied his mother.

One morning they were having breakfast and the radio was on. A man was singing:

"Mr Sandman,

Bring me a dream,

Make her complexion

Like peaches and cream..."

William looked at Claudia, and she smiled.

It was now July, and the weather was hot. There were fans on in the kitchen and sitting room, and William slept with the French windows in his bedroom partly open, though with the curtains drawn.

Then one day Claudia received a telephone call from Italy. She had to fly home urgently. There were tears in her eyes as her taxi came and she said goodbye.

A new au pair girl arrived a week later. She was tall and thin, with a sallow complexion and red hair, which she wore in a long pigtail. She spoke very little, never smiled, and had a dry kind of laugh, more like a cackle. She was very strict with William, and altogether not much fun to be with. Her name was Ilse. She was a dental student from Latvia.

"I really don't like her, Mum," said William, "can't you tell her to go?"

"Now that Susan's away I need someone here to help in the house and to look after you. We can't do without an au pair. I've got a job now, remember?"

"Well, can't we get another girl then?"

"No. And Ilse's actually very nice. She's just a little shy at the moment. You'll soon grow to like her."

"Aw Mum," protested William.

"That's enough!" said his mother angrily. "Look, I'm going to be late for work." She picked up her handbag and walked out of the front door.

One Thursday evening William's parents told him they

would be away for the weekend, and were leaving early the next morning.

"We're going hiking in Snowdonia," said his father. "We'll be walking up the mountain, and descending on the train."

"Can I come too?" asked William, excitedly.

"I'm afraid not," said his mother. "The climb is too hard for young children."

"Oh please!"

"I'm sorry, but it's not possible," she said firmly, "and anyhow, what about school? Ilse will look after you while we're away."

"Don't leave me alone with her!" pleaded William.

"Now we've had this conversation before," said his mother, carrying on with her packing.

William went to school as usual that Friday, and spent Saturday with friends in the park and watching TV. In the evening, when he went to bed, he had trouble getting to sleep. But Ilse did not tell bedtime stories. She just left him some books to read and went off to her room.

William eventually did fall asleep, but woke up again in the middle of the night. He sat up in bed. He could see two shoes sticking out from underneath the long velvet curtains. Unable to move in terror, he could not take his eyes off them. Someone must have come into the garden from the Common, slipped through the French windows, and was now standing behind the curtains.

He could hear whispering coming from one of the bedrooms. After a while he plucked up courage and shouted for help. Ilse came into his room in her dressing gown and with her hair undone.

"Whats the matter?" she demanded angrily.

"It's the Sandman," said William. "He's waiting behind the curtains!"

"Don't be silly," said Ilse. She turned on all the lights. "Look! There is no Sandman here."

She opened the curtains. There was no one standing behind them.

"You see!"

She picked up the shoes and waved them in front of him.

"And what are these? They are your own shoes, you stupid boy!"

She put them under the chair where he left his clothes.

"And don't you disturb me again!"

She switched off the lights and stormed out of the room.

On Sunday Ilse took William over to see Tom. After tea they played some computer games, until it was time to go home, have supper, and go to bed.

It was easier gettting to sleep than the night before. But later William woke up again. It was past midnight. Under the curtains were two large brown boots.

He could hear the television on upstairs in the sitting room.

"Help!" he shouted in terror. But nobody came. The curtains moved slightly. Was it the wind, or the man behind them? He was paralysed with fear.

"Help!"

Ilse rushed in carrying her handbag.

"What is it this time?" she asked furiously. "You just interrupted my favourite programme!"

"It's the Sandman," William gasped, pointing at the curtains.

"Don't be so stupid!"

"This time it really is him," said William desperately. "Those big boots. That's what he wears!"

Ilse turned all the lights on.

"I told you before, he is not there. Look!" She pulled back the curtains sharply. Behind them were only the boots.

"So what are these then?" she asked, holding them up. "They are just another pair of your father's walking boots!" she laughed mockingly.

"Yes, but the Sandman's got some just like that," said William, feeling ashamed.

Ilse came and sat on his bed.

"The Sandman is not here. But I am here. I am the Sandwoman. And this is what I do to children who will not go to sleep."

She reached into her handbag and took out a trowel filled with sand.

"Now open wide!"

She grabbed William's chin and tried to force his mouth open. For a moment he held it tightly closed, then suddenly opened it and sank his teeth into her finger. Ilse screamed in pain, and he pulled back on her pigtail with all his might.

Then came the sound of the front door being unlocked.

EIGHT
The Caravan Holiday

My parents always said that I had 'imagination'. That's what artists and writers have, what makes them 'creative'. I would imagine all sorts of things and then make up stories. Perhaps this is because Natasha (my sister) and I are half Russian. But then I started having nightmares. They were mainly about monsters, witches and devils, but sometimes about pirates, shipwrecks and earthquakes too. Every night I was so sure I'd have a nightmare that I'd force myself to stay awake by humming tunes or even singing out loud. Of course I would finally fall asleep, but so late that I couldn't get up next morning, and started missing school.

Mum and Dad were very worried, and sent me to a special doctor called a psychiatrist. He was in Harley Street, London, where they only have doctors. You see all sorts of ill people arriving in taxis. We sat in the waiting room. There was an aquarium with tropical fish, magazines, and comics and puzzles for children. Then the nurse took us in to see Dr Glover. It was more like a sitting room than a surgery, with comfortable brown leather chairs, antiques and a Persian carpet.

"A nervous little fellow, eh?" said Dr Glover. He told my parents that they should closely monitor what I watched on TV and the internet.

"And no horror comics!"

Things got better then, until a friend of mine called Keith told me about something. One night, in the summer, he was lying in bed with the window wide open. Suddenly, with a horrible whirring and rustling sound, a goblin flew in and sat on the end of his bed. It was small, brown and hairy, with a hunched back, pointed head and bat's wings. Keith lay there terrified, sweating, and not daring to move an inch. The goblin sat there for TEN WHOLE MINUTES, then flew back out of the window.

The following night I had another nightmare. I was talking to a goblin, and then a hobgoblin came and joined us (that's a senior, more evil kind of goblin). I asked him how his wife was. He proudly replied that she had just died and gone to Hell.

Then came a whole new lot of nightmares. I was sent back to Dr Glover. I got to enjoy sitting in the waiting room watching the fish swimming around the rocks, weeds, and sunken ships in the aquarium.

We live in a very old house. It is huge, and has many rooms. In the hall there are some Tudor portraits, and their eyes follow you as you walk past. I'm dead sure the house is haunted. But my parents say, "Nonsense, Thomas, just your fertile imagination."

It was now the summer holidays. Dr Glover had said that in view of my condition, we should go somewhere "more cosy and intimate." Mum persuaded Dad to take us on a caravan holiday. He was pretty grumpy about this. First we'd have to hire a caravan. Then have a tow hook fitted on our car, and also an electric plug so that whenever the car's lights went on, the caravan's would too. And he was worried that the car might not easily cope with the extra weight of the caravan.

It was amazing when Dad drove up with the caravan. It was called a Bluebird Supreme, and was longer than our car. Inside was a kitchenette and lounge area, shower and toilet, a separate room for Mum and Dad, and two bunk beds, for me and Natasha. She bagged the top bunk.

"Can we ride in the caravan?" asked Natasha.

"No – it's against the law," said Dad.

We set off. After a few hours on the road my parents said we should find somewhere to park for the night.

"Let's stop in this lay-by," said Mum.

We pulled in. Dad unhooked the caravan to rest the car's springs. We turned a handle to make a little wheel, called the jockey wheel, come down to support the caravan's tow bar when on the ground. Then Natasha and I jumped into the caravan and Mum made tea.

Afterwards we went out to have a look around. Further along the lay-by there were three horses grazing and some old gypsy caravans.

"We can have our fortunes told!" said Natasha.

But as we got nearer the caravans Mum said, "I can feel a sense of hostility. I really don't want to stay here."

"Well, I suppose we are encroaching on their territory," said Dad. So we walked back to our caravan, hitched it up, and drove off.

It was getting quite dark before we found somewhere else to stop. We turned off the main road along a rough track, went down a steep slope, and parked at the bottom. Mum made supper.

"This kitchen is beautifully equipped!" she said. It had everything you would find at home: cutlery, crockery, pots and pans. At bedtime Natasha and I were too excited to get to sleep!

Early the next morning we were woken by a terrible noise – banging, crashing and engines revving.

"What a din!" said Dad.

We had parked in the middle of a quarry! So we drove out through all the bulldozers, diggers, and dumper trucks.

That evening we went a long way down a narrow farm track, through a gate and into a field. There were cows at the other end. Mum was a bit worried, but Dad said they were harmless.

Next morning a loud knocking on the window woke us up. Dad opened the door. A Land Rover was parked right next to us with a red-faced man in a tweed cap standing by it.

"'Ere! Git off my land!" he shouted.

"Er...I'm very sorry, I didn't realize," mumbled Dad.

"Well, you should have, shouldn't you. This is private here."

"We'll get going as soon as possible."

"I should certainly hope so!"

The man's face was turning from red to purple. I thought he was going to explode. He stood there with his hands in his pockets.

"Bloody liberty," he kept on muttering, "a bloody liberty."

Dad, still in his pyjamas, quickly hitched up the caravan and got into the car. Slipping and sliding in the mud we somehow got through the gate, back up the track, and onto the main road.

After that my parents said they'd had enough of always having to leave, and from now on we would stay at an official caravan site. We had been given the Caravan Club's booklet of all the sites in the UK. The nearest one in Oxfordshire was the Wychwood Caravan Park.

We drove in through a gateway with 'Welcome' in big letters on it. The site was huge. Caravans, longer than ours, were parked neatly in rows. A sign said Manager's Office. Dad stopped the car by it, and went inside.

"Do we really have to stay here?" I asked. After camping out in the wild it seemed so tame and organised.

"We have no other choice, Thomas," said Mum.

A few minutes later Dad came out with the Manager.

"We cater mainly for residential vans, but we do have a section designated for tourers."

He walked ahead and we followed slowly behind in the car.

We were shown to our parking place, and Dad signed a form that was on the Manager's clipboard. We had lunch in the caravan and then Natasha and I went out to look around. Some of the caravans had a low fence around them and a small garden of flowers and shrubs, with deckchairs and picnic tables. An old man was watering his plants.

"These aren't caravans – they're houses," said Natasha.

To me they looked more like prefabs – those temporary houses they gave people who were bombed out in the War.

"They're caravans all right," said the old man, "you'll notice they've all got little wheels. They're known as mobile homes."

So they didn't have to pay taxes like fixed houses.

"But unlike your touring caravans, they're not road legal. They have to travel on a lorry."

Often the wheels and the space between the base of the caravan and the ground were covered by a strip of canvas, wood, or plastic called the 'skirt' or 'valance'. Later we saw one being unloaded. The back of the lorry tipped up and the caravan was winched down the slope onto its pad, where it was plugged into water and electricity.

There were several permanent buildings on the site: the Manager's office, the shower and toilet block, and a small shop. Natasha and I went in there to buy some sweets. The lady inside was very friendly,

Dad had brought his computer as he had hoped to do some work during the holiday. Next day he said he would stay in.

"But can we go exploring?" I asked.

"Yes, as long as you don't leave this caravan site," said Mum. "You are not allowed out of the gates."

"But that's so boring!" complained Natasha.

Mum wouldn't budge, so we decided to make a thorough inspection of the site. The caravans were parked in neat rows with equal spaces between them. Some were a bit older or newer, longer or shorter, but they all looked pretty much the same. Most of them were painted cream, beige, or pale green.

"Look at that funny one over there," said Natasha.

We walked up to the caravan. It stood by itself in a far corner of the site, right next to the boundary fence. It was shorter and higher than the others, and looked more like a hut than a caravan. On one end there were steps going up to it, and on the other end a spindly iron chimney coming through the roof. Unlike the other caravans it was dark brown and made of wood.

We carried on round the site until we got back to our own caravan. During tea Mum said we'd probably be staying there for at least ten days. My face fell.

"Don't worry," said Dad, "we'll go on lots of excursions from here. We're only using this as a base."

Next day I met a boy called Gary. He and his parents lived on the site, and he went to the local school. He was American – his Dad worked at a U.S. Air Force base nearby.

Gary was mad keen about baseball. He tried to explain the rules to me. Everywhere we went he'd take his bat, ball and padded gloves, and would practise shots as he walked along. I said I'd teach him about cricket.

One day Gary hit a ball under one of the caravans. It was the old man's one. He was doing some gardening. We said we were sorry, but could we go and retrieve our ball?

"Yes, of course," he said, smiling, "go ahead."

I crawled past the valance and under the caravan. The ball was behind one of the wheels. The old man was very friendly. He had lived on the site for years, and knew nearly everyone there.

"And the lady who runs the shop, that's Mrs Smithers."

Next day Natasha, Gary and I were walking near the far end of the site, and I hit a really good ball. It soared up in the air and went for miles. In cricket that would have been a 'six'. It flew right through an open window of one of the caravans – the old wooden one!

We walked up the steps to the door. There was a faint sound of someone singing or chanting in a low voice. I hesitated for a moment and then knocked. The singing stopped. I heard footsteps and the door opened slowly. An old woman stood there, dressed in black.

"Come in, children," she said, speaking in a very foreign accent. "I've been expecting you."

"Er, actually, could we just have our ball back?" I asked nervously, "I'm very sorry, it went through your window."

"You may indeed," she said, "but first you must have some tea with me."

We looked at each other for a second, then gingerly went

into the caravan. It had a musty old smell about it. It was very dark inside – there was only one dim electric light and some candles. The walls were hung with small Persian carpets.

"Now sit down here," said the old woman, pulling out three stools. She went over to an old brass kettle which had a flame under it, and came back with a tray. On it was a teapot, a jug, glasses, and a plateful of cakes.

"I will be drinking tea, but perhaps you would prefer lemonade."

I picked up a glass of lemonade and tried one of the cakes. It was very sweet and quite delicious.

She said she had seen us walking around the site and asked how long we were staying. She was very friendly, especially to Natasha.

By now my eyes had got used to the darkness. I saw that the caravan was quite narrow inside. Sometimes it felt as if it was slightly swaying. At the far end was a stove with a faint glow coming from it. One side wall had a kitchen cupboard, and the other had a large set of shelves. On them were rows upon rows of round objects, standing upright. At first I thought they were jars and bottles, then I noticed that each one had a face on it!

It was getting time to go, and we finished our tea and got up.

"Oh, and your ball!" said the old woman. She opened a drawer, took it out and gave it to me, smiling. Her hands were old and gnarled.

"Come and visit me again," she said, as we walked down the steps, "promise!"

"I promise," said Natasha.

While we were walking away I turned and looked back at the caravan. There was something odd, but I couldn't quite make it out. As he lived nearby I asked Gary what he thought of that caravan.

"Kinda weird," he said.

But actually he had never been to that part of the site before. He had very little free time as he always had masses of homework to do.

"Pop wants me to be an 'A' student, get good grades and go to Harvard."

Then I got it. The caravan was turned the other way round from when I had first seen it.

"Look – the steps! Don't you remember? They were on the left-hand side, next to the fence. Now they're on the right. So now the other end of the caravan, with the chimney, is by the fence."

"You dead sure about that?" asked Gary.

When we got back to our own caravan I told Mum all about it. She said we should try not to disturb other people living on the site. After supper I unpacked my books and CDs. Natasha had brought along some of her dolls and she placed them in a row by her bunk. There was Greta, who had a blonde pigtail and wore a dirndl, and Manfred in a Tyrolean hat and leather shorts and braces. And also Kalinka, the Russian doll. She was really just a smooth round piece of wood with a face, hands and dress painted on it. But if you twisted her she came apart at the waist and there was a smaller doll inside. And *that* one had an even smaller one in it, and so on, until you got to a tiny one that was solid wood. Aunt Olga had brought Kalinka from Russia.

I suddenly realized that all those round things with faces on the old caravan's shelves were actually dolls!

I spent the next few days mainly with Gary. I was lucky to have found a friend on the site. As for Natasha, Mum took her for walks and trips in the car, and they saw the model village at Bourton-on-the-Water. Poor Dad stayed glued to his computer, as his office had emailed him about an important new project.

I got quite friendly with some of the other people on the site too. Like the old man we'd met. I asked him about the woman in the wooden caravan.

"Been here longer than anyone can remember – and I've been here fifteen years."

One day Natasha and I went to the shop to get some Coca-Cola's. Mrs Smithers smiled and asked if we were having a good time. Then her smile faded. Someone had come into the shop. It was the old woman.

"Natasha," she sighed, "I knew I would find you here. And when are you coming to have tea with me again?"

"Can I help you?" asked Mrs Smithers sharply.

"Please, just some tea," said the old woman, "and perhaps a little honey."

She turned to Natasha and looked her in the face.

"Now remember your promise. I hope you will come very soon. I am expecting you."

The she hobbled out of the shop.

We got back to our caravan and Natasha told our parents about it.

"That nice old lady asked me to tea!"

Mum said she'd take her over to see her one afternoon.

Later on we got a text from Aunt Olga saying she was coming to see us in a day or two. Olga is an amazing person and has been all over the world. When she was in Russia she worked as a journalist. Dad said perhaps she was also a spy!

Next day I went to see Gary. He showed me his model aeroplanes and also a remote-controlled car he'd got for Christmas. It was a bright red pick-up, with giant tyres and four-wheel drive.

"Wow! Let's take it for a spin!" I suggested. But Gary said he just had too much homework. But I could try it out myself if I liked. He showed me how to operate the radio controls.

"Be sure not to get out of range," he warned.

There wasn't much room to drive the car amongst all the caravans, so I took it to the end of the site where there was more open space. I switched on the car and the transmitter. It was great fun driving, twisting and turning, and I performed a perfect figure of eight.

Then I thought I'd do a speed run, in a straight line. The

car shot ahead like an arrow.

But when I tried to stop, it just carried on. I ran after it but couldn't catch up. It headed straight for the old wooden caravan and disappeared underneath it.

The car had gone through some old sacks that had been pinned to the bottom of the caravan, like a curtain, to cover the gap between it and the ground. Clipped to the sacking was a thin electric cable leading into the caravan. I put the transmitter on the ground and crawled through the sacks and under the caravan. It was all dark in there with a thick, unpleasant musty smell. I took the torch I always carry out of my pocket and shone it around. The ground was strewn with feathers. The car must have got stuck behind a wheel or perhaps a stone or brick.

Then I saw two big bright yellow stalks sticking up from the ground into the base of the caravan. Each stalk had four long thin things like fingers stretched along the ground with a claw on the end.

Horror upon horror! Instead of being on wheels the caravan was mounted on CHICKEN'S LEGS!

I had to bite my finger to stop myself from screaming. My first reaction was to get away as quick as possible, but I had to retrieve the remote-controlled car! It had stopped against a block of wood. To reach it I had to crawl between the chicken's feet. One of them lifted itself for a moment and the whole caravan lurched. I grabbed the car and crawled out through the sacking. I picked up the transmitter and started running back towards our caravan.

I decided not to tell anyone about this. My parents would have thought that my 'imagination' had got so far out of hand that I was having hallucinations. I would be sent back to Dr Glover who might even put me in a lunatic asylum!

Realizing that I was still clutching the car, I altered course towards Gary's caravan. I knocked on the door and he opened it.

"Hey, you OK? You look as white as a sheet! Seen a ghost or something?"

I gave him the car and said I had to go back to our caravan straight away. I was so exhausted I fell asleep almost immediately after supper. By some amazing luck I didn't have a nightmare.

I resolved to find out as much as possible about the old woman. I was quite sure she was really bad. I saw Mum getting out some clean white socks from Natasha's suitcase and hanging up her dress. I was convinced that if she went to see that woman she would be in serious danger.

I went to the shop to buy a Mars bar and asked Mrs Smithers about the old woman. She couldn't actually remember her coming into the shop before. She obviously kept to herself. But Mrs Smithers didn't live on the site and came into work every day. I decided to ask the Manager and knocked on the door of his office.

"Can I help you, son?" he asked, looking up from his computer.

Needing an excuse for seeing him, I asked if it would be alright if I rode my bike around the site (we had brought two foldable ones with us). He said that was fine as long as I showed consideration for others. Then the phone rang – someone was making a booking.

"Anything else?" he asked impatiently, putting down the phone.

"Er...you know that old wooden caravan that's at the corner of the site?"

"Yes, what about it?"

"Can you tell me anything about the lady who lives there?"

The Manager looked at me and spoke in an official tone.

"You will understand that I cannot give out any information whatsoever on our clients. It is strictly confidential."

"Well, thank you anyhow." I felt a little foolish.

Just as I was leaving the office Dad came in, presumably to pay for our parking.

"What on earth are you doing here?" he asked angrily.

That evening I was told not to interrupt people's work by asking them questions they were generally too busy to answer.

Next day Aunt Olga phoned to say she would be arriving soon. Later on, a blue convertible drew up alongside our caravan. Olga came in and gave us all a big kiss.

"I've got presents for you!" she announced.

She gave me a book on aeroplanes, and for Natasha some fairy stories. After supper she showed them to me. It was an old Russian book that Olga had bought in St. Petersburg.

There were Russian tales like Peter and the Wolf, and ones we already knew, like Snow White and Cinderella. Stories about kings and queens, elves and wizards, and fairies and witches.

The book said that fairies were kind, beautiful beings, which flew around bringing happiness to mankind. But unfortunately some of them became proud and turned bad. Then they lost their wings and ended up as bitter and twisted old women. Their only pleasure was in casting spells and causing trouble and disaster.

Many witches flew through the night on broomsticks, meeting secretly in covens.

"Time for bed!" said Mum, and the fairy stories were put away.

But I was so fascinated that when everyone was asleep I got the book out again, and, using my torch, read further. One of the most wicked witches was called Baba Yaga. It was said that she devoured people and her house was surrounded by skulls. Her magic was so powerful that she could actually change the weather and bring forth thunder and lightning. And she also enticed children into her home and turned them into dolls. She lived in the middle of the forest in a house mounted on chicken's legs.

"That's it!" I gasped, nearly waking everyone up.

Olga stayed the night with us, and next morning I asked her if it was true about witches. She said that Russia was a vast country with a long history, so it had many legends. And there were lots of old women called babushkas, usually dressed in black with a headscarf. They were widows, often due to the War or Stalin. In the countryside, if a haystack caught fire, a horse went lame, or a churn of milk went sour, it was always blamed on the old woman who lived alone in the village. Because people were superstitious and needed a scapegoat.

I decided to tell Olga what I had seen, but first she would have to swear solemnly to keep it a secret. I said I had proof that Baba Yaga really did exist. And she was not only here in England, but actually living in this caravan site!

"O darling boy, such imagination!" she laughed.

Later, as Olga got into her car to drive off, she gave me a wink.

"Secret!" she whispered.

I went back to talk to the old man. I found him raking the pathway outside his caravan. I asked him if he knew anything more about the old woman.

"Not really," he said.

But many years ago he had met a gamekeeper whose father had said that the whole area had once been covered with trees.

"You see, we're in the Wychwood Forest. Of course, nowadays there are only small pockets of woodland left. But we still have the village names: Shipton-under-Wychwood, Milton-under-Wychwood, and Ascott-under-Wychwood. Look at this...".

He walked over to the next caravan. Its tow bar was resting on an old tree stump.

Then he pointed to a round wooden seat, set in the ground. It had been carved out of the base of a tree.

Next day Dad and I went food shopping in the nearest town, as there wasn't much choice in the shop here on the site. When we reached the town centre I saw a sign saying Public Library. This gave me the idea of doing some research. Realizing this would take some time, I asked Dad if I could go back later on the bus (I had seen buses stopping outside the caravan site). At first he said No, but then we saw a bus stop with a timetable showing there was a bus back at 5.30 p.m.

"All right," said Dad, "but make sure you don't miss it. And keep your mobile switched on."

I went into the library and asked the lady at the desk if there was anything about witches. She was very surprised, but then said that there had been a lot of black magic going on in Oxfordshire and Gloucestershire in the past. Until about 1960 there had even been a Museum of Witchcraft at Bourton-on-the-Water.

"I know what – have a look through these."

She took me into another room. It had shelves and shelves of large leather-bound volumes.

"You can sit here at this table. Take your time. And call me if you need any help."

I looked through at least a dozen of the volumes. Reports of weddings, cricket matches, magistrates' courts, council business, rotary club meetings, etc. The volumes were old bound copies of the local newspaper.

"One more book, then I'll call it a day," I said to myself.

Then I spotted an article dated 10th July 1934. It was about the building of the Wychwood Caravan Park. It had been necessary to cut down some of the forest. A Mrs Barbara Jaeger, who lived in there in a caravan, had lodged an objection to the project. She was overruled, but when work started on site a series of accidents began to occur. A man lost his hand with a chainsaw. A bulldozer overturned and the driver was killed. The lady at the desk helped me take a photocopy of the article.

I spent so much time at the library that when I got to the bus stop the bus had already left. I waited there hoping to catch the next one.

There was a police car parked across the road. After a while a policeman got out and asked me what I was doing. I told him I was waiting for the bus to the Wychwood Caravan Park. He took a look at the timetable and said that I had missed the last one.

"Not to worry, we can give you a lift home!"

There was also a policewoman in the car.

"You can ride in the front, if you like," she said, "strictly against regulations, of course!" They laughed.

On the drive back they showed me how the radio worked. They were in constant two-way communication. A car reported stolen had just been stopped in the High Street. At 24 Oakwood Avenue: "*automatic alarm operating, suspect on premises.*" They even switched on the siren and blue flashing light for a moment.

I suddenly decided to tell them all about Baba Yaga and the terrible danger Natasha was in. But they just looked at each other and said nothing. After that they didn't seem so friendly.

When we got there my parents were most surprised to see me arrive in a police car! The policeman went up to Dad.

"Can I have a word with you, sir?"

He spoke to him for a few minutes, then got back into the car and they drove off.

Dad was absolutely furious. The policeman had said that I was either a lad, seriously disturbed, or had made up "some daft story just to take the mickey out of us." Dad had said it was, of course, utter nonsense, and had to explain all about my 'overactive imagination'.

Next day I spoke to Mum about it. She was a lot nicer but didn't believe me either. She said that when I was only three we had stayed in a farmhouse in Sussex. The lady there kept chickens, and she had just killed one of them to cook for lunch. She was busy plucking it when I walked into the kitchen. I saw the two feet she had just cut off standing by themselves on the kitchen table, and I screamed and screamed (Dr Glover had been told of this). And now, ever since, I couldn't eat chicken, not even the chicken nuggets we have at school. If chicken was on the menu that day I had to be given something else, by special arrangement.

"For you that was a traumatic experience," said Mum, "and it's the explanation for your phobia."

"Yes, but she's still a witch," I protested.

"How can you say something so horrible!" she said, getting cross. "She's probably just a lonely old woman. Actually I thought she was rather nice."

"WHAT?" I shouted.

I learnt that yesterday afternoon the woman had called in at our caravan and Mum had given her a cup of tea.

"Don't you understand?" I was desperate, "she's the most wicked of all the witches! Her name is Baba Yaga!"

"Don't be ridiculous."

"OK, I'll prove it then!"

I went over to the shelf to get the book of stories that Aunt Olga had brought. But it wasn't there!

"The book! Where is it?" I cried out.

"That nice lady borrowed it," said Natasha. "She'll give it back tomorrow. When I go over to have tea with her."

I realized now how urgent it had become. I just had to stop Natasha from going to see Baba Yaga. But it was hopeless trying to warn her, or my parents, or anyone else. No one believed me. I thought of telling Gary, but he was too straight and logical. He'd just think I was crazy. No, whatever I did, I would have to do alone.

That night, lying in my bunk, I tried to think of how to expose Baba Yaga. Throw a banger under her caravan to scare the chicken's feet into running away? But it was only July and Guy Fawkes Night was months away, so there were no fireworks in the shops. Light a fire under the caravan with a can of petrol? Far too dangerous – it might explode and set fire to everything else on the site.

The best idea I could come up with was to tear off the sacking around the base of the caravan to show everyone clearly the chicken's feet. Mum was going to take Natasha to Baba Yaga's caravan, leave her there for an hour or so, and collect her afterwards. I planned to come along too, with the excuse of going on further, past her caravan, for a walk in the fields. But before they got up the steps into it I would quickly rip off the sacking and shine my torch underneath for them all to see.

There was a small shed nearby. It was unlocked, and one day I'd had a peep inside. There were lawnmowers, wheelbarrows and all sorts of tools in there. I was going to smuggle out some garden shears and hide them in a patch of nettles near Baba Yaga's caravan so they'd be ready when I came later with Mum and Natasha.

Next morning I told my parents I was going to the shop, but at a safe distance changed course for the shed. But one of the site's gardeners was in there, so I had to hang around for a while. He came out with a lawnmower, and I hoped and prayed he wouldn't mow my patch of nettles.

I crept into the shed. Among all the rakes, hoes, forks and spades I found a large pair of shears, and slipped them into a plastic bag I'd brought with me. Then I walked towards Baba Yaga's caravan, and looking carefully around, dropped the shears into the nettles.

In the afternoon, around four o'clock, Mum got Natasha ready and we set off. Natasha was very excited.

"Look – I've done her a drawing. It's got all my dolls in it!"

When we got near the caravan I darted off towards the patch of nettles.

"What are you doing?" cried Mum, "you'll get stung."

"I lost my pen-knife in here yesterday. I couldn't find it, so I'm going to have another look for it now."

Suddenly the sky got all dark and it began to rain. I thrashed around wildly in the nettles, but just couldn't locate the shears. I looked up. Mum and Natasha were approaching the caravan's steps.

I saw a light in the window, and Baba Yaga in it. She turned her head, looked out, and smiled. At last I found the shears and started to run towards the caravan. Mum was putting a scarf over her head and was helping Natasha into her cardigan. Then a lightning bolt hit the ground, so close to me that I heard it fizzle. Holding the metal shears I was bound to be struck next time. Then came a deafening clap of thunder.

"Inside quick, or we'll get soaked!" said Mum. They were now at the bottom step.

"Stop!" I yelled, pushing forward with the shears in my hand.

Mum and Natasha stood there open-mouthed.

"LOOK!" I screamed, diving to the ground.

I chopped desperately at the sacking. It came apart easily. Then I hit something hard and rubbery. There was a flash, a tingling force shot up my arm, and I was hurled backwards onto the ground. In the split second before I passed out I realized that I'd cut through the electric cable.

I woke up in hospital. The doctor, the nurses, everyone, were incredibly nice.

"You're a very lucky boy, Thomas," said the doctor. "Two hundred and forty volts!"

In the meantime my parents had packed up and driven to the nearest hotel, where they took two rooms for the rest of the holiday, and kept the caravan in the car park.

"At last I can have a proper bath!" said Mum.

The severe electrical storm had knocked out the wi-fi at the caravan site, but now Dad could make use of the excellent computer facilities at the hotel.

And Natasha was safe. That evil witch had been thwarted.

I still can't eat chicken!

NINE

The Jack-in-the-Box

Mark Woodley lived in a flat in London with his parents and his sister Sophie. He was ten; she was two years younger. They also had a cat called Bumble.

Their mother was passionate about antiques. She had a good eye for a bargain, and was a skilled negotiator. Over the years she had built up a fine collection of all sorts of old things. She was particularly interested in Victorian toys and dolls, and at auction had recently acquired a marvellous dolls house, complete with miniature furniture. Unfortunately their flat was very small and space was limited, so she often kept items for a while, then sold them on, usually at a profit.

At weekends Mr and Mrs Woodley often went to country sales, taking the children with them. They would come back to London with the car laden with antiques. And in the holidays they sometimes went abroad, as well. On the return journey the boot of the car would also be filled with boxes of wine, as it was much cheaper on the Continent.

On one of their trips they went to Liège. It is a city in

Belgium renowned for its ancient buildings. It also has many antique shops and an annual fair selling bric-a-brac. Mrs Woodley had heard of a particular shop there, and was keen to visit it.

They found it at the end of a narrow street in the old town. Above the door was a faded wooden sign saying:

G. de BRUGES

ANTIQUITÉS BROCANTE RÉCUPERATION

The owner was an old man, with a long beard and dishevelled grey hair. The shop was vast, and crammed full of all sorts of old things – lamps, crockery, furniture, statues, old radios and telephones, pictures, books and toys.

In one corner was a rocking horse. It was dappled grey, and its mane and tail were of fine white silk thread. Its saddle and harness were of red leather.

"Ooh! Can I ride him?" asked Sophie, excitedly.

"Of course – but hold on tight," said Monsieur de Bruges kindly.

Sophie begged her parents to buy it for her, and they negotiated a good price. They also bought a delicate Japanese vase.

They walked deeper into the shop. There was a large prewar electric train set, with an engine, coaches, and goods trucks all made of tinplate. With signals and a model station! Mark asked his mother if he could have it.

"It's far too expensive," she said, "and anyhow, there just isn't any space in your bedroom for all that track."

She bought him a toy car instead

As they were leaving, Mark noticed a pale yellow leather box, about forty centimetres square. On the side of the lid was a small brass catch. He touched this. The lid flew open, and a little man shot out and faced him grinning, swaying on the end of a spring. Mark got a terrible fright.

"What is it?" he asked.

"It's a jack-in-the-box," said his father. "It's an old traditional toy. You don't see them nowadays."

The jack's arms were outstretched. He had a white face, red lips, piercing blue eyes, and a comical expression. He wore a yellow shirt, a red waistcoat, and a black hat with a feather. Below his body was the spring, which was encased in light green material, pleated like an accordion.

"How much do you want for this?" asked Mr Woodley.

"I don't know – fifty euros?" suggested Monsieur de Bruges.

Mrs Woodley looked at her husband.

"That's incredibly cheap," she whispered.

She didn't even bother to bargain, but shook the owner's hand and gave him the money.

"There you are," she said to Mark. "I've bought you another present."

"But I don't like it," he protested, "I wanted the train set."

"All right, it'll be mine then," said his mother, "it's a rare antique – probably Victorian. One can't turn down something at that price."

Monsieur de Bruges pushed the jack back into his box

and closed the lid.

"Be careful, the catch is a bit loose," he said.

He helped them put all their purchases in the car.

"Bon retour! Et merci!" he said as they left. "You have done me a great favour."

The rocking horse had been put in the back of the car, but the children still had enough room to sit, though it was rather cramped. The square yellow box was in the boot, with the luggage. In Ostend Mr Woodley bought several cases of wine. They arrived at the docks in time to catch an afternoon ferry.

When they reached Dover they drove off the ship and into the customs shed. The other cars were waved through, but they were ordered to pull into an inspection bay at the side.

"Just our luck," grumbled Mr Woodley, "they *would* have to pick on us."

The customs officer was old and wore glasses. He asked them which countries they had visited, and what was the purpose of their trip. Then a younger officer joined them. He had a dog with him.

"What's that for?" asked Mark.

"It's a sniffer dog," said his father, "they're looking for drugs."

"Would you all mind getting out of the vehicle, while we have a look inside?" asked the older officer.

They quickly searched the front and back of the car, and smiled when they saw the rocking horse.

"Could you open the boot, please?"

They took a cursory look at the suitcases and wine cases, without opening them. They seemed more interested in the square yellow box. The dog sniffed at it suspiciously, and the older officer leant over it and touched its catch. The lid sprang open and the jack shot out. The officer, taken by surprise, fell backwards onto the ground and his glasses flew off. The dog went beserk and attacked Mr Woodley, biting him on the hand. The children started to cry.

The customs officer picked himself up and looked around for his glasses. He swore when he found that one of the lenses was broken.

"You should have warned us about that thing," he said angrily, "now if you wish to make a complaint...".

"That won't be necessary," said Mr Woodley, "we just want to get on our way as soon as possible. We have two young children with us."

The younger officer now had the dog back under control, and on the lead.

"I should get that wound seen to, if I was you," he said. "Have a tetanus injection, just in case. And our apologies for what just happened. He's a young dog, you see. Very nervous, he is."

It was late in the evening by the time they got home, and the children went straight to bed. All the luggage, wine, and antiques were carried up into the flat. Although it was Sophie's, the rocking horse could not be kept in her bedroom, as there was absolutely no room for it in there.

So it was put next door in Mark's room, together with the square yellow box.

"I don't want that box in here," protested Mark.

"Why not?" asked his mother.

"I don't like it," he said, "it's scary."

"There's no room for it anywhere else. Until we get a bigger flat."

Mark soon fell asleep. But in the middle of the night he woke up. He could hear a rhythmical creaking sound. He turned on his bedside light. The horse was rocking back and forth, of its own accord. This was not due to the wind, as the window was closed. Then the rocking stopped. Mark turned out the light and fell asleep.

He woke up again a few hours later. There was a slight rattling sound in his bedroom. He switched on the light and listened. At first he thought it was a mouse. Then he heard a tiny voice.

"Let me out! Let me out!"

It was coming from the square yellow box. Mark was terrified.

"Let me out! Will you please let me out!"

Mark didn't move.

"Didn't you hear what I said? LET ME OUT!"

He got out of bed, went over to the box, and touched the catch. The lid opened and the jack-in-the-box flew out.

"Thank you," he said.

Mark stared at the little man with his funny face and hat, bobbing on the end of his spring, his arms waving.

"I...I didn't know you could speak," Mark said.

"Yes, and three languages," said the jack. "English, French, and Flemish."

They talked for a long time. Jacques was clever, friendly, and amusing. He told Mark all about Liège and its long history, and Monsieur de Bruges and the antique shop. Mark told Jacques about London, Sophie and his parents, school, and what they did in the holidays.

It was agreed that he would be let out of his box for an hour each night, very late, when everyone else was asleep.

"I like my box," said Jacques, "after all it's my home. But sometimes I get bored, or I feel cramped and want to stretch my spring."

It was to be a strict secret between them that the jack-in-the-box could talk. He would speak to no one else but Mark, and then only late at night, when he was alone in his bedroom.

Mark yawned.

"I want to go back to sleep now," he said.

He pushed Jacques back into his box and closed the lid.

"Don't forget our secret," said the tiny voice from inside the box.

Next morning Sophie ran into Mark's room.

"I'm going to ride my horse!" she said excitedly. "I'm calling him Pegasus."

He was a big horse, and she had to stand on a chair to get into the saddle, while Mark steadied him and held his bridle.

"Hold on tight!" he said.

The horse started rocking, gently at first, then faster and faster, with longer rocks.

"It's magic!" cried Sophie, "it's like he's alive, and doing all the rocking himself!"

Every Tuesday a woman called Maria came to clean the flat. The children loved her – she often brought them sweets and little cakes she had baked at home. But their mother was not entirely satisfied with her.

"She's so slow," she complained, "last week she took two hours to clean the sitting room!"

"She seems alright to me," said her husband.

"You don't know anything about housework," said Mrs Woodley angrily, "she often misses out whole bits of the kitchen. They're still dirty and dusty when she's gone. She breaks things and never owns up – just hides the bits in a drawer. I could easily get another cleaner, who'd be faster and cheaper. There are plenty of girls from Eastern Europe nowadays."

One day, when the children were at school, Maria was cleaning Mark's bedroom. She had picked up the Japanese vase, which had been put on the mantlepiece, in order to dust it. Still holding it, she went over to the square yellow box and began dusting that too. She touched the catch, the lid burst open, and Jacques sprang out. Maria screamed, and dropped the vase onto the floor. It shattered into small pieces. Mrs Woodley, who was in the hall and about to go out to lunch, rushed in.

"YOU CLUMSY IDIOT!" she yelled, "that was a prize antique! Could have made good money out of that!"

"I'm sorry! I'm so sorry!" said Maria, in tears, "I did not know about the box and that clown."

"You're sacked!" shouted Mrs Woodley.

"But please..." sobbed Maria, falling down on her knees in front of her.

Mrs Woodley stepped back quickly. She was wearing a new pair of black suede boots, and did not want her cleaner's hands all over them.

"Please, Madame," begged Maria, "I need the job. My family...I will be extra-careful in future. I promise."

"Get up from that ridiculous position," said Mrs Woodley, "and take your things and get out!"

Her husband heard the commotion and came into the room.

"You can at least give her two weeks' wages," he said, rather shocked.

"All right, then," said his wife, angrily. "But I want to see the back of her - now!"

When the children heard that Maria was not coming back, they were very upset.

"But why, Mum?" asked Sophie, "she was so nice!"

"She was a useless cleaner. And I've noticed that some of our things are missing, too."

Sophie knew this was a lie.

Meanwhile, every night Mark and Jacques had their secret talk. They had to be very quiet in case Sophie, who was in the next-door room, or anyone outside in the corridor, heard them. Jacques seemed very wise and knew a lot of things.

Mark told him he was very bad at French. At school you were often given, as homework, a passage in English to be translated into French. At the next lesson the English text would be out on the whiteboard, and you had to translate it out loud without the help of any notes or dictionaries.

He said that their teacher, Madame Charrier, was extremely short-sighted and wore glasses with very thick lenses.

"I know!" said Jacques, "I'll translate your homework into French and dictate it to you here, then you read it out in class. If her eyesight is that poor she'll never notice."

Mark was shocked at the suggestion.

"But that's cheating!" he said.

"No," said Jacques, "it's called being pragmatic. To accept an offer of help, and take the opportunity."

Eventually Mark was persuaded. At each French lesson he would bring the written translation, put it cheekily on his desk, and read it out. The rest of the class giggled, and found him rather daring. Madame Charrier was delighted, but could not understand how Mark, who had always been weak at French, had so suddenly improved. He gave a perfect translation every time!

Then it was half-term – it lasted over a week. At the next French lesson Mark, as usual, read out his translation, which was lying wide open on his desk. He had not noticed that Madame Charrier was not wearing her glasses. She went straight over to him and seized the sheet of paper. She had just had corrective laser surgery on her eyes, and now had perfect vision.

She was furious, and sent Mark straight to the Headmaster. Next day Mr Woodley received a letter from him.

"It's furtive and dishonest," he said, bitterly. "I never thought my son would grow up to be a cheat."

Sophie had always wanted a pet. Her parents would not let her have a puppy. Dogs always had to be taken for walks, and that was awkward in London. And they didn't have a garden. But Sophie was insistent, so they let her have a kitten instead.

"As long as it doesn't ruin my furniture," said her mother.

Bumble grew into a fine marmalade cat. Sophie adored him and loved playing with him and stroking his fur. Unfortunately he got into the habit of sharpening his claws on a fine leather Regency chair in the sitting room. One day Mrs Woodley came home to find that the seat had been completely ruined by scratching. The leather was even ripped in places.

"Just look at it, my beautiful chair!" she cried, "I won't have my good furniture destroyed like this. I'm getting rid of that cat!'

Sophie burst into tears and begged her not to.

"All right, I'll give him another chance," said her mother, "but one more thing like that, and out he goes!"

When everyone was out, Bumble would wander around the flat, including Mark's bedroom. When the rocking horse arrived, he was at first wary of it. But he then learned that if he pushed down hard on the tip of a rocker with his paw, the horse would rock up and down. He often amused himself like that.

Bumble remained suspicious of the square yellow box, and always avoided going near it. But one morning he heard a faint sound coming from it. Curiosity got the better of him. He approached it cautiously and listened. It was as if someone inside was snoring. He touched it very gently with his paw. The snoring stopped, but there was now a silent rattling sound. He touched the box again, harder this time and on the brass catch. The lid flew open, and Jacques shot out. Bumble recoiled and miaowed in terror. Then he attacked him savagely, nearly biting off his arm and tearing the cloth around his spring, exposing the metal. Mrs Woodley, who had just returned, heard the noise and rushed into the bedroom. She kicked the cat away, and picked up the jack-in-the-box to inspect the damage.

"Where's Bumble?" asked Sophie desperately, when she got back from school that afternoon.

"We had to give him away," said her father, "the animal shelter have just collected him."

Sophie burst into tears.

"You gave away my cat!" she cried, "how *could* you? Why did you do that?"

"I'll show you why," said her mother, taking her by the

arm into the bedroom. "Just look what he did to the jack-in-the-box! It'll have to be expertly repaired now. I warned you. I can't afford to have my valuable things damaged like this."

Sophie ran into her room, got into bed, and cried herself to sleep.

She still had Pegasus. She came into Mark's room and rode him every day. She would rock gently at first, then faster and faster and higher and higher. Afterwards she would pat his neck affectionately.

"Good boy, Pegasus, good boy!"

Mark, who always helped Sophie mount and dismount, was glad to see her enjoying herself so much.

But there was someone who did not appreciate Pegasus quite so much.

"That horse!" said Jacques one night, after he had come back from the menders.

"What about him?" asked Mark.

"I can't stand the rocking. It makes the floorboards creak. I can't relax in my box. And it always wakes me up. Can't the horse be put in another room?"

"No. There's nowhere else he can go, except in here."

"Anyhow, it's far too big for your sister," continued Jacques, "and too heavy for her to control. That's dangerous."

"But he gives her so much pleasure," said Mark.

One day, when Sophie was rocking away happily on Pegasus, she failed to notice that each rock brought the front tip of one rocker closer and closer to the square yellow box. Then it touched it and hit the brass catch. The lid flew open and Jacques shot out. Peagasus shied and reared backwards on his rockers. Sophie was taken by surprise and lost her balance. As she fell off she put out her arm to save herself. She crashed hard onto the floor and screamed and screamed. Her mother rushed in.

An ambulance was called and she was taken to hospital and given an X-ray. Luckily her arm was just badly bruised but her wrist was broken. She was kept in overnight for observation. When she got home the next day the rocking horse was gone. Her mother had sold it – at a good profit.

Sophie had lost Bumble and now Pegasus. She confronted her father.

"You took away my rocking horse. Well, I want a real one now. I'd like to have riding lessons. And then my own pony."

"That's impossible," said Mr Woodley.

"Why?"

"Perhaps you've forgotten that we live in the middle of London."

The real reason was that he was too mean to pay for the lessons.

Sophie started not to eat her food, and often refused to go to school in the mornings. She had frequent rows with her parents, and sometimes spent the whole day in her bedroom.

One day their Aunt Jessica came to see them. They had tea in the sitting room.

"I just don't know what to do with Sophie," said Mrs Woodley, "she's become so difficult."

"Why don't you send her to boarding school?" suggested Aunt Jessica.

"Isn't she a bit young for that?" asked Mr Woodley.

"Not at all!" said Jessica, "I know a school that would take her now – St. Margaret's Convent, in Petersfield. I'm a good friend of the Mother Superior. I'll have a word with her."

"It might do her some good," said Mrs Woodley.

Mark had been having tea with them. He went straight to Sophie's room and told them what he had heard. She ran into the sitting room.

"I don't want to go to boarding school!" she cried, "I want to stay here with Mark!"

But her parents resolved to make enquiries about the Convent – such things as fees, and where to buy Sophie's uniform.

By now Mark had realized that only bad things had happened since Jacques had arrived.

"I don't like the jack-in-the box," he said to his mother, "it's evil. Can't we get rid of it?"

"Certainly not!" she said, "it's a valuable antique. Very rare, and worth a great deal of money."

"Then why don't we sell it?"

"I plan to keep it as an investment. It will greatly increase in value over the years."

Mark now knew that if there was anything to be done, it would be up to him.

To replace Maria, Mrs Woodley had decided to get an au pair girl. A small room, until now used for storing furniture and suitcases, was made into a bedroom for her. It was up a short flight of steps at the end of the corridor, and separate from the main part of the flat.

Helga, the au pair, went to English classes every morning, and helped with the housework and cooking. She spent most of her free time in her room, watching TV or listening to pop music.

Mr and Mrs Woodley now often went out, leaving Helga in charge of the children. One day they left after breakfast. They were taking Sophie to St. Margaret's Convent, and would not be back till late in the afternoon.

Helga was left to look after Mark. After lunch he said he would stay in his bedroom for an hour or two, to look at his computer. So Helga retired to her room, and soon you could hear loud music coming from it.

It was now time to act. Mark took a large metal tray from the kitchen into the bathroom, and laid it flat in the bath. Then he filled the tray with methylated spirits from a bottle he had found under the kitchen sink.

He got a ball of string and cut a length of it. Then he tiptoed into his bedroom. He heard snoring – Jacques was asleep. He wound the string around the square yellow box, carried it quietly into the bathroom, and gently placed it in the middle of the tray.

The snoring stopped.

"What's happening?" asked a voice from within the box,

"something's not right. Mark – are you there?"

But he was terrified, and didn't answer.

"Mark – where on earth am I? I know I'm not in your bedroom. And what's this awful smell? Let me out!"

Mark remained silent.

"Let me out! LET ME OUT!"

Mark had a box of matches with him. He struck one, but it broke in half. His hand was trembling now. Pop music could be heard coming from Helga's room. He struck another match. It lit, and he threw it into the tray. It burst into flames immediately.

"Mark! It's getting hot! Let me out! Please! LET ME OUT!" cried the voice, desperately.

"No!" said Mark.

"Ah! I see! You're going to burn me alive! Like Joan of Arc!"

"Joan of Arc was a saint," said Mark, "but you're a devil."

"No – I'm your friend, Mark. I've always tried to help you. Please let me out. PLEASE! I BEG OF YOU! FOR GOD'S SAKE, LET ME OUT!" screamed Jacques.

Then there was a horrible rattling sound. The box began to jiggle and shake. Jacques was trying to jerk the catch open. Mark could see it moving slightly. That was why he had bound up the box with string. It was now almost bouncing in the tray. Mark added more methylated spirit.

"MARK! PLEASE! HAVE MERCY! PLEASE!"

"No, Jacques," said Mark, firmly.

The flames were now licking around the sides of the box,

scorching the leather.

"So you'd murder your friend, would you? Your good friend, who never meant you any harm, and was always kind to you? Mark! MARK! HELP! I DON'T WANT TO DIE!"

Suddenly the lid burst open – the fire had distorted it and had burnt through the string. Jacques shot out, his arms waving wildly. Above the flames he looked terrifying. He looked at Mark straight in the eyes.

"So you were going to destroy me, Mark? But you won't. You see, you can't. Now put out this fire, and carry me back into your bedroom."

Mark was mesmerized.

"Go on. Do as I say. Now!" ordered Jacques. "Turn on the bath quick! You've got to put out the fire! And get me out of here, quick!"

"I'll get the fire extinguisher in the hall," said Mark, rushing out of the bathroom.

But he came back with a large black plastic rubbish bag. He put it over Jacques' head, then pulled it down over his whole body and his spring. You could see the bag wriggling. It was too hideous to look at.

"Mark! Please don't kill me!" came a piteous, muffled cry from inside the bag.

The flames were dying down. Mark picked up the bottle of spirit, to pour more into the tray. Then he heard a key turn in a lock, and the front door opened. Mrs Woodley rushed into the bathroom.

"MARK!" she yelled, "WHAT THE BLOODY HELL ARE

YOU DOING?"

His father quickly put out the flames with the fire extinguisher.

Six months later a taxi drew up outside the flat. Mark and his mother came in, both carrying suitcases. He had been away at a psychiatric clinic, with a period of convalescence at a cottage in Devon afterwards. He had fully recovered, and was now fit to go back to school.

Mark went into his bedroom, and looked around. Nothing had changed. Everything was still there – including the square yellow box.

"Why don't you lie down for a while, Mark," said his mother, "you're very tired. You've had a long journey. Have a bit of a sleep. I'll wake you up at suppertime."

She left the room. Mark lay on his bed.

"Welcome back," said a little voice.

TEN

The Mirror

My name is James Warburton. Our house is in London, near Marble Arch. My sister is now sharing a flat with some friends, but I'm still living at home with my parents.

I'm interested in many things. I used to collect stamps. This helped me learn about geography. I had the stamps of every island in the Caribbean. Then I became good at conjuring, and was able to perform magic tricks at parties.

This made me interested in real magic, which is known as Occultism. I collected books of grimoires and spells. Some had diagrams of magic circles with Hebrew letters. One had a series of squares, rather like crossword puzzles, reading the same in each direction. And I studied the lives of famous magicians like Aleister Crowley.

One day I was standing in the drawing room, reading out loud a ritual from one of my books. I was wearing a cloak and a turban I had made out of black velvet, and had a wand in one hand. Then Imelda, our Philippina cleaner, came into the room. She gave a scream and started crossing herself. She handed in her notice straight away.

My parents were very angry.

"This is all so...unhealthy, James," said my father. "Why can't you develop other interests? And you never do any sport, like other boys."

So I took up fencing. I loved the world of duels and swordfights, and read *The Three Musketeers*. I became so good that at school I won a prize for Epée.

In the drawing room we have a lot of books, and some antique swords kept by the fireplace. There is also a curious old mirror. It is long and narrow, and you can see yourself in it full length. It has a gold frame with letters painted around it in a foreign language. In the base of the frame is a small drawer. Inside are a few loose nails, screws, etc., and a card with an English translation of what is written on the frame. On the back of the card there is just one word.

One of my books tells you how to make your reflection in a mirror come to life. You have to stand in front of it, and by sheer concentration, transfer your centre of consciousness from your real body to its reflection. I had tried this many times but without success.

In legend, some mirrors themselves had special powers. In Snow White, the Magic Mirror on the Wall told the Queen "who was the fairest of them all." This was the inspiration of stories like *Alice Through the Looking Glass*.

One evening my father took me to dinner at his club. I asked him about the mirror in the drawing room. He said it was Persian. It had come off a pirate ship captured in the 18th Century.

One of the most notorious pirates at the time was a man

called William Varley. In the Caribbean no ship was safe from him. But when the wars against France and Spain were over their ambassadors complained, and his ship was intercepted by the Royal Navy. Varley, who had been sailing to find some hidden treasure, was captured and brought in irons back to Portsmouth. Then he was taken to London. Unlike most pirates who were sent to Execution Dock at Wapping, he was tried at the Old Bailey and hanged at Tyburn. It is said they used a silken cord. Then his body was left hanging in chains.

At Portsmouth his ship was broken up, and some of her timbers were used for building houses. The furniture in Varley's cabin was sold, but the Persian mirror was given to Judge Warburton, who had had him hanged. My father was that judge's direct descendant. And later I found out that our house was built on the very site of Tyburn gallows!

William Varley dressed very elegantly. On his death his clothes were auctioned off in Mayfair. In a coat pocket a small map was found, giving the location of some buried treasure on an island in the Caribbean. This map is now in the British Library, in London. One day I went there and got special permission to see it. As it is enclosed in a glass case no photos or photocopying were possible. So I carefully memorized all the details:

The island was called Dead Chest, in the Virgin Islands. The treasure itself was buried 60 yards south-west of a hut standing on a line joining two points 150 yards due east and 100 yards due south of Parson's Rock.

Now I happen to have a very good memory. I always win at Pelmanism, where you have to remember what the playing cards are after they are turned face down. Also my school won the Hampshire championship for General Knowledge, and I was Team Leader.

I asked the librarian if anyone had ever found the treasure. He said it was most unlikely. At the time few people took those sort of maps seriously. And anyhow, the Royal Navy just didn't have the resources to send a ship all that way on a wild goose chase.

One day, during the school holidays, I was invited to a fancy dress party. At first I couldn't think of what costume to wear. Then it came to me: I would go as a pirate – William Varley!

I got hold of a book about pirates. It had a lot about Varley. He was actually the son of a lord, the Earl of Chellingham. He was insanely jealous of his elder brother, who was to inherit the title and estate, and killed him in a duel. But before standing trial he escaped from Newgate Prison and joined the Navy. Then he led a mutiny, and eventually seized a Spanish ship called the Gloria Dei. For seven years he roamed the seas, robbing, burning, and pillaging. His aim was to amass a fortune, buy a sugar plantation and live like a gentleman. Though known for his ruthlessness he inspired total loyalty in his crew, in particular Nat Skinner, the bosun. Later, when captured, that individual was described as a 'simple-minded thug.' (He was sentenced to 500 strokes of the lash at the Marshalsea Prison, and then sent to a penal colony in America).

The book showed a portait of Varley standing by a table with a sextant and telescope. He was clean-shaven with a sallow face and tight thin lips. There was a black patch over his left eye. His right eye was grey and piercing. He wore a black three-cornered hat, a dark blue coat trimmed with gold braid, and a white lace shirt. A brocade waistcoat, breeches, silk stockings and shoes with silver buckles. He had a sword and carried a pistol in a purple sash worn around his waist. All this would be my fancy dress costume!

I hired some of my outfit from a theatrical costumier, bought the rest from secondhand shops, and my mother used some scraps of material from her sewing box.

My parents were going to the Opera the night of the party, so I would be alone in the house. I took a taxi as I would have been very conspicuous going there by bus or Underground!

I had a great time at the party, and won Joint First Prize with a girl called Sarah Shawcross, who came as Cleopatra.

When I got home I went up to my bedroom, sat there for a moment, then went into the bathroom. I looked at myself in the mirror. I still had all of my costume on. I really did look authentic and frightening! Then the telephone rang. I went down to the drawing room to answer it. It was my mother asking if I had enjoyed the party.

I was about to go upstairs again when the old mirror caught my eye. I opened the small drawer in the frame and took out the card. I read the words out loud:

Speak to me
And what you see
I will make
Reality.

Now Past and Present are the same
To see them both
Just call my name.

I turned the card over and called out "Soraya!"

I put it back in the drawer and looked at myself in the mirror. I could feel something was wrong. Then I realized why: I had a patch over my left eye, so the patch on the face in the mirror should have been straight opposite mine. But no: Its patch was opposite my *right* eye. I lifted my right arm. The figure in the mirror also lifted its arm. It was not opposite mine.

The man stepped out of the mirror. My arm was still outstretched and he shook my hand.

"William Varley, Royal Navy. Or rather, ex-Royal Navy," he said with a faint smile.

I couldn't move for sheer terror.

"Imitation is the best form of flattery," he said.

Another person came through the mirror. He was big and burly with a thick beard. He wore boots, a striped shirt, a leather jerkin and a red handkerchief around his head.

"This is Nat Skinner, the finest bosun in the West Indies," said Varley.

"Thank 'ee, Cap'n. And skins 'em I do, with that little cat o' mine!"

He laughed, showing a row of blackened teeth.

"Take him, Nat," said Varley.

I tried to resist, but it was no use, and I was dragged back through the mirror. Then everything went black and I passed out.

When I woke up I soon realized I was not at home, but in a dark and confined place. I felt stiff and uncomfortable, as I had been lying on wooden boards. My hat, coat, and waistcoat were gone. I felt a rocking motion. There was a smell of wood and tar. I could hear a slushing sound and mens' voices cursing and swearing. When my eyes got used to the darkness I saw there were sacks, barrels, coils of rope and chains all around. Then I heard a key turn and a door creaked open. In came a boy of about my age, dressed in a shirt, breeches and stockings.

"Where am I?" I gasped.

"Well, where the bleedin' hell d'you think you are," said the boy, "in some fancy London residence?"

"Am I...in a boat?'"

"You're at sea, and aboard the Glory Day," he said.

He handed me a bowl and a metal cup.

"Better eat this quick. Won't be no more of it."

Then he left and locked the door. I had been given some porridge, a dry biscuit, and a cup of water.

Later on the door opened again. Nat Skinner came in.

"Come on, lad."

He took me by the arm and we went up on deck. The sunlight was dazzling as I had been so long in darkness in the hold. There was sea all around, and no sight of land. Rough-looking men were pulling on ropes and unfurling sails. Several of them were up the masts.

"See them decks?" asked Skinner, "clean 'em."

"But...I don't belong here," I protested.

"Oh? Then perhaps you'd like to meet my little feline friend?"

He went over to a locker, took out a cat o' nine tails, and swung it round and round. He pointed to a scrubbing brush and a bucket of water. I got to work.

As time went on I was given many other tasks. At first they were simple, such as coiling rope or manning the pumps. Then I started handling the ropes, sails and rigging. The first time I went up the mast was terrifying!

The Gloria Dei was a ten gun sloop. I learnt all about her history. She had been carrying gold from South America to Cadiz when she was captured by Varley and the mutineers. They ordered her whole crew to walk the plank. Captain Alvarez and three of the officers refused, and they were shot. Alvarez's head was cut off and put on the bowsprit. Varley then set fire to his own ship, which was smaller, and they all sailed off in the Gloria.

I got to know some of the ship's company. There was Arthur the helmsman; Jeb, Smith, and Peters, gunners; Slim, Tom, and Robbie, deckhands; a negro called Lennox (a very big man); and a chap with a wooden leg called Peg Leg

Greg. And also Davis, Varley's cabin boy, who had brought me food when I was in the hold.

The crew called me "The Young Gentleman," and said things like, "Would he remove his kid gloves, care to get his manicured hands dirty, and turn the bleedin' windlass?" But eventually they became friendlier and began to accept me as one of them.

"So you're at Eton?" asked Davis, one day.

"No."

"Harrow, then?"

"No. Actually I am at Winchester."

"The Young Gentleman is being heducated at Winchester, actually," said Peters.

They all laughed.

"Winchester, eh?" said Greg, "that's Hampshire. Pompey!"

In his command of the ship Varley was assisted by the First Mate, a Mr Hollis. He was a quiet man and a very good navigator. I learnt that he had once been a banker, but was jailed for embezzlement. Freed on condition that he joined the Navy, he had taken part in the mutiny with Varley.

There were also two women on board: Mrs Hollis, who was always extravagantly dressed. She was from Jamaica. And Madge, the ship's cook, old and fat. She also served breakfast to Mrs Hollis in her cabin.

The crew quarters were hot and cramped. The air stank of sweat. I had hardly any room to hang my hammock. I was often seasick. The food was dreadful, consisting usually of hard bread, potatoes, or gruel with bits of meat in it. The biscuits were sometimes full of weevils. There was no fresh fruit, nor any vegetables, and I reckoned some of the crew had scurvy. On Sundays everyone was given a ration of rum.

Davis came up to me one day.

"Captain wants to see you."

He went aft and opened a door with a key. We entered a beautiful and spacious cabin. It had a large window overlooking the stern. Books lined the walls, and there was a cabinet full of delicate china and pewter. A sofa, an armchair, and a small dining table with four chairs around it. And in the corner was the Persian mirror.

"Sit down, James," said Varley.

Davis left the cabin. A moment later Madge came in with a tray.

"Will you join me for luncheon?" asked Varley.

"Er...thank you, sir."

Compared with what I had been eating up to now, this food was delicious.

"Have some wine," he said, pouring me a glass from a decanter.

After a moment he spoke again.

"I will come straight to the point. The treasure map – will you give it to me?"

"I haven't got it," I said.

"Then where is it?"

"In the British Library, in London."

"But you will have remembered everything," said Varley.

I said nothing. His single eye flashed and his lips tightened.

"James, if you do not tell me, I fear we shall have to dispose of you."

I had no choice.

"All right," I said, "it's on Dead Chest, in the Virgin Islands."

"And the treasure's location on that island?"

"60 yards south-west of a hut standing on a line joining two points 100 yards due east and 150 yards due south of Parson's Rock."

"Thank you," he said, writing it all down on a sheet of paper.

After a moment he rang a small silver bell. Davis came in and I was escorted out of the cabin.

Over the next week I noticed the weather was getting warmer. One day I saw land.

"Where's that?" I asked.

"The Azores," said Tom.

We put into Corvo, very briefly, for water. I was kept in the hold again, in case I tried to escape.

The rest of the voyage was long and arduous. One night there was a violent storm. We rode it out with all the sails reefed. Another time we were becalmed. It was hot and humid and we sat motionless on an oily sea. Then, for a while, we were chased by the Royal Navy, but Varley outmanoeuvred them by skilful seamanship.

We finally reached the Virgin Islands. Carefully avoiding Anegada and Virgin Gorda, we passed Cooper Island and Salt Island and came within sight of Dead Chest. We anchored two hundred yards out. They launched one of the boats and Varley was rowed ashore with some of the men. I sat in the stern with Nat Skinner keeping a careful watch on me. Varley looked through his telescope and pointed at something in the distance.

"Parson's Rock, I imagine," he said.

We pulled the boat onto the beach. There were palm trees there, but as we moved inland, the vegetation got thicker and a way had to be cut through it with machetes. Then we came to a clearing. There was a hut with some chickens around it. An old man came out shouting and waving his arms.

"Not to worry, Cap'n, I'll sort 'im out," said Skinner.

He took out his pistol and shot the man. The chickens all scattered, squawking. Then he went into the hut. I heard screaming and two more shots. Skinner came out laughing.

"Easy as kiss-yer-hand," he said, putting away his gun.

Varley made careful sightings with his compass, taking a fix on Parson's Rock and the hut. Then he paced it out. He pointed down at the ground.

"I think it's here," he said. "Start digging."

But after two hours nothing had been found. Some other holes were dug near the first one. The men were exhausted in the sweltering heat, and began to grumble.

"Bleedin' kid," said Skinner, angrily, "knew 'e was a waste

of time. And to come all this way for nothing!"

Varley came up and looked at me straight in the face. He was pale with anger. His single eye flashed, and his thin lips quivered.

"Well?" he asked.

It was terrifying.

"What shall I do with 'im now, Cap'n?" asked Skinner, fingering his pistol.

I really thought my last moment had come. But my mind was working at lightning speed, and I thought of something.

"I'm very sorry, sir," I stammered, "I got them all mixed up. The coordinates, I mean."

"I see," said Varley.

"Actually, I think it's 150 yards east and 100 yards south of the rock."

"You had better be right this time," said Skinner, menacingly.

Varley worked out the new position, and they went to the spot.

"Dig!" he ordered.

After about twenty minutes Slim hit something hard with his spade. They uncovered a large wooden chest, bound with brass.

There was a big cheer, and then everyone was patting me on the back.

"You know, I always had the utmost confidence in that lad," said Skinner.

The chest was loaded onto the boat and rowed back to the Gloria. When it was opened it was beyond anyone's wildest dreams. Diamonds, rubies, emeralds and sapphires. All kinds of jewellery and gold watches. Bullion, and a huge quantity of gold and silver coins – ducats, dollars, doubloons, and pieces-of-eight.

Each member of the crew had his share of the treasure, what he received depending on his status in the ship's company. Mrs Hollis was given a string of pearls. And I got a silver dollar! But most of it was not distributed. It was itemised in detail, and then the chest was sealed and kept in a room next to Varley's cabin, guarded by two men.

Then we weighed anchor and set sail. We soon lost sight of land. I had no idea where we were heading.

Two days later, at noon, there was a roll of drums. All hands were called on deck. To witness a punishment. A man was led out, stripped to the waist. He was one of the guards of the treasure chest; he had stolen nine doubloons from it. Nat Skinner took out his cat o' nine tails. The man received nine lashes. Then his hands were placed on a wooden block. Skinner got a knife and, one by one, chopped off seven fingers and both thumbs.

"We're not monsters, you know," he said, looking up at his audience, beaming. "I did have to leave 'im with *one* finger. How else is 'e goin' to pick 'is nose?"

Then the man was pushed overboard.

Two days later I saw land in the distance. They said it was Martinique. Then a ship was spotted. To trick them, Varley raised a French flag. As we got near we signalled for her to surrender. She took no notice, so we approached alongside.

She was a French merchant ship, the Rochefort. We fired a broadside. They fired back, but were outgunned by the Gloria. The Rochefort began to take in water. Nat Skinner led a boarding party. Some of the French sailors were killed, and others managed to escape in one of their boats. Skinner made the captain, two officers, a finely dressed gentleman, and a lady of quality get into their other boat. They were escorted back to the Gloria. Tom and Robbie had already ransacked the Rochefort and loaded our boat with several chests, and also silverware, china, tobacco and hogsheads of wine.

On meeting the French captives Varley removed his hat. The gentleman stood and faced him.

"I am the Comte de Vernay."

"Your servant," said Varley, bowing.

"King Louis will hear of this, and you will pay for it dearly," said the Count, furiously.

There was a sound of cannon again. Peters had fired at the Rochefort, just below the waterline. She went straight to the bottom.

"Ooh!" went a shrill voice.

The chests had been brought up on deck and opened. Mrs Hollis was rummaging through them, pulling out the finest silks, satins, calico and muslins – all the Countess's clothes.

"Beautiful gowns!" she exclaimed, "latest Paris fashions."

She went up to the Countess.

"I'll have that blue silk you're wearing."

She tore the dress off her

"Really, Jane!" said Mr Hollis, shocked.

"And its frilly underskirt too," said Mrs Hollis.

The Countess was left standing in just a short petticoat and stockings. It was a cold evening and Varley was wearing a cloak. He took it off and put it around the Countess's shoulders. It was the only decent thing I ever saw him do. Then the five French people were ordered back into their boat and cast adrift.

We continued sailing southwards. I realized that, now they had found the treasure, I was no longer of any use to them. Varley and Mr and Mrs Hollis usually had dinner together in the Captain's cabin. Davis, who had been serving them, overheard snatches of their conversation.

"Planning to get rid of you, they are."

They had been discussing what to do with me. Indeed, if they were ever caught, I was a potential witness. The crew knew about it too. Madge had begged the First Mate's wife to implore the Captain 'to have mercy on the lad'. But Mrs Hollis told her to hold her tongue or she would get a good hiding. In her view I was a liability and should walk the plank.

"A hungry lot, them sharks!" said Davis.

I didn't have long to wait. A few days later they signalled to a passing ship. She came close and sent out a boat to the Gloria. Four men came aboard. One looked particularly brutal and carried a whip. I was sent for. The man looked me up and down, but shook his head. Then, casting an eye over the crew, he picked out Lennox. He tossed a bag of coins onto the deck and took him back to their ship.

I knew I had very little time left. I was desperate. Then suddenly the idea came to me. It was obvious – I had to escape the same way I had come – back through the magic mirror!

Varley's cabin was always kept locked, even when he was in it. He trusted nobody. The only other person with a key was Davis. It was on a cord tied to his belt. I devised a plan. I had saved most of my rum ration in a bottle. I sold it all to Davis for a farthing. That night he got blind drunk and passed out. I cut the cord, took the key, and crept aft towards the Captain's cabin.

With my heart in my mouth I unlocked the door and opened it gently. Only one lamp was lit. Varley was sitting at his table poring over some charts. He had his back to the door. The mirror was in the corner of the cabin, past his table. I could reach it as long as he didn't look up. It was now or never! I tiptoed up to it and whispered "Soraya!" I stepped through the mirror and was back in our drawing room in London.

I could hear my father in the corridor, singing bits of Wagner .

"What did you see?" I asked.

"The Flying Dutchman."

A strange coincidence, I thought.

"How was the fancy dress party?"

"Great."

Next evening I took Sarah Shawcross out to dinner. When I got home I found that my parents were out. I decided to go and watch TV in the drawing room. But as soon as I opened the door I knew something was wrong. A man in a black three-cornered hat was sitting on the sofa. He stood up.

"Captain Varley" I asked, "what are you doing here? You belong in the 18th Century."

"Quite so."

"And in 1726 you were hanged for mutiny and piracy."

He laughed.

"Well then, James, you and I will rewrite history. I am taking you back to the Gloria Dei. I need a new cabin boy."

I shuddered to think what had happened to Davis.

"Certainly not!" I said.

Varley drew his sword. I grabbed one of our antique ones from the fireplace. There was a furious fight. I was glad to have had all those fencing lessons at Winchester. Twice he nearly killed me. But then I slashed his wrist and he dropped his sword. He stepped back to the end of the room, got out his pistol, and took careful aim. I picked up a book that was next to me and flung it at his head. It hit him at the very moment he pulled the trigger. He missed and hit the mirror instead. It shattered into tiny fragments. And apart from some dust and smoke there was no sign of William Varley. After all, he had been dead for three hundred years.

***

Three weeks later my mother was in my bedroom going through my clothes. The holidays were nearly over and she was packing up my suitcase for school.

"What are these?" she asked.

She held up the breeches I had worn for the fancy dress party.

"Don't worry about those," I said, "just chuck them."

"No. That's silly. You might want to wear them again," she said, "but they're filthy! I'll take them to the cleaners."

A few days later she collected the dry cleaning. A little plastic bag was pinned to the breeches. Inside was a silver dollar.

ELEVEN

The Toby Jug

Emma Faulkner and her parents lived in a very pretty house in Kensington, West London.

"It's Regency," her father would say proudly.

It had a nice garden at the back, and a small front garden too. The house had three storeys, and was built of dark yellow brick with a cream stucco ground floor. Its windows were tall and of excellent proportions. It was situated in a quiet street, with several small shops nearby.

"It's a little village," her mother would often say, "we're a real community here."

She knew all their neighbours and was on friendly terms with the local shopkeepers.

Everything was perfect – except for one thing: an Underground line ran right beneath the house. Every so often (except late at night) you could hear a rumbling sound, and the house would shake a little. The Faulkners had lived there for many years and had got used to it. At one time they had been concerned that the Underground trains had weakened the foundations of the house. But a surveyor had made a detailed inspection and assured them that they had nothing to worry about.

This shaking had once made a precious Ming vase fall off a side table in the sitting room and shatter into pieces. It was unrepairable, but fortunately the insurance paid for the damage. Mrs Maitland, the cleaner, was under strict instructions to ensure that the shaking did not cause the china ornaments on the mantelpiece there to move too near its edge. This also prevented the pictures on the walls from hanging level, and she would straighten them each time she came.

The mantelpiece in the sitting room had a clock in the middle. On the left of it were two Chinese lions and a small jade box. On the right side, nearest the clock, was a Toby jug, and then a shepherdess. Furthest away, near the right-hand end of the mantelpiece, stood a soldier.

The Toby jug was a fat old man with a rather red face, in a black three-cornered hat. He sat on a chair that was also part of the jug. He wore a blue coat, a red waistcoat, brown breeches, and yellow stockings. Someone had once dropped three marbles into him and forgotten about them. Pencils and biros were sometimes put in him too, and they stuck out over the top of his hat. One day Emma left two wet paintbrushes in him sticking upwards, and the paint had dripped down onto his coat. Luckily they were watercolours and it washed off easily.

"I am a Toby jug," he would angrily say to the other figures next to him. "In Devon, where I come from, we carry cream. Good thick Devonshire cream, for scones and jam. I am not here for putting pens and pencils in. It is most undignified for a man of my position!"

The Shepherdess was from Meissen, in Germany. She held a shepherd's crook in her hand, and a young lamb lay at her feet. She wore a simple brown dress over a white blouse. Her hair was blonde and in plaits. She had blue eyes, a fair complexion, and rosy pink cheeks.

The Soldier was tall and handsome. He wore a red tunic with gold buttons and epaulettes, black trousers, and a sword at his side. On his head was a high bearskin.

Being in close proximity for so long, these two became fond of each other, and eventually fell in love. The Soldier would often speak softly to the Shepherdess. But someone else had become obsessed with her beauty – the Toby jug.

Emma was an only child.

"I'd love to have a baby brother or sister," she once said.

"Well, I'm afraid that's rather unlikely," said her mother.

But Emma had lots of friends. They often came to her house for tea and sometimes stayed on for a sleepover. Whenever she was alone she didn't watch television much, or play on her computer. She was fond of painting and drawing, and also read a lot. This had helped develop her imagination. She sometimes played with the china figures on the mantelpiece in the sitting room.

She made up a story about the Chinese lions. They had once guarded the Emperor's palace, and killed a dragon that had threatened him. One lion bit off its tail, and the other went for its throat.

But she was more interested in the figures on the right of the clock. She knew that the Soldier and the Shepherdess were in love. She would pick them up and put them close to each other, sometimes with their faces actually touching, so that they could kiss. She often forgot to place them back in their usual positions afterwards, and Mrs Maitland had to do it when she dusted the mantelpiece.

Emma didn't think the Toby jug would have had much success with the Shepherdess.

"Why, he's far too old, and so fat and ugly," she once said out loud.

She had no idea how much her words had hurt the Jug. He was infatuated with the Shepherdess, and insanely jealous of the Soldier.

One day it rained all afternoon and Emma had to stay indoors. She got out her crayons and drew a charming little cottage on a white card. It had a pretty garden with flowers and trees, and green fields beyond. Then she went to the mantelpiece and made the Soldier and Shepherdess face each other.

"You two are getting married!" she said.

She turned them both so they could see the drawing on the card.

"And this will be your home."

The Toby jug was consumed with jealousy, and vowed to destroy his rival, the Soldier. Now, unlike the other figures, the Jug had the ability to move himself. The marbles that had been left inside him were irritating, but, with a supreme effort of will, he could make them all roll together and hit any one side of his interior. Then each time he would be pushed half a centimetre along the mantelpiece. So, with a series of jerks, he could move in any direction he chose. He would wait until an Underground train was passing, as its vibration lessened the friction between his base and the surface of the mantelpiece.

Mrs Maitland came in to clean early in the morning on Tuesdays and Fridays. She would hoover the carpet in the sitting room, adjust the pictures, and dust the mantelpiece, correctly replacing any ornaments that had been moved by the Underground's vibration. She had worked there for years, and was old and short-sighted. Mr and Mrs Faulkner got up later, and normally never went into the sitting room until around midday, when the clock was wound up.

The Toby jug decided to act early one Thursday morning. It was the rush hour, and the trains were more frequent. As soon as the first train ran he began to move towards the Shepherdess. After some time he was touching her.

"Keep away, sir, please!" she exclaimed, blushing.

The Jug said nothing, and was now pushing her towards the Soldier.

She cried out in fear.

"Halt! I order you!" said the Soldier.

But the Jug ignored him. After many more trains had passed he had pushed the Shepherdess up against him.

"Stop, I say!" shouted the Soldier, "or I will draw my

sword to protect this lady!"

The Toby jug laughed, as he knew the sword was useless. It was just moulded into the Soldier's side. He continued pushing. As he now had to move the other two figures as well, he was progressing at less than a quarter of a centimetre at a time. But, slowly and inexorably, all three were moving towards the right – and the end of the mantelpiece.

The Soldier realized what was in store for him.

"You will hang for this, sir! That I guarantee," he said in powerless rage.

"Huh!" laughed the Jug. "I'm so fat they'd have a job even finding my neck!"

"Do not harm him, kind sir, I implore you!" pleaded the Shepherdess, "he is my betrothed."

But the Jug took no notice and carried on pushing. After several hours the Soldier found himself on the very brink of the mantelpiece. One final jerk, and he went over the edge and crashed down onto the stone fireplace surround. There he lay decapitated, with his head and bearskin a foot away from his body.

The Toby jug now stopped, exhausted and victorious. He had gained his revenge, but hardly the love of the Shepherdess. Tears flowed from her eyes. She had lost her beloved.

It was Emma who found the Soldier smashed on the floor, shortly after breakfast. She was incredibly upset. She called her parents. Her mother picked up the Soldier and his head, and dropped the two pieces into a plastic bag, which was then put away in a cupboard.

No one could understand why the Toby jug and the Shepherdess were close up next to each other on the far right-hand edge of the mantelpiece, when the ornaments on the left of the clock had not moved one inch.

"Must be those damned trains!" said Mrs Faulkner.

She would have a word with Mrs Maitland, to ensure that the ornaments stayed safely on the mantelpiece, in their correct places.

"She's as blind as a bat!" said Mr Faulkner.

The Toby jug and the Shepherdess were put back in their normal positions. The Jug now had her all to himself. He hoped that, in the course of time, loneliness would help him win her over. Over the next few weeks he tried hard to be as charming, interesting and amusing as possible. But to no avail. She would not be consoled for her loss, and rejected his every advance.

One Friday morning, when Mrs Maitland dusted the mantelpiece, she carelessly replaced the Toby jug a bit too near the front edge. After she left, the Jug resumed his courting of the Shepherdess. She ignored him as usual. Trying to be witty, he began cracking jokes. He found some of them so funny that he laughed at them himself. The marbles inside him jangled and made him rock about. Without realizing it he was also getting nearer to the edge of the mantelpiece. He cracked more and more jokes, but the Shepherdess still took no notice. Then he thought of a pun, which to him was particularly funny.

"That soldier – he certainly fell for you, didn't he?"

He guffawed maliciously. He just couldn't stop laughing, it was so funny. He laughed and laughed, the marbles jangled about. He rocked and rocked, and got nearer and nearer the edge of the mantelpiece. Then a train passed underneath. The Toby jug toppled over the edge, and crashed down onto the fireplace below. He shattered into tiny pieces.

Emma heard the sound and rushed into the sitting room.

"Mum! Dad!" she shouted, "the Toby jug's fallen down!"

Her parents came in.

"Can't we mend him?" asked Emma, very distraught.

Her mother saw all the broken pieces. There were so many of them.

"It looks almost impossible," she said, shaking her head, "and if one could have it mended, it would be hideously expensive."

"Hardly worth it," said Mr Faulkner. "I remember buying it when I was in Exeter. I think I only paid twenty pounds."

"I never liked him much anyway," said his wife, "so squat and ugly."

She fetched a dustpan and brush, swept up all the bits, and put them in the dustbin.

The Shepherdess now stood alone on the right-hand side of the mantelpiece. She did not fear the Chinese lions, as they were on the other side of the clock. She was relieved to be rid of the Toby jug's attentions, but pined for the Soldier.

Three weeks later a cardboard box arrived. Inside,

carefully protected in bubble wrap and tissue paper, was the Soldier. He had been expertly repaired, and it was impossible to discern where the break had been. Emma was overjoyed. She put him back on the mantelpiece in his old position. Her cousin, who was studying for the priesthood, conducted a marriage ceremony for the Soldier and the Shepherdess. Emma made them a small house out of clay at school, and had it fired there. It was painted in bright colours. She placed it between the Soldier and the end of the mantelpiece.

***

One evening, a year later, Mr Faulkner came back home carrying a box.

"Whatever's in that?" asked his wife.

"You'll see," he said.

He opened the box and took out a carefully wrapped china figure. It was a princess. On her head was a tiara, and she wore a long purple gown which flowed out around her feet. She was very beautiful.

"Gosh!" said Mrs Faulkner, "why did you buy that? I bet it was very expensive. No! I don't want to know how much you paid."

"Yes, she did cost a fair amount," admitted her husband, "but I just couldn't resist her. Fabulous, isn't she?"

Mrs Faulkner looked at the Princess carefully. Her long black hair was exquisitely pinned up under her tiara. Her translucent white skin, fine nose, full red lips, arched eyebrows and high domed forehead portrayed a woman of exceptional beauty and intelligence. Her slender arms were extended outwards as if she was swaying in a graceful dance. Her dress was sheer elegance. Beneath its hem was a glimpse of a golden slipper.

Emma came into the room.

"Wow!" she exclaimed.

"Now you see why I had no choice!" said her father, "the dealer told me he'd fallen in love with her, and if I didn't pay him the full price he would change his mind and keep her!"

They found a place on the mantelpiece for the Princess. It was on the left of the house and next to the Soldier.

TWELVE

The Plates

I was playing in the garden with Tim, my little brother, when I heard my mother calling.

"Amanda!"

I went back inside.

"Amanda. Remember you're having tea with your grandmother today. You should look smarter. Wear your blue dress. And some proper shoes."

"Why?" I asked.

"For two reasons," she said. "You look scruffy in that T-shirt. And as for those jeans and trainers!"

"And what is the other reason?"

"Because I said so."

"Yes 'mother'," I said, raising two fingers level with my ears and flicking them twice.

"Will you stop doing that every time I speak to you!" she said angrily.

That's the sign for inverted commas, i.e., my "mother". Because I didn't consider her to be that. Nor her husband, my father. And also I absolutely HATE wearing dresses and

149

skirts. They flip and flop around with a mind of their own. Once I was crossing a barbed wire fence and I tore my skirt. My mother was unbelievably vile about it, and made me sew it all up myself.

For a long time I had been pretty sure they were not my real parents. At first it was just an idea – or even a fantasy. Perhaps I was really an orphan or a foundling? Then I read a book called *The Princess*, by Margaret Richardson. In it a girl finds out that the nasty and boring parents she lives with are not her real ones, but impostors. She is actually a royal princess. Her real father and mother, the King and Queen, have been imprisoned in the dungeons of Castle Haldenstein. But one day a young woodman comes out of the forest. Riding a white horse he rescues the Princess, and sets her real parents free. They win back their kingdom and the false parents are put in jail. Then the Princess marries the woodman (who turns out to be a prince in disguise) and they all live happily ever after.

Tim said the book was a lot of romantic rubbish. But I think he felt the same way about our parents. They didn't even look like us – Tim and I have fair hair, while my mother's was dark, and so was my father's, with a bit of grey at the edges.

I first began to get really suspicious when some minor things didn't quite ring true. As they say: "the devil is in the detail."

Several of our white bath towels had the letters WPH embroidered in one corner. Now none of us have those initials. One day I asked my mother about it.

"Oh, it's nothing," she replied.

But after that I didn't see those towels for a long time. Then I saw one again in the airing cupboard. The corner with the initials had been replaced by a matching piece of plain towelling, carefully stitched on. The same had been done to all of the others.

Another time I was unloading the dishwasher. When I took out one plate, I found that by holding it at a certain angle you could see the faint outline of a house on the rim. It had three gables and a tower. Under this were some letters, but they were too faded to make anything out. Then my mother came into the kitchen. She took the plate out of my hand and threw it into the rubbish bin.

"We don't need that old stuff," she said, "doesn't match the rest of the crockery."

We lived in a Victorian house. The garden was at the back. A gate in the garden wall led into a big park with many tall trees. Through them, in the distance, you could see the roof of a large building. And at one side of our house was a garage. It was never used, and was always locked. We didn't have a car, and one day I asked my father why.

"We can get by perfectly well without one," he said.

"What's the garage used for, then?" I asked.

"Storage."

I had never been inside the garage, and became more and more curious to know what was in it. One day both our parents had gone out shopping.

"Let's have a look inside the garage!" I said to Tim.

"No, We shouldn't. Anyhow, it's locked."

"Coward!" I said. "I think I know where the key is."

In the hall was a row of hooks where all the keys were hung up. At one end was a key hanging by itself.

"I bet that's the one!" I said.

I was right. But the doors were so stiff that we could only open them just enough to squeeze in. It was so dark inside you could hardly see anything. Running my hand along the wall I found a light switch, but when I turned it on nothing happened. When my eyes got used to the darkness I saw that the place was crammed full of furniture, crates, and cardboard boxes. I opened one. It had crockery in it. I took out some plates. They had a design on them with writing underneath.

"It's horrible in here," said Tim, "it's so dark and damp! Let's go."

High up on one wall was a small window, coated with grime, and I clambered up over a pile of furniture to reach it. I managed to open it and let in a bit more light. The garage was full right up to the ceiling, and as far as the back wall. Then suddenly I lost my nerve.

"Yes, I think it *is* time to go," I said, "before they come back."

I took one of the plates back with me so I could have a chance to study it later. Then we closed and locked the garage doors. As I was putting the key back on its hook I heard the front door open. I dashed upstairs and hid the plate in my bedroom.

That night I had a good look at it. It was similar to the one from the dishwasher, but the image on its rim was clear and distinct. It showed a Victorian mansion, dark red in colour, with three pointed gables. There were bay windows on the ground floor and arched gothic ones on the upper storeys. At one end of the house stood a clock tower with a tall spire. Under this was written Wynstanley Park Hospital.

Next morning I got up a bit late and had to hurry in time to catch the school bus. I stupidly left the plate on my chest of drawers. When I got home that evening my mother confronted me with it.

"Where did you get this?" she asked, holding it up.

"Er ... I just found it somewhere."

"You've been in the garage, haven't you?" she said, accusingly.

I said nothing.

"Well?" she asked, standing there.

"Come on, Mother! It's just a plate! Why are you making such a fuss about it?"

She walked off angrily with it in her hand. Later I noticed that the garage key was no longer on its hook.

Tim's bedroom was at the top of the house, overlooking the garden. One day, with his binoculars, we focused on the building in the distance.

"It must be the same as the one on the plate," I said, "look, I can see the tower through the trees!"

We resolved to go there as soon as we had the chance.

Next Saturday our parents said they would be away for the afternoon. So we went through the garden gate into the park. After a while we came to a barbed wire fence. (This was where, a year earlier, I had torn my skirt. My mother had spotted us there and had shouted for us to come back). This time we got across alright. After a few hundred yards we reached a high brick wall. We scaled it and landed in some bushes on the other side. There, in front of us, stood the house.

"It's really creepy," said Tim. "Let's go back."

"No!" I said firmly, "not after we've come all this way."

But I must admit I felt pretty scared too. The large bay windows seemed to leer at us, and the gothic ones were like little eyes. Each of the three gables was crowned with a pinnacle. On the roof were tall chimneys, and evil-looking gargoyles leaned out from the gutters. The walls were of dark red brick, with ivy growing up them. Birds fluttered in and out of the clock tower's spire.

"I bet there are bats in there," said Tim. "Do you think it's got bells?"

"As long as they don't start ringing now," I said, "that would be *too* scary."

We walked up to the front door. On it was a big yellow sign: KEEP OUT. DANGEROUS STRUCTURE. But strangely, the door was ajar. We crept in and found ourselves in a big hallway. It smelt damp and musty. Many of the floorboards were rotten, and in some places plaster had fallen off the ceiling. A huge wooden staircase rose in front of us. We went into a side room. It was full of school desks. We went back into the hall. Then I heard a sound. Footsteps?

"I think we should go," I said.

"Me too!" said Tim.

So we headed back. We saw an old signboard lying in the bushes, by the wall. It said: WYNSTANLEY PARK SCHOOL. We got home well before our parents returned. They suspected nothing!

Standing in our garden the next day, I was struck by how much our house looked like Wynstanley Park. It was a miniature version of it: one gable instead of three, and the same gothic windows, all much reduced in scale. And identical dark red bricks. There was surely some connection between the two places. Also the name of our house was Winsley Cottage.

My relationship with my mother was frosty, to say the least. She said I was a difficult child. If I ever argued with her she would say: "Don't backchat!" But I am an independent spirit. Sometimes I would call her 'Stella' instead of 'Mother'. Once I addressed her as 'Mrs Stella Boardman'.

"How dare you call me that!"

"I'm sorry," I said, "that was incorrect. It's 'Mrs Michael Boardman'."

My father wasn't as bad. But he was weak. He always agreed with my mother and did everything she said. He was insignificant. A mere cipher.

Soon after our trip to the mansion I had the dream again.

I had often had it before. I was a little girl and was in a car with Tim. He was just a baby. A man and a woman were in the front. The car stopped and two more people got in. There was something wrong about them. We went off again. Then the car stopped a second time and a bald man with a black moustache got in too. We were now squeezed up so tightly! Then something unspeakably awful happened. At this point I always woke up, usually screaming.

The first time I had this dream I was so frightened that I had to go down to the sitting room, as my parents were still up. They were watching television.

"Amanda! Why aren't you wearing your dressing gown? You'll catch cold," said my mother.

But when I told them about the dream they weren't at all sympathetic, only annoyed that I had interrupted their viewing.

"Now go back to bed."

The worst thing was that if I ever dreamt about a car it would invariably turn into that nightmare. And somehow I always knew what was going to happen, and even expected it.

Grandma lived in a small flat, and had a carer to look after her. This time, after tea, I played some tunes on her piano. On top of it was an envelope addressed to 'Mrs Meadows'.

"Who's that?" asked Tim.

"Why, it's me!" said Grandma.

It had never occurred to us that she had a surname!

There was also a photograph of a man in a silver frame. He had a moustache, and was quite young, but already bald.

"Who's that man?" I asked.

"My son," she said proudly, "he's a School Principal now."

Then the carer took me by the arm and led me into another room.

"It's a great shame," she said quietly.

"Why?"

"Her son is dead. Tragic. But she just can't accept it. You mustn't mention him again."

We were having breakfast one Saturday morning. Our parents were already dressed. Then the door bell rang. It was a taxi.

"We're going away for the day," said my mother. "I've put your lunch in the fridge, and some supper too, in case we're back late."

Whoopee! A whole day to do whatever we liked. I watched TV for a bit, then turned it off. We had no time to waste.

"The garage!" I said excitedly.

"But we haven't got the key," said Tim.

We got dressed and went outside. The small window in the garage was still open. We put a stepladder up to it and just managed to squeeze through. I had taken a spare bulb with me, and when the light was on we were amazed at how much stuff was in the garage. I found some large suitcases. One was full of ladies' clothes, with some nice dresses in it. Another had mens' clothes. All the jumpers were motheaten. Among the suits and shirts was a white cotton coat, the kind that scientists wear.

There was also a filing cabinet. Inside were files all about Wynstanley Park Hospital. Patients', doctors' and nurses' names and addresses. And accounts: catering, maintenance, wages, etc. One file said: "Domestic – Wynstanley Cottage".

I looked at my watch.

"We'll spend an hour and a half in here, have some lunch, then do some more afterwards," I said. "We must be out by four o'clock at the latest, in case they're back early."

I looked around. Most of the furniture was very good, though the armchairs and sofa were damp, and mouldy in places. There were antiques and pictures too. I wondered why we couldn't have them in our house.

We carried on after lunch. There was garden furniture too, and several statues. And always more boxes! Mainly filled with books, often about medicine and psychiatry.

Tim was standing on a pile of boxes, handing them down to me. There were always more underneath. Then he stopped.

"There's something hard here," he said.

We cleared away everything that was on top of it. A large object, dark green, and made of metal.

"It's a car!" I said.

We cleared away enough to open one of the doors. It was dark and musty inside. We sat in the front seats. They were brown leather and covered in dust. Tim tried to move the gear lever, but it wouldn't budge. He twiddled the steering wheel and pressed the horn button in the middle. Nothing happened.

"Peep peep!" he joked.

"You idiot!" I said angrily, "what if someone had heard it?"

On the back seat was a tartan rug and two coats, a man's and a woman's. I felt very ill at ease, and yet it was strangely familiar.

"I'm getting out," I said.

We opened the boot. Inside was a handbag, with lipstick, makeup, and a letter about a place in a kindergarten for Amanda Harrison. And also a briefcase, containing a diary for nine years back, and a wallet with credit cards in the name of Professor W.L. Harrison. And two photographs: one of a little girl, and the other of a baby.

"That's us!" I said.

There was also a driving license with a photo on it. Was that our real father?

Tears came into my eyes. I had been right all along. But it was already past three o'clock. We put everything away as we had found it and climbed back out of the window.

As soon as we were in the house we washed the grime off our faces, hands and clothes, and were quietly watching television when our parents returned.

I thought about everything we'd found in the garage, including the car. What colour was the one in my dream? Was it green? I remembered the smell of the leather seats. I asked Tim if he'd ever had a dream like that.

"Yes, I think I did have one about being in a car once," he said. After a moment he added: "But it was a long time ago. My memory of it is very hazy."

That evening we talked about the car again.

"You know, we forgot to do something really important," he said.

"What?"

"To write down the number plate. That's how you can trace the owner."

I was now convinced that our so-called parents were impostors. But who would help me find our real ones, and who would believe me anyway? I was only a schoolgirl. I decided to confide in Mr Featherstone, the art master.

I love art. Once I won a prize for the best still life. Mr Featherstone is younger and less uptight than the other teachers. He drives a red sports car. After the art lesson I stayed behind and told him everything. He looked very surprised, but said nothing.

When I came back from school the next day the red sports car was parked outside our house. I went straight upstairs, but heard snatches of conversation coming from the sitting room.

"...and thank you again, Mr Featherstone."

"Well, I thought it was the right thing to do."

Nothing was ever said about this, either at supper or afterwards. But I could sense the growing hostility of my parents.

One day, a week later, I saw two lorries parked outside.

Everything in the garage had been loaded into a removal van, and the car was being winched onto a breakdown truck.

Tim and I resolved to go back to Wynstanley Park. We got hold of a local Ordnance Survey map. On our first visit we'd had to climb over walls and fences, but we found how to reach the main entrance by road.

One Sunday we got the opportunity, and rode there on our bicycles. It was easier this time. There was a long gravelled drive, covered in weeds, then some high iron gates. Through them you could see the tower and gables of Wynstanley Park. There were cranes and bulldozers all around it. The gates were locked. Next to them was a small lodge. A door opened and an old man came out.

"Sorry, private property."

"Er...we were just looking," I said.

"Won't be much to see soon," said the man, "it's all coming down. Fifteen houses they're building here. Luxury flats too."

"I thought it was a school," I said.

"It was once. Never worked out, though. Went bust."

"Oh."

"Yes," he continued, "unlucky place, this. And before that, a hospital. Mental hospital."

I shuddered.

"Come in, I'll tell you all about it. I could do with a bit of company."

We leant our bikes against the gates and followed him

into the lodge.

"Like some tea? Or lemonade, a glass of milk?"

"Thank you very much," I said.

He went into another room and came back with a tray.

"Now make yourselves comfortable."

Tim and I sat down in some old armchairs.

"My name's Alf. Used to be the Head Porter. When it was a hospital, that is. And at the school, too. They kept me on as caretaker. To keep people out of the house and grounds. Dangerous structure, you see. What are you two called?"

"I'm Amanda Boardman, and this is my brother Tim," I replied. "But our real surname is Harrison."

"Harrison, eh?" he said, looking up with interest, "where do you live?"

"At Winsley Cottage."

"Once known as Wynstanley Cottage," he said. "That's where Professor and Mrs Harrison lived."

"I believe they were our parents," I said.

"Bad business, that," said Alf, darkly, "a tragedy, it was."

"What do you mean?" asked Tim.

"No. I shouldn't tell you. Not good for young ears."

I looked at him straight in the face.

"Alf – you' ve got to tell us."

He poured himself another cup of tea, and offered us some more biscuits.

"Well, I suppose it really does concern you two children," he said gravely. "Professor Harrison was the Director of Wynstanley Park Hospital. Catered for all types of mental illness. Finest in the country. But one day two inmates escaped from M1 – that's the locked ward. Climbed over the wall and got out of the grounds. Someone phoned the Professor. He was on his way back from a family outing. Had his wife and two children in the car."

Alf turned and looked at us.

"The Professor caught up with them two miles away. Told them to get into the car. He was going to take them back to the hospital."

A chill went through me.

"Then what happened?" I asked.

"They murdered him and his wife."

I was stunned.

"How horrible!" I said.

"But not the kids. Look, wait here, I'll show you something."

He went out of the room. Tim and I looked at each other. He came back with a scrapbook and opened it. A yellowed press cutting said: TRAGEDY AT MENTAL HOSPITAL. *Professor William Harrison, an eminent psychiatrist, and his wife Dorothy, were yesterday brutally murdered by two inmates escaping from Wynstanley Park Hospital.*

There were three photographs: One of the Professor, one of his wife, and a third one of a bald man with a moustache.

"Who's he?" I asked.

"That's Meadows," said Alf.

The man in the photo at Grandma's flat!

"And he died too," I said.

"Oh no!" said Alf, "Meadows ain't dead. He said he'd tried to save the Professor and his wife. But I reckon he put them two lunatics up to it."

"Why?" I asked.

"He was Deputy Director. Ambitious sort. He wanted the Professor out of the way. To get his job."

He poured himself some more tea and munched a biscuit.

"Where is he now?"I asked, horrified.

"Dunno. Somewhere, I suppose. Yes, Meadows, he did it all right. Set it all up, if you ask me."

I began to cry.

"Now, now, Amanda," said Alf kindly, putting his hand on my shoulder. "Don't you cry. Remember, you begged me to tell you."

"Yes," I sobbed.

"And you two kids are OK. Well, I heard they'd found foster parents for 'em. But I didn't think they'd still be living at the cottage."

"We had better be going now," I said, "thank you for the tea."

"Yes, thank you," said Tim.

"Come and see me again, any time," said Alf.

The journey home was the hardest bike ride I ever had to make.

Tim and I spent the rest of the day in a state of shock. But we took care not to behave any differently in case our parents (if you could call them that) suspected anything. We were obviously victims of a carefully planned conspiracy.

Next day, after school, I went straight to the police station. There was a small waiting room where I had to sit as there were two people ahead of me. Then I went up to the enquiries window.

"How can I help?" asked the policeman sitting behind it.

I told him about the garage, the mental hospital, and how our parents had been murdered and replaced by impostors. It was all poured out in a great hurry, all garbled and jumbled up.

"Slow down, young lady," said the policeman.

He listened for a bit longer, then got up.

"You'd better wait here a moment."

He came back a minute later with a woman who was wearing jeans and a jumper.

"This is Detective Inspector Curtis," he said. "I'll leave you in her capable hands."

She smiled at him.

"Come in here and tell me all about it."

We went into a room. It was sparsely furnished with a table and some chairs, and no pictures on the wall.

"Perhaps you'd like something to drink? And something to eat?"

I nodded. She spoke into a phone and someone brought some tea and sandwiches.

"Call me Anthea," she said.

I repeated what I'd said, but this time in a more orderly manner. Sometimes she asked me questions, and wrote down notes on a sheet of paper.

Her expression suddenly became serious.

"You're not making all this up, are you?" she asked.

"No."

"I must warn you that wasting police time is a serious offence," she said sternly.

"I absolutely promise you, every bit of this is true," I said. "You can ask my brother Tim."

"Right then. Let's continue," said Anthea.

When I had said everything I asked her what she was going to do.

"I'm not sure, at this point," she said. "First I shall write a report, then we will do some investigation. But you should go home now, Amanda. And don't talk about this to anyone. Just behave as you would normally."

She opened the door and showed me out. It was good to be taken seriously, for once.

One day, at breakfast, Tim and I were told not to put on our uniforms as we wouldn't be going to school that morning.

But we were to look "neat and tidy." Later on two cars arrived, and a man and a woman came into the sitting room. My mother served them coffee. Then we all had to sit down.

The man wore a dark suit and had a briefcase.

"Let us introduce ourselves," he said. "My name is Simon Harwood. I am a solicitor. This lady is Mrs Mary Swinton, a Children's Welfare Officer, from Berkshire County Council

Social Services. I am a trustee of the Foundation set up for you two children upon the deaths of Professor and Mrs Harrison, your father and mother. I will not go into further details about that unfortunate occurrence. Mr and Mrs Boardman here were appointed as your foster parents and guardians, to attend to your upbringing. May I say that they seem to have done an excellent job!"

"Thank you," said my foster father.

"Now we had intended that this be disclosed when the elder one of you reached the age of eighteen," continued Mr Harwood, "but since you appear to have already discovered it, we decided to visit you both in person. In order to confirm the fact officially, and to eliminate any doubt in your minds as to its veracity."

"What a pompous man," I thought.

"You see, now the truth has come out we don't want you to suffer any distress," said Mrs Swinton.

"I understand," I said.

"But what should we call them, then?" asked Tim, pointing to our foster parents.

"How about 'Aunt Stella' and 'Uncle Michael'?" suggested Mrs Swinton, smiling.

"That's fine," I said.

Tim nodded.

"Well, this is all I have to say at this juncture," said the solicitor.

He picked up his briefcase and shook hands with our foster parents.

"Goodbye Amanda, goodbye Tim," said Mrs Swinton.

Then they got into their cars and drove off. We changed our clothes and went to school after lunch.

After that life went on pretty well as usual. But I noticed that our relationship with our foster parents had improved. After all, there were no more secrets between us. They seemed to be making a real effort to be nice – to make up for the shock of discovering our past.

When the summer holidays came, Aunt Stella said that Tim and I would be going to a college in Sussex for a few weeks.

"You'll really like it there," she said. "It's by the sea. They do all kind of sports – tennis, riding, sailing. And there's pottery and drama too. They've got a fantastic swimming pool."

"Sounds great!" I said.

We were very excited when the taxi arrived to take us to the station. Later, when we got off the train, another one had been specially booked to collect us.

"It's a wonderful place," said the driver, "they have children from all over the world. I wish I could send my kids there."

We were shown our rooms, then had tea and met some of the other children. We went into the games room and played ping-pong and table football. Afterwards we had supper and watched a film.

Next morning we were given a tour of the grounds. There was an African boy and a Chinese girl with us too.

Our guide was called Marjorie.

"Great facilities, aren't they?" she said, "the swimming pool's almost Olympic size, you know."

We walked back to the college buildings.

"We like all new arrivals to meet the Principal."

We walked along a corridor, then stopped outside a door.

Marjorie knocked, and we went in. Sitting at a desk was a bald man with a grey moustache.

"Here are our four newcomers, Mr Meadows," she said cheerfully.

"Welcome," he said, smiling. "Please remind me of your names."

"Eddie," said the boy.

"And yours?"

"Ang Soong," said the girl.

"And you two, of course, are Amanda and Tim," said Meadows. "It will be a great pleasure having you here."

His smile widened.

THIRTEEN
The Train Spotters

My sister and I are sitting in a small seaplane being flown by our cousin. He doesn't hold a pilot's license – he has only had a few flying lessons. A helicopter is chasing us. We have run out of fuel and are making an emergency landing on a narrow loch we can see ahead. Both sides of it are lined with police cars. If our cousin muffs the landing we will crash and drown. If not, we will be arrested and probably shot. How did we get into this mess?

Through curiosity...

For the past few years Beth and I have stayed with our aunt and uncle in Scotland for the summer holidays. Our cousin Angus is nearly ten years older than me, but he is great fun, and we have often had exciting adventures with him. We stay at a place called Balgarvie Lodge. It is on the edge of the Drumcraigie Forest. In the autumn and winter there is grouse shooting and deer stalking, and salmon fishing in the summer.

But my favourite pastime is train spotting. We live in England, near Crewe, and I often go into the station to collect engine numbers, which I record in my notebook. Then I check these against the lists in the specially printed enthusiasts' books.

There are many different types of diesel and electric locomotives used in Britain. I've even seen several special trains, hauled by steam engines, pass through the station. I've got some friends I meet up with there, who also do it. I even took Beth along with me a couple of times.

"I can't see the fun in it," said my mother once, "standing out there in the cold at the end of the platform with your little notebooks. Seems a bit autistic to me."

One day, during our holiday in Scotland, we went for a very long walk and came across a railway line, single-track. I came back the next day with my notebook, some sandwiches and two cans of Coke, and waited. After a while a passenger train went by, followed by a goods train some time afterwards. I wrote down the numbers on their engines and then went home.

Two days later, my aunt took us shopping in Kirkton, the local town. We went to the railway station and I looked at a timetable. There were four passenger trains a day in each direction. I asked the Stationmaster how often there was a goods train.

"There's one going towards Inverness on most weekdays, and one the other way too," he answered.

"Are there ever any special trains?" I asked.

"Och no."

The next day I went back to the railway line. Beth came

with me. She had a book with her so she didn't mind waiting around. The two trains went by as before. The weather was hot and humid and I began to feel rather sleepy. I lay down in the long grass. I dozed off and was woken up by a loud droning sound and saw something most unusual. A Class 37 diesel was pulling an old passenger coach, a box van, and a very long wagon. This was of full height, cylindrical in shape, and made of thick steel, like armour plating. Each of its bogies had three axles. Another Class 37 was pushing at the rear. The train was travelling at around twenty miles an hour, and seemed to be transporting something extremely heavy.

"I wonder what's inside that wagon?" I asked Beth.

"Perhaps nuclear waste?" she suggested.

"Or some valuable and dangerous liquid?"

The next time we went to Kirkton I asked my aunt to drop us off at the station while she went shopping. The Stationmaster's office was locked but there was a signal box a hundred yards past the end of the platform.

"Let's go and ask in there," I said to Beth.

We walked beside the track till we reached the signal box and climbed up the steps to it.

"Do you think we really should?" she asked nervously.

"Why not?" I said boldly.

I opened the door and went in. The signalman was pulling a lever.

"Yes?" he asked

"Excuse me," I said, "I'm sorry to disturb you, but

on Thursday we saw a special train going through the Drumcraigie Forest. Do you know anything about it?"

"No specials along this line, just the regular service," he replied bluntly.

"Yes, but this train was carrying an extra-heavy load in a purpose-built wagon."

"I just told you," said the signalman angrily, "now if you don't mind, I've got a job to do."

"Well, thank you anyway," I said.

Beth was already halfway down the steps and I followed quickly. I glanced back at the box, and through the windows, saw that the signalman was on the telephone.

Three days later a letter arrived addressed to my uncle.

Dear Mr Stewart,

I must advise you that two children in your care were observed unsupervised at Kirkton Station last week. Will you please make clear to them that tresspassing on railway property is strictly forbidden, and request them to refrain from bothering staff with questions they are generally too busy to answer.

Yours sincerely
S.J. Fraser.
Manager, Highland Division, Inverness.

The next day Beth and I went back to the railway line. We took the dogs with us as they needed a walk. Near the track stood a small croft. There was a dog in its garden, and as we passed it started barking. An old man with a long grey beard, wearing a heavily patched tweed jacket and a ragged kilt, stumbled out of the croft.

"Shut up, ye stupid old thing!" he shouted.

We had trouble holding our dogs back even though they were on leads; they snarled aggressively. Then the man dragged his by the collar into an outhouse.

"Dogs! And where are ye two from? Ye're tourists?"

"Not really. We're staying at Balgarvie Lodge," I answered.

"Mr Stewart's place?"

"Yes," I said.

"When I was Keeper we always had a drive there on the muir. The grouse fly fast over the butts."

"Yes, I've seen a lot of them," said Beth.

"But it was the whusky that did me in," said the man.

He came up close to me.

"Ye wouldna have some on you, by any chance?"

"I'm afraid I've only got some Coca-Cola," I said apologetically.

He shook his head.

"Too young. Best keep off the drink, then. Aye, I was once Head Keeper for Lord Strathmorran. He owned all the Drumcraigie Forest in those days."

He burst into song.

The Lairds of Strathmorran
Hae gold in the sporran
And a golden-haired lassie as well.
Aye, happy are they

Who feast night and day,
And in fair Strathmorran do dwell.

He turned to look at me.

"But then bad luck befell the family, and they lost most of the land."

I thought I'd ask him about what we'd seen.

"Er...we saw a very odd special train going towards Kirkton. Do you know anything about it?"

"It no be going to Kirkton," he said

"Oh?"

"Branch line," he said, "two miles from here. Leads into government base, top secret. But I can tell ye all about it. Worked for a while on the railway, when I lost my job."

The sound of barking came from the outhouse.

"Shut up, will ye, ye noisy thing!" he shouted.

He continued.

"Now one winter, one o' them special trains got stuck in the snow. Verra cold it was. While we were waiting for the snowplough I shared a bottle of whusky with the crew. Aye, the drink, it loosens the tongue! They told me what's in them trains. Ye'd never guess: Whales!"

"What?" we asked, in astonishment.

"Live whales. Great big 'uns, too."

"That's not possible!" I said.

"Och aye. The Navy lands them at Duncansport. Then they're put in them trains."

"Whatever for?" I asked.

"Research," he answered.

He went over to the outhouse and came back with his dog.

"Got to give 'im 'is dinner now."

"Well, we'd better be off," I said, "it was nice talking to you."

"Best keep away from them trains," he said.

He pulled his dog into the croft and shut the door.

That evening I told my uncle about the old man.

"That'll be Jock Macdonald," he said, "he was a good keeper. Then he took to drink. I remember an ugly scene one night at the Spittal Hotel. He called John Campbell, the Underkeeper, 'a bloody Sassenach-lover' and fired his gun at him. Luckily the shot only grazed his hand. But they had to sack Macdonald. He went downhill fast after that, and only took a few odd jobs here and there."

"He told me there's a top secret base in the Drumcraigie Forest," I said, "and they have special trains with whales in them!"

"Well, much of the estate was sold years ago. When Bobby Strathmorran died his brother inherited it, and then *he* was killed shortly afterwards in a car crash. Tragic! They had to pay two lots of death duties, and to settle them they handed most of the forest to the government. Some of it is now run by the Forestry Commission, and the rest by the Ministry of Defence."

"And what about the whales?" asked Beth.

"Utter nonsense!" said my uncle. "Just the ravings of an old drunk. A brain soaked in alcohol for years! When he started imagining things they had to send him to Glascow, to the Gartnavel Royal Hospital."

"So what's in those trains, then?" I asked.

"Just food and supplies," said my uncle.

A few days later we went back to the railway line and walked along it the way the special train had been going. After about two miles there were some points, with another line branching off to the left. We followed this for a while. It led to an area enclosed by a high wire fence with watch towers along it. A red and white barrier lay across the track, with a guardhouse next to it.

"I don't think we should go any further," said Beth, nervously.

I agreed, and hoped we hadn't been spotted.

Soon after we had got back to the Lodge, our Dad telephoned. He and Mum would be coming for a few days. I mentioned the secret base, the special trains and their 'contents', and he sounded interested.

When he came he brought with him a tattered old book. It was a journal, written long ago by his grandfather, describing a visit to a Doctor Aziz Suleiman, in Egypt. A particular entry caught my attention. It read:

I found his flat with great difficulty. It was in a narrow back street of Cairo. His wife brought us tea, then left us. Dr Aziz was a wizened old man, and wore a fez with a turban wound around it. He spoke of his studies and research. They had cost him his job at Al-Azhar University. He claimed that part human, part animal creatures were traditional to many cultures. For instance, there were the Centaurs and the Minotaur in Greek mythology. The Egyptian gods had human bodies and the heads of birds and animals. And what about mermaids? Perhaps, after all, humans and animals were not physically incompatible, as biologists always said, and had, in the past, actually interbred.

He had a theory about the Pyramids. He claimed they were not built by teams of labourers, but by giants. How else could they have handled such huge blocks of stone? These giants had perhaps been created by means of elephants.

Aziz also maintained that Alexander the Great's spectacular conquests could have been due to 'great soldiers' born in a similar way. Had Hannibal used them too?

I went away amazed by the originality of his thesis. It even refuted Darwin! Over the next few years I searched for his papers in many university libraries, but in vain; they had all been destroyed.

Our cousin Angus, who is now at university, was also staying at Balgarvie. When I spoke about the secret base he didn't seem surprised.

"Last year me and two friends went on a long hiking trip," he said. "We got badly lost and ended up in a remote part of Drumcraigie Forest, the other side of Ben Garran Dhu. We eventually found a path leading to the top of a hill. There was a radio mast there, and a high barbed wire fence with a gate in it that was locked. There was a track behind the fence. I looked through it with my binoculars. You could see right down into the valley below. At the end of it was a loch, with some things in it. In the distance they were so small I couldn't make out what they were."

"Gosh!" I said.

"Then a Land Rover came down the track and two men with guns got out. They went through the gate and made us hand over our mobile phones, and ordered us to go back the way we came."

Angus also said he had heard aeroplanes in the middle of the night.

"They sound like large turboprops. But there's no airfield anywhere near here – not for miles!"

He was very interested in aircraft. He had had several flying lessons in Scotland, and also in Canada, where he had flown a seaplane.

The next day we made our plan. To find out what was going on we had to get into the base – and the best way to do this was aboard the special train.

"We'll make it stop, then climb onto it," said Angus.

Over the past week I had made several visits to the railway line and had recorded exactly when the special trains ran. At 11.30 am, two days later, Angus, Beth and I walked along the track. At the junction I noted that the points had been switched towards the branch line. We walked along that for about five hundred yards to a place where Angus, the day before, had cut down several thick branches with a chainsaw, and left them in the undergrowth. We laid them across the track and hid behind some bushes. I looked at my watch, then heard the train coming. It was dead on time!

It stopped with a screech of brakes. Two men jumped down from the front engine. One of them had a saw in his hand, and set to work cursing and swearing. The other man was talking on his mobile phone.

"Quick! Get into the coach!" said Angus.

But just then its door opened and a man with a submachine-gun got out. He looked around, then walked towards the front of the train.

"Go round the back, and get in on the other side," Angus whispered.

We crept past the rear engine's buffers, bending low in case anyone was in the cab. We passed the long steel wagon and the box van and reached the passenger coach. Luckily its door wasn't locked. It was high off the ground and I had to help Beth up. When we were all in I shut it quietly. The sound of the diesels idling helped muffle the click.

"Don't go down the corridor," I whispered, "go into the toilet."

All three of us piled in. There was no room to move! I locked the door. A while later the engines revved up and the train moved off.

After a minute or two it stopped for a brief moment. There were voices outside – we were at the barrier. It got going again. Then we heard footsteps out in the corridor. Someone tried the toilet door. The footsteps went away, but were back shortly afterwards.

"I don't understand it," said a voice, "Jim just went into the toilet at the other end, and there's only the three of us in this carriage."

We heard banging on the door.

"Come on now, open up!" said another voice, sternly.

More banging.

"Use your key," said the first voice.

I saw the lock turning. The door opened and a man stood at the entrance.

"All tickets please!" he said, laughing.

We were herded into one of the compartments.

"Sit ye down. Ye may as well make yerselves comfortable for the rest of the journey," said the man.

A few minutes later the train slowed down and came to a halt. We were escorted off by the man with the submachine-gun. Some guards arrived and made us get into the back of a truck.

"I've radioed the Colonel," said one of them, "they're to be taken to the Director's office."

The truck's canvas sides were down, so I couldn't see anything. But I reckoned the base was quite large as it was several minutes before we stopped again.

"Out!" ordered one of the guards.

We went into a concrete building and were told to wait in a corridor. A thin, neatly dressed woman, with her hair in a tight bun came up to us. She knocked on a door.

"Herein!"

We were shown into a large but sparsely furnished office. At a table at the end of it sat a tall man with a pale face and sleek black hair. He was wearing a dark suit. Behind him was a plate glass window with a view of water beyond.

"Ah, our guests!" he said. "Over the years we have had the odd reporter stray in here. 'Investigative journalists' they call themselves. But never before children."

He turned to Beth.

"You know, a young girl like you should not have got mixed up in this kind of business."

He spoke to the woman who had shown us in.

"Please bring some refreshments, Fräulein Schmidt."

"Jawohl, Herr Doktor."

She turned, and left the office with a click of heels.

"May I introduce myself. My name is Hoffmann. I am the Director of this institute. It is a military establishment, where secret medical research is carried out."

He stood up, turned to the window, and pointed at the water.

"This loch, as you call it over here, is a home to the world's largest mammal – the whale. We keep them in special pens. And for what purpose? For reproduction. I will explain. From time immemorial it has been known that human beings can breed with animals. But modern religions have always suppressed this knowledge. In Europe it was the Catholic Church, through the Inquisition. Yet now, because their DNA is virtually identical to ours, we are using whales to produce human soldiers. Super Soldiers!"

The door opened and Fräulein Schmidt brought in a tray of tea and sandwiches.

"Please help yourselves," said Dr Hoffmann. "Many years ago, in Germany, it was discovered that the only thing governing the size of any mammal was the size of its mother. The experiments were conducted by my grandfather. They even came, I believe, to the attention of the Führer himself!"

He allowed himself a little smile.

"Now we have found that it is possible for a whale to carry a human foetus successfully to term. There were many difficulties to overcome, mainly rejection. But we persevered!"

I couldn't believe my ears.

"In essence, the process is quite simple. In the laboratory human cells are cultured 'in vitro'. When they have sufficiently divided and the embryo is at the correct stage of development, it is implanted in the whale. She will then produce a human baby like any other, except for its greater size. It will eventually grow into an adult at least four metres tall!"

We were aghast. Hoffmann looked around at us.

"You may well find this distasteful. But Super Soldiers are just another item of modern warfare. And in the next war none of your generation will ever be sent to the front! Any role you may have will be purely administrative – if that has not already been taken over by robots and computers."

He picked up a telephone on his table. A man in military uniform came in.

"This is Colonel Robertson, our Chief of Security," he said. "Now that you are here you might as well have a tour of our establishment. You will find it most educational. I will see you again later."

We were escorted out of the building, and, under armed guard, were told to sit in an open vehicle that was waiting nearby.

"You won't try anything foolish, will you?" asked the Colonel anxiously.

"No," Angus assured him.

We drove down to the loch and passed some large corrugated iron sheds. Railway lines ran into them, and one of the long steel wagons was being shunted there. A splashing sound was coming from the sheds.

"This is where the whales are received," said Robertson, "into these covered docks. They are filled with water from the loch. Then each whale is allotted her own individual pen."

He pointed to a small white building at the side.

"And this is where the human embryos are prepared, under the most sterile conditions, before they are brought to the whales."

A man in a white coat came out of the building carrying a metal canister, and went into one of the covered docks.

Then we drove uphill towards a row of high brick

buildings.

"These are the nurseries where the infants are raised, through childhood and adolescence, until they are fully-grown. They receive a basic education, but most of their training is military: strategy, tactics, logistics and operations."

Then we passed another building, single-storey and made of wood.

"This is the gymnasium," said Robertson.

In the distance was a playing field with some woodland beyond it.

"The soldiers must reach peak physical fitness, hence the gym and sports ground. Combat training is initiated in those woods over there," he said, pointing to them.

As we approached the sports ground I saw that a game was in progress. All the players were over twelve feet tall!

We drove back to the loch. There was a slipway at the water's edge, and on the tarmac behind were parked a helicopter and several large aeroplanes.

"These can carry troops anywhere," said Robertson. "Being amphibious, they can land both on a runway or on the water."

There was also a wooden jetty with a small seaplane tied up to it. And further out on the loch, on moorings, lay three giant aircraft, bigger than anything I could have imagined.

"These flying boats will transport large quantities of Super Soldiers to any part of the world that is on water," said Robertson proudly. "They can alight on lakes, rivers, in harbours, and even on the open sea."

We now headed back to the base. Colonel Robertson left us outside the Director's office, and Fräulein Schmidt showed us in. A small man in a grey suit was in there too.

"This is Mr Nakamura," said Dr Hoffmann, "he arranges the procurement and disposal of the whales."

The little man bowed.

"With the assistance of your Royal Navy," continued Hoffmann. "Now you may wonder what happens to the whales when they are too old to bear offspring? They are slaughtered."

"How awful!" cried Beth.

"Indeed," he said, "but inevitable. The whale meat is then sent to Japan, where it is still much appreciated by the older population."

He looked at some papers on his table.

"And now, this is how we will deal with you two children, and this young man who should have known better. Despite warnings, you have seen fit to penetrate our establishment. We have a policy of strict secrecy. No intruder ever leaves this place alive. And no exceptions can be made. So regrettably, you will have to be put to death."

We gasped.

"But, I can assure you, it will be quite painless. And, in a way, you will be contributing to our project! Your bodies will provide a source of genetic material, and will then be processed for meat. They say that human flesh tastes like pork. The troops will not know the difference. They need protein. You will be made into sausages, perhaps. In Germany we have many kinds: frankfurters, of course, but also bratwurst, weisswurst..."

He laughed.

"I come from Bavaria. I love the mountains and the wildfleisch. Your Scottish venison is superb, but I must confess to not liking haggis!"

I realized then that the man was mad. I looked at Angus. Then we both had the same thought simultaneously. Dr Hoffmann was sitting at a lightly-made pinewood table. We sprang forwards like tigers and overturned it, and he fell backwards, banging his head against the glass window behind. He was stunned for a moment. Nakamura took out his phone, but Beth snatched it off him.

"Quick! Outside!" said Angus.

We tore out of the building and rushed down some steps leading straight to the loch. Alarm bells were now ringing.

"Onto the jetty!" shouted Angus.

There was gunfire, and bullets were whistling past us.

"Into the seaplane!"

I opened its door and pushed Beth in. Angus untied the ropes, jumped onto a float, and got in after us. We started drifting away. Angus climbed into the pilot's seat. After three attempts the engine burst into life.

"That's lucky," he said, "it's a Cessna 172. The same type I flew in Canada."

We taxied out into the loch.

"Water rudder up, mixture rich, flaps one-third out,"

Angus mumbled.

He opened the throttle fully. The plane rose up a bit and gathered speed. A fast motor launch was now racing parallel to us.

"Stop!" said a voice on a megaphone. "You cannot escape! You are surrounded!"

They began firing at us.

"I repeat: you cannot escape! Stop at once!"

The plane started to pitch up and down violently.

"For God's sake, take off!" I screamed.

"I can't!" said Angus, "we're porpoising. And I haven't got the airspeed. If I pull the stick back now, we'll bounce up, stall, and crash back into the water. I can't fight the rocking. We'll have to stop and try again."

He slowed down, turned, and taxied downwind. The launch followed us.

"Stop! Switch off the engine! We are coming alongside!"

More gunfire.

Angus turned back into the wind, and applied full throttle. This time we skimmed along fast and smoothly, and easily got airborne. Beth and I cheered. We climbed for a short time, then levelled off.

After five minutes, we had passed the end of the loch, and were now over the glen.

"There's a big loch thirty miles away," said Angus, "I suggest we land there and beach the plane on the shore. We'll hide in the woods for a while, then quietly slip home."

The spray had now totally cleared from the windscreen.

I saw a helicopter flying slightly ahead of us. Then our engine coughed.

"Damn!" said Angus, looking at the gauge, "we're out of fuel! They must have holed the tanks."

He prepared to land. There was a narrow loch just below us. A police boat was waiting on it, and there were cars on either bank. Blue lights everywhere!

"Well, it was a good try, I suppose," said Angus.

FOURTEEN

Victor the Van

Victor was a small white Vauxhall van. He was what is known in the trade as a 'car-based van', i.e, he had a car's engine and chassis, but the body of a van. His front was like that of a Vauxhall car, with the same bonnet, radiator grille and windscreen. But behind his front doors, instead of side windows and back seats, there was a cargo floor. His side walls were lined with plywood. And over his back bumper he had two doors for loading goods.

On top he had a roof rack, which carried two ladders. Inside there were buckets, mops, brushes, and containers of detergent. His owner, Mr Maggs, was a window cleaner. Every day they would go off on a round of jobs, with the same regular customers for years. Victor knew the way to all of them by heart. In his overalls and tweed cap, Maggs would drive around whistling contentedly, or listening to the radio.

He was a good man. He drove smoothly and carefully, and took good care of Victor. He never swore at him if he found it hard to start on a cold winter's morning. Once a week he checked his oil and his tyre pressures, and he washed and polished him regularly. Once a year he would have him serviced. With his engine newly tuned, his chassis greased, and a change of oil, Victor would come back feeling renewed and refreshed.

There had once been a Mrs Maggs. She would often bring a cup of tea up to the van when it was parked outside their house. At weekends she rode in the passenger seat, and they would drive to the supermarket – and sometimes to the cinema in the evening. Once they even went to the seaside.

One day it occurred to Victor that it had been some time since he had last seen her. Maggs had become sad and gloomy, and no longer whistled as they drove around.

Three months later, a big black dog came on the scene. He was called Scruff. He went everywhere with Maggs, sitting on the passenger seat with his head out of the window to catch the breeze. On Saturdays and Sundays they always drove to the park. While Maggs took Scruff for a long walk, Victor would chat to the other cars parked there. He made friends with the ice-cream van who was always there in the summer.

After several years Victor noticed that Scruff had got fatter and rather sluggish. He no longer jumped into the van and had to be helped onto the passenger seat. He seemed less keen to go for his walks in the park, and those became shorter too. One day Scruff no longer appeared. Victor saw an unfamiliar-looking van parked outside the house.

The years went by. Maggs was getting older. He drove

more slowly and the window cleaning took longer. When he had put away his stuff into the van and tied on his ladders, he would be out of breath as he got into the driving seat.

One morning when Maggs had not turned up, Victor thought it must be a Saturday. He did not appear the next day either. Maggs often didn't use the van at weekends, though he sometimes drove to the bowling club, which he had recently joined. And on Sundays he would often walk over to the corner shop to buy a newspaper, giving Victor a pat on the bonnet as he passed by.

With still no sign of him on the third day, Victor now assumed it was a Bank Holiday. But on the fourth day he became anxious.

"Where on earth is he?" he wondered.

From where he was parked Victor could only see a small part of Maggs's house. There was no sign of any activity. People hardly ever called there anyway, except for the postman and the meter reader. During the General Election, a canvasser had knocked on the door, and once there had been someone from the Council. Later it got dark, but no lights went on in the house.

Days went by. People walked past on the pavement, and vehicles drove up and down the street. By now Victor was really worried. And bored too.

"If only I could turn on my radio," he thought.

A beautiful sports car parked in front of him.

"Excuse me," asked Victor nervously, "I wonder if you've seen an old man around, wearing overalls and a tweed cap?"

The sports car snorted and didn't answer.

Later on a plumber's van parked next to Victor. He asked it the same question.

"Sorry mate," it replied, "I'm not from round here. I'm on call. Emergency. Burst pipe at Number 34."

Over the next week Victor had no luck with any of the other vehicles that stopped there. One car had a Spanish number plate and couldn't speak a word of English. Then there was a motorcycle. It didn't even listen to him, and just went on about how fast and powerful it was. Then a large silver limousine glided into a space near him.

"I drive Lady Ponsonby," it said haughtily. "Apart from her chauffeur, I have no dealings with the staff. And certainly not with tradesmen."

One day a Ford parked right up to him. Victor asked if it had seen an old man in overalls and a tweed cap.

"No, can't say I have. Now my owner, he's in sales. Does hundreds of miles a week. Midlands, South Coast, West Country...you name it. Always in a hurry. Mind you, got to keep an eye out for them cameras. Quickest way out of London? Take the Uxbridge Road, nip down Hanger Lane, and turn left onto the A40. Yes, a busy man, my owner. Well turned out too. Smart leather briefcase, shoes polished, good suit with trousers nicely pressed. Gives me a wax polish, regular. Hey, don't your guy look after you? You could do with a clean."

By now Victor was in a sorry state. He was parked under a tree and there were leaves and bird droppings all over him. He was coated with a layer of dust, and a boy had written in it: U NEED A WASH.

"My tyres are going flat!" he said to himself in desperation, "and my battery will go flat too!"

He felt lonely and abandoned. People passed by and ignored him, as if he didn't exist.

But late one night, two men came and tried to open his doors. Victor thought they were going to smash a window and break in.

"I wish I had a burglar alarm," he said to himself.

Instead they cut the ropes on his roof rack and stole the ladders.

After weeks had gone by someone came and stuck a yellow piece of paper onto his windscreen. Next day a lorry stopped in the road alongside him. Some men got out and put slings under his wheels. Then he was lifted up, placed on the back of the lorry, and tied down. The men drove off with him, laughing and joking.

The truck swayed as it braked and cornered, making Victor feel sick – and self-conscious too, carried up in the air like that. After half an hour they drove through some gates into a huge yard, where rows and rows of cars were parked. At one end was a Portakabin. An official with a clipboard told them where to unload Victor.

***

There were all sorts of cars in the pound, some vans too, and even a minibus and a Rolls-Royce. Throughout the day people came to collect their cars that had been towed away.

They went into the Portakabin to pay the release charge. All distraught, some tried to argue, and many were rude.

Victor started talking to a car he had been put next to.

"Been here long?" he asked.

"Oh no," it replied, "just a couple of hours. My owner will be here any moment."

Soon afterwards there was a brisk tapping of heels. A well-dressed woman arrived, got into the car angrily, and drove out of the gates. Then Victor heard a door slam. A man drove off quickly in a BMW with a squeal of tyres.

Over the next month there was a constant stream of cars arriving on the back of trucks, and owners retrieving them. But nobody came to get Victor.

Then one day four men appeared. They had a key. One got into his driving seat and released the handbrake. The others pushed him round the corner into the police car park.

They soon got Victor going. They charged up his battery, turned the key, and he started first time! His tyres were pumped up, he was given a good wash, and his interior was valeted.

The police used him for all kinds of jobs. He carried traffic cones, boxes of files, uniforms, caps and helmets, radios and large items used for evidence. On Mondays he would fetch supplies for the canteen, and on Thursdays food for the police dogs. At weekends one officer, PC Sweetman, would 'borrow' him and take him home. Victor wondered whether this was strictly on police business.

At the police station there were three patrol cars, two unmarked cars, a Land Rover, two personnel carriers fitted with riot screens, a large van, and a smaller one for the dog unit. There were also several motorcycles, which were kept in a special shed. The other vehicles found them small and noisy. And the unmarked cars considered themelves superior to the patrol cars.

"They're Uniform, we're CID," they would say.

The patrol cars were very friendly to Victor. One was for general policing, the second was painted in blue and yellow squares for traffic duty, and the third one was a high performance car, Foxtrot Whisky. He had a powerful engine and was used for fast pursuit, sometimes in conjunction with the police helicopter.

Victor also got to know some of the officers. As they drove him he would listen to their conversation. About the job. The latest gossip about the WPC's. The snooker competition and the Police Ball. And what the Super had said.

Foxtrot Whisky was a very experienced police car. He had been to Bramshill and had taken a course in high speed driving.

"Police work can be summed up in four letters," he said.

"D.A.C.C. – Detect, Apprehend, Charge and Convict."

He had once served in the Thames Valley Police. His proudest moment had been when the Queen came to visit. He carried the Chief Constable, and escorted the royal car and the Lord Lieutenant.

One day an auction was held in the police car park. Victor, three uncollected cars, and some bicycles were put up for sale. A few people turned up to bid, mainly dealers. Some had trade plates with them. They walked round the cars checking for rust and dents, kicked the tyres, opened the bonnets, and looked at the interiors. One car, a Jaguar, attracted most of the interest.

"Nice model this – very clean," said the auctioneer.

The bikes went in a single lot to a cycle shop.

"And now we come to Lot number 5, today's final lot," he said, "the Vauxhall van, colour white. Good runner, in daily use. Anyone want a van? Starting at seven hundred pounds. No? Five hundred then?"

But there was only one bidder and Victor was sold for £250.

The new owner paid cash and drove him away at once. He did not even have time to say goodbye to his friends at the police station. An hour later they turned off the road into a yard where vans and lorries were parked. A sign said 'Holtspur Logistics'. Victor was driven into a large glass-roofed shed. After a brief check over he was parked in the corner of the building.

Holtspur Logistics was a transport company. It served the whole country, with occasional trips to Ireland and the Continent too. It was owned by a Mr and Mrs Philpott. They were extremely rich, and would turn up from time to time in a big limousine. They had a house in the South of France, and, it was believed, a yacht as well. Mr Williamson, the Managing Director, felt they were not investing enough in maintaining and renewing the fleet of vehicles, and suspected that they were 'milking' the company to fund their extravagant lifestyle.

Ken, Matt, Larry, Vince and Ginger operated the lorries, and Benny, Fred and Graham drove the vans. Any staff shortages due to sickness or holidays were filled by agency drivers.

There was, on the whole, a friendly atmosphere at Holtspurs – apart from Hanson, the Philpotts' chauffeur. During their visits he always turned down the offer of a cup of tea in the canteen, preferring to sit alone in the front seat of the limousine.

"I don't normally associate with your service drivers," he would say.

Other employees were Dan MacAlister, the Chief Engineer; Andy Wilson (Handy Andy), assistant mechanic; Jenny Bleasdale, the secretary; Eric Dunwoody, the carpenter; and Dick Robson, the forklift driver. The Transport Manager, Mr Royston, was constantly in and out of his office, clipboard in hand. He was the one who really kept the business running on a day-to-day basis.

Victor was soon put to work. He carried materials, tools and supplies, and also spare parts for the other vehicles. He got to know all of them. There were two small vans, Maurice (a Renault) and Boris (a Ford). There was a larger van called Lenny, a Luton van, his body extending over the top of his cab. And a box van, even bigger, called Fritz (a

Mercedes-Benz).

There were three big lorries, each one a tractor unit, forming the front part of an articulated vehicle. There was Björn (a Volvo) and Sture (a Scania). Sture would often point out that Saab, his manufacturer, also built jet aircraft. In the garage they spent most of their time chatting in Swedish. On long trips they often travelled together in convoy. There were four trailers available for their use.

The third and largest tractor was called Karl. He was a Mercedes. Unlike the Swedes he had three axles, and a more powerful turbocharged engine. Mr Williamson had acquired him at great expense, believing that Holtspurs needed greater carrying capacity to remain competitive. A special trailer had been imported for Karl, from Austria. He was called Ulrich and was exceptionally long, also with three axles. He and Karl had a special coupling, and they could only be used together. (Karl's coupling was not compatible with the other four trailers). With Ulrich behind him, Karl would sweep majestically out of the yard, more than sixty feet long, the pride of the fleet.

He was vain and arrogant.

"I'm the longest and strongest," he would boast.

He called the Swedes 'pretty average. OK for medium loads' and the vans 'errand boys for local deliveries'. He treated everyone with scorn – except Fritz, a fellow Mercedes, who worshipped Karl and laughed at all his jokes.

Now articulated vehicles are usually detached when in the yard overnight, or if left unused for any length of time.

This takes the weight off the tractor's chassis and tyres. The electric cables and hydraulic pipes are disconnected, two steel legs are wound down by a handle to support the front of the trailer, and the tractor is driven off. But few people had ever seen Karl without his trailer. Then he was just a great big cab with a short little chassis and a round steel plate smeared with grease called a 'fifth wheel', his part of the coupling. He looked top-heavy, out of proportion, and rather silly. However, he was always parked behind a wall at the back of the garage.

Victor enjoyed his new life at Holtspurs. He got to know all the drivers, sometimes giving them a lift to work, or picking up Mrs Darbyshire, the lady who ran the canteen, when she'd missed her bus.

The only problem was Karl. If someone said "Mercedes" he would shout "Mercedes-BENZ, if you please!" Then Fritz would explain that in the 1890s Dr Benz's daughter was called Mercedes.

And the stream of insults went on. Karl said to Lenny:

"With that bit over the top of your cab you look as if you're wearing a hat."

He told Maurice he smelt of garlic, not petrol.

"You're really a sort of car," he said to Victor, "actually half car, half van. A cheap car, and not much of a van either."

Every joke that Karl made was followed by shrill laughter from Fritz. He agreed with everything he said. He was a yes van.

Karl was also horrible to Ulrich, calling him, "Ulrich the

Untermensch, the Trailer from the Tyrol."

"You have no engine," he said once, "wherever I go, you follow, and whenever I stop, you stop."

"Yes," said Ulrich, "at least I have brakes. But may I remind you, without me you are useless."

It was the first week in December. Jenny Bleasdale was putting up the decorations for the Christmas party, to be held, as usual, in the canteen. The drinks had already arrived, and Mrs Darbyshire was preparing canapés, and had baked a huge cake. Mr and Mrs Philpott would be attending.

The run-up to Christmas is the busiest time of the year in retailing. A vast amount of stock has to be shifted from the docks and factories to warehouses and distribution centres, and then on to the shops, or directly to customers purchasing on the internet.

The telephone rang in Mr Royston's office. It was Mr Williamson. He had just negotiated an important contract. A large consignment of wine had to be collected from Tilbury Docks and delivered to Swindon, that day. This could have easily been done in one trip using both the Volvo and the Scania. But unfortunately the Swedes were up in Scotland.

"Well, what about the big Mercedes, then?" asked Mr Williamson.

"With that tonnage it would be overloaded – well over the legal limit," said Mr Royston.

Mr Williamson then asked if the excess load could be

taken by any of the smaller vehicles. But Fritz was having a major overhaul in Kent, Lenny was delivering furniture in East Anglia, and Maurice and Boris had been leased out to a courier service in Surrey. This left only Victor – the smallest of the fleet!

"I can't see any solution," said Mr Royston, "unless we could perhaps *rent* another vehicle?"

After several fruitless hours on the telephone and at his computer, Mr Royston had to admit defeat. He rang Mr Williamson.

"I've tried everything," he said, "but there's absolutely nothing. Nowhere. I even asked Jack Taylor, down at Carshalton, if he could help me out and lend me one of his. He said he only wished he could. Commercials are like gold dust at this time of year!"

"Look, this really puts me in a spot," said Mr Williamson, "I've already agreed the deal. We need the revenue. And, what's more, I've got the Philpotts breathing down my neck."

Mr Royston said nothing.

"Come on, Jim," pleaded Mr Williamson, "can't you make an exception? Just this once?"

After a moment Mr Royston replied.

"All right, I'll let it go. But only this one time."

"Thanks."

"I really don't like doing this," said Mr Royston, uneasily.

"Don't worry – it'll all be fine," said Mr Williamson.

Next morning Karl and Ulrich left for Tilbury. Vince was

at the wheel. When they reached the docks the pallets of wine crates were already stacked up outside the warehouse. There were two forklifts to speed up the job. When Ulrich's doors were finally closed and padlocked, every square inch of space had been filled.

"Very heavy load, this," said Vince. He looked worried.

"You'll be OK," said one of the forklift drivers, "powerful trucks, these Mercs."

"Yeah," said Vince, "anyhow, there's no steep hills on our route."

The heavy weight made Ulrich's tyres bulge, and it pushed down hard on Karl's chassis, making his cab tilt upwards. Vince signed the documents and climbed in. He started the engine and they pulled out slowly in bottom gear.

To reach the dock gates they had to make a sharp left turn to avoid a raised kerb. On it were fixed some low concrete posts, hardly visible from high up in the cab. Vince did not take the corner wide enough and Ulrich's wheels got wedged against one of the posts. They were stuck and couldn't move, so Vince reversed a few feet, then went back into first gear, accelerating hard, to take it at a run. As Ulrich's wheels hit the post again the lorry shuddered, there was a graunching of metal, a sharp jerk, and Karl shot forwards. Vince leapt down from the cab. To his horror he saw that the coupling had broken and Ulrich's front had smashed into the ground.

He took out his mobile and rang Holtspurs. Two hours

later a car arrived with Mr Royston and Dan MacAlister, followed by Andy and Mr Dunwoody in Victor. First of all a breakdown crane had to be brought in to lift up Ulrich, so that his steel legs could be wound down to support him. Luckily the cargo had been well-packed so it was undamaged. But Ulrich's coupling had been sheared off and was beyond repair. There was no spare one at Holtspurs, so a new one would have to be ordered and sent over from Austria.

"These things always happen at Christmas!" said Mr Royston, bitterly.

"Aye, they do indeed," said Mr MacAlister.

Before leaving the yard Mr Royston had telephoned Mr Williamson to inform him of the accident. He now rang again to report that the damage was far worse than expected. The big Mercedes could not pull its trailer, so they would now be unable to transport the goods.

"No. We entered into a contract and we have to fulfil it," said Mr Williamson, firmly.

It was of little consolation to Mr Royston to know that, back at Holtspurs, there were several perfectly good trailers – but unusable by Karl.

"I've got an idea!" said Mr Dunwoody, suddenly.

On Karl's short chassis, between the back of his cab and the fifth wheel coupling, there was a space about three feet long. It had a steel grille over it, and could be used for carrying, say, a toolbox or a rolled up tarpaulin, but little else. Mr Dunwoody suggested that a simple platform could be built out of wooden planks, and bolted onto the grille. The pallets of wine would then be loaded onto this and tightly secured by a tarpaulin and ropes. Karl would thus become a very short 'rigid' lorry – hardly any longer than Victor!

"That's daft!" said Mr MacAlister.

"We have no other choice," replied Mr Royston, "let's see what the chippy can do."

While the others drove off to a builders merchant to buy timber, bolts and tools, Mr Royston supervised Ulrich's unloading.

"Never 'ad to do this kind of thing before," joked one of the forklift drivers, "not in twenty-five years!"

The platform was quickly assembled, and fixed to Karl's chassis. Then the pallets were loaded on, piled right up to the roof of his cab.

Victor was able to carry several of them too.

They set out for Swindon. When they arrived the warehouse manager couldn't believe his eyes, and burst out laughing. And what would have normally been one simple trip down the M25 and M4 became a long-drawn-out nightmare. Mr Royston had calculated that they needed to make around twenty return journeys to deliver all the goods.

"What? Back again?" joked the manager at Swindon each time they returned, "you lot are up and down here like a yoyo!"

Vince could not be expected to do even half the extra

driving, as this would have exceeded his maximum permitted hours, as recorded on the tachograph. This also applied to Victor. And as most of Holtspurs' drivers were away on other jobs, agency drivers had to be hired.

Mr Williamson emailed the clients warning them there would be a delay due to a technical hitch. He was granted a time extension, though at a financial penalty.

As Karl passed by on the motorway, cars, lorries and coaches would laugh.

"Lost your trailer, then?" asked one.

"Big truck, small load," said another.

Due to the vastly increased mileage, much more fuel was needed.

Whenever they filled up at service stations they would get strange looks, and felt embarrassed. But it was Karl himself who really suffered. Once King of the Road, he now felt ridiculous and humiliated. He looked like an overgrown pick-up! A long articulated lorry drew up alongside him at the diesel pump.

"Here's the long and the short of it!" said the attendant.

After nineteen exhausting trips all the wine was finally delivered, and Karl and Victor went home to Holtspur Logistics. Meanwhile Ulrich had been carried back on a low loader, to await the new coupling from Austria. He was very upset. By now some of the other vehicles had already returned. None of them (except for Fritz) laughed at Karl; in fact they felt deeply sorry for him. He was never rude and arrogant again.

At the Christmas party Mr Royston told everyone what a great help Victor had been.

"A small vehicle, but so versatile. Invaluable in an emergency!

"Yes," said Victor to himself, "thank goodness I am just a simple van."

FIFTEEN
Edith

I am writing this so that if anyone ever finds me, they will know what happened. I have very little paper – just the pocket notebook I always carry on me. Soon my torch battery will run out. Then I will be totally enveloped in this darkness, in which I will probably die.

***

Stupidly, it all started in the cinema. It was on a weekend in the summer. I was watching a film with my friend Harriet. It was some American cops and robbers movie. The acting was bad and the plot was weak.

"This film's rubbish," I said.

"It's all right," said Harriet, "I'm sure it'll get better further on."

"I'm not wasting any more time watching this!"

"Shhh!" said someone in the audience.

"I'm going," I whispered.

"Well, I'm staying to the end, Edwina," said Harriet firmly.

I got up, disturbing the whole row of people next to me. But when I reached the aisle I found I'd left my cardigan under my seat, so I had to go back again and get it. They all muttered angrily.

I realize now it was a selfish thing to do. Harriet and I would have spent the rest of the day together and had a good time. I decided to go home and read the book that was in my handbag. It was about history, which I love.

The shortest way home was through the Cathedral grounds. I walked down the High Street, along the passage leading to the Close, then reached the large green area around the Cathedral itself. At the far end of this, near the boundary wall, the grass wasn't mown, and was quite long. I took out my book and sat down on one of the large stone slabs that were there.

After a while I stopped reading and looked at some of them. They were graves mainly of top clerics and townspeople, and their names, dates of birth and death, and life histories were recorded in Latin or rather archaic English. But the one I had been sitting on was quite different. The stone was very worn, so I reckoned it was many centuries older. Five letters, inscribed in an ancient script, said simply 'EDITH'.

It was a hot and humid day. I lay down on my back, with my cardigan rolled up as a pillow, and looked up at the sky. It was very peaceful. I must have dozed off for a time. I was woken by a man's voice.

"Oi!"

An old man in a waistcoat and rolled up sleeves was standing over me.

"I'm sorry," I said, sitting up, "I know I shouldn't really be here."

"Oh no," said the man, "you have your rest. Public place, this."

He stood there staring at me. I felt quite uncomfortable.

"But if I was you, I'd choose another spot than this. Anywhere else."

"Oh," I said, getting up.

I expected he wanted to mow the grass there.

"History, eh?" he said, looking at my book, "Normans and Saxons. Then you'll know all about 'er."

He pointed at the grave I had been lying on.

"I don't, I'm afraid."

"That's Edith the Evil," he said.

A shiver ran down my spine.

"Well, I'd better be going home now," I said. "It's getting late."

He nodded, then walked slowly on.

At home I looked at my book. There was no mention of anyone called Edith the Evil. But this just increased my curiosity. Lots of kings had epithets: Ethelred the Unready, Charles the Bald, Richard the Lionheart. And queens too, like Bloody Mary.

At school I asked Miss Barton, my history teacher, if she knew anything about Edith the Evil. She had never heard of such a person. When I enquired how to do research on her, she suggested that I concentrate on the school history syllabus, as A levels were drawing near. I tried the internet and other books in the library, but got no results either.

Then I had an idea – I'd go into the Cathedral. I went up to a man in a long black cassock, with a leather belt around his waist.

"Er, excuse me," I asked gingerly, "do you know anything about the graves here?"

"Very little, I'm afraid," said the clergyman, smiling. "Not my forté!"

"Oh sorry."

"But maybe the Dean could help you. I believe he made a study of them a while ago," he said. "He's usually in his office about now. Would you like to see him?"

"Yes please!"

We walked through the Cathedral and into the Cloisters. There was a gothic wooden door with a brass plaque saying 'The Very Reverend the Dean'.

The clergyman knocked and we went in. The Dean was sitting at a desk.

"Sorry to disturb you, but this young lady needs a bit of help. She would like to know about the graves."

"Ah yes, the graves!" said the Dean, standing up. "Nice to see someone like yourself take an interest in this place."

"Thank you, sir," I replied.

"Well, I'd better return to my duties," said the clergyman, leaving the office.

I felt shy and nervous, but the Dean soon put me at ease and asked if I'd like some tea or coffee.

"I usually have a cup of tea around this time and a biscuit

or two. Now what would you like to know?"

"About Edith the Evil."

He seemed taken aback.

"May I ask why?"

"Well," I said, "I was looking at some of the stone slabs in the churchyard, and came across a very old one that just said 'EDITH'. Then this man, I think he was a gardener, said it was the grave of Edith the Evil."

"That'll be old Tom, the Sexton," he said, smiling. "But you still haven't told me *why* you want to know about this?"

"Well, partly because it's such a mystery. There seems to be no record of her, anywhere. And my history teacher doubts she ever even existed!"

He looked at me straight in the face.

"You might find it preferable to study some of the later tombs. Many famous people are buried here, like Sir William Lorimer, who fought in the Civil War, or Anne Lanckton, who built the Westgate Alms Houses in 1552."

I wondered why he was being so evasive.

"I'm sorry, sir, but the person I really want to know about is Edith," I insisted, hoping I didn't sound rude. "Her grave is here, yet apparently she never existed."

"She *did* exist," said the Dean.

He seemed uncomfortable, and said nothing for a moment.

"Look, I'm afraid I've got an awful lot to do now. Meetings with the Choir, the repairs to the Chancel roof, the accounts..."

"May I come and see you again?" I asked boldly. "Perhaps when you're not so busy?"

"If you must," he said wearily, "you are a very persistent young girl! But it would be best if you came round to the Deanery. Please telephone first."

"Thank you very much, sir," I said, "I'd better be going now."

"Thank you for coming," he said, opening the door. "By the way, you never told me your name."

"Edwina Mayfield."

I left the office, walked back through the Cloisters, and went straight home.

I was greatly encouraged at the Dean's admission that Edith really existed. l did more research. In early Saxon times, England was made up of several regional kingdoms – Kent, Wessex, Mercia, Northumbria, etc. One very old book referred to a King Edward of Mercia, "the king with two queens". Both were called Edith. Although many Anglo-Saxon texts had been lost in the fire at the Cottonian Library in the 18th century, a fragment of parchment recording this had survived.

'After the reign of Edward and the first Edith, the second, she ruled alone.'

When I told Miss Barton about this she was most impressed. She knew a professor of history at Oxford, and said she would request her to do further research on my behalf.

A week later she asked to see me. Her friend had spent a

lot of time in the Bodleian Library. It has vast underground vaults containing thousands of books. She had found a very rare one called *English History and Legend in the Dark Ages*. It had a section on King Edward. He was known for his 'pious and saintly works. A monastery he built.' Edith, his wife, 'was most beloved by the people for her virtue, and charity to the poor.' But later on the King was seduced by another woman, also called Edith, and fell completely under her influence. The Queen and her son died mysteriously, and Edward married this second Edith. After his death she reigned on as a cruel and ruthless tyrant.

She was a striking figure, tall and elegant, and spent much of the kingdom's wealth on clothes, luxuries and jewellery. Every plot to depose her failed. It was as if she was protected by some malignant force. Whenever her opponents were destroyed she boasted of being 'refreshed by their blood.'

Edith refused to yield to the inevitability of old age. She surrounded herself with young women, needing their vitality; they were, no doubt, terrified of her. On her deathbed, finally giving up the struggle for life, her last words were: "I drink the strength of youth, and thus one day I shall return." Then she turned to the wall, laughed, and died.

King Edward's life is fully recorded in the Anglo-Saxon Chronicle. But strangely, there is no mention of the second Edith. In 1925 a scholar claimed that the original passage on Edward had been erased, and rewritten fifty years later. The ink and handwriting looked slightly different. Perhaps the memory of Edith the Evil was so painful that all reference to her had been removed!

I plucked up enough courage to phone the Dean. He invited me to tea at the Deanery. Mum made sure I looked reasonably smart. I knocked on the door of a pretty 18th-century house in the Cathedral Close.

"Come in, Edwina," said a lady in a floral dress.

I was shown into a sitting room. In there was the Dean.

"I know, let's have some tea. This is my wife, Millicent."

She also brought in cakes and sandwiches, which were arranged on a three-tiered stand.

They were both very nice, and asked me many questions.

"What school are you at?" asked the Dean.

"St. Wilfred's, sir."

His eyes lit up.

"Ah! Used to teach there myself. Long ago, of course."

When we had finished tea his wife cleared everything away and left the room.

"Now I suppose we'd better talk about that particular interest of yours," he said.

He went over to a bookcase and took out a slim volume.

"This is something I wrote a few years ago on the graves here," he said, "remind me of what you wanted to know."

"About Edith, the second wife of King Edward."

He frowned, and turned over some pages of the book.

"Her tomb is by far the oldest one in the churchyard. Unlike other royalty, she was not buried in the Cathedral, but at a distance from it, in unconsecrated ground. In the course of time, however, the cemetery had to be enlarged, so her grave is now surrounded by more recent ones."

"Why wasn't she buried in the Cathedral?" I asked.

"Because she was one of the most evil women who ever lived."

A shiver ran down my spine.

"You know, there are more interesting and rewarding things to study here," he said, closing the book, "the Cloisters, for example. Some of the finest monastic architecture in the country."

"Yes sir, but I've spent so much time researching Edith's life that I'm now completely absorbed in it. I've also chosen it as my special subject for A levels." (Actually that last bit wasn't true).

The Dean looked at his watch.

"Well, I suppose we could go down into the Crypt, if you like. It's got some interesting tombs and relics. There'll just be time before Evensong."

He went to a drawer and took out a bunch of keys.

"Come and see us again soon, Edwina," said his wife, as we left.

When we were inside the Cathedral, the Dean unlocked a small door and we descended a circular staircase. It was dark and spooky. He switched on some lights, and I saw we were in a vaulted chamber supported by stone pillars.

"Many famous people are buried here," he said.

We passed the elaborate tomb of a mediaeval knight and

his lady. Further on the ceiling got lower. The chamber was now of rough stone with thick round arches.

"We are now under the oldest part of the Cathedral," he said, "dating from early Saxon times."

We reached two graves set in the ground.

"These are believed to be the tombs of King Edward and his first queen."

At the far end of the Crypt were some ornate wooden cabinets.

"We call this the Treasury," said the Dean.

He unlocked one of them and lit it up. Gold chalices and bishops' croziers lay inside glistening, as well as mitres and heavy brocade vestments.

"What's this?" I asked, pointing to a piece of bone capped with silver at either end.

"The relics of St. Wilfred."

He opened another cabinet.

"You might find this interesting."

Inside was an emerald brooch, a long gold necklace and a tattered garment that looked like a woman's gown.

"These are some of the possessions of the second queen, known as the Evil."

I reached into the cabinet and put on the necklace. A strange and powerful force flowed through my body. The Dean stood there aghast.

"I'm sorry, I didn't mean to do that," I stammered, taking off the necklace and handing it to him, "I don't know what came over me."

"That's all right, my dear," he said, sounding embarrassed, "but it was a rather unusual thing to do."

As we left the Crypt the Dean said that nothing else belonging to Edith had ever been found. But according to legend her crown had been buried with her.

I became more and more obsessed with it all. When I was invited to a fancy dress party, I went as an Anglo-Saxon queen. I even bought a fake emerald brooch to hold my cloak together.

This year we were going to Spain for our summer holidays. Until now, we had always had them in England (once we went to Scotland). I needed to apply for a passport, as children can no longer travel on their parents' ones. I sent up for a copy of my birth certificate. An envelope duly arrived addressed to: 'Ms EEF Mayfield'.

"Look," I said, "they've given me another 'E' by mistake!"

When I saw the certificate itself I got a shock. It said, 'Edith Edwina Frances Mayfield'.

"They've got my name wrong," I said.

"Actually, your real name *is* Edith," said Mum.

A creepy feeling grew inside me.

"You never told me that!"

How could it be possible? I'd always had three initials: E.F.M. They used them at school. And once, as a prize, I got a leather-bound book with those three letters embossed on it.

"The truth is," said Mum, "when you were a tiny girl, each time we called you Edith you burst out crying."

"Quite uncontrollably," added Dad.

"You just screamed and screamed," said Mum. "Why, we had no idea. So the only solution was to use your second name, Edwina."

"Thank you very much," I said, sarcastically.

The holiday in Spain was great fun, and we always had lots to do. But sometimes, when I was lying alone in bed or on the beach, I'd wonder if I had any special link to Queen Edith. And was it predestined? I also started planning what to do when I got home.

I resolved to find Edith's crown. The first place to look was obviously in her grave. But I needed someone to help me. I knew a boy called Rick Davenport. His father was in the Army. Rick hoped to go to Sandhurst as soon as he left school. He was keen on sports and keeping fit. He was an Army cadet, and often went off to Corps Camp in the holidays – sometimes abroad.

"I can survive for two weeks in the wild, living rough," was his boast.

I told him about my plan, and said he was the only person I had let in on the secret. He was very keen.

"It'll have to be done at night, of course. The gravestone will be very heavy, so we'll need to bring in some equipment," said Rick.

One day I took him into the Cathedral grounds to see Edith's tomb.

"Shouldn't be too difficult," he said, "we'll dig out any soil around the lid with a large screwdriver, and use a crowbar to prise it open and lever it up. Then we quickly insert a piece of wood to prop up the lid high enough to climb inside."

We decided to do it on Saturday night, at 2 o'clock in the morning. Rick said he would bring all the tools. I would take my torch and some lemonade and sandwiches.

But on Friday morning he phoned me.

"I'm afraid I won't be able to help you, Edwina."

"Why?"

"I've got to fly to Norway this evening. To Camp – for the rest of the holidays."

"That's a lie!" I said angrily.

"Look, I was only just told about it this morning. I can't get out of it."

"No – it's because you've got cold feet," I said, "you're scared!"

"That's not true!" he protested.

"Well Rick, I'll just have to do it on my own."

However, he did say he'd just have time to help prepare the opening of the tomb before he left. Early that afternoon he met me in the Cathedral grounds with all the tools. Keeping an eye out for the sexton, we finally managed to open the stone lid, wide enough for me to crawl in later. It was propped up by a thick piece of wood.

"Now we need some camouflage," he said.

We gathered lots of long grass and nettles to cover the gaping hole. Then Rick put away all the tools into his bag, and slung it over his shoulder.

"Good luck!" he said, walking away.

"Thanks, I'll need it."

On Saturday night I went to bed at the usual time, but did not go to sleep. At 2 a.m. I got dressed again, putting on some dark blue jeans and a black jumper. I had my keys, my pocket notebook, a biro, a small bottle of water, a torch, and a carefully folded plastic bag to put the crown in (hopefully). All this was stuffed into my jeans pockets. I crept downstairs. Everyone had gone to bed, and all was silent except for the ticking of the grandfather clock in the hall. I quietly opened the front door and let myself out into the street .

Walking through the town I saw no one at all, although one or two shops were still lit up. Far ahead a lorry crossed the traffic lights on the High Street. I soon reached the Cathedral grounds and climbed over the low stone wall into the graveyard. It was a moonlit night. The Cathedral looked pale and ghostly in the distance.

I had little trouble finding Edith's tomb. Some of the camouflage over the gap seemed to have gone. I cleared the rest away and shone my torch into the tomb. It looked very deep. I turned round, squeezed through the gap, and lowered myself in backwards. Digging footholds in the soil with my trainers, I carefully climbed down one corner of the tomb. It had a dank and earthy smell. When I reached the bottom I had a good look around. But apart from a few small fragments of wood and pottery, there was absolutely nothing there!

I was really disappointed. Then I heard a wicked laugh. I shone my torch up at the opening.

"I knew you would come, Edwina," said a voice.

Against the night sky I could see the outline of a woman in a long cloak. On her head she wore a crown.

"I've waited more than a thousand years for this moment. Now, thanks to you, I shall live again!"

Her voice was exultant and evil. I froze in horror.

She crouched down and leered at me through the gap. Then she took off her crown and threw it into the tomb.

"Edith the Third!" she cackled.

She pulled away the wooden prop. The lid of the tomb slammed shut.

***

Pitch blackness! Sheer panic! I switched on the torch and climbed up to the top. But however hard I pushed, the heavy stone lid would not budge.

I sat down on the floor of the tomb and cried in despair. I had forgotten to bring my mobile phone! And nobody knew where I was. Except Rick, but he was away in Norway. I looked at my watch. It was 3.30 a.m. In five hours I would begin shouting for help.

***

So that's my story. I must end it now as my torch is getting dim. Buried alive in a Saxon grave! It had my name on it.

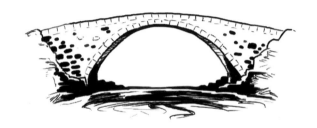

SIXTEEN
Dalesbridge

My name is Peter. I would like to record a strange series of events that have occurred in a definite pattern throughout my life.

When I was a boy we lived in a town called Dalesbridge. Its most interesting feature is the bridge, which crosses a deep gorge and connects the old part of town with the more modern half.

It is a twelfth century stone bridge, and it spans the gorge with a single arch. It is a remarkable feat of engineering. How it was built is a mystery to mediaeval scholars, as it was far ahead of the architectural skills of the time. At one end of the bridge stands the parish church.

My parents were religious and we went to church every Sunday. I always had to comb my hair and wear smart clothes. At first I found it boring, but later became quite interested in it all, particularly the New Testament.

One Sunday was very different - the Bishop took the service. This was because the Vicar had suddenly died. During the sermon the Bishop said that, sadly, this was not the first time it had happened. When I asked my parents what he meant, they were evasive and changed the subject.

Next Sunday a priest from a nearby parish officiated, but he had to drive twenty miles there and back. This was until a new resident vicar could be appointed. And there seemed to be a lot of gossiping among the congregation. But every time I drew near, people would stop talking.

I had stupidly left my coat in the church and went back to get it after lunch. The two women who arrange the flowers and collect the prayer books were in there. They were talking about the late Vicar. I hid behind a pillar. One of them had heard he'd committed suicide. How? By jumping off the bridge. When I got home I said nothing to my parents, of course.

A few days later I happened to be standing on the bridge. A lady was taking photographs of it, and of the church. She said she was writing a book about bridges with a religious connection. This one was known as a 'devil's bridge'. According to legend it had been built with the help of the Devil.

I said I found this hard to believe. She replied there were other such places in Europe: Pont du Diable in France, Teufelsbrücke in Switzerland, Ponte del Diavolo in Italy. Sometimes a town had been founded beside a particularly wide or deep river, and it was essential to have a good crossing to allow further expansion. But bridges were often made of wood and frequently collapsed.

Now the local parish priest was always held in high

esteem, and people often looked to him to find a solution. In some towns a bridge had miraculously appeared overnight, in others the priest had somehow acquired amazing skills as a builder and stonemason.

"But why would the Devil actually want to help people?" I asked. She said he never did anything for nothing. There would be an agreement. The Devil would build the bridge and the priest, while he was alive, would get all the kudos and prestige of it. But when he died, his soul would go to Hell.

I shuddered. She told me the story of Faust. He was a doctor at the university. One night Mephistopheles, an agent of the Devil, appears to him and makes the following offer: Faust can obtain the highest academic honours, and indeed anything he should desire – fame, riches, beautiful women – if he will just sign a deed handing over his soul to the Devil. Faust makes light of it and signs. He has a fabulous life. But when the time comes, Mephistopheles returns and Faust is dragged screaming down to Hell.

I told her about our own vicar's suicide. She said she knew about it, and that it had already happened three times before at Dalesbridge. And also that devil's bridges always carried a permanent and on-going curse with them.

The lady took some more photos then got into her car and drove off. As I walked home I thought about everything she had said, but still felt pretty dubious about it.

A week later my parents gave a luncheon party. One of the guests was a priest. He was a Jesuit – one of those extremely clever Catholic priests who have studied all aspects of religion and theology. Before lunch my sister Anne and I had to pass round the drinks, and nuts, olives, and crisps. Then I opened one of the French windows so that the priest would come into the garden, as I wanted to ask him a question: did the Devil really exist?

He was quite taken aback. He answered yes, he did exist. But his advantage was that many people didn't believe in him, and carried on sinning and wrongdoing with impunity.

I became very interested in the subject. In Heaven the glorious archangel Lucifer led a rebellion against God. He was defeated and, together with all the angels who had joined him, was cast down into Hell, whereupon they became devils and he was now known as Satan. In the Garden of Eden he took the form of a serpent, and persuaded Eve to eat the forbidden fruit. Many cathedrals have frescoes of the Last Judgement. The good souls went up to Heaven, but the bad souls were sent down to Hell, to be devoured by the Devil. And with his great horns and goat's feet he presided over witches' covens.

People were obsessed with the Devil. In the 18th Century, in the Hellfire Caves under West Wycombe, Sir Francis Dashwood dressed up as the Devil and gave his friends a good fright. In the town of Verrières in France, in 1851, an old woman was forcibly ejected from the village church, having accused the priest, who was saying the Mass, of being the Devil. The woman said she had seen his tail sticking out from under his cassock. But actually it was just the end of a long cord that he had used as a belt under the cassock, and had carelessly allowed to trail out behind him!

I also investigated what link the Devil had with the bridge in our town. I asked a teacher at school why it was called 'Dalesbridge'. He said it meant 'bridge over a valley'. But after some research in the library, I found it was originally spelt 'Deilsbridge'. And one day, in an antique shop, I saw a very old print of 'Ye Churche at Devils-Bridge'.

***

They eventually found a new vicar for our church. He was younger than the previous one. My parents had some people round for drinks and invited him and his wife too. She admitted that she had felt very uneasy about coming to Dalesbridge.

On Sundays, after the service, the Vicar would stand outside the church and say goodbye to the congregation. Afterwards, he could sometimes be seen talking to a particular man. Once I saw them walking on the bridge and looking over into the gorge.

One afternoon, when I was on one end of the bridge, I saw the Vicar standing in the middle, looking down into the gorge. Then, to my horror, I saw him climb up onto the edge of the parapet. I was sure he was going to jump. I decided the best thing to do was to walk slowly up to him and speak to him calmly. As I reached him he turned towards me and stepped down. Then I noticed there had been someone else with him on the bridge – that same man.

The Vicar walked back to the church. I never saw him again. Later I heard that his wife had quickly packed up all their belongings, and they had driven through the night to the North of England. They applied to be posted to New Zealand.

After I left school I went to Oxford and read Theology. My parents had sacrificed a lot to send me there, and I worked hard and got a First. I stayed on and studied for a PhD and then began teaching. I made a number of friends, and two very good ones: Jack Hargreaves and Maisie Dobson. My sister went to the University of Toronto.

I sometimes gave lectures. One of them was entitled 'The Temptation of Christ – Fact, Fiction, Myth or Allegory?' This story is in the Gospel, and is also the theme of *Paradise Regained*, by John Milton. When Jesus has spent forty days in the wilderness, Satan appears to him and tempts him three times. First he tells him to turn the desert's stones into bread. Then he takes Jesus up onto a high mountain. He challenges him to throw himself off, assuring him that angels will catch him and bear him aloft. Finally Satan offers him anything in the world if he will just kneel down and worship him. I described how I myself visualized the scene and the encounter in the desert.

The lecture was well attended. At the end, when nearly everyone had gone, I saw that two people still remained in the room. One was a Japanese girl who left after asking a couple of questions. Then the second person, a man, spoke to me.

"That was a very good lecture," he said, smiling, "and just as it was, except for a few details."

After a moment I recognized him. It was the man I had seen on the bridge at Dalesbridge, with the Vicar.

***

I eventually became Professor of Theology. Anne married someone she met at Toronto, and stayed in Canada to make her life there. After many years of teaching I decided to take a sabbatical. I spent several months touring Europe, visiting churches, museums, and libraries. This vacation was also to enable me to gather material for a book I was writing, *The Personification of Good and Evil in Christianity*.

The last country on my trip was Italy. I went to Milan, Venice, Ravenna and Florence, and spent a week in Rome. Then I visited Orvieto, with its beautiful cathedral, richly decorated with marble and mosaics. It was late in the afternoon and the Duomo was almost empty. I was looking at the frescoes by Signorelli depicting the end of the world. One was the Preaching of the Antichrist. Here a man with the resemblance of Christ (except without a halo) is addressing the people. But just behind him you can see the Devil manipulating him as if he were a puppet.

I gazed at the fresco, fascinated. Then I heard someone behind me speak quietly.

"A good likeness – almost perfect."

I did not turn round – I recognized the voice.

***

Some years later I had to go back to Dalesbridge. My father

was already dead. My mother had stayed on living there for a time, but finally moved into an old peoples' home. When she died I sold the house and most of the furniture – the rest I sent to my rooms in Oxford.

There had just been a memorial service for my mother at the church. When it was over and I had said goodbye to her remaining friends, I walked out onto the bridge, knowing it would be for the last time. I looked down into the gorge. An intense feeling of melancholy took hold of me. What was the point of life anyhow? If I wanted to I could end it all, right now.

Then I was conscious of someone else standing next to me. I turned my head slightly, and out of the corner of my eye I could see the man. I found myself climbing onto the parapet. I could sense him silently willing me, urging me to jump. Why not do it now, and get it over with?

Suddenly my mobile rang. It was Maisie, inviting me to lunch at the weekend. I stepped down from the parapet, wondering what on earth had come over me. I looked around. There was no one else on the bridge.

***

When I retired I bought myself a small flat in North Oxford, just off the Banbury Road. I lived a quiet existence and only returned to my college for the odd social occasion. After some years my health began to deteriorate. I was eventually admitted to the John Radcliffe Hospital for heart surgery. After the operation I remained in hospital for another week, for convalescence.

I had a private room, so was fortunately able to read and rest quietly. I had several visitors, including the Dean of my college. Then the day before I was due to go home, the nurse said there was someone else to see me. I wondered who it could possibly be – I knew so few people now. Maisie had already visited me (Jack was dead), and Anne had just telephoned from Canada.

The door opened and in walked the man. There was a chair by my bed. He sat down and looked at me in the eyes.

"It won't be long now, Peter, will it?"

He smiled, then got up and left the room.

SEVENTEEN

The Hairdresser

"Behind every hero stands a traitor." Slav proverb.

It was a hot day in May, unusually so. Janet was at home, revising for her A levels. She was sitting out on the balcony. This was on the first floor and gave a good view of the street below. It was about three o'clock in the afternoon. Both her parents were out at work, and would be back at the flat much later.

Suddenly she heard a terrible crash. She dropped her textbook. A car had pulled out of a parking space without indicating, right into the path of a large van. Both vehicles were badly damaged.

The drivers got out and stood on the pavement arguing. Soon afterwards a police car arrived, and two policemen began to interview them. Then a grey BMW appeared on the scene. Blue lights were flashing alternately from its headlights. A man in plain clothes got out and spoke to the policemen.

A few minutes later the doorbell rang. Janet went back inside and picked up the entry phone.

"I'm a police officer," said a voice, "will you let me in, please?"

Janet pressed the button and shortly afterwards there was a knock on the door of the flat. She opened it and in walked the man in plain clothes. He showed his identity card and walked straight over to the French windows leading to the balcony. He shut them and drew the curtains.

"I must ask you not to go out there for the next two hours," he said, "nor to leave the building."

Janet was so surprised she said nothing.

"Is there anyone else here?" asked the policeman.

"Just my parents. But they're not in right now. They're at work."

"I see."

"Will you need me as a witness?" asked Janet, trying to be helpful.

"Thank you, but that won't be necessary. And just remember what I said."

Then he opened the door and left the flat.

Some time later Janet realized she had left her book outside. She parted the curtains slightly, opened the French windows, and crept out onto the balcony.

By now two breakdown trucks had arrived. One of them had covered sides, to prevent anyone seeing what it was carrying. The van that had crashed was long, dark brown, and with six small frosted windows. It looked as if it had been built for a special purpose. A similar van was now parked near it. What appeared to be statues, totally shrouded in black cloth, were being transferred upright from the damaged van into the new one. The grey BMW had gone. The whole street had been cordoned off by the police. Janet picked up her book and returned to the sitting room to continue her revision.

When her parents got back she told them all about it.

"A lot of fuss about nothing, if you ask me," said her father.

***

When Janet left school, she did not go to university, but straight into a job. She decided to become a hairdresser, and was taken on as an apprentice at a salon near her home. This was very convenient, as she could walk to work. She learnt everything – washing, cutting, blow-drying, dyeing. How to help clients choose new hairstyles that suited them better. She took phone bookings and managed the appointments book. She cleaned the salon, arranged the magazines, made coffee for the clients, and helped them on and off with their gowns.

She finally received her diploma as a qualified hairdresser. Soon afterwards she got a phone call from another salon offering her a better job.

"I've been headhunted!" she said to her mother, excitedly.

Janet now had a higher salary, and with it more responsibility. She was given an assistant, a French girl who was starting as an apprentice, as she had.

Unfortunately the new salon was quite some way

from her home. After a time she got tired of taking the Underground, and bought herself a bicycle. She could now get to and from work in thirty minutes.

Her route took her across a roundabout that was particularly dangerous. Several accidents involving cyclists had recently occurred there.

"Janet, *do* be careful!" pleaded her mother.

She insisted she wore a high visibility yellow jacket with a helmet and flashing light.

One day Janet found the roundabout completely blocked off. A police car and ambulance were there.

"Oh no!" she thought, "not another accident!"

Then she saw a narrow alleyway which she had never noticed before. She rode down it, passing a sign saying: GOVERNMENT PROPERTY. STRICTLY PRIVATE. ADMISSION ONLY ON OFFICIAL BUSINESS. Further on was a large concrete building, standing in a courtyard enclosed by iron railings, inside which several brown vans were parked. They seemed strangely familiar.

This short cut saved her ten minutes and she began to use it regularly. But one day an official put up his hand for her to stop.

"Sorry Miss, Government Property. No right of way. Strict orders from the Ministry."

"Oh, I'm sorry," said Janet.

"I'll let you through just this once," said the official.

But she continued using the alley in order to avoid the roundabout. After a week, however, the official stepped out in front of her again.

"I told you before, no right of way!" he said angrily.

This time he held out his arm to stop her passing, so she had to pedal back and tackle the roundabout again. But she was not to be defeated, and rode to work fifteen minutes earlier. She was never challenged again.

Janet became an experienced hairdresser. She thoroughly enjoyed the job. The different hair – straight, curly, long or short. Black, brown, blonde or red. The variety of clients – young girls, fashionable women, middle-aged ladies, men. And the odd eccentric, like the old woman who asked for a haircut and forgot to say she was wearing a wig! Some of her customers became friendly with her. They'd tell her their holiday plans, even confiding in her their personal problems.

One client was different. She came in regularly once a week. She was always smartly dressed. Janet had only once seen her in trousers, and those as part of a suit. She was called Mrs Clarence. Once, towards closing, she came in carrying an evening dress on a hanger, and changed into it afterwards.

Dorothy Saunders, Janet's boss, said she was the best hairdresser she had ever had. Whenever she went away on holiday she would leave Janet in charge of the salon. Janet also handled all the bookkeeping, and cash and credit card transactions. By now she had four girls working under her.

As the years passed the salon became more and more successful, much due to Janet's reputation as a fine hairdresser. Many clients specifically asked to have their hair done by her in person.

One day Dorothy called her into the small office at the back of the salon. At first she thought it was just some routine matter. But then she saw another person sitting in there.

"Good morning, Mrs Clarence," said Janet, in surprise.

"I have several customers waiting," said Dorothy, getting up, "Mrs Clarence would like to have a few words with you privately."

She left the office and shut the door.

"You are an excellent hairdresser," began Mrs Clarence.

"Thank you," said Janet, wondering what it was all about.

"I would like to make you a proposition. Oh, please sit down."

Janet sat down rather clumsily in a chair opposite her.

"I belong to an organisation that is part of the Government. It is a small group doing very specialized work. We require someone of your experience to provide the services of a hairdresser.

"It's very kind of you to consider me," said Janet, choosing her words carefully, "but I don't quite understand what you want me to do."

"We cater for a small select number of people," said Mrs Clarence, "and their welfare includes grooming and hairdressing. But owing to their position they must receive this care in private."

"I see," said Janet.

"Now we would like you to work for us. This entails making personal visits to wherever the clients live."

"But what about my job here at the salon?" asked Janet.

"We have made special arrangements with Dorothy," said Mrs Clarence, "you will continue working here normally. But from time to time you would go off on these special assignments. About once a month."

"It sounds very interesting," said Janet.

"May I add that this work is very well remunerated. Anyway, perhaps you would like to think about it."

Janet said nothing for a moment. Then she made up her mind.

"I'd be delighted to give it a try, Mrs Clarence."

"Are you sure? I must warn you that this is a serious commitment."

"Yes, I am," said Janet firmly.

"Please go to this address," said Mrs Clarence, taking an envelope out of her handbag, "an appointment will have been made for you. And remember, the conversation we have just had is strictly confidential."

She stood up. As she left the room she looked Janet straight in the eyes.

As she cycled home, Janet wondered what she had let herself in for. She went straight to her room and opened the letter. It asked her to present herself at 11.00 a.m. on Friday 15th April at an address in Whitehall.

When the day came she dressed smartly and put on some make-up. She decided to take the Underground. On the way to the station she ran into a friend of hers.

"You look nice. Going anywhere special?"

"Not really," she replied.

Coming out of Westminster tube station she began to feel nervous. She found the building in Whitehall and showed the letter to the porter at the desk. He gave her a pass, opened an electric gate, and she sat down in the waiting area. Soon a woman came up to her.

"Janet Mason?"

"Yes."

"Please come this way."

They took a lift, then walked down a corridor. The woman knocked on a door and Janet was shown into a small office. A man was sitting at a desk. He was very thin and had a hawk-like look on his face.

"Please sit down, Miss Mason."

He showed her a form.

"This is the Official Secrets Act. It is a requirement that you sign it before commencing the work you are scheduled to do. Upon signature I would then warn you that any breach of its provisions is a criminal offence, incurring heavy penalties."

He handed her the form.

"You might wish to read it first."

Janet glanced at it, signed where indicated, and gave it back to him.

"Thank you, Miss Mason. That will be all."

He pressed a button and Janet was taken back to the

reception area. She handed in her pass and went out into the street.

One morning, a month later, Dorothy asked her to come into the office. A holdall had been packed for her and a car would shortly be picking her up.

They drove down Kensington High Street, then turned left into a private road. A policeman let them through some gates and they entered the courtyard of a large, dark red brick building. It was Kensington Palace. Janet was met by a man in a suit and escorted through an archway, up some stairs, down a corridor, and into a room. A very old woman was sitting there in a wheelchair.

"I expect you have everything you need – to attend to the Princess," said the man. "Would you like a cup of coffee, Miss Mason?"

Janet set about cutting and washing the woman's thin grey hair. She tried to be friendly and talk to her, but all she would do was nod her head and sigh.

She went to the Palace once a month. But on her ninth visit she found the Princess lying on her back on a couch. Her skin was a waxy colour and her eyes were closed. Two men in black suits and ties, and white shirts were standing by her.

"Tidy up the old lady for us, will you?" said one of them. "Do your best, love."

Two months went by. Then one day Janet was again asked to come into the office. This time the driver took a different route – to another part of London. Janet recognized the roundabout. They drove down a side street and stopped at some gates. The driver punched in a code and they opened. They went through a short tunnel and into a courtyard. There stood the concrete building with the brown vans parked outside.

A man in uniform opened the car door and Janet was ushered up the steps. She was asked to stand on two footprints painted on the floor, and look straight ahead while a camera scanned her face. Then an electric gate opened. She was taken into an office. A woman was sitting at a desk. It was Mrs Clarence.

"Good morning, Janet," she said, "please sit down."

She looked briefly at a file open in front of her.

"I see that you have been with us for nearly a year now. We are very satisfied with your work. We now require you to do something quite different – and far more challenging."

"I am very glad to help," said Janet.

"Good. First I will tell you about our organisation. It is so secret that no one outside the group knows anything about it, except for the Prime Minister, the Home Secretary, and the Secretary of State for Defence. We have achieved a scientific advance of the utmost importance, way ahead of any other country. Eternal life, so to speak."

"Gosh!" exclaimed Janet.

"There are naturally many physical constraints," continued Mrs Clarence, "but it is well worth the trouble. You see, we have preserved for ever the finest brains in politics, science, and the arts. For the benefit of this country and posterity!"

For a brief moment Janet thought she was mad.

"Now what you are about to see you may well find disturbing. But I know you are a girl with the strength of character to overcome that, and you will do an excellent job."

She spoke into a telephone. A man came into the office.

"Please take Miss Mason to her supervisor."

They walked down a long corridor. It was clearly a hospital. There were doctors and nurses, and also porters pushing trolleys.

They entered another office.

"Hello, Janet," said a man in a white coat, "I'm Doctor Turner."

He gave her a pack of clothes.

"You can change in the room next door. Then come back in here."

She put on a dark blue uniform trimmed with white piping, and a close-fitting cap. Dr Turner took her by the arm and they walked further down the corridor into a small room. A nurse was sitting at a desk.

"How are they all doing today, Sister?"

"Fine, Doctor.

They went through into a ward. A faint electrical hum and the sound of pumps could be heard. Instead of beds there were two rows of columns, five to a row. They were about four feet high. Each one was mounted on castors and had a control panel with lights, dials and switches.

Wires and tubes ran from the base of the columns into a thick cable which was clipped to the wall, leading out of the ward. On the front of each was a computer screen and keyboard with a mechanical arm on either side of it. And, protruding from the top of every column, cut off at the base of the neck, was a human head!

Janet had to bite on her finger to stop herself from screaming.

"But...where's the rest of them?" she asked, horrified.

"Well, of course, mortality has compelled us to discard their bodies," said Dr Turner, "but these units can fully replicate their functions. They maintain the blood and cerebrospinal fluid, thus keeping the brains alive. The blood is oxygenated, enriched by nutrients, minerals and vitamins, and filtered by dialysis."

He slapped one of the units enthusiastically.

"I wish you wouldn't do that, Dr Turner," said the head that was on top of it.

"My apologies."

"So what do I have to do?" asked Janet, still in a state of shock.

"Cut their hair," replied Dr Turner, "that's about all they've got left now, poor dears!"

He took her over to a cupboard. It was full of hairdressing equipment.

A nurse carrying a clipboard went up to them.

"Dame Marion needs a shampoo and set."

Janet recognized Marion Williams, the famous opera

singer. She set about washing her hair. A towel had to be tightly wrapped around the base of her neck where it entered the 'collar' (the plastic connection to the unit) to prevent water leaking in.

Dame Marion was very talkative and tried hard to put Janet at her ease. She said that many of the heads were well-known public figures. Their deaths had been kept secret and only their bodies disposed of. Their heads, already removed, were being kept alive on these units.

"I had no choice in the matter," she said bitterly.

She normally had one recording session every few months. Her unit was fitted with an extra-powerful air compressor, so that, as well as talk, she could also sing loudly.

She had even once appeared on television singing an aria; great care was taken to show no more than one inch below her chin.

"They do kill us off eventually," she said, "even celebrities have to die sometime. But I've got to suffer another fifteen years of this hell!"

Janet attended to another head that day: Professor Moorcroft. He had fluffy unkempt grey hair and a beard.

"It's marvellous," he said, "this has enabled me to carry on with my research. Atomic fusion. So much still to do! I fell ill while writing my latest paper. But my so-called death was merely a brief interruption of my work."

He switched on his computer with his mechanical hand. He was directly connected to Cambridge University, and, via Skype and video-conferencing, could speak to other scientists all over the world.

Janet finished, and put away her equipment.

"I'll get you escorted out," said the nurse, "only a few hours to go, now!"

She said that at ten o'clock at night all the lights were dimmed. Talking was then forbidden, but heads were allowed to watch their computer screens switched to silent mode, or listen to music through headphones. Others had black hoods put over them to help them sleep.

Over the following months, and the next year, Janet made regular visits to the hospital. She got to know many of the heads. There were actors, writers, scientists, religious leaders, politicians – even businessmen. Some of these had chosen it voluntarily on succumbing to a fatal illness, and had paid for everything themselves. They spent their time buying and selling shares, and doing business on their computers.

Then there was Baroness Haylesworth. She sometimes attended committee meetings at the House of Lords via video-link. Before each one her hair was always immaculately styled. She wore large diamond earrings.

There were five other such wards at the hospital. A beautician called Tracey also came once a month.

"They had to go and get you in a hurry," she said one day.

"Why?" asked Janet.

"The girl before you. Couldn't take it anymore. Had a nervous breakdown, then killed herself."

"How awful!"

"To me it's just another job," said Tracey, "and the pay is good."

She had worked there for a long time. She said that to make life at all bearable for the heads, the hospital provided counsellors and religious help. Psychiatrists administered drugs and sedatives.

Janet also learned all about the brown vans. Their main use was to transport heads to and from Falconhurst Hall, a big house in Surrey. Twenty were already there, and the Ministry planned to move the rest of them out of London. Security was far better as the Hall was set in its own grounds of fifty acres. And in good weather the units could be wheeled out into the gardens, for the heads to enjoy a bit of greenery.

Each van could take up to four heads and units. They were strapped in and connected to the van's power supply (which also had a backup generator). Apart from the driver, the vans carried a doctor, nurse, engineer and security guard.

As time went on Janet inevitably got to know her heads better. Some were glum and silent as she attended to them, others chatty. Professor Moorcroft was a brilliant mathematician and nuclear physicist. He was keen to impart to her his knowledge. While she cut his hair and trimmed his beard he would teach her chemistry, physics and astronomy, illustrated by diagrams on his computer screen. Much more interesting than what she had done at school!

Marion Williams recounted her whole life story. Her childhood in Wales, then as a student at the Royal College of Music in London, where she met her husband, a violinist. They lived for a time in Sydney, and performed at the Opera House.

"Those were the happiest days of my life."

Later they returned to Europe, appearing everywhere: Glyndebourne, Covent Garden, Bayreuth, La Scala.

"When my darling Peter died I just threw myself into my work."

She had contracts with big music corporations, and was still making several recordings a year, well into her late sixties.

"You see, they couldn't afford to let me die," she said, "I was too valuable."

One day she asked Janet to come right up close to her.

"I want you to kill me," she whispered, "it's easy. All you have to do is turn off my master switch. Our mechanical arms are designed so we can't reach it."

"I can't do that, Dame Marion," said Janet.

"Yes you can. Just say you hit it by mistake with your scissors. Or with the hairdryer. By the time the control room monitor detects it, I'll be long dead. I beg you, please help me get out of this nightmare!"

From then on it became very difficult for Janet. On each visit she had to endure hearing Dame Marion's piteous entreaties.

One day Mrs Clarence sent for her.

"We need you to accompany some of the heads to North America. I cannot be more precise than that. You will be away for three weeks."

"But what will I say to my parents and to Dorothy?" asked Janet in surprise.

"You will have to make up a story. Say you are going on holiday," said Mrs Clarence, "you will be leaving in ten days time."

That week Janet went clothes shopping. She showed her friends at the salon the cotton sundress she had bought. She told them she was going to Thailand.

"I've just got to have some sun."

She said she had been saving up for the trip for a long time. It was quite fun inventing a completely false story, and making her workmates jealous!

"Don't forget your sun cream!" said Dorothy.

When the day came Janet's father offered to drive her to Heathrow, but she had already booked a taxi. On arrival at the hospital she was met by Dr Turner, given her hairdressing kit, then taken to one of the brown vans. Professor Moorcroft and three other scientists – one male and two female – were already strapped in.

After about forty minutes they reached their destination. Stepping out of the van, Janet was surprised to see they were actually on the tarmac, right next to a private jet.

"I think it's Northolt Aerodrome," said the doctor who was with them. "It's used for royalty and VIP's nowadays."

After the heads had been loaded onto the aircraft, Janet went aboard. The front of the cabin had seats for the doctor, nurse, engineer, security guard and herself, plus a stewardess. The rear part had been fitted to accomodate the heads.

After takeoff lunch was served. An hour or so later they landed in Iceland for a brief refuelling stop. Once they were airborne again Janet opened a book she had brought with her. After a while she dozed off.

"Would you like to come up onto the flight deck?" A young man in uniform was standing next to her seat.

"Oh, thank you," she said, getting up.

He opened the door and pointed to an empty seat behind the pilots.

"You can sit in the jump seat if you like. My name's Bruce. I'm the First Officer, and this is Jim, your Captain."

"Hi!" said Jim, turning round.

Janet looked out of the cockpit window. There wasn't a cloud in sight. You could see the ocean far down below.

"We're flying at 36,000 feet," said Bruce, "amazing visibility, isn't it?"

Then Janet saw two jet fighters flying alongside them.

"Who are they?" she asked, in alarm.

"That's our escort. RAF," said Bruce, "but halfway across, the United States Air Force take over."

He then invited her to sit in the right-hand seat. She was fascinated by the radar screen, instruments and switches. She put on a headset and listened to all the radio communication between Jim, Air Traffic Control, and other aircraft.

Later she saw they were flying over land.

"That's Greenland," said Bruce.

One could clearly see the fjords, glaciers, and then the white expanse of the ice cap. Shortly afterwards the jet fighters peeled off.

"Bye chaps," said Jim on the radio.

Twenty minutes later a strange deep voice sounded in Janet's headset

"Gulfstream, Bravo Victor Zulu. Do you read?"

"Victor Zulu," answered Jim.

"Descend immediately to 3,000 feet. Alter course to two-niner-one. You will land at Kangerlussuaq. Later I give you altimeter, wind speed, and approach and runway headings."

The accent was distinctly Russian.

"Not bloody likely!" said Jim.

Then Janet noticed some other jet fighters flying next to them.

These ones were different.

"Jesus! They're Su's!" said Bruce.

"If you are looking for your American friends, you will be disappointed," said the Russian voice, laughing, "you are surrounded now!"

Janet went back into the jump seat and put on a headset.

"Mayday, Mayday," said Jim, on an emergency frequency.

"You stop that right now!" said the voice, grimly.

A rocket shot past them.

"I think they mean business," said Jim.

He put the plane into a dive and told the passengers to prepare for landing. Terrified, Janet returned to the cabin and fastened her seatbelt.

As they landed she saw the runway was lined with armoured vehicles. They taxied to a halt.

"Now open!" said a loud voice.

The crew reluctantly lowered the steps. A man in a long khaki overcoat and fur hat, accompanied by four soldiers with submachine-guns, boarded the aircraft.

The two pilots, the stewardess and the security guard were taken off first, and driven away in a van. Then the heads and units were disconnected from their positions in the cabin, and were loaded into a specially adapted personnel carrier. With them went the doctor, engineer, nurse and Janet.

They drove across the tarmac to an enormous plane parked several hundred yards away. Janet could not believe what had happened. If Greenland belonged to Denmark, where was the Danish Army? And how had the Russians pulled this off despite the fighter escort and the tight security in England?

Once on board the giant aircraft she noticed that its interior had been arranged in much the same way, apart from being more spacious. There were also Russian doctors, engineers and nurses to attend to the heads.

The doors were shut, the engines started, and they

taxied towards the runway.

"Welcome to all our guests," said a voice on the intercom, "now, back to Mother Russia!"

Once they were airborne a meal was served: beetroot soup, meatballs and cabbage, a sticky cake, and tea. And as the hours passed Janet wondered how long she would be staying in Russia. Perhaps the rest of her life?

A tall man in uniform was standing by her seat, smiling.

"Hello. I am Vladimir. Captain. This is Antonov transport. Biggest and best! Flight will be very long. Over North Pole. You should stretch legs. Walk around cabin. We have also comfortable lounge for passengers."

He pointed down the aisle, behind her.

"But why you look so sad? You know, life in Russia not so bad now. Food better, shops full. In winter skiing at Sochi, spend summer on beach in Crimea."

He winked.

"And Russian boys, very handsome!"

Later on Janet went along to the passenger lounge. People were sitting together in groups, except for one person, who was alone. She was smartly dressed, and could be easily recognized. Her hair had been so often styled at the salon!

"I'm so sorry, Janet," said Mrs Clarence. "You see, I needed the money."

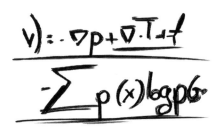

EIGHTEEN
Coincidence

"Hatred is a sour fruit. But Revenge, how sweet is that fruit! Yet in the end, all fruit turns rotten."
Ahmed Al Behkiri, Philosopher, 11th Century.

***

Coincidence! It defies logic and rational thought. Is it just the product of the most unlikely odds? Or is it already fated and pre-ordained? Or perhaps due to some supernatural meddling with our lives?

When Oedipus was told by the Oracle at Delphi that he would kill his father and marry his mother, he rushed away in despair. At a fork in the road from the sanctuary his chariot crashed into another one, and its driver, an old man, was killed. Many years later he discovered it was his father. And the woman he had married was the man's widow – his own mother. Was this tragedy a mere coincidence, or, since it was foretold by the Oracle, already predestined? And had it been arranged by the gods?

In Ripley's *Believe It or Not* some robbers tie a man to a tree, and, before leaving, shoot him. But the bullet misses and gets embedded in the tree trunk. Some twenty years later the man cuts down the tree. His chainsaw hits the bullet, and it flies up and kills him. That bullet was meant for him!

In 2009, in the National Lottery of Bulgaria, the same set of numbers came out in the next draw five days later. Almost impossible odds, leading many to think that the lottery was rigged.

Years ago, when I was a boy, I was walking down a narrow street when I heard a terrible crash. Two glass vans, travelling fast in opposite directions, had tried to squeeze past each other. They were carrying large panes of glass (for shop windows, etc), vertically on the outside of each van, on the right-hand side. These had hit each other and smashed to pieces. The road was covered with shattered glass. I stood there with my mouth open in amazement.

"You can wipe that smile off your face!" called out one of the drivers to me, "find this funny, do you?"

"I'm sorry," I said, "it's just the two of you meeting like this – such a coincidence."

"Coincidence, eh? Bleedin' expensive, that's what it is!"

Until then the drivers had been shouting at each other, but they now began to turn on me.

"Buzz off and mind your own business," said the other driver, by now red in the face.

Then a policeman arrived on the scene.

"You had better move on, my lad," he said to me sternly, "provoking them could be considered 'Conduct Likely to

Cause Breach of the Peace'.

But in my own life I have suffered a much graver set of coincidences. My training is in mathematics. I have always taken an objective view of any unlikely event and assessed its probability, rather than immediately calling it a coincidence. But what happened to me cannot in any way be explained by logic.

When I was nine I went to my prep school. My best subject was mathematics. Soon I was top of the class. There was only one thing wrong – the maths teacher, Mr Harbottle.

He and I just did not get on. As I was good at the subject most teachers would have been pleased. But no – each time I made a mistake he would point it out to the rest of the class with a smug little smile. He always marked my homework unfairly, with comments in red ink in that little spidery writing of his. As my maths got better and better he seemed to resent it, as if a rivalry had developed between us. He was probably jealous.

He was a thin man. His body seemed to squirm, rather than move. His face resembled that of a fish – an elongated head, little beady eyes behind glasses, and a tiny mouth. He carried a briefcase with the initials F.S.H. on it. Even those spelt 'fish'!

They stood for Frederick Stainsforth Harbottle.

He sometimes took games. I wasn't very good at football. But once I did a brilliant shot and kicked the ball right into the goalmouth. It hit the top bar then bounced down just behind the line. My side all cheered, but Harbottle blew his whistle and disallowed the goal. When I protested he sent me off for 'insubordination'.

In class things got worse and worse. One day Harbottle was doing a complex calculation on the blackboard. But he couldn't get it to work out. I had spotted why – he'd made a simple mistake somewhere, a plus instead of a minus, but I kept quiet about it. Then I started giggling. He came up to my desk and demanded why I hadn't told him where he'd gone wrong. He showered me with insults and accused me of sabotaging the lesson. I couldn't take it any longer.

"You look like a fish, sir."

He went bright red, his eyes nearly popped out of their sockets, and his little mouth opened and closed rapidly in speechless rage. He would have hit me had it been legal. I was sent straight to the Headmaster's study.

That was when I really began to hate him. I would think about him even when out of school, at weekends, and during the holidays too. I remember having trout for dinner once, and slowly cutting the head off my fish, wishing it was Mr Harbottle's.

But when I went on to my public school it was quite different. I got on very well with Mrs Anderson, my maths teacher. She really believed in me and encouraged me to work hard.

"Michael, if you continue to do as well as this you could win a scholarship to Cambridge!"

She even gave me some extra coaching in her spare

time. After three terms I was the top mathematics pupil in my year, and had won the Junior Maths Prize .

After the summer holidays I went back to school full of enthusiasm. However, I heard that Mrs Anderson had left and the vacancy had been filled by someone else. The day of the first maths lesson I came into the classroom a bit early. The teacher had not yet arrived, but on a chair was a briefcase with F.S.H. on it!

Mr Harbottle quickly read through his list of pupils. But when he reached my name he paused.

"Michael Watkins. Ah yes."

From then on he made my life utter hell, so much so that I even thought of specializing in another subject. In class he would argue with me and try to humiliate me in front of the other pupils. Then he would look around to see everyone's reactions. He complained about me to the other teachers and tried to influence them against me. And at the end of term I always got a stinking report.

But strangely, on just one occasion, he appeared to be actually nice. It was a fine summer afternoon, and I saw him drive into the car park (I thought he only had a bicycle).

"Hello. Lovely day, isn't it?" he said, smiling, as he shut the car door.

That was totally out of character. Due perhaps to the fine weather – and maybe a good lunch?

It all came to a head at the end of my third year, during my A level exams. I was taking the Advanced Mathematics paper and was confident of doing well. Mr Harbottle was invigilating. He suddenly accused me of cheating. He rang for someone else to replace him, and got up and marched me off to the Headmaster.

In the showdown that followed I defended myself vigorously. Harbottle, in his usual slimy way, had no doubt prepared the Headmaster with a pack of lies about me. But in this case he was unable to prove I had been cheating in the exam. In fact, I later got excellent results and decided to sit for a Mathematics Scholarship to Cambridge.

I knew that universities very much relied on secondary schools' recommendation of former pupils, so I took care not to disclose the actual college in Cambridge I had applied to. In addition, to lay a false trail for Harbottle, I even said I was trying for Oxford. In June I went to Cambridge and sat the scholarship exam.

A week or two later, while back at home for the holidays, I received a letter from Cambridge asking me to come back for an interview. I got on the train full of hope and expectation.

I spent the night at the college and made friends with several of the other candidates. Next morning I was ushered into a large room and interviewed by a panel of six 'dons'. Then I went into another room to meet the Professor of Mathematics. He said they had all been highly impressed by my exam papers. He was very friendly, and spoke about life at the college and its history and traditions.

Then suddenly there was a knock on the door and a woman came in.

"Yes?" asked the Professor.

"Sorry to disturb you, sir, but a Mr Harbottle is on the line."

"Can't it wait?"

"He says it's most urgent," said the woman.

"Oh, all right, I'll take it," said the Professor, clearly irritated. "Will you excuse me for a moment, Michael?"

He left the room. When he returned, some ten minutes later, his manner was quite different, almost icy. The atmosphere became strained and artificial, and the rest of the interview was more of a formality than anything, and quickly concluded.

When I was back home a letter arrived from the college in Cambridge. They regretted to advise me that I had not been awarded a scholarship. Nor were they able to offer me a place at the college either.

I eventually went somewhere else, to what is known as a 'redbrick' university. I got a good degree, but it did not have the prestige of one from Cambridge - with a scholarship too.

I couldn't help feeling that Mr Harbottle had ruined my career. Although I now had a good job in the statistics department of a large brewery, I knew I would have done better if I had gone to Cambridge. As the years went by my memories of Harbottle did not gradually fade, as would normally happen. Instead they grew into deep resentment and hatred, and I became obsessed with thoughts of revenge.

One day a card arrived in the post. It was an invitation to my old school's two-hundredth anniversary. I specially hired a car not just to get there, but as a means of killing Harbottle. The plan was simple: to sit in the car, wait for him to appear in the school drive, car park, or playing fields, and then run him over. I would say that my foot slipped on the pedal. But unfortunately Harbottle was not present at the reunion – apparently he was ill. All that trouble and expense for nothing!

When my father died his pension and life insurance were not sufficient to properly support my mother. She and I lived in quite a big house. We had the choice of either selling it and buying a smaller one (and living off the rest of the proceeds), or keeping it and taking in a lodger.

We redecorated one of the bedrooms – it had an ensuite bathroom. We partitioned off part of the sitting room to create a dining area, as we planned to offer bed and breakfast.

Our first lodger was an attractive girl called Heather. Unfortunately I didn't see much of her as she was either at work or out with her boyfriend. They got engaged, and then she got married and left.

The next one was an American called Bill Bradley. He was aged about forty, and had come over here to work in a merchant bank. He was very fit, and keen on sport. I became quite friendly with him, and at weekends we would often have lunch at a pub or at the local golf club.

As I got to know him better I would confide in him, and

he'd give me advice, rather like an older brother (which I had never had). One day I told him all about Harbottle, and how I desperately craved for revenge for what he'd done to me.

"You sure gotta hangup about that guy," said Bill, "and I guess you feel real bitter. But he's just some old jerk who messed you up when you were a kid, back at high school. That's all in the past now."

He banged his fist on the table, to emphasize the point.

"Look, Mike, what matters is the present. And the future – your future!"

When Bill left we had a series of lodgers, none of whom stayed very long. There was a married couple who spent most of their time having rows, a chap who stayed all day in his room singing Buddhist chants, and people attending conferences. We had to ask one man to leave as vans kept on delivering cardboard boxes – he was running a business from his room. Then there was the German who was booked to stay half board (bed, breakfast and evening meal). He sent, in advance, a thirty-line email exactly specifying his dietary requirements.

Our next long-term lodger was Mrs Indira Patel, an Indian lady in her late fifties. She stayed with us for more than two years, and became a good friend of my mother, who had been rather lonely after my father died. They did yoga together, and each Thursday night we had curry, then listened to Indian records in the sitting room.

I too became friendly with Mrs Patel, and at weekends

would often take her for short outings in my car. On the way home we usually stopped for a cream tea at a country hotel or tea shop.

"How quintessentially English!" she would exclaim.

On one of these trips I talked about my life – my job, friends and aspirations. And also about my past. How Mr Harbottle had ruined most of my schooldays, stopped me getting into Cambridge and harmed my career.

When I had finished Mrs Patel said nothing for a moment. Then she covered her head with the end of her sari, which she always did when about to say something important.

"'Laisse tomber', as the French say. Your fixation with this man is poisoning your mind, and hindering your progress towards maturity. You will not develop spiritually until you free yourself of this burden of hatred."

She spoke slowly and deliberately.

"And as for revenge, the Bhagavad Gita expressly forbids it. If, by hating, you do evil, you will find punishment through the law of karma. And what did Jesus say? 'Love your enemies.'"

She poured herself some more tea.

"You are a young man, Michael, with so much to live for. Forget the past, enjoy the present, and look forward to the future!"

I took note of what she was saying. She had a degree in Psychology.

Mrs Patel eventually left and went back to India. For a

long while we had no one staying with us. Then my mother found out about a scheme promoted by the County Council. If you took on an invalid or handicapped person you could make far more money than with a private lodger. Their rent was guaranteed by the Council, and there were tax benefits too. I wasn't keen on the idea, but my mother insisted.

We had to make a few changes, such as installing a wheelchair ramp, and handrails in the bathroom, for the house to be registered as 'a dwelling approved for the care of elderly and handicapped persons as specified in the Act'. Then an ambulance arrived with our first resident.

Two paramedics and a nurse helped an old man into the house.

My mother stood by to welcome him.

"I'm sure you'll look after Mr Harbottle," said the nurse breezily, "he'll be in good hands!"

My heart missed a beat. Then, in quick succession, I felt horror, outrage and despair. I would never be free of him. But this was not the same Harbottle I had last seen at school so many years ago. The fish-like face had not changed. But instead of an aggressive teacher, an old man sat in a wheelchair with his head slightly bowed.

My mother helped him into the sitting room and brought tea.

"This is my son Michael," she said.

He nodded. I didn't think he had recognized me. Afterwards my mother took him to his room and unpacked his things.

As I lay in bed that night I resolved to kill Mr Harbottle. It was a disaster that he had come back into my life, but fate had also delivered him into my hands.

However, I took my time in deciding how to dispose of him. Meanwhile, I gradually gained his confidence. I asked him about himself. He said he had worked in education all his life. But he did not mention which schools he had taught at, which was a good thing, as I didn't want him to identify me as a former pupil of his. I would engage him in light conversation, and he found me a pleasant companion. But actually he didn't speak very much; I heard he'd had a stroke.

I eventually formulated my plan. I started by taking him for walks in the garden, and then down the lane, as far as the village green. Harbottle could walk slowly for very short distances with the aid of two sticks. Later we progressed to trips requiring his wheelchair and a journey in the car.

We lived near the sea in East Sussex, and a few miles away were the Seven Sisters and Beachy Head, some of the highest cliffs in England. I would take him there for outings, pushing him in his wheelchair along the clifftop path. Then I would stop for a while, and turn the wheelchair towards the sea so that he could look at the view.

I took him out most weekends when the weather was fine. I would get him into the car, fold up his wheelchair, and then drive off to the cliffs. There was a café there and we always stopped first for a snack before our walk along the cliff path. I soon got to be known as a kind and caring young man.

The week before I had planned 'to do the deed' I loosened the wheelchair's brake so it could be released with a slight touch. But as the appointed day approached – one Saturday in June – I began to have serious doubts about killing Harbottle. Was it really worth it? After all, he was a different person now. No longer a vicious schoolmaster, but a rather pathetic old man. And whatever justification I had, this was still murder. I risked spending the rest of my life in jail. Why not just forget about it, as I had been so strongly advised to do?

On the Friday, the day before, I went to work at the brewery as usual. Three weeks earlier I had applied for a more senior position that had become vacant. It was a good step up and carried a higher salary. I had been there for a long time and was fairly confident of getting the job.

That afternoon I was called into the Managing Director's office.

"Do sit down, Michael."

"Thank you, sir."

"Now about this promotion..."

"Yes."

My pulse rate quickened.

"Michael," he said, looking embarassed, "I have to tell you this."

He opened a drawer in his desk and took out a letter.

"Look," he said, "I know how much this job meant to you. And, in normal circumstances, we would have given it to you. But you will understand that we had to advertise it. There were a number of candidates. None of them had your level of experience or your length of service with us."

He paused for a moment.

"However, just before the deadline we received one more application."

He held up the letter.

"And that candidate had by far the best academic qualifications. Now I can assure you that the Board gave this their fullest consideration. I did my best to argue in your favour, but I was overruled."

He put it back in the drawer.

"Michael, I am so sorry to disappoint you."

I knew what he was going to say next.

"You see, he has a degree from Cambridge University."

This put paid to any hesitation I had about finishing off Harbottle. The next morning, Saturday, was fine and sunny, though rather windy. I suggested we went on the cliff walk. My mother wrapped him up in his coat and scarf and put on his cap. As I folded his wheelchair to put in the boot of the car, I checked the brake I had loosened. On arrival we had some tea at the café then took the path along the cliffs. After a few hundred yards I looked around to see if anyone was nearby. I turned the wheelchair to face the sea and put on the brake. It was at a place where the safety fence had fallen down. Here the land sloped down to the cliff edge, which was under ten feet away. Harbottle shielded his eyes from the sun, and looked out to sea.

"Fishing boats," he said.

"And here's a nice big one for them," I said under my breath.

I released the brake and sent off the wheelchair with a good shove. Harbottle gave a short cry as it careered down the slope and over the edge of the cliff. I ran after it shouting "Help!" and looked down. The wheelchair lay twisted on the pebbled beach below, with Harbottle a few feet away. He wasn't moving.

What I did next had been rehearsed in my mind many times over. I ran all the way to the café and breathlessly told them what had happened. They rang the police and the coastguard. Soon afterwards I saw a helicopter flying past. Then I phoned my mother.

Eventually a police car arrived at the café. I was allowed to drive home in my own car, with them following behind. Two police officers took a statement from me in the sitting room. My mother, though in a deep state of shock, made them cups of tea.

Then one of their phones rang.

"Yes, I thought so. I'll inform him."

The officer said that Mr Harbottle was unfortunately dead. My mother put her hands over her face.

They were surprisingly nice. Not once did I come under any suspicion. Nor was I accused of negligence with the wheelchair. I'd had a terrible experience and received nothing but sympathy. I had lost a friend and 'father figure'.

"Well, accidents do happen, I'm afraid," said one of the

policemen as they left, "that's the hardest part of our job."

A week later the Coroner's Inquest was held. Only three people attended: my mother, myself, and a reporter from the local newspaper.

The Coroner asked me to say in my own words what had happened. He thanked me when I had finished, and said that if any further information were needed, it could all be supplied by the police.

There was a report from the paramedics, who had been dropped by helicopter onto the beach at the foot of the cliff. And also one from a pathologist.

An inspection had been made of the wheelchair, but it had been too badly damaged in the fall for this to be conclusive. It was noted, however, that the brake on that particular model was known to be unreliable.

Another contributory factor was the weather. The meteorological report for that Saturday recorded a north wind of some degree of force. A gust could well have dislodged the wheelchair and blown it towards the cliff edge.

In summing up the Coroner commended my devotion to that elderly gentleman, and regretted that our friendship had been ended so tragically. He recorded a verdict of Misadventure.

As I left the inquest a social worker handed me a leaflet. Because of the trauma I had suffered it was recommended that I see a counsellor. I felt it would look better if I did, so I had several sessions with someone listed on the leaflet.

Then came the funeral. A handful of Harbottle's friends turned up and also an old woman who was some distant cousin. My mother and I were a bit early, so we waited outside the church. A taxi arrived and an elderly man got out. He had an overnight bag, which he left inside the porch, and also a briefcase with the initials F.S.H. on it.

As I went into the church I was given a white folded card which I didn't look at very closely – it gave the hymns and prayers of the funeral service. Then a man got up and made the Address. He had worked for many years with 'Frank' at the Department of Education. What a wonderful colleague he had been!

After some more hymns another person came and spoke. It was the man who had arrived in the taxi.

"My dear brother Francis, my identical twin! Yes, Frank and Fred, no one could tell us apart. When we were small we wore the same clothes, had the same toys. And when we grew up we had parallel careers. Frank was a civil servant, in the Department of Education, and I was a schoolmaster ..."

Afterwards, back home, my mother laid on tea and drinks for those who had been to the funeral. I saw her chatting to that Mr Harbottle, and stood nearby listening to their conversation.

He had spent the previous night at a hotel a few miles away, but had now checked out. To my horror I heard my mother inviting him to stay with us.

"Why not come and spend the night here?" she

suggested, "we have a spare room now."

"That's so kind of you, Mrs Watkins, but I wouldn't dream of causing you any trouble."

"It would be no trouble at all. Please come. There's only Michael here. The house feels so empty, now that your brother has...gone. And you could also sort out some of his possessions."

He looked round, caught me listening, and gave a smug little smile.

"And didn't you say you'd just given up your flat in Brighton? I know what!" said my mother enthusiastically, "come and move in with us. Permanently! We need a new lodger."

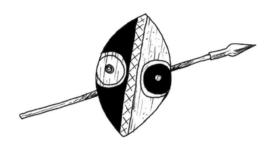

NINETEEN
MoomBoo

It is hard being an exile. When you have given your whole life to your tribe, to your people, and then you are banished – for ever – it is a bitter fruit to swallow. Day after day I wander through the jungle, alone and aimless, not having seen a human face since I had to leave my village.

At first I was afraid of the gorillas. Then I noticed that they were ignoring me, as if they somehow accepted my presence among them. Recently some uneaten food appeared to have been left out for me. Compare the kindness of these simple creatures with the ingratitude of my fellow men! But I brought it all upon myself.

***

Our village was situated in the middle of the jungle. This was so dense that almost no one had ever penetrated it. A river ran through the village, where the men would fish. They also went on hunting trips in the jungle. Nearby were fields, where the women grew crops.

The village was totally cut off from the outside world – as if it never existed! We were happy and contented, and completely self-sufficient. The place was called Kuara-MoomBoo, which means 'the Gift of MoomBoo'.

I can only recall one person ever leaving, a man called Narere. He dug out a tree trunk and floated down the river. He returned to the village a long time afterwards, smelling awful, due to the alien food and drink he had consumed. He spoke about the 'amazing, wonderful things' he had seen. But I didn't think anyone was the slightest bit interested. I was sure he had come home because he was unhappy in the outside world.

My name is Narugo. I had three sisters, but no brothers. My father had just one wife. I felt he was disappointed in me, for I was not like the other boys – I was born lame.

"Do not worry," said my mother, "one day Narugo will do the greatest thing ever in the history of this tribe."

My childhood was a difficult one. Because of my infirmity, I could not fully join the other boys in their activities. I could go fishing, but they would not let me go with them on hunting trips. They said I was too slow, even though I could keep up with them pretty well using my crutch. So I sat outside our hut making spears, and bows and arrows. (I did not weave baskets or work in the fields as only the women did this.)

One day one of the boys called me a cripple. I got my crutch and gave him a thorough beating. No one ever said that to me again. And, bit by bit, I began to gain their respect.

"The others live by their arms and legs, but you will

survive by your head," said my mother.

In our village we had, of course, what the white man calls a 'witch doctor'. He was the second most important man after the Chief. I spent much of my time with him, learning all the rituals, prayers, and incantations. The use of herbs in healing. And also the sacred legends and traditions of our tribe. I was designated his successor, and when he died I moved into his hut.

My position gave me huge authority. People came to see me for medicine if they were sick, and also for advice. I helped women who had problems with children. And, if sufficiently rewarded, I'd give out love potions to seduce others. Or put a curse on their enemies.

It was a good life. My hut was comfortable and well positioned, next to the river. Outside was a large tree which gave excellent shade, under which I received visitors. I was unmarried, but my meals were provided by the Head Women of the village, for whom it was a great honour. I usually spent my evenings alone, deep in study.

One day some missionaries arrived, pitching their tent just outside the village. They aimed to convert us to their religion. They also said we should wear clothes.

Now we wore practically nothing, apart from beads and ornaments. Those of the women were particularly colourful. And on special occasions, the Chief, the Elders and myself wore ceremonial ones. But the missionaries brought along a large amount of clothing. We put it on to please them – there was much giggling among the women! (After they had gone, however, most of it was cut up, the trousers being made into bags and the skirts into sunshades).

The missionaries said we were to worship someone called Jesus Christ, and no one else. They had pictures of him and read stories about him from a special book. Although he was white and from a faraway land he was apparently the god of everyone, including our village, and would come back again one day.

But after two weeks they packed up to go. They had completely wasted their time, having not converted one single member of the village.

"There is but one god – Jesus Christ," they said as they were leaving.

I smiled and shook my head.

"No, you are wrong," I said. "Jesus is *your* only god. We too have one god. His name is MoomBoo."

Later on another lot of missionaries came. They also worshipped Jesus, and especially his mother and people called 'saints', but in a different way. They also had no success.

For us, everything had come from MoomBoo. He was the Giver. Long, long ago he had come down from the stars. He had founded our tribe, and had given us our village and our fertile fields, and the river abundant in fish. And I, Narugo, was his representative on earth, in charge of worshipping him.

Once a year, on the anniversary of his arrival, there was a festival. The Chief, his wives, his sons and their wives, the Elders, the Head Women and myself all put on our finest ornaments. I carried the Shenda Maroné, a large rod, beautifully carved out of wood and richly decorated. It had been made centuries ago, under the divine inspiration of MoomBoo himself. It was only exhibited at this festival, being kept the rest of the time in a special casket in my hut. This was our tribe's most treasured possession, our direct link with MoomBoo in all our invocations of him.

The Shenda Maroné was so sacred that it had never been used to enforce authority. A lesser rod, the N'dbela, took care of the most serious cases. It had merely to be pointed at the offender for him or her to die immediately. In thirty years I'd only had recourse to it twice. Normally I just had to point my staff directly at someone for them to fall into line (I had given up using a crutch).

We had two sacred books. Their covers were of antelope skin, finely tooled. The pages were made of special paper. Reeds from the river were cut up into tiny pieces and mixed with flour and water. This was then chewed by the women into a fine paste, before being rolled into sheets and dried in the sun.

The Book of Legends recounted the arrival of MoomBoo on earth. And it prophesied that, at the appropriate moment, when the stars were right, he would come down again.

The Book of Dreams recorded every dream about MoomBoo. Anyone having had one was required to inform me, and it was written up in the Book. All the dreams were remarkably similar. Over many years we had built up an accurate picture of MoomBoo, his two Attendants, and their ship. Thus to await their return!

We were then visited by some anthropologists. They had no wish to change us, and were glad that our way of life had never been tainted by the outside world. They stayed for a month and studied us carefully. I became friendly with two of them, Hans and Trudi Baer. They came from a country called Switzerland, and showed me pictures of mountains covered with white stuff known as 'snow' formed when rain becomes very cold. Mountains far higher than the volcanoes one can see in the far distance, if one climbs to the tops of the trees here.

They said that their second name, and also that of their capital city, was a spelling of 'bear', a furry animal that once lived wild in Switzerland. Another common name was Wolf. Imagine any of us being called 'Elephant' or 'Crocodile'!

When they left, the anthropologists gave me a present. It was a box made out of something called plastic. You turned a handle for a while, and then out of it came voices or music. Sheer magic! By twisting a knob you could hear other sounds which came from different places. After a time you had to wind the handle again.

***

I enjoyed many years of comfort and privilege, my influence growing steadily as time went on. But one day I was summoned to see the Chief. He told me to appoint my successor.

I rather reluctantly made a list of young men who might be suitable. I finally chose a youth called Naralongwe. He was slight and thin, but very intelligent, more suited to a priestly life than one of hunting. I taught him to read so he could study the sacred books. He learned about the rituals and ceremonies, potions, charms and curses, divination and soothsaying and the two sacred rods. And human psychology – how to manipulate and control the villagers, and influence the Chief. Naralongwe became a valuable assistant.

But in the evenings, alone in my hut, I listened to the box the Swiss had given me, often staying up much of the night. I turned down the sound with the other knob so that no one else could hear me listening. I gradually pieced together some idea of the outside world. It was unbelievably large and diverse. With great difficulty I sorted the various voice sounds into distinct words, then into sentences, and eventually came to understand the national language. I practised it in a whisper. I even learned a bit of English.

The more I understood, the more I learned. My thirst for knowledge became so intense that I knew I'd have to go into the outside world to satisfy it. So I told the Chief I needed to withdraw far into the jungle, alone, for at least six weeks. I could then meditate undisturbed and communicate with MoomBoo more deeply.

He was most uneasy about this, and said that in all our history it had never happened before. Who would cater for the spiritual needs of the village? I assured him that

Naralongwe could deputize for me perfectly well in my absence.

I took with me as much food and water as possible, and also some clothes from the missionaries that I had kept hidden. When I had gone deep enough into the jungle I put them on. I chose a shirt in a colour called 'khaki', and, rather than shorts, matching long trousers. I found these most uncomfortable. I cut my hair and trimmed my beard. The aim was to look like an offficial or civil servant, and thus get better attention wherever I ended up. I hid my staff under some leaves. With enormous pain and effort I had trained myself to walk without it, and my limp was now barely noticeable.

The jungle was so thick that I often had to literally cut my way through it. Many times I was tempted to turn back. It was interminable. Then the vegetation got less dense, giving way eventually to a clearer type of forest. Some hours later I found myself in open bush. I saw many animals there: buffaloes, elephants, zebras, giraffes, and lions, which were my greatest fear.

I walked on for several days. I took a rest at a place where the long grass had been flattened down. Then I heard a noise. A strange kind of cart arrived, with no animal pulling it. The men riding on it beckoned to me, and I climbed aboard.

After an hour or two we passed a village, then another one, and got onto a rough track. Then onto one that was black and very smooth. We drove along incredibly fast, and

I had to hold on tight! There were other carts like ours going along it. We finally arrived at whole rows of huts that were bigger than I could have ever imagined, and we stopped. The men called it 'Town'. It was full of people; I looked just like them.

I spent that night sleeping under a tree, and the next day wandering around. I was completely amazed at what I saw. There were very few white men, but their mark was everywhere. The large huts ('houses'), the 'cars', and the 'roads' with people walking about in an orderly way, most of them neatly dressed.

Food was obtained not by hunting or fishing, or from the fields, but by going into huts called 'shops'. One of them was very large, and you walked along rows upon rows of food or drink and put whatever you chose into a metal basket on wheels. Then you gave someone at the door small round metal disks or bits of coloured paper, and you were allowed to take it away.

I could get water from a fountain in the 'park', but had almost run out of the food I had brought with me, and had nothing to give them in the shops. Then I had a stroke of luck. I entered a building which was full of books, rows of them. Some people were sitting there reading. A man went up to me, pointed at a sheet of paper pinned to the wall, and asked if I had come as the new 'library assistant'. I said "Yes", speaking as little as possible so as to hide my outlandish accent. I was told I could start the next day.

My wages enabled me to buy food. And now I could

learn from all the books in the library. I taught myself to read their script. Many had pictures. There were moving ones too, which I learnt were called 'videos', 'DVDs', or 'television', and a remarkable device called a 'computer' which could tell you anything you asked.

I was allotted a small room at the back to sleep in. This meant I could carry on studying in the library well after it closed.

Every seventh day I had a day off, and I would use this to learn more about my surroundings. Once I took a large public cart (or 'bus') to the 'airport'. Huge metal birds, very noisy, ran along the ground like fat geese to get into the air. But up in the sky they looked tiny. So *these* were the silver birds we sometimes saw passing high over our village – actually great big flying buses full of people! And if humans could go right up into the skies, where were the gods? Perhaps they didn't really exist?

Another time I went to a place where a lot of people were singing and dancing. Some had drunk too much of a certain strong liquid, and were staggering about talking loudly in a slurred manner. They absolutely stank – the way Narere had done when he returned to our village.

I observed that many people spent much of their wages on clothes, televisions, cars, and things they didn't really need. They were never satisfied, governed by the urge to always acquire something new.

And once I saw a large building with a big metal thing ringing repeatedly from up on the roof. I went inside.

There were rows of people there, singing songs together. Then they were addressed by a man in the front. He wore special clothes and I assumed he was the priest. Little did he realize that the old man sitting at the back was also a kind of priest, and probably a good deal more powerful than he was!

He made a long speech about 'the Second Coming'. One day Jesus Christ would come down again from the sky. While this was the official line, I was sure that none of the priests seriously believed it would ever happen. And if it did, it would undermine their whole organisation, and put an end to their jobs.

The time came for me to go back to my village. I thanked the librarian for his kindness, and took my leave. He was sad to see me go.

The journey back was easier. The town was on a river and I reckoned it was the same one that went through our village, and used by Narere in his dugout. So I simply walked along its banks, and when I saw I was getting near the village, I went back into the jungle. I found my staff, and took off my clothes and buried them. I arrived home as night was falling, to a warm welcome.

***

There were more good years, and life went on very much as before. Except that in the evenings I secretly listened to my 'radio' much less often. My experience of the outside world had shown me that our life in the village, however isolated, was far superior. How privileged we were!

Then one year it just didn't rain. At first people welcomed the continual sunshine, but it turned into a prolonged drought. The river was reduced to a trickle, running through a bed of dry cracked mud. The crops withered and died. Food became so scarce that we began to eat next year's seeds.

I performed many rain dances, but they had no effect whatsoever. So I devised a longer and more elaborate ritual, which also involved a sacrifice. I asked everyone to be patient, as it always took some time before our prayers were answered from up high. I had, of course, studied meteorology in the library in the town, and I knew which clouds indicated that rain was coming. And I listened to the weather forecast on my radio. One day the drought would end, inevitably. But it didn't! We were desperate.

As a last resort I organised a ceremony on the grandest scale, involving all the top members of the village – the Chief, his family, his sons and their families, the Elders and the Head Women. Nothing like this had ever been done before. We walked slowly and solemnly three times around the village, chanting the sacred songs. I was at the head of the procession, wearing my leopard skin cloak and carrying the Shenda Maroné.

We stopped at the open space in the centre of the village. I began the invocation. I said the sacred prayers and whispered some secret words in the priestly language known only to me. Then, in a loud voice, I addressed our god:

"O MoomBoo, the Giver, we beseech you, come down now

and grant us rain. MoomBoo...MoomBoo...MOOMBOO!"

And I raised the Shenda Maroné towards the sky. For a moment nothing happened. Then there was a bolt of lightning, a clap of thunder, and the heavens opened. Heavy rain, all day and night. How the people rejoiced! They sang and danced with joy. But I had put my very last ounce of strength into this, and I retired to my hut, utterly exhausted. I fell asleep at once.

I awoke very late the next morning. But I did not hear the usual village sounds. It was quiet and eerie. Evidently something important had occurred. I left my hut – there was not a soul about. I walked towards the centre of the village. A huge silvery-grey cylinder, higher than the tallest trees, stood there, its conical top pointing up at the sky. Around it, at a safe distance, was everybody. I whispered to the chief. We went back quickly to our huts, and returned in our full regalia. The Chief wore his crown and his First Wife bore a tray of fruit. And I carried the Shenda Maroné.

The three of us slowly approached the ship. Then, with great reverence, I tapped gently on its side with the Shenda Maroné. We retreated backwards, and waited.

After a while a small crack appeared in the side of the ship. It became a doorway. A ramp extended itself down to the ground and three figures slowly descended. MoomBoo and his two Attendants! The whole village prostrated themselves.

Eventually we rose to our feet. I made a short speech humbly thanking MoomBoo for the blessing of rain. The

Chief welcomed him and his Attendants to our village, and the First Wife presented the fruit.

MoomBoo spoke. He said that as the Giver, he would grant us anything we desired. I replied that, since he had given us water, he had restored life to us. What more could anyone want? To live in security and happiness, with the rare honour of witnessing, with our own eyes, our god himself!

Everyone stood in awe, overcome by the grace and majesty of it all. But then suddenly a man burst through the crowd and went right up to MoomBoo.

"Yes," he said, "there *is* something we could do with. A plough."

I was stunned. I couldn't believe my eyes! It was Narere. MoomBoo nodded to one of his Attendants. A modern plough appeared just like that.

"And a tractor to pull it with," added Narere.

A brand new tractor now stood in front of the plough – like the ones I'd seen near the town. Everyone gasped with astonishment at this magic. Then another man came forward. He asked for a motorboat. The Attendant pointed to the river. And tied up at the bank was a sleek and powerful-looking craft.

I realized then what must have happened. Narere, impressed by what he had seen in the outside world, had told everyone, and probably even shown them photographs. I had been wrong all the time in assuming that they hadn't been interested. And now they had the chance to have it all.

I was so shocked I just walked away, taking the Shenda Maroné with me. No one saw me leave, they were all so dazzled by the magic. I went back to my hut. I felt quite confused by it all.

After a couple of hours I realized I had to go back there. The atmosphere was now very different: instead of reverence it was like a carnival – verging on hysteria. People were shouting and waving their arms with excitement. By now they had mobile phones, televisions and computers. Women sported fancy clothes, furs and evening dresses. There were motorbikes, cars, and even trucks. As I arrived a helicopter appeared. And some of the men had guns.

It had now got dark, and MoomBoo and his Attendants retired to their ship. People drifted away, clutching their new possessions with glee. I left too, in disgust, and slipped away back to my hut.

When I awoke the next morning one could hear all the noise and excitement in the village. But no one came to see me. I was being completely ignored, despite this momentous event being entirely my doing. How I resented this! I had to admit it, I was jealous. Of MoomBoo. How foolish to be jealous of a god!

Taking young Naralongwe with me, I went to see the Chief. He was a good man, though lacking, to my mind, the judgement and experience of his father. He was sitting with the Elders, deep in discussion.

"O Chief," I said, "I have come to you with something

of the utmost importance to say. After hours of careful deliberation I have reached the following conclusion: MoomBoo is bad. He is evil."

Naralongwe was horrified.

"How can you say that?" he cried, "MoomBoo is good. MoomBoo is glorious. He is the Giver. It is written so in the Legends!"

"He brought us rain," said the Chief.

"Yes," I said, "and, of course, without it we would have perished. But that is all we required. Not these extra gifts. They are quite unnecessary.

"They will help in the development of the village," said the Chief.

I began to raise my voice, doing something I would have never dared before: argue with him and question his authority.

"A few of the gifts may, no doubt, be useful," I said, "but all the rest are just frivolous luxuries. They will change our village forever. It may be primitive, but it is quiet and peaceful. A haven! How lucky we are to live here! Now everybody will become greedy and corrupt. And competitive too, like in the outside world."

I did not mention that, on my trip, I myself had been there.

"But how can MoomBoo be bad?" he asked, "it is unthinkable. He is our god, the creator of all, the founder of our tribe, the Giver. We owe everything to him."

"I know that," said I, "but what he is now doing is wrong.

It is causing the village irreversible harm. Our people are simple and hard-working, and are not equipped for all these elaborate modern things. They will not bring them happiness."

I paused for breath.

"And there is one thing even greater than MoomBoo."

"Oh, of course!" said Naralongwe, "the missionaries..."

"It has nothing to do with them," I said angrily, "it's something that is higher than anyone, higher than even a god. It is called Right and Wrong, Good and Evil. And MoomBoo is destroying us. He is evil. We must ask him to go!"

They all looked at each other.

"Has he gone mad?" asked someone.

Then the Chief stood up and made a pronouncement:

"This village welcomes MoomBoo. We are eternally grateful for all he has done for us, both in the past, and now in the present. His bounty continues for ever! Our worship of him will now be all the more devout. And you, Narugo, in your sacred role of priest, will lead the village in that worship."

I had failed to convince them. I stormed out and returned to my hut.

I realized that something drastic had to be done. Without delay! I put on my ceremonial ornaments and my leopard skin cloak, and picked up the Shenda Maroné. Then I marched up to the centre of the village. I pushed my way through the throng around MoomBoo's ship and went straight up to him.

"MoomBoo," I said, "you have brought us rain, essential to life. Now again can we drink, water our crops, and eat. You have saved us! But now your task is completed. And we, your people, can again live in peace and harmony, ever worshipping you, our god."

He said nothing and just smiled.

"Depart now, back to your home in the stars," I continued, raising the Shenda Maroné, "taking with you the love, devotion, and gratitude of this village."

But he just stood there smiling. Then I don't know what got into me. I completely lost my temper.

"What on earth are you waiting for?" I screamed. "JUST GO!"

I rushed forward to strike him with the Shenda Maroné. But when it got within a foot of him it hit an invisible shield and shattered into pieces. I was hurled backwards by a powerful bolt of electricity, and thrown to the ground.

The crowd gasped.

"Sire, as you see, they are still but primitive savages," said one of the Attendants.

"Well, we'll just have to wait *another* five thousand years," said MoomBoo, "then see if they have evolved any further."

At that, the three of them wallked up the ramp into their ship. The door closed and the ship silently lifted off and shot up into the sky. The crowd wailed. Then all hands were upon me, and I was dragged away.

I spent the night in my hut, under guard. I awoke the next morning to the sound of drums. Two men escorted me to the Chief's hut. Outside stood many people in a circle: the Chief, the Elders, and the Head Women. I noticed that Naralongwe was carrying the N'dbela.

I was made to stand in the middle of the circle. Then the Chief addressed me.

"Narugo, you have driven away MoomBoo, our saviour and our god. He would have done a lot for the village. May he hear our prayers and return one day! What you did was misguided, to say the least. In view of your long service with us, we will spare your life. But you are hereby banished from this tribe for ever. You must leave by nightfall. And if you ever try to come back to this village we will kill you."

So that I could fend for myself in the jungle I was given food and water, a spear, and a bow and some arrows. I walked through the village with my head down. But when I had passed the furthest field I turned round for a last look. The little round huts with their mud walls and thatched roofs, so safe and cosy! Smoke curling up from the fires of the cooking pots. Old people sitting outside, children playing. Others fishing in the river. This paradise had been my home. Now I was leaving it for good. I wept.

**

Each day I wander through the jungle, with no direction, no purpose. Let the leopard take me! And deliver me from this boredom, this loneliness, this pointless existence. Then the hyenas will eat my body.

I have all the time in the world for reflection, now. Sometimes I wonder what personal request I might have asked MoomBoo for myself. Apart from youth, I had everything one could possibly wish for – comfort, authority, power. Except this: to have my leg straightened, to cure my limp. In all that excitement the thought had never occurred to me! And, do you know what? I don't even care.

TWENTY
The Chauffeur

Trevor Roberts started off on light vans, moved to lorries and was soon driving Thornwood Transport's largest articulated vehicles. He then came to the attention of Mr John Elphinstone, chairman of the group of companies of which Thornwoods was part. He needed a new chauffeur, and Trevor was glad to accept the job, after taking a short training course at Rolls-Royce.

When Mr Elphinstone got his knighthood, Trevor had a cockade sewn onto the front of his cap, as is the privilege of a titled person's chauffeur. When not driving he would lovingly polish the Rolls, and valet its luxurious upholstery. They made several trips abroad, including one to the South of France, visiting glamorous places like Cannes and Monte Carlo. Here Trevor wore a lightweight suit in a paler colour.

When Sir John retired and no longer needed a chauffeur, Trevor feared he would have to go back to driving commercials. But he was lucky and found another position, with a Mr Sidney Goldstein, who had contacted him through an agency.

Mr Goldstein had never learnt to drive.

"I was too busy making money," he would say.

But as a young man he had been very poor, working for the family fruit business in Whitechapel. First a barrow, then a shop, followed by a chain of stores, and finally the biggest wholesale fruiterers in the UK, supplying supermarkets throughout the country. "Soft fruit, hard fruit, hard cash!" was his motto.

Mrs Goldstein's maiden name was Silberman.

"It's the wrong way round," her husband would say, "I'm silver, she's gold."

"Oh Sid, you're such a dear!" she would reply.

Trevor's duties consisted mainly of taking Mr Goldstein to the office, and him and his wife to dinner or the theatre, and to synagogue at the weekend. Apart from trips to the airport, or to Hendon, where Elaine Silberman, Mrs Goldstein's sister lived, they rarely left central London.

One evening after work Trevor was driving home in Mr Goldstein's Bentley. He overtook an old woman on a bicycle and brushed past her so closely that he nearly knocked her over, making her drop the bag she was carrying.

"Can't you look where you're going?" he yelled out of the window.

"You'll pay for this, you will!" she shouted back, picking up her bag from the gutter.

Next morning Trevor got into the Bentley to collect Mr Goldstein and take him to Heathrow. But when he turned the key the engine wouldn't start. After ten attempts he waited a bit. Then he tried again, another ten times. This was unthinkable! It had never happened before. He opened the bonnet, looked inside, but everything looked normal. He closed the bonnet, got in and tried again. Again and again.

A group of children were standing around on the pavement.

"Bet he feels stupid!" he heard one of them say.

Trevor, bright red in the face, opened his window.

"Buzz off! On your way!"

The children ran off laughing.

After many more futile attempts, Trevor got out his mobile and called Mr Goldstein.

"I can't start, sir. I've tried everything, but it just don't want to know."

Then he ordered a minicab to take him to the airport.

He smoked a cigarette and then rang the AA man. After what seemed ages, the yellow van arrived and turned on its flashing light.

"Let me try it," said the AA man.

He turned the key. The car started immediately.

"I must have the magic touch!" he joked.

Keeping the engine running he opened the bonnet, looked around, closed it, got back in and revved up.

"Don't seem nothing wrong," he said.

The AA man filled out the paperwork. He said that if they had needed to transport the car to a garage, a covered recovery vehicle would have been mandatory, as it was a

Bentley or Rolls-Royce.

A week later Trevor pulled into the side of the road to buy a Coca-Cola at a shop. He opened the car door then heard a bell, followed by a terrific thud. A bicycle had ploughed into it. The rider fell over. It was the same old woman!

"Didn't you see me coming?" she screamed, "didn't you look in your mirror?"

"You saw I'd stopped. Stands to reason I was going to get out," said Trevor.

"No. It's your fault. It's your responsibility to look out for other road users. Especially cyclists."

She got back on her bike and started to move off.

"Stupid old cow," muttered Trevor.

She stopped.

"I heard you. No one calls me that and gets away with it,"

Then the woman pedalled off.

Next day Trevor was on his way to collect Mr Goldstein for a meeting in the city. As he was a bit early he stopped at a café for a sandwich and a cup of tea. He came out whistling a tune. But his good mood soon ended when he found the Bentley wouldn't start.

"Oh no! Not again!"

After many frustrating attempts to start, Trevor noticed that the car was pointing downhill on a gentle slope. Further on it became much steeper. If he could just coast down the hill, fast enough to turn the automatic transmission, that would surely start the engine. He let off the handbrake. But the car didn't move. He got out and pushed with all his might, but it was so heavy that it hardly budged. Then it slowly began to roll forwards. He held onto the steering wheel and pushed harder. The car gathered speed and Trevor had to run faster and faster to keep up with it. He was about to jump in when he slipped and lost his footing. Dragged along by the car he held onto the steering wheel for dear life. But after a few seconds he had to let go and fell flat on his face. He picked himself up to see the Bentley careering down the hill. He ran after it shouting and waving his arms. It mounted the pavement and crashed into a shop window.

There was sheer pandemonium! Shoppers and passers-by screamed and there was shattered glass everywhere. Two police cars soon arrived, their sirens wailing, then an ambulance and later a fire engine. Luckily the shop was closed with no one in it.

When the police realized it was a driverless car, Trevor had a fair bit of explaining to do. They took a serious view of the matter, and warned him that he risked being prosecuted for dangerous driving.

A breakdown truck was called out to recover the Bentley and Trevor phoned Mr Goldstein to say that he had been involved in an accident. He could sense the irritation in his employer's voice.

The car was not badly damaged but the repairs at the Bentley specialists still took two weeks. And it was also given a service so as to fully investigate "that ****** starting trouble."

During this time a replacement car was hired, a Mercedes-Benz. One day, while driving, Trevor broached the subject.

"Mr Goldstein, sir..."

"Yes, Trevor."

"Nice motor, this."

"Yes. Yes it is."

"I was wondering, sir ..."

"Yes?" Mr Goldstein was reading the Financial Times.

"Er, whether you might consider trading in the Bentley and getting one of these instead."

"Well yes – possibly."

"More reliable and economical. Altogether a better car. And sir...

"*Yes*, Trevor?"

"I've taken the liberty of getting a catalogue of the Mercedes range. For your perusal."

"Thank you, but later. I'll certainly give it some thought."

Trevor found the Mercedes lighter, faster and more stylish.

"It's a driver's car," said the motor dealer in Mill Hill.

He had also promised him a commission if he could persuade his boss to buy one.

The Bentley was soon back on the road. One evening Trevor was driving back to the mews where the car was garaged. It was getting dark. It was rush hour and the traffic was heavy. He stopped at a zebra crossing but was unable to get going again as more and more pedestrians kept crossing. There was a long line of vehicles behind him. One hooted impatiently. Then an old woman wheeling a bicycle crossed right in front of him. It was her! As soon as its back wheel had passed the car's bonnet Trevor moved forward. He felt a crunch and the bicycle fell over. He put on the handbrake and got out. More hooting.

He found he had knocked over a small trailer that the bike was towing. Its load of cardboard boxes had been tipped out all over the zebra crossing. One box had burst open and what looked like small models had fallen out of it. He checked the damage. One of the trailer's little wheels was badly bent.

"I'm really sorry...I didn't see..." began Trevor.

"You again!" shouted the old woman. She picked up her bicycle and began collecting up all the boxes.

The traffic started moving past slowly. Some pedestrians helped pick up the boxes. One even offered to be a witness on the woman's behalf.

"That's all right, thank you," she said, "I can deal with him myself, can't I?" And she looked up at Trevor with a malicious sneer.

He took out his wallet and held out some money. She shook her head.

"Oh no. Don't think you can get off so easily. I'll get even with you. Just you wait."

And she pushed the bicycle, with the trailer wobbling on its twisted wheel, off the crossing.

Next day Trevor stopped for some lunch on his way to

collect Mr Goldstein. He left the restaurant and took out his car keys. But the Bentley had vanished! He stood on the pavement and looked to the left and to the right, but it was nowhere to be seen.

"Where's me car? WHERE'S ME BLEEDIN' CAR?" he gasped.

Trembling with desperation he dropped his keys into the gutter. They landed on top of a small metal object. He automatically picked it up along with the keys without looking, and put it in his jacket pocket. Then he took out his mobile and called Mr Goldstein.

"The car's gone, sir."

"What do you mean, 'gone'?"

"Well, it was alright when I parked a short while ago. And now it's not here any more. Just disappeared!"

Trevor could feel the exasperation in his boss's voice.

"Then don't you think you had better call the police?"

"Yes, sir."

"And Trevor. Please order me a taxi."

At first Trevor assumed that the car had been towed away, even though it hadn't been left on a yellow line. But when he rang the car pound they had no record of it. So the Bentley must have been stolen!

It was reported to the police. But it was known to be almost impossible to steal a Bentley due to its advanced security system. So Trevor inevitably came under suspicion. And the police were also aware of his recent accident.

"You're in enough trouble already, my boy," said the

inspector who interviewed him.

The insurance company said they would not pay for the loss without further and exhaustive investigation. And a hefty claim for damage to the car and the shopfront was still pending.

Although one couldn't say that any of this was directly Trevor's fault, his boss was beginning to lose patience and had even thought of giving him notice. But Mr Goldstein was a kindly man. With his connections in banking he had arranged a mortgage on favourable terms for Trevor and his wife Janice to buy a flat in Tottenham. And Mrs Goldstein had even been considering inviting them to a Friday-night dinner.

Once again a replacement car had to be hired – this time a Vauxhall. It would have cost almost the same amount to have hired one complete with driver, but Mr Goldstein preferred to keep his own man.

Three days later, when Trevor came home from work, he was confronted by Janice.

"I don't know what's got into you, Trev."

"What d'you mean?"

"Now you've started collecting toys!" she said angrily.

"What?"

"I took your other suit to the cleaners, and this was in one of the pockets."

She pointed to the mantelpiece. On it was a tiny little car, like a Dinky Toy. Trevor picked it up and gasped. It was an exact model of the Bentley in miniature – the same year, the same type, the same colour grey.

"Where's that old stamp collection of mine?" cried Trevor.

"First it's toy cars. And now it's stamps," said Janice.

Trevor rushed into the bedroom and came back with an old battered suitcase. He rummaged through it and took out a magnifying glass. He peered carefully at the car through it and turned white with shock. Even the registration mark was the same as on the real Bentley!

"You look tired, Trev," said Janice, "come and have your tea."

Over the next few days Trevor got used to the Vauxhall and found that he actually enjoyed driving it. Meanwhile the police were pursuing the line that the Bentley had been stolen to order. Several gangs were known to be operating in the London area. They had software that could override the electronic security devices of luxury cars. These usually ended up abroad, mainly in Russia or the Middle East.

One evening Trevor turned on the TV to see Match of the Day. Then he watched the next programme. It was about witches. There were many popular misconceptions about them. That they were just in fairy tales. And in the olden days people were ignorant and superstitious, and falsely accused old women of witchcraft and burnt them at the stake. No – witches still existed nowadays. But they did not wear black cloaks and pointed hats and ride around on broomsticks. They looked just like anyone else, and indeed you would find it hard to recognize one.

Their magic spells fell into two main categories: Transformation and Miniaturisation. The first was when, say, a prince was turned into a frog. The second was when the victim was reduced to a tiny version of itself. In Belgium a carthorse was once shrunk to the size of a mouse, and its bridle, reins, collar and the cart it was pulling, all became equally small.

Next day Trevor happened to be reading the local newspaper. A small advertisement in Classifieds caught his eye:

CURSES, SPELLS, HAUNTINGS & BEWITCHMENT. MRS ENUGU WILL HELP YOU OVERCOME THEM (plus a telephone number)

At first sight, to Trevor, it was a lot of hocus-pocus nonsense. But then he started thinking. What if he *had* been bewitched by the old woman with the bicycle? He tore out the advertisement and put it in his wallet.

The following evening, before going home, he phoned the number. The address was in Brixton. There was a row of doorbells and he pressed the one with 'Enugu' by it.

A voice crackled on the entryphone: "It's the Top Floor Flat."

After climbing four flights of stairs he reached the top landing. A door was slightly ajar.

"Come in," said the voice.

Trevor stepped gingerly into the room. It was dark inside and there were just a few dim lamps in the corners. There was a rich smell of incense. Sitting among a pile of cushions was a very large black lady wearing a gold Moroccan-style kaftan.

"I'm glad you came," she said.

She offered him some tea and some little cakes, which were beside her on a brass tray. They were very sweet and sticky. He looked around the room. There was a photograph of the Pope and one of a young man in a scholar's gown and mortarboard.

"My son," she said proudly, "he now has his Master's Degree."

Trevor felt a bit awkward telling her his story, but Mrs Enugu had a warm, motherly air about her and he soon felt quite at ease.

"I know of this woman," she said finally.

She said that she owned a toy shop, and believed that some of the models on sale were actually real things or people that had been miniaturised. She went over to a bookshelf and brought back a scrapbook. In it was a yellowed press cutting. Thirty years ago a whole brigade of soldiers, complete with tanks and lorries, had simply disappeared without trace in North London. And it wasn't terrorists or the Russians. The Government had immediately suppressed any news of it, but not before one reporter had quickly got his article through before he too disappeared.

"MI5 or MI6," said Mrs Enugu, smiling, "but *you* were lucky."

"Why?" asked Trevor.

"She could have made you into a toy chauffeur!"

And she laughed and laughed, as if she were going to split her sides laughing.

After a moment she spoke again, in a more serious tone.

"This is very powerful magic. You must have done something serious to antagonize her in this way."

Trevor said that each time he had met the woman there had been an unpleasant argument, and admitted that he himself had been a bit rude.

"So you see, you too have played your part," explained Mrs Enugu, "but in the end Good always overcomes Evil. And if you can achieve goodness you will finally succeed in reversing this spell."

Suddenly she stood up and closed her eyes.

"The car! I can't do anything without the car! You must bring it next time."

She sat down.

"The consultation is over," she said, "that will be twenty pounds."

Luckily Trevor had enough money with him.

"I'm sorry, but I have to live," she said apologetically as she took the payment.

Janice was furious when Trevor got home.

"Where on earth have you been?"

"I just went for a bit of a walk as it's a nice evening."

She was not convinced.

"That's unlike you. Anyway, go and have your tea now."

Afterwards Trevor went into the living room. He saw that the mantelpiece had been rearranged. And the model car was gone!

"Where's all the stuff that was here – and the little car?" he asked desperately.

"Oh, I took it all to the Oxfam with some other junk and some old clothes too. Anyhow, what's so important about that toy car?"

"Er – nothing really," stammered Trevor.

"Look, I just don't get it, Trev," said Janice angrily. "Ever since the Bentley was stolen you've been acting all peculiar. You'll end up by getting the sack. Then where will we be? You not earning, and us with a mortgage and a baby on the way!"

And she stormed out of the room.

Next day was Saturday. Trevor usually went to the gym in the morning, and this time he left home earlier and called in at the Oxfam on the way. There were books, CDs, DVDs, kitchenware, and rails of secondhand clothes. At the back of the shop was a shelf with children's books and toys – and on it was the little model Bentley!

Trevor edged along the clothes rails and had nearly reached it when someone holding a dress pushed past him, making him knock over a vase. As he was putting it back, he saw a woman and a small boy at the toys shelf. The boy picked up the car and the woman went to the cash desk to pay for it.

Trevor went up to the boy.

"Er son...do you think I could, er... buy that car off you?"

The boy shook his head.

Trevor pointed at the toys shelf.

"I know, tell you what...how about if I buy this here double-decker bus and then swap it for the car?"

The woman came back.

"You leave my boy alone!" she said angrily.

She took him by the hand and they left the shop.

When Trevor got back from the gym, lunch was on the table.

"When I was in the supermarket just now something really odd happened," said Janice.

"Oh, what?"

"This woman. Came right up to me and patted my bump. Said she was a witch."

"WHAT?"

"She said she could tell if it was a boy or a girl," said Janice angrily. "I told her to take her filthy hands off me and to mind her own business!"

"What did she look like?" gasped Trevor.

Janice looked at him in surprise.

"What's that got to do with it?"

"Was she black, white...I dunno...young, old?" he asked.

"She was one of them hippy types. Youngish. Hair done up in braids. Distressed jeans. Grotty-looking."

Trevor breathed a sigh of relief.

"Yeah. There's weirdos everywhere, nowadays," he said.

Two days later Trevor finished work early and was driving back to the garage in the mews. It was around four o'clock. The traffic was congested – he had hit the school run. He passed by a school. Parents were collecting their children, some by car. Suddenly he spotted the woman who had been in the Oxfam, waiting by the school gates. He quickly parked the car, leaving his cap in it, and slowly approached her.

"Excuse me, Madam."

"What do you want?" she asked angrily.

"Er..."

"I know you. And your sort. You keep away from my child and me!"

She pointed to a car parked down the road.

"My husband's in that car over there!"

"I'm really sorry to trouble you, but..."

"You heard what I said!"

She was becoming quite agitated.

"Bill!" she shouted, waving at the car.

"Please listen to me," said Trevor, calmly. "I am a specialist dealer in antique toys. Now it happens that your son's model car is a very rare example in a series where only a dozen were ever made."

He paused for a moment.

"I have been instructed by one of my clients to acquire the car for his collection. For which he is willing to offer a large sum of money."

A man came up to them.

"What's all this about? What does he want?"

"He's been hanging around pestering me about that toy car I bought Tommy," said the woman.

"Now you clear off, or I'll get the Law!" he threatened.

"Yes, but apparently the car is very valuable," said his wife.

The man changed his tone.

"How valuable?"

"Extremely valuable," answered Trevor.

He took out a piece of paper from his pocket, wrote down a number, and handed it to the man.

"Please give this some consideration, and call me should you wish to proceed further." He smiled. "With your lad's permission, of course."

And he walked off.

When Trevor got home he changed out of his suit and made a cup of tea. Then his mobile rang.

"I'm ringing about that toy car," said a man's voice.

"Oh yes."

"My wife and I have given it some thought."

"Thank you," said Trevor.

"How much are you offering?"

"How much would you like?" asked Trevor.

After a short silence the man spoke.

"I want five hundred quid for it."

Trevor said nothing.

"All right then, four hundred?"

"Three hundred and fifty pounds and it's a deal," said Trevor firmly.

"OK."

"How would you prefer the money?" asked Trevor.

"Cash."

"I could meet you somewhere with it," suggested Trevor, "how about outside the Red Lion in Holloway? Say 9.30 tomorrow night?"

"That's fine. See you there, then," said the man, and he hung up.

Janice came into the room.

"What was that?" she asked.

"Oh nothing," replied Trevor, "just something about the car."

The next evening he phoned Janice to say that he would be home late as he was taking Mr and Mrs Goldstein to a dinner dance in St. John's Wood. He got to the Red Lion at 9.15, parked round the corner, and waited outside the pub. The man arrived soon afterwards.

The transaction was done quickly. The man received a brown envelope containing a wad of banknotes, which were counted out slowly. Trevor got a small plastic bag with the model car in it. He examined it carefully to check that it was the right one.

When he got home Trevor slipped into the bedroom and opened the wardrobe. He took the car out of his pocket, wrapped it up in newspaper, then put it in a shoe box with his new trainers.

Trevor arranged to meet Mrs Enugu the next afternoon. He showed her the little car.

"Ah yes," she said, holding it in the palm of her hand, "this will be a long process."

She went over to a cupboard. There were rows of large glass jars and bottles. She took out a jar, unscrewed the top, and poured a small amount of powder onto a white card. It had a very strange smell.

"This is Growing Powder. Made from the Garooba plant and secret ingredients," she said with a smile. "In my country we use it if an animal or child is not growing to its proper size. In your case you will sprinkle it on the car."

For an instant Trevor thought the woman was crazy and that he was wasting his time – and money.

"As I said, this will take time. For Good cannot vanquish Evil immediately. It is a long battle."

She sat down.

"Now! You must do one hundred good deeds. After each deed is performed you will write about it on a sheet of paper. You will then place the car on the paper and sprinkle some powder over it. Each time this is done it will grow a little. And when you have accomplished the hundredth good deed the car will be restored to its normal size."

She poured some powder into a small jar and gave it to him.

"Come and see me again to report on your progress. And I will give you more powder if you run out."

She stood up.

"Now go! For you have much work to do."

Trevor thanked her and put the jar in his pocket. This time it was only fifteen pounds.

He drove home. He knew there were all kinds of

charlatans out there, ready to take advantage of sad and gullible people. But he had little to lose – and perhaps a lot to gain.

Next morning Trevor began to think about the good deeds. Presumably this didn't mean just giving money to charity. And he found that it was hard to be even permitted to do a good deed. When he offered to help a Japanese lady carry two heavy suitcases up some steps, she refused – being either too proud or too suspicious.

That Sunday he took a walk in the park. It was a hot day and an ice-cream van was there. A little girl had just bought an ice lolly when the man closed the sales window and drove off.

Then Trevor heard some crying. The girl's lolly had come off its stick and fallen into a puddle. He sprinted after the ice-cream van, cut through some prickly bushes, ran in front of it and forced it to stop. He bought another ice lolly and presented it to the girl.

That night, when Janice was asleep, Trevor got out the shoe box and tiptoed into the kitchen. He wrote down the good deed in neat handwriting on a plain A4 sheet of paper, put the car on it and sprinkled some of the powder. Nothing happened.

"Bloody con," he muttered, "I knew it."

But then he heard a slight squeaking sound. The car was getting bigger! After five minutes it was much larger. Then it stopped growing. He wrapped up the car and put it back in the shoe box. The trainers would now only just fit in. He crept back into the bedroom and put the shoe box in the wardrobe.

Next day he had another opportunity. A woman was standing by her car arguing with a parking warden - he was going to give her a ticket. She looked desperate. At first Trevor thought she had broken down, but actually she had dropped her car keys down a drain in the gutter. He quickly dealt with the warden, then went to the nearest hardware shop and bought an iron crowbar. He rolled up his sleeves, levered up the drain cover, and fished out the keys.

That night he repeated the procedure. The car was now too big for the shoe box so he hid it in his sports bag. After some more good deeds it soon outgrew the bag. So he decided to take it to the mews garage and place it next to the Vauxhall.

Here are some of the other good deeds done by Trevor:

He climbed up a tree and rescued a cat that had been stuck there for hours. When the Fire Brigade finally came and found their job already done, they were quite shirty about it.

He gave his Spurs v. Arsenal ticket to a boy whose own one had been stolen.

He helped a removal man with a bad back carry furniture up to a fourth floor flat.

He rescued a boy's model glider from the Regent's Canal.

One day an old man's hat blew off into the middle of the road. Trevor dashed out to retrieve it. A bus thundering towards him screeched to a halt.

"What the hell d'you think you're doing?" shouted the driver, leaning out of his cab.

And Janice had begun to notice it, after an old lady wrote in the local paper to thank him for fixing the electrics in her flat. One day they were walking down the street together. A woman's necklace had just broken. Pearls were scattered all over the pavement, some being trodden on or kicked into the gutter. People were walking by and ignoring it. But Trevor got down on his hands and knees and diligently picked up every single pearl for her.

"You're a right Sir Galahad now, Trev," said Janice, laughing, "not that selfish husband of mine no more. Yeah! Saint Trevor of Tottenham!"

Meanwhile, with every good deed, the Bentley was getting bigger. In three months it had grown from the size of a pedal car to that of a Mini. Trevor now had to get down onto the garage floor and push the sheet of paper underneath the car. And Mrs Enugu had told him to increase the amount of powder to be sprinkled; she had ordered an extra supply of it from Nigeria.

One day, while he was on his way to collect Mr Goldstein, Trevor's mobile rang. Some builders urgently needed to get inside the garage to carry out repairs. Could he let them in? If not, they would go and pick up the spare set of keys from the office. Trevor started to panic. No one must see what's inside! He went into a bedding store and bought some super king size sheets. Then he drove quickly to the mews. A van with a ladder on top was already parked outside the garage. A man with a bunch of keys was about to unlock the doors.

"No! Stop!" shouted Trevor.

The man turned round.

"'ere! Who are you?" he asked angrily.

"I'm in charge of things around here," said Trevor.

"Well, there's complaints coming from next door about a water leak in this garage. I need access. You got a problem with that?"

"I have to go in first," said Trevor firmly.

"Suit yourself, mate." The man lit a cigarette.

Trevor unlocked the doors so that they were just ajar and slipped into the garage. He quickly flung all the sheets over the diminutive Bentley.

"You can come in now," he said, opening the doors wide and switching on the light.

The man walked in and touched a wall on the left-hand side of the garage. There was a pipe running along it, and water was dripping onto the brickwork.

"Yeah – seeping through the party wall. Could be a loose union."

There was a large nut halfway along the pipe. He took a spanner out of his toolbox and tightened it.

"Easy job!"

He looked around.

"What you got underneath all that? Dead bodies?"

He pointed at the sheets and laughed. Then he picked up his tools, got into his van and left the mews. With a sigh of relief, Trevor locked up and drove as fast as he could to Mr Goldstein's house.

He had also kept a record of all the good deeds in a notebook. One day, six weeks later, he realized that he had completed ninety-nine of them. Then Janice asked him to get some milk at the supermarket. He was in the queue behind a woman with a very full trolley. When she got to the till she desperately fished in her handbag, but found she had left her purse at home. The check-out girl was quite rude and the woman began to cry. But Trevor offered to pay for it all. He received a cheque and a letter of thanks by return of post.

That night he wrote out the hundredth good deed and put it under the Bentley, which was duly sprinkled with the powder. He watched the car finally reach its correct and original size. Now it was the Vauxhall that looked small by comparison!

Trevor now had to arrange for the Bentley to be 'found' again. He decided to take the car to some back street and just leave it there. He would be running the risk, of course, of being stopped for driving a car reported stolen. One afternoon he opened the garage doors, checked that no one was watching, got into the Bentley and slid quietly out of the mews. Expecting fearfully to see at any moment a blue flashing light in his rear mirror, he drove around for forty minutes, and then parked the car off the Caledonian Road.

He wrote out a note which he fixed to the windscreen with sellotape:

"Thank you for the loan of the car. I am very sorry for the inconvenience this must have caused, but I had no choice. It was an emergency. The car has been washed and valeted, and has a full tank of petrol."

Making sure he had left nothing inside, he locked the car and took the bus home. A few days later the police notified Mr Goldstein that the Bentley had been recovered.

Trevor had, of course, shown himself to be pleasantly surprised at this good news; he thought this would now be the end of the matter. But the police would not release the car straight away. They were suspicious of how it had just 'reappeared.' It would be dusted for fingerprints and a forensic team would check for any fibres of clothing left inside by the driver. And the note examined by a handwriting expert.

The prime suspect was Trevor, and the police were keen to interview him. However, to permit further investigation with a view to an eventual prosecution, it would be up to Mr Goldstein to make a formal complaint.

"It just don't ring true," said the inspector who came to see him, "that chauffeur of yours, Roberts – he's either a clever villain or some kind of a nut."

But Mr Goldstein did not want to take it further – he was just relieved to get his Bentley back. He was also busy at the time with a major takeover bid. And he had a bit of a soft spot for Trevor, too.

"Let bygones be bygones," he said.

The inspector tried hard to persuade him otherwise.

"To succeed in our work, we in the Police Service do always need the cooperation of the victims of crime."

But Mr Goldstein was adamant.

"If you don't mind me saying so, sir," said the inspector, "you shouldn't let yourself be taken in so easy. But if that is your wish, so be it."

And he walked out of the house.

***

It was a fine Sunday afternoon. Trevor and Janice were taking a walk in the park. Their baby was in its pram. By some trees was a lake, crossed at its widest point by a wooden footbridge. At one end of this was a small metal sign: GRINDLEMERE POOL.

There was much controversy over this. Some said it was named after Archbishop Grindal, whose palace, now in ruins, had been in the park. Others claimed that the lake was the very site of Grendel's Mere, in Beowulf, out of which came the monster Grendel and his evil mother.

They crossed the bridge.

"Rickety old thing," said Trevor.

"Downright dangerous, if you ask me," said Janice, "the Council should do something about it."

At the other side they sat down on a bench and Janice gave the baby its bottle. They looked back over the lake. A large black lady was at the bridge. She wore a short-sleeved flared jacket, a long tight skirt and a turban, all in the same bright purple material. As she crossed you could hear the tapping of her high heels on the planks, and the bridge creaked and swayed. As she passed the bench she gave Trevor a wink.

"Seems to know you," said Janice.

"Never saw her before in my life," said Trevor.

They sat there watching the ducks and moorhens on the lake. A pair of swans swam past. After a while they saw another person crossing the bridge. It was an old woman pushing a bicycle and trailer. When she was halfway across, the bridge began to shake. Then it lurched sideways, and with a tearing and snapping of timber, the whole thing collapsed into the lake.

Next day it was all in the newspapers. The bicycle and trailer had been retrieved. But strangely, despite a thorough search of the lake bed by divers, no trace of a human body was ever found.

TWENTY-ONE

The Antique Dealer

I am an antique dealer. I travel around the country buying anything old and interesting, then I sell it in my shop in London. Sometimes there is a sale at a big country house, often because the owner has died.

Last autumn there was to be a big sale at a place called Ormsbury Park, in Oxfordshire, and I decided to go to it. Like many others in the antique trade I have a Volvo Estate. It has a great carrying capacity. I've also got a roof rack for larger items that won't fit inside.

The day before the sale, in the afternoon, I took the A40 to Burford, turned right at the roundabout, and headed down the steep and picturesque high street to the river. I crossed the bridge, then, following my Sat Nav, took a left turn down a narrow road. After a mile or so I reached a village called Swincote, and drove down the main street. But this didn't seem right.

The directions I'd been given had said I should turn right at the entrance to the village, just after the telephone box and before the church. So I turned round at the village green and drove back slowly. Just past the church I saw a concealed entrance on the left. A wooden signpost said: 'Ducking End. Single Track Road.'

I drove along a very narrow lane for about two miles. It was full of potholes and had trees with overhanging branches on either side. Surely this couldn't be right! But there was nowhere to turn round. Suddenly the road dropped. The car plunged downwards, there was a great splash, and water shot all over the bonnet and windscreen. I braked hard, then tried to accelerate out. But nothing happened. The engine had stopped. I turned the key several times, but it was no good. The engine was drowned.

Cursing, I got out of the car and tried to push it. But it was well and truly stuck. I was stranded in the middle of a ford!

I took out my mobile to ring the AA. But the screen just said 'No reception'. For a moment I wondered what to do. Then I thought I saw some smoke in the distance. I locked the car and waded through the ford. I walked further along the lane. After about half a mile I came to a row of three cottages.

I knocked at the first house. An old woman came to the door.

"What d'yer want?"

"I'm terribly sorry to disturb you, but my car is stuck down the lane."

"Oh is it?" She gave me a knowing look, "that'll be in the ford, I expect."

I blushed. "Er, yes."

"Always happening. There is a warning sign, you know."

"I'm afraid I didn't see it," I said sheepishly.

"I don't expect you did. All covered up in the bushes. Council don't bother much round here, you see."

"Er - would it be all right if I could use your telephone to call the AA?" I asked. "I can't get any reception on my mobile - well, it's so low here, and all these trees ..."

She grinned, showing a set of blackened teeth with one gold one in the middle. She was very fat, and wore an apron, thick brown stockings and carpet slippers.

I waited, feeling helpless and embarrassed.

"Well, do you think I could perhaps use your phone? I'd be glad to pay for the call."

"That won't be necessary," she replied.

"That's very kind of you," I said, "are you sure?"

"As sure as sure can be." She put her hands on her hips and tilted her head slightly.

It was beginning to get dark. I was starting to feel impatient but I realised I'd have to play the game her way.

"Well, if I could just quickly use your telephone. Once again, I'm really sorry to have disturbed you."

"That's all right," she said, "but there's only one thing wrong."

"What's that?"

"I'm not on the telephone!"

She roared with laughter, and I got a fine view of the blackened stumps.

Very funny indeed.

"But I might be able to help you somehow," she ventured, "you'd better come in and get dry."

It had also started raining. I had no option but to do what she said. The door opened straight into her kitchen.

I walked across an old stone floor.

"Sit you down," she said, pointing to a wooden chair by the stove. Blackened pans hung around the chimney.

"Nice cup of tea, warm you up, that will."

She poured me a cup from a big brown teapot, then padded out of the room. I heard her go up some stairs.

A moment later she was back. Over her arm was an old pair of trousers.

"Take yours off and I'll dry them. You can put these on for the time being. They belonged to the man 'oo died."

"What?"

"Yes, from the man 'oo died. Got stuck in the ford – lost the starting handle. Walked all the way here, and then dropped dead. Heart attack, I suppose. Never got to know 'is name." She grinned and waved the trousers at me.

"Don't worry, I'm all right, thank you," I said.

Actually I was more concerned about my shoes. They were brand new suedes which I had just bought in Jermyn Street. Now they were full of muddy water and squelched when I walked.

Though I felt awkward, I was determined to get somewhere.

"Madam," I began.

"I'm Mrs Howe."

"Mrs Howe, I really must get to a phone."

"I can't help you there, but what I *can* do is tell you how you are going to die."

This was getting creepy.

"What's your name?"

"Andrew Parsons."

"Well, Andrew, you're going to die in an aeroplane crash."

For a moment I was speechless.

"Look, Mrs Howe," I began again. "I've got to contact a breakdown service. I've got to get my car going. I have to be somewhere tonight."

I had booked a room at the Swan Inn, near Ormsbury Park, so as to get to the sale early next morning.

"But you did say you could help me," I said desperately.

"Another cup of tea, then I'll take you next door."

She poured another cup, then opened a biscuit tin. She leant towards me, rattling it.

"Have one of these. Too 'ard for my teeth, they are."

When tea was over she opened the door and I followed her out. We went up to the next cottage. She made two sharp taps with the doorknocker.

After a while the door opened.

"Gentleman's in a bit of trouble," announced Mrs Howe.

"Come in," said a voice.

I walked in alone, and found myself in a hallway.

"In here," said the voice.

I entered a sitting room. Sitting on a sofa was a woman with short hair, in a shirt, sleeveless jumper and grey flannel trousers.

"Come and sit next to me," she said, patting a place on the sofa.

I explained my predicament. She listened attentively.

"Now first of all you must have some tea."

"Thank you," I said, "but actually I've just had some."

"Then you will have some more."

There would be no argument about this. She got up and strode out of the room.

When she was gone I had a chance to look around at the furniture. Sometimes one can find a real gem in the most unlikely place, and buy it from the owner on the spot.

De Maupassant tells a story about an antiquarian who'd had to stop at the house of a peasant. When he went inside he couldn't believe his eyes: there in the corner was an extremely rare and priceless chair! So as not to alert the owner as to its true value, he asked if he could buy it for firewood. The man, surprised to be offered even a few francs for it, took it out of the room. He returned telling the dealer that he had loaded the chair into his carriage. And, to save him the trouble, he had already chopped it up into pieces!

Before I could sit down the woman came back in with some tea and biscuits.

"Nice pictures," I said. There were some old prints on the wall, of the town of Wareham, in Dorset.

"We used to go there by charabanc, for our seaside holidays," she said. "Now, have some tea. Do you take sugar?"

"One, please."

She dropped a small cube of sugar into my cup with some silver tongs.

"It's over there, on my desk," she said when we had finished tea, pointing to a candlestick telephone. I unhooked the earpiece and listened.

"Number please," said a voice.

Speaking into the mouthpiece I told the operator I needed a breakdown service, but she couldn't get through to the AA nor the RAC.

"I know, I'll try Headley's Garage in Burford. If not, there must be one in Oxford."

But there was no answer anywhere. They had obviously closed for the night. I was marooned!

On the piano was a silver-framed photograph of an old biplane. I recognized her standing next to it in a leather helmet and flying suit.

"Father's plane," she said, smiling proudly. "I learnt to fly in it."

There was also a wooden model of a bed – old and very wide.

"The Great Bed of Ware, in Hertfordshire," she said, "you see, that's my name, Cynthia Ware."

"I'm Andrew Parsons. Nice to meet you, Mrs Ware."

"I never married."

I blushed.

"I don't know what to do," I said despairingly.

"I know exactly what you should do. The woman next

door has a spare room. She used to take in paying guests. You'll be able to sort everything out tomorrow."

I realized I had no choice. But if I left early enough in the morning I could get my car going and still be at Ormsbury Park in time for the sale.

"But first I shall tell you where you are going to die."

"I'd rather not know," I said.

"You will die in France."

She opened the door and we left the cottage.

"I'll accompany you to her house."

There was a wicker gate, and it opened with a creaking sound.

"Goodbye and...thank you for the tea."

"Don't mention it," said Miss Ware. She turned on her heels and walked off briskly.

I knocked on the door, waited for a bit, then knocked again.

A voice asked, "Hello?"

It came from behind the house. A moment later a tall and rather thin woman appeared, carrying a trowel and a flowerpot. She wore a blue twinset, tweed skirt and wellington boots.

"Ah yes, I thought I'd heard someone."

"The lady next door suggested I come and see you," I began, gingerly.

"Oh yes. Well, what can I do for you?"

"She told me you sometimes have a room available. You see, my car is stranded."

"You'd better come in then," said the woman, "I'll lead the way."

She put down what she was holding in the porch, and changed into some shoes. I was ushered into her sitting room.

A cuckoo clock chimed, six times.

"Good-o!" she exclaimed breezily, "sun's over the yardarm. Would you like a drink? Perhaps a little sherry?"

"That would be very nice," I replied.

She went over to a buffet and poured out two glasses from a decanter.

"Do sit down."

She handed me a glass and sat down in an armchair opposite me, leaning forward eagerly.

"You poor man!" she said, "Cheers anyway!" She raised her glass and took a sip.

"This is extremely kind of you, I really didn't mean to disturb you," I began.

"That's quite all right. By the way, my name's Julia."

She sat back and smoothed her skirt.

"I'm Andrew Parsons."

"Hello, Andrew. Tee-hee! How exciting, having a man in the house!"

Then she said, "I'll show you your room, and afterwards we'll have a bite to eat."

I finished my sherry and put down my glass. I followed her out of the room and up a steep narrow staircase.

She opened the door into a bedroom. It had a leaded

window and was simply furnished, with a chair and a chest of drawers.

"I'll just get you a towel." She went out for a moment and came back with a jug of water.

After she had gone I took off my jacket, shoes and socks, and lay down on the bed, exhausted. I had to stop myself from falling asleep – it would have been rude to have stayed too long in my room. After about ten minutes I opened the door and went downstairs.

Julia told me to make myself comfortable in the sitting room while she prepared supper. I looked around the room. On the walls were charts of the sun, moon and stars with strange symbols and intersecting lines. There were bookcases full of leather-bound almanacs, some dating from the 19th Century. And a collection of china owls, whose beady eyes seemed to follow you wherever you moved.

Hearing the door open I quickly sat down again. She brought in a tray and put it on a small oak table, which had been laid with two places and a bottle of wine.

During the meal Julia asked me what had brought me 'to this neck of the woods.' I talked about my job and the ins and outs of the antique trade.

"I often listen to the wireless now," she said, after we had finished eating, "sometimes to the Third Programme."

She went over to a walnut cabinet and turned a knob. Out came the sound of classical music.

"A liqueur perhaps?"

"A cup of tea would do fine," I replied.

After a while Julia switched off the radio.

"Very quiet around here, isn't it?" she said, "not much going on. Though you might catch a glimpse of me in my housecoat," she chuckled. "Good night!"

She left the room and I heard her climb the stairs, then the creak of the floorboards above. A minute or two later I went up myself. I climbed into bed and fell asleep immediately.

I was woken the next morning by a twig tapping on the windowpane and the sun streaming onto my face. I went downstairs into the living room. Julia came in carrying a tray. Her hair was in a turban, and she was wearing a silk kimono.

When breakfast was over I raised the subject of paying my bill.

"I really ought to get going now. Er, do you think I could settle up?"

"That would be very kind," she replied.

I reached into my jacket for my wallet. It wasn't there. Nor was it in my trouser pocket. Stupid – I must have left it in the car! It had all my money and credit cards in it.

"You can give me a cheque if you like," said Julia, seeing me flustered and embarrassed.

I felt my pockets again and, thank heaven, found my cheque book.

"Whom should I make it out to?"

"'J. Wenn' if you please. Spelt without an 'h' and with

two 'n's."

She put the cheque in a drawer in the breakfast table. She looked up at me.

"There are two things I'm going to tell you. Firstly, how to get back to the village. You can get help there. Turn left out of the front door. Then you'll see a gate. Take the path through the fields and over the style. It's nearer than it seems."

Outside, the trees were swaying in the wind.

"Look," she said, pointing through an open window, "you can just see the spire of Swincote church."

"And what is the second thing you are going to tell me?"

"When you are going to die."

"Mrs Wenn," I said firmly, "you have been very kind and I'm most grateful for your hospitality. But that is something I would prefer not to know."

She looked straight at me. Her eyes were dark blue and piercing.

"The date you will die is the 14th June. The year is..."

"That's enough!" I interrupted angrily.

"But Andrew, you have to know!"

"Look, I told you, I don't want to!" I was almost shouting.

Julia opened the drawer, wrote something on a piece of paper, and folded it. She stood up, leant over me and tried to put it in my breast pocket. But I seized her hand and pushed her down again. The sleeve of her kimono slid back revealing a long skinny arm.

"Andrew!" she shrieked, "can't you see? This is a

privilege! It's something everyone needs to know, even if they're afraid of it."

She got up again.

"Your fate, Andrew! You can't escape your destiny!"

She stretched out her arm and again tried to put the folded paper into my pocket. But I got up quickly and dodged sideways. I grabbed her hand and prised her bony fingers apart. The piece of paper flew out of the window.

I walked straight out of the room, through the hall and out of the front door. Following the directions I'd been given, I opened the gate and took the path through the fields. I crossed the style. There was a tractor ploughing. When it reached the corner of the field I put up my hand. The driver stopped and opened the door of his cab. I told him what had happened to my car.

"In the ford, eh? I'll be with you shortly, when I've dropped me plough."

He pointed the way to the river.

When I got to the car I found that luckily the water hadn't seeped into the passenger compartment. I sat down by the side of the road and waited. After about half an hour the tractor arrived. The driver fixed a chain from the front of the tractor to a towing eye at the back of the Volvo.

"Get you out in next to no time!"

He jumped back into the cab and put the tractor into reverse. With a bubbling and squelching the car moved back onto dry land.

"We'll get you going now," he said cheerfully, opening

the bonnet. He took out an aerosol can and sprayed it into the engine.

"Try it now."

I turned the key. After a few seconds the engine spluttered then burst into life.

"Amazing stuff, this WD-40!" said the tractor driver.

I thanked him profusely, and wanted to offer him something for all his trouble. He was reluctant to accept anything, but I insisted.

"OK then, give me a fiver for the diesel. But what I don't understand," he asked, "is how come you end up in the ford when there's a perfectly good bridge right here?"

He pointed to a wooden bridge on the right. How could I have possibly missed it, and driven into the river?

"It's been here for twenty years," he said, "only other time I've been called out was when some youngsters was larkin' around in a jeep. And they'd gone into the ford deliberately."

He climbed into the cab and drove off.

I reversed carefully until I reached somewhere I could turn round. This time I had no trouble finding Ormsbury Park. Even if I missed the first few lots I would still get there in time for most of the sale.

I parked the car and hurried into the hall, where the sale was being held.

"Lot 25. The oak mirror-front wardrobe. Starting at one hundred pounds. No? All right, sixty pounds then. Come on, what'll you give me for the 'robe? Fifty pound? Thank you, sir,...fifty-five...lady's bid at fifty-eight..."

By the end of the sale I had bought a desk, a Persian carpet, two candlesticks, a chest of drawers, (Regency), and a small armchair.

A few weeks later I went to another sale, this time in Cheltenham. On the way home I stopped at a pub near Burford. In the bar, hanging from a beam, was a long wooden pole with a small chair on the end of it. Underneath was a brass plaque: 'The Swincote Ducking Stool. Once used to try witches in the River Windrush.'

Then I heard a voice that sounded familiar: "If I'm not mistaken, you're the gentleman I pulled out of the ford."

It was the tractor driver! He had a friend with him, quite an old fellow.

"Yes, and I'm eternally grateful. I don't know what I would have done otherwise."

"So you was going to Swincote Chickens," said the tractor driver.

"What?" I asked, mystified.

"Biggest poultry unit round here," said the old man.

"I was trying to get to an antiques sale at Ormsbury Park, but I took the wrong turning."

"Them rearing sheds are just across the river. You can't miss 'em," said the tractor driver.

I still didn't understand.

"When my car stalled I had to wade across the river. On the other side, further on, there were three cottages."

"No, no," said the tractor driver authoritatively.

"Wait a minute," said the old man, "now you mention it, I think there were some houses there once. But they were demolished years ago."

Later I found myself talking to someone else. He turned out to be a fellow antique dealer. We chatted a bit about the trade, and then he asked for my business card.

A.R.H. Parsons
Parsons Antiques
158 Kings Road
Chelsea
London SW3

"So, Andrew, what does A.R.H. stand for?"

"Actually my real name isn't Andrew," I admitted, blushing, "I'm Archibald Rupert Hornsby Parsons. But I got teased so much at school that I decided to call myself Andrew, my grandfather's name."

On the drive back to London I thought about what those three women had said. Then the answer came to me in a flash! The death they had foretold was not mine, but my grandfather's. He had been shot down during the War in a Spitfire, over Normandy, on 14th June 1944.

When I got home there was a letter waiting for me. It was from my bank. They were returning my cheque, as they couldn't pay it. I had written it out in pounds, shillings and pence!

TWENTY-TWO

The Penny

"See a penny, pick it up,
All the day you'll have good luck!"

So goes the old saying.

Up to 1971 there were twelve pennies in a shilling, and twenty shillings in a pound. Pennies were large coins made of bronze, and dark brown in colour (unless brand new). They mainly bore the heads of Elizabeth II and George VI, but sometimes those of George V and Edward VII too. Very occasionally you got a Queen Victoria penny in your change. As she reigned so long there were several 'heads' of her. The 'bun penny', so called as she wore her hair in a chignon, showed her as a young woman. These coins were always very worn. The 'old queen' pennies were minted at the end of her reign; in these she wore a veil over her head.

At Decimalisation in 1971 the currency was simplified. There were now a hundred pennies in a pound, and no more shillings. The coins became much smaller. At first they had the wording: 'one new penny' on them, but the 'new' was soon dropped. In 2021 the only monarch's head on coins was still that of Elizabeth II. Many people in Britain have seen no other. Due to the length of the Queen's reign she too has had several 'heads'.

Many years ago a penny would buy something – such as a loaf of bread. And there were also halfpennies (ha'pennies) and quarter pennies (farthings). But nowadays a penny is almost worthless. So if you saw one on the pavement you might well not bother to pick it up. Unless you were very poor. Or superstitious.

In France, for a long time, there were no public telephone boxes in the street. One had to go into a café and buy a token called a 'jeton', to use in the coinbox there. But sometimes you got a jeton that didn't work, or got stuck in the slot. This was called 'un faux jeton'. The term came to mean a thoroughly bad person, who, on occasion, appears on the scene and causes trouble. A 'rotten apple', a 'bad penny'.

***

Rebecca Warner lived with her parents and her sister Anne in a village in Berkshire. She was fifteen. Anne was three years older.

It was a Saturday, early in June, the day of the annual village fête.

"Anne – it's the fête this afternoon. Let's go to it!" said Rebecca.

"I can't," replied her sister.

"Why not?"

"I'm going out with Kevin."

"So I'll have to go there by myself," said Rebecca, angrily. She walked over to the field where the fête was being held.

It was a fine summer's day. A brass band was playing. There were many sideshows: ninepin bowling, plate smashing, tombola. There was a raffle, and she bought some tickets. There were stalls selling secondhand books and clothes, a dog show, and a children's fancy dress competition. Cream teas were served in the tent.

At the far corner of the field was a table, with an old man sitting by it. He had a grey beard and was wearing a long dark blue robe with gold moons and stars all over it, and a pointed hat. Next to the table was a large cylindrical object, with a design of red bricks and mortar painted on it. A sign said:

WISHING WELL

Three Wishes for £1

Rebecca was intrigued, and went up to the man.

"Are you a wizard?" she asked him.

"I suppose you could call me that," he replied.

"I'd like to make some wishes," she said, giving him a pound coin.

On the table was a pad of writing paper, a pile of small envelopes and a bowl of pennies. The man told her to write out each wish separately on a sheet of paper, fold it, and put it in an envelope with one of the pennies. Then seal the envelope, write her name on it, and put it in the wishing well.

Rebecca spent a moment choosing her wishes, then wrote them out. The first one was to win the raffle. The second was to be selected to play Cleopatra in the school play (it was Antony and Cleopatra by William Shakespeare). And the third wish? "For something bad to happen to Mrs Stevens."

She wrote REBECCA WARNER 1 on the first envelope, and her name with 2 and then 3 on the others. She looked into the well. It was full of water, and the envelopes already in it lay at the bottom. She put her first two envelopes in quickly, but hesitated a bit before dropping in the third.

"May all these wishes be for the good," said the old man.

"Er, yes," said Rebecca, as she left.

She went into the tent and had some tea and scones. When she came out the winning raffle numbers were being read out on a loudspeaker. But none of them were hers. She looked at some secondhand clothes, then walked home. Anne was still out with her boyfriend.

The next Monday, at school, there was a message on the notice board. After the last lesson in the afternoon the names of those chosen to act in the school play would be announced. Rebecca couldn't wait for school to end, she was so excited. At four o'clock everyone went into the Assembly Room and Mr Matthews read out the list. But the part of Cleopatra was given to another girl, Dorothy Baker. Nor did Rebecca get one of the other female parts. She went home bitterly disappointed. The first two wishes dropped in the well had turned out to be completely useless!

The first lesson on Tuesday was geography. But strangely, no teacher was waiting in the classroom. Then, after twenty minutes, the door opened. Mrs Stevens came in. Her arm was bandaged and in a sling.

"I expect you all wondered what had happened to me?" she said. "Well, I fell and broke my arm last night. I can't drive now, so someone had to give me a lift into school."

Rebecca gasped. The third wish had worked! She hated Mrs Stevens. If she was just one minute late for class, she got reported. There were constant arguments between them, such as whether to say Iran or Persia, or Sri Lanka instead of Ceylon.

"What's so funny, Rebecca?"

"Nothing, Mrs Stevens."

"I thought I saw a smirk on your face."

"Well, actually I was thinking of a joke someone told me yesterday," said Rebecca.

"Share it with us."

"Oh no, I couldn't possibly! It's not appropriate."

The whole class burst out laughing.

"Then I shall have the pleasure of hearing it myself, in private," said Mrs Stevens. "Wait for me at the end of the lesson, Rebecca."

Lying in bed that night Rebecca thought about the well, the old man, and the three wishes. The first two had been ineffective. But the third one had worked! So presumably the penny enclosed with it had some kind of power. It was a valuable asset that could be used again and again. She had to get it back!

On Saturday she went to see one of the women who had organized the village fête.

"You know the wishing well you had?" she said, "is there any way I can get in touch with the man who ran it?"

"I don't think I can help you," said the woman, "he came at the last minute. He's not from around here. I'd never seen him before."

Rebecca was already halfway out of the door.

"Wait! I think he left something behind!" the woman called after her.

She rummaged in a drawer and took out a card. It read:

WILLIAM MOUNTFORD

Clairvoyance. Tarot Reading. Magic.

(There was an address and telephone number at the bottom.)

"Can I have this?" asked Rebecca, excitedly.

"You're welcome to it."

Next day she phoned the man and arranged to meet him at his house. It was just a half-hour bus ride away. She knocked and the door was opened. Mr Mountford was wearing an old jumper and corduroy trousers. He showed her into a room lined with books.

"How can I help you?" he asked.

"Er...you know the wishing well at the village fête?" began Rebecca, nervously.

"Yes."

"I put in three envelopes."

"I remember," said Mountford.

"Do you think I could have one of them back?"

"Of course," he said, "but this is very unusual. I can't

recall anyone ever asking for one back."

"You see, one of the envelopes really worked," said Rebecca. "I wished that my grandmother would be well again. She was very ill, and everyone thought she was going to die. Now she has completely recovered!"

"I'm delighted to hear that," said Mountford.

"It was like a miracle!" she said, surprised at how easy it was to lie.

Mountford took her into another room, in which there was a deep round basin, made of black marble. It was full of water. In the bottom was a mass of envelopes.

"You'll find it somewhere in here," he said, "but it may take you a bit of time. Many people put in envelopes. You could say they are all superstitious. But the notes and pennies just focus their wishes. The water is charged with them. Like holy water in a church."

Rebecca rolled up her sleeves and put her arm in the water. It felt strangely warm. She took out handfuls of envelopes, read the names on them, and put them back in the basin. They were wet and soggy, and the writing on some was almost illegible. She found one with REBECCA WARNER on it, but it was wish number 2. She left it out on the side. After half an hour of fishing she was about to give up. Then she pulled out REBECCA WARNER 3.

"I've found it!" she cried.

Her heart began to beat faster.

"As long as you believe in that penny, its power will increase each time you use it," said Mountford, "but remember: the forces of magic are neutral. The operator must choose whether to use them for good purposes or for bad. And be warned: if you curse someone, it could well rebound on you."

He gave her a towel to dry the envelope, and she put it in her handbag. Then she thanked him and took the bus home.

Back in her room, she took the penny out of its envelope, wrapped it in some cotton wool, and hid it in her chest of drawers. Then she destroyed the note about Mrs Stevens. Had this really been caused by the wish and the penny, or was it sheer coincidence?

Anne was three years older than Rebecca. She had just won a place at university, and was now her parents' 'golden girl'. Her boyfriend, Kevin, often took her out in his car in the evening. Rebecca didn't like him.

"He's suave, and treats me with condescension," she once said.

Anne had a dog called Skip, which she absolutely adored. Rebecca hated him. He had once chewed up one of her shoes, and ruined her new sweater. It was soaked in saliva with a sleeve nearly torn off. And she found his high-pitched bark most irritating.

"You should call him Yap," she said.

"That's not a name," said Anne, angrily.

"Yes it is. It's an island in the Pacific."

One day Anne said that she had got three tickets for the Reading Jazz Festival. They would all go there in Kevin's car.

Rebecca looked forward to it eagerly. But on the day, Anne said that she only had two tickets after all. Rebecca was bitterly disappointed. Later she found out that Anne had sold the third ticket to a friend of hers.

She vowed to get her revenge. The penny! She bought an antique china bowl and filled it with water. Then she wrote out a curse, put it in an envelope with the penny, and dropped it in the bowl.

Late one evening she was lying in bed when she heard a car arriving outside the house. There was a screech of tyres, followed by a sharp squealing sound, then yelling and crying. She rushed downstairs and opened the front door.

"You idiot, Kevin! You've killed him!" Anne was screaming.

Skip lay under the car's front wheel, covered with blood.

"I told you not to drive so fast!" cried Anne.

She was beating Kevin hysterically on the shoulder with her fists.

"There was nothing I could do, honestly," he said, "he just ran out in front of me."

Mr and Mrs Warner appeared in their dressing gowns.

"You had better go now, Kevin," said Mr Warner, sternly. "I will deal with this."

Mrs Warner tried in vain to comfort her daughter. She was inconsolable.

The school play was to be at the end of term, in just over a month's time. Rebecca went up to Mr Matthews.

"Sir, I wonder if I could make a suggestion?"

"Yes, Rebecca?"

"Well, I know I wasn't selected to be Cleopatra, but I would like to be an understudy for the part."

"If you wish," he said, "but you must realize that it is most unlikely that you will appear on stage. A lot of work for you, with little chance of acting."

"I am prepared to accept that," said Rebecca.

She wrote out a curse "that Dorothy Baker be prevented from acting in the school play" and put it in the china bowl with the penny. And over the next month she diligently learnt the part of Cleopatra and attended the rehearsals.

Things, however, progressed as normal. Dorothy was doing particularly well.

"She's a natural Cleopatra!" people were saying.

And Nigel Redwood, who played Antony, was so handsome!

But on the morning of the play came bad news. Dorothy was in hospital with acute appendicitis. Rebecca glided into the part easily. She drew wild applause.

"She's a born actress!" said the Headmaster.

When Dorothy came back to school in the autumn term, Rebecca performed a different kind of acting: that of showing sympathy to the unlucky girl whose part she had taken.

After that the penny was not used again for a long time. It was just kept hidden in its drawer, and flowers were put in the china bowl. But one Tuesday, the following summer, Nigel asked Rebecca to go out with him to a nightclub in

Maidenhead that Saturday evening.

"I'm afraid you can't go," said Mr Warner.

"Why not?" asked Rebecca.

"Because you're too young to stay out all night."

"Please, Dad!"

"When I say 'no' I mean 'no', and that's final," he said firmly.

"You're just jealous of the young," said Rebecca, angrily. "You can't dance anyway. Because you're so old and fat!"

Mr Warner was, indeed, quite overweight. His doctor had warned him of the dangers of obesity, such as diabetes and heart disease. After an electrocardiogram at the local hospital, the cardiologist had told him to take more exercise and go on a diet, or else run the risk of a heart attack.

The next day Rebecca asked her mother to get him to change his mind.

"No, I cannot go against your father's authority," said Mrs Warner. "As parents we both act as a team, and your dad said 'no.'"

On Thursday Rebecca tried her father again. But he was inflexible. So she decided to use the penny. The note said: "To make Dad let me go to the disco. And to punish him if he refuses."

On Friday she made one last attempt to persuade him.

"Please can I go to the disco, Dad!"

"I already told you. No."

"But I really am old enough to go out all night. And I'm quite responsible. I can easily look after myself," she pleaded.

"You are still a young girl, Rebecca. But perhaps in a year or two..."

"Look – I'm not a young girl any more. I'm a woman now. Please Dad!"

"Will you stop torturing me, Rebecca," said her father, exasperated.

He suddenly turned red.

"I don't feel well..." he said, clutching his throat.

"Dad, you've just eaten too much!" said Rebecca, mockingly.

Mr Warner keeled over and fell heavily on the floor. His mouth opened and closed quickly, and his limbs twitched. Then he was still. Rebecca screamed and ran to fetch her mother.

A few days after the funeral Rebecca was in church again. She was a Roman Catholic, and wished to go to confession. She knelt at the confessional.

"I have committed murder," she said.

"What?"

Father Ryan was aghast. In his time as a priest he had had theft, adultery, violence – but never this!

"Yes, I killed someone," she repeated.

"Who?"

"My father."

"Have you told the police?" he asked.

"Well, it's not really like that," said Rebecca, "you see, I did it with a penny."

"A penny?" he asked, in disbelief.

She explained in detail how she had used it on her father, and the whole circumstances of his death.

"You cannot take the blame for that," said Father Ryan, "given the state of his health it would have probably happened sooner or later."

"I suppose so," said Rebecca.

"The most one can say is that the argument upset him and brought on the heart attack. Did you deliberately provoke him?"

"No. I just wanted him to let me go to the disco," she said.

"Your father's death, though predictable, was an unfortunate coincidence, and no fault of yours. You feel guilty because you harboured bad thoughts about him, and wished him harm. That was your sin. And as for the penny, it had no effect whatsoever. Merely superstitious nonsense. It just helped you concentrate your negative thoughts."

"I see," said Rebecca.

"Now instead of hating, you must love. Instead of cursing, you must bless," he said.

He gave her absolution; her penance was three Our Father's and six Hail Mary's.

Rebecca got up from the confessional.

"One more thing," said Father Ryan. "I'd get rid of that penny, if I were you."

***

When she grew up Rebecca went to university, left home, and began a career in advertising. She did well, took home a good salary, and was able to buy herself a nice flat in London. She made frequent use of the penny – to gain an advantage over rivals when seeking promotion, or to dispose of anyone who stood in her way.

She eventually married a man called Derek. After ten years the relationship deteriorated into a series of rows, mainly about money. They had no children. Finally Derek packed up and left. But in all the years of marriage, he never found out about the penny. It was kept in a secret drawer in Rebecca's jewellery box.

She kept the flat after the divorce, but the settlement was not as favourable as she had hoped. Derek had a tough lawyer. He moved abroad and married again. Rebecca cursed him with the penny: "To destroy Derek and his new family." And if she ran into any of his friends, she would interrogate them, eager to find out if anything had happened to him.

After many years Rebecca retired, and lived a solitary but comfortable existence. She used the penny from time to time. Once on her downstairs neighbour, who was always complaining about the music she played at night. He became stone deaf. Another time, against an airline that had refused to refund her ticket. One of their planes subsequently crashed.

One afternoon she went out shopping. On her return she found that her flat had been burgled. It had been totally ransacked, and her belongings were strewn eveywhere. Her jewellery box was open, and a necklace and some rings had been stolen. But her main concern was the penny. It was gone!

After hours of tidying up and searching for it she saw something small, round, and dark on her bedroom floor, under the curtains. It was the penny – of no interest, of course, to the thieves.

After that she resolved to have it with her at all times. She never put it in her handbag – that could always be snatched, or the penny mixed up with her loose change and spent by mistake. It was always kept on her person, usually in the back pocket of her trousers. She made sure all her skirts had pockets in them too. If she wore a shirt with a breast pocket, she would keep the penny in that. She even sewed a tiny pocket into each of her dresses. And at night she slept with it under her pillow.

One day she put her jeans in the washing machine, then into the dryer. As the drum revolved she heard a tinkling sound. It was the penny! She had nearly lost it again.

She realized now that to keep transferring it each time she changed her clothes was asking for trouble. So she decided to wear it on a fine silver chain around her neck. This would involve having a tiny hole drilled near the rim of the coin, where it would be attached to the chain.

It was a warm day in early October. Rebecca put the penny in the pocket of her cardigan and set out for a jeweller's shop in the High Street. But when she was in there and tried to produce the penny, she found, to her horror, that it was missing! It had fallen through a small moth hole in the base of the pocket, which she hadn't noticed before.

Desperately she retraced her steps, looking everywhere, on the pavement, in the road, and in the gutter. This was made harder by all the dead leaves already on the ground. But it was hopeless!

Every day Rebecca walked the streets, searching in vain for the penny. She began to get known as 'that eccentric woman' who always seemed to be looking for something on the pavement. She came across buttons, bottle tops, old watch batteries, sometimes even coins. But never her own magic penny.

Then one day, as she was out looking, she spotted a small brown coin in the road, six feet from the kerb. Her heart leapt – she knew at once it was the penny! She stepped off the pavement into the road, and bent down to pick it up. She did not see the big red bus bearing down on her.

**

If you walk down Kensington High Street, Earls Court Road, or the surrounding streets, you might well see an electric wheelchair moving slowly along the pavement. In it sits an old woman. Her hair is grey and her face is lined, the lips pursed in bitterness. She appears to be always looking for something on the pavement or in the gutter. If she ever sees a coin lying there, she will stop passers-by and ask them to pick it up for her. Then she examines it, but strangely, always throws it back.

TWENTY-THREE

Morowona

I was going through my post one morning when I opened an invitation from my old college at Oxford. It was for a 'Gaudy' – a reunion of all the old alumni who had been there within, say, a five year period. I am in my late fifties, so most of my contemporaries, like me, are now old men (there were very few women at our college in those days). Gosh! We were there nearly forty years ago!

I arrived at Oxford in the afternoon, and was shown my room, where a gown had been laid out on the bed. There was a service in the Chapel. Then, after tea, I went back to my room, had a bath, changed into my dinner jacket, and put on my gown. Drinks were served on the lawn, and then we went into Hall. After Grace, sung beautifully in Latin by the Choir, we enjoyed an excellent dinner.

Sitting on my left was Tom Bradfield, who had been in the same year as me. On my right was a chap I didn't know very well, who had rowed for the college.

"Well, Simon, tell me what you've done with your life," said Tom.

"After I went down I spent a year travelling. Then I

continued with my Law studies, and was called to the Bar."

I'd had a successful career as a barrister, and had taken silk five years ago. I sometimes still attended court, but most of my work was now in chambers.

Tom and I talked about people we had known when we were at the university. We had lost touch with most of them and some were now dead. I asked him if he remembered Bob Reynolds.

"Yes," said Tom, "he never did a stroke of work, and was nearly sent down for playing all those practical jokes."

"Oh yes!" I said, laughing.

"And do you remember Morowona?" he asked.

"Morowona? Yes, I think I do."

***

When I was an undergraduate, I often ate in pubs and restaurants, as well as in Hall. There, I sometimes sat next to a fellow who was always rather quiet and withdrawn. I heard he was from some island in the Pacific. One day I asked him what his name was.

"Morowona," he replied.

"Do you have any other names?"

"Yes, but they are long and you would find them hard to pronounce."

When I got to know him better I learned that he was the Crown Prince of his island. He was reading PPE (Politics, Philosophy and Economics). I asked him why he had chosen that subject.

"For kingship," he replied.

He said that when his father died he would have to go back and assume the throne.

I noticed that whenever we had meat, Morowona was served something else, such as fish, vegetables, or salad.

"I see you are vegetarian," I said once.

"Yes. Our diet is fish, and whatever else we can grow on the island by way of vegetables, fruit and crops."

One evening I was about to go into Hall when Morowona came up to me.

"I would like to go to a restaurant," he said.

"OK. Why not?" I said, a bit surprised.

I knew a nice little restaurant called Julie's, just off the High Street. When we got there Morowona didn't go straight in, but stood outside, closely examining the menu by the entrance.

"No. No good," he said, shaking his head.

"But the food's great here!" I protested.

"We should try somewhere else," he insisted.

He seemed to be acting rather strangely.

"All right – we'll go to the Devonshire Arms," I said.

When we arrived there I saw there was no menu outside. We went in, sat down, and a moment later a waitress came up to us.

"I wish to order liver," said Morowona straight away.

"But sir, wouldn't you like to look at the menu first?" she asked, handing it to him.

"No, I want liver, please," he said firmly.

"It's not on the menu today," said the waitress, "but I'm

sure I can get the chef to cook you some. Anything to start with?"

"No thank you," he replied.

"And you, sir?" she asked, turning to me.

"I think I'll have the turbot."

Our food arrived. The waitress brought Morowona liver and bacon, with boiled potatoes and peas. He ate some of the vegetables, then cut a piece off the liver. He put it on the end of his fork, turned it slightly to look at it, then put it in his mouth. He chewed it carefully, and swallowed it with difficulty.

"Morowona," I said, "may I ask you a question?"

"Yes."

"Have you ever eaten meat before?"

"No."

He ate some more of the liver and grimaced. He didn't touch the bacon, but finished the vegetables. I was sure he would have rather had the fish I had ordered.

We had fruit salad for desert. He enjoyed that, and became more relaxed. Then we walked back to our college.

A week later Morowona came up to me in the Junior Common Room.

"Simon – I would like to eat some tongue. Can you help me?"

We tried several restaurants, but none of them had it on the menu. So we finally went to Julie's. He had fish and I had pasta.

"Look Morowona," I said, "what's all this about?"

"I just need to have some tongue," he answered.

"But why tongue?" I asked, "why that in particular?"

He did not reply. I sensed there was something very odd.

"All right," I said, "I'll get you some tongue tomorrow. They don't usually serve it in restaurants, so I'll buy some in the supermarket. Come over to my digs in the evening, and we'll eat it together."

As I was in my third year, I no longer lived in college, but had a room in North Oxford.

The next evening I opened the tin of tongue I had bought, and prepared two plates of it, with some salad. I opened a bottle of red wine. There was a small table in my room, and Morowona and I sat opposite each other.

He tasted the tongue, and ate some of it. I could see he was making a great effort. Then he finished the salad.

"Thank you," he said, "now I must try heart."

"What?" I asked, astounded.

"Heart, Simon."

"Now look, Morowona," I said angrily, "I just don't get this. First it's liver, then tongue, and now heart. Why on earth do you have to try these things?"

By now we had both had several glasses of wine.

"I *have* to eat them," he said, "you see, I am obliged to eat them."

"Liver, tongue, and heart specifically?" I asked. "Why not steak, chicken – I don't know...lamb chops?"

I was beginning to get impatient with him.

"Anyhow, it's not so easy to get heart. It's not that

popular nowadays. You'd have to go to a butcher for it."

After a few more drinks he finally told me. He was a vegetarian, like everyone else on his island. No one ever ate meat – not even eggs. But long ago there was cannibalism. It had now totally disappeared – except in the 'Karamoga'.

This was the traditional coronation ceremony. Whenever a king died, his liver, tongue, and heart were removed, cooked, and then eaten by the heir to the throne. They embodied the mercy, wisdom, and courage of the deceased monarch, and were thus transferred to his successor. Only then could he be crowned king. The ritual was very solemn, and was carried out by three priests, one for each of the organs, under the direction of the Karata Gatura (the High Priest).

"Do you really have to go through with this?" I asked, quite shocked.

"Unfortunately yes," said Morowona.

His father, the King, was in very bad health, and could well die soon.

"Isn't there any way you can get out of it?" I asked.

"No. It is my duty. My people expect it of me."

It was the end of May. We were both in our third year, and our final exams were soon coming – they were in June. Most of one's time was spent revising the previous two years' work. It was hard for us all, but Morowona had an extra problem: if his father died he would immediately have to go back home for the Karamoga ceremony. But what if it was at the same time as Finals?

One evening I attended a drinks party on our college lawn, at which some of the dons were present. I got into conversation with one of them.

"I see you know Morowona," he said. "He is one of my star pupils."

I was speaking to Doctor Wilkinson, the Professor of Politics at our college.

"He's brilliant," he continued, "and so think his Philosophy and Economics tutors. He may well get a First."

I said that Morowona was very concerned that his father's impending death might interfere with his exams.

"Yes, he's spoken to us about it," said Dr Wilkinson. "It must be a great worry for him. Duty before academia! But it would be tragic if he couldn't sit Finals because of that."

When I next saw Morowona, I learnt that he was in regular touch with the people on his island regarding his father's health; it was fast deteriorating. The country was now being effectively governed by his mother, Queen Aramana, as Regent, with the assistance of the Karata Gatura.

In the days when we were students, communications were far less easy than they are now. There was no email, and international phone calls were costly and had to be booked in advance. Very long distance calls were often unclear due to the number of relay stations required. So urgent messages were frequently sent by telex or telegram. Morowona kept in contact with his island with great difficulty. It was called Raragongara, and was situated in a remote part of the Pacific Ocean. The nearest archipelago was the Solomon Islands.

What if the King died and Morowona stayed at Oxford to sit Finals, and didn't go back to perform the Karamoga? That was unthinkable. The island would descend into chaos. There was a republican party, backed by the Chinese, and they might use this to start an uprising. The country was of strategic importance, and was rich and self-sufficient. There were phosphate mines, and they were now drilling for oil just outside the reef.

Meanwhile I still had to get hold of some heart for Morowona. I was friendly with a girl called Jenny, who worked in the Steward's office, in charge of catering. Her job was to provide food for the college from all the various suppliers and wholesalers. She had to keep to a strict budget, and had a reputation for economy and getting value for money.

"Heart?" she said, "no trouble at all! I'll order some from our butchers, and have it cooked for you in the college kitchens. Then it can be taken up to your friend's room."

I didn't tell her then why we wanted the heart: Morowona needed to 'familiarize' himself with it (as he had already done with liver and tongue), so that, when the time came, he could fulfil his sacred duty by eating his dead father's organs.

Two days later I received a message from Jenny. I went down into the kitchens, and one of the cooks handed me a tray. On it was a small dish containing the heart and some boiled potatoes and carrots, and also a gravy boat, all under a round aluminium cover to keep it warm.

"Enjoy your meal!" she said, smiling.

I took it up to Morowona's room. Unlike most third year students, he still lived in college. I had laid a table for two, and opened a bottle of wine.

He lifted the cover, and appeared shocked by what he saw: a fleshy round, pear-shaped thing, with its artery holes visible. He took a knife, cut off a piece, and put it in his mouth. He tried hard to deal with the chewy, rubbery meat, but eventually spat it out in disgust.

"Have some vegetables," I said, "then cut off another bit and pour some gravy over it. You'll find that easier to eat."

He did what I said, chewed a lot, and finally managed to swallow it.

"It's the hardest one of the three," he said, with a shudder. "Well done!"

I had brought some fruit and cheese to have afterwards. He could now relax, and we finished the wine. I noticed he got quite drunk on just a modest amount of it.

Finals were fast approaching. Morowona became increasingly anxious. He now had to make phone calls almost daily, to check the status of his father's health. There were no telephones in undergraduates' rooms, so special arrangements were made for him to use the college secretary's office. The calls had to be made at night, because Raragongara was ten hours ahead of Greenwich Mean Time.

The strain on him was beginning to show. You could see

the tension in his face. He stuttered when he spoke. He had trouble sleeping, and told his tutor he found it hard to concentrate on his work. He was, indeed, on the edge of a nervous breakdown, and there was talk of sending him to the Warneford Mental Hospital for treatment.

Then one day the Dean sent for Morowana, and showed him a telegram with the sad news that his father, the King, had just died.

It was ten days before the start of Finals. What Morowona had been fearing had indeed happened: to have to fly straight back to Raragongara to attend his father's funeral, and – what he dreaded the most - perform the Karamoga ceremony. This meant he would not be able to sit the exams.

He was on the point of booking his airline ticket home. There would be the long flight to Australia, another to Honiara, in the Solomon Islands, then a third, in a small plane, to Raragongara.

Dr Wilkinson was most upset.

"What a shame! Such a fine student! After all the work he's done he deserves to get a First."

There seemed to be no way out. Then one of the dons came up with an idea: Morowona might still be able to sit Finals as planned if the Karamoga could be held first, not on the island, but here at Oxford!

He was called into the Senior Common Room and the idea put to him. He thanked them for their suggestion, but said it was quite impossible. From time immemorial, the

Karamoga had always been in Raragongara.

"My duty to my people is paramount. It must come before my studies. Had things turned out differently I would, of course, have gladly sat the examinations. But now this is not possible. However, I have very much enjoyed my course, and will always remember my time at this college with gratitude."

But Dr Wilkinson persisted. What if the officials performing the ceremony were to fly over to England, and the Karamoga was relayed to the island electronically – to be witnessed by all the people there on television?

Morowona was finally persuaded. Queen Aramana and the Karata Gatura would, of course, have to agree to encourage the nobility and people to accept this break with tradition. And then, when his exams were over, he would be free to return home, be received by his subjects, and assume his duties as King.

There was much to organize in a very short time. A man came from the Foreign Office in London. A set of rooms, known as Bishop Warham's Chambers, was reserved for the Karamoga ceremony. They were normally used for functions. There would be strict security, and no public access to the college for several days before the event. And these designated rooms would be accessible only to persons directly involved, all needing passes.

The BBC sent engineers to survey the site. An Outside Broadcast van would be parked in the Quadrangle, complete with dish and wireless antennas. The ceremony, however, would not go on the air in Britain, but would be relayed by satellite link directly to Raragongara, to be broadcast live on local television. A giant TV screen would also be erected in the main square of the capital city.

Shortly before the appointed day, three men arrived at the college in a taxi from Heathrow Airport. Good Lord! I can still remember their names: Ravaranamantha, Tioga Togo, and Naruala Na. They were given rooms in the secure area. Their luggage amounted to seven suitcases. Each man had two of his own. In one were his traditional vestments, to be worn during the ceremony. In the other was a casket containing one of the late king's organs, for which he was personally responsible. The remaining suitcase had the costume and regalia that Morowona would be wearing for his coronation.

The next morning I was doing some revision in my room in North Oxford when I heard a knock on the door. It was Morowona. He was quite breathless, having cycled fast all the way.

"Simon," he said, "I just can't go through with it!"

It was now just two days before the Karamoga.

"You know you have to, Morowana," I said.

Of course he didn't want to let everyone down after all the preparation and expense, and shirk his duty to his people.

"The ceremony itself is no problem. What I just cannot handle is the eating of the organs."

"But you practised all right, didn't you?" I argued, "I

thought you did rather well."

"Yes, but they weren't the real thing. But to eat Father's own liver, his tongue, and his heart! It's revolting! It's abhorrent! I just can't!"

He told me he had considered running away, and even suicide. He had come to me as the only person he could confide in.

I took a bus straight to the college, thinking hard of a way to help him out. Then I had an idea. I decided to go and see Jenny. I found her in the college kitchens.

"Jenny," I asked, "could I have a word with you in private? It's urgent."

She looked alarmed.

"OK. Come and see me in my office in half an hour."

It was on the third floor of Staircase 7. I knocked and went in. I said it was about Morowona . She knew, of course, about all the arrangements for the Karamoga ceremony. But when I told her he had to eat his dead father's liver, tongue, and heart, she turned white in the face.

"How awful!" she exclaimed, "It's barbaric!"

I said that no one else at the college knew about this, apart from me. Morowona was in an impossible situation, and in utter distress. But he had given me full details about the Karamoga, and I had now thought of a solution.

"You see, those three fellows who came are priests. Each man has a casket with one of the organs in it. During the ceremony they are taken out, cooked, and then served to Morowona, one by one. He must be publicly seen to eat them."

"Ugh!" she said.

"Now suppose we could substitute some ordinary meat from Oxford instead, without anyone knowing (except us and Morowona)? He could manage that – he's already practised eating it."

"Yes," said Jenny, "but how do you intend to do it? Those men will be watching over the caskets like hawks. It's their sacred duty – the whole point of them being here."

"There must surely be a way of doing the switch," I said, "Jenny, do you think you can get hold of some liver, tongue, and heart which we can slip into the caskets?"

"I'll go to the Covered Market today and get you some butchers' meat ," she promised.

It was now the day before the Karamoga. Preparations were almost completed. Carpenters had been at work, carpets were laid, and furniture brought in. Thick black cables ran out of Bishop Warham's Chambers, down the staircase, along the Quad, and into the BBC van. Security guards checked all the passes.

Early that morning I went to see Morowona and explained to him my plan.

"That I cannot do," he said. "If I fail to consume my father's body, I do not absorb his soul, and Karamoga will not have taken place. Then I would not be his true and worthy successor. It would be contrary to the most fundamental principles of our religion!"

I told him he had no choice. If he could not eat his

father's organs and the ceremony was aborted, he would be betraying his people; the consequences of that would be disastrous. But if he followed my plan and secretly ate 'butchers' meat', he would appear to all to have done everything expected of him. And nobody would know!

I slowly managed to convince him.

"But how can it be done?" he asked, "those three Gaturas guard their caskets day and night. They don't let them out of their sight for one moment. They even sleep with them!"

I wondered if he was completely right. During the long flight here it would have been necessary to refrigerate the King's organs. Had they been kept in the aircraft's own fridge (along with the passengers' food), or did each suitcase have a small built-in fridge to keep its sacred contents cool?

That afternoon Morowona invited me and the three priests to tea in his room. They came in together, walking rather stiffly, each one carrying his suitcase. They bowed deeply and were formally greeted by Morowona. An excellent high tea had been laid on: cakes, toast and jam, and sandwiches (egg and tomato, cucumber, and smoked salmon). The men ate greedily and soon became more relaxed. Ravaranamantha spoke a bit of English, but Naruala Na was fluent in it. He gave me a full guide to the Karamoga ceremony, and an explanation of its meaning.

They stayed on for drinks. I had prepared a fruit punch in a large glass bowl, having spent the morning buying and mixing the ingredients. I had laced the fruit juice with some 'spirit'. This was 98% pure alcohol. I had got it from a

Polish student called Lewandowski.

"It's almost tasteless," he said, "so if you want to get somebody drunk, just mix it in!"

By the time the men left Morowona's room that evening, they were noticeably tipsy. They staggered down his staircase, and one of them stumbled and nearly fell. I watched them walk back through the Quad to their rooms, all three swaying merrily and clutching their little suitcases.

That evening I had dinner in Hall with Morowona. I wanted to give him some moral support, as tomorrow was his big day. On the way into Hall I ran into Jenny.

"I bought all the meat. I had to trim it down – in an ox it's much bigger than with humans," she whispered, "and I'm the one who's going to do the switch - tonight! I have a security pass, and I also got hold of keys to each of their rooms. I told the housekeeper I needed to check if they had coffee, tea, and biscuits!"

"That's great!" I said, "they've had a lot to drink, so hopefully they'll sleep it off tonight!"

The Karamoga was to be seen in Raragongara at five o'clock in the afternoon. But due to the time difference, the ceremony would take place in Oxford at seven in the morning. I set my alarm clock, had an early breakfast, and arrived at the college in good time at 6.15 am. Jenny came up to me.

"I did it!" she said, excitedly. "It was terrifying! I quietly unlocked each of the doors and tiptoed into their rooms. They were all snoring away. The caskets were next to their beds – luckily they'd taken them out of the suitcases. I lifted the lid off each one, identified what was in it, and slipped in the butchers' meat instead. Then I took away the human stuff in a plastic bag. All bloody and slimy! Not very nice. And I had to do this three separate times!"

"Jenny – you're fantastic!" I said.

What a brave woman! I heard later that the Gaturas always carried knives. If they had woken up they would have killed her.

It was now time for the Karamoga ceremony. Only the Dean, Dr Wilkinson and myself had been invited to watch it. We were issued with passes and climbed the stairs to Bishop Warham's Chambers.

We went in and were asked to stand to one side, at the back. In the middle of the room were TV cameras, lights, and a mass of cables. The cameramen were already in position. At the far end was a throne. Sitting on it was Morowona. I had never seen him looking like this!

He was wearing sandals, and a purple skirt with a pointed, serrated hem, ending just below the knee. Above that he had a plain white shirt. He was bareheaded.

To his left stood the three Gaturas, with their caskets by their sides. They wore skirts of a similar type, but each one of a different colour. They had gold jackets, and on their heads were curious-looking hats.

The ceremony began. The ancient ritual was performed with great solemnity. After some prayers Ravaranamantha lit a fire under a metal tripod. He opened his casket, took something dark red out of it, and put it in an ornate frying pan. There was a sizzling sound, and the smell of liver cooking, and aromatic herbs. When it was ready he produced a silver knife and fork, and, singing an unearthly-sounding chant, served it to Morowona on a golden platter.

Tioga Togo and Naruala Na presented their respective tongue and heart in the same way. Morowona ate it all with aplomb. I was impressed by his dignity and resolution.

At the end of this Naruala Na, deep in chant, put a purple velvet cloak around Morowona's shoulders, and a sceptre in his hand. Then he placed a gold crown, encrusted with jewels, on his head. It was tall and pointed, like the spire of a Siamese pagoda. All three priests then prostrated themselves before their new sovereign.

The ceremony was over. Everyone clapped. Morowona came over to me and shook my hand.

"Thank you," he said, and grinned.

***

In September I went back to Oxford to take my degree.I had succeeded in getting a good Second. And I learned that Morowona had got a First!

Many students did not go to the ceremony, and had their degree certificates sent to them by post. And unfortunately Morowona had had to stay behind in Raragongara. But my parents had come, so, suitably attired in gown and mortarboard, I attended the formal Degree Ceremony in the Sheldonian Theatre.

Afterwards we went back for drinks on our college lawn.

Dr Wilkinson said how proud he was of Morowona.

"He has been a great credit to this college!"

Jenny was also there. She congratulated me on my results.

"Thank you," I said, "but Jenny, there's just one thing I wanted to ask you."

"Yes?"

"What on earth did you do with the dead king's liver, tongue and heart?"

"Oh that?" she said, giving me a sly look. "Do you remember the beef stew we had for lunch the next day? Well, I found I was a little short of meat. So I popped it all in too. I couldn't let it go to waste, could I?"

"What?" I asked, horrified.

"None of you seemed to notice. In fact, everyone loved the stew, and I got nothing but compliments!"

TWENTY-FOUR

The Grand Gala Ball

I suppose most girls would like to know about the man they are going to marry. All of us at school did, except for one girl who wanted to become a nun.

Whenever we had plum or cherry pie we would count out the stones afterwards: tinker, tailor, soldier, sailor, rich man, poor man, beggar man, thief. But each time one got a different answer.

One day, during the holidays, my parents took me to a funfair. There was a caravan with a sign on it saying: *Fortunes Read*.

"Ooh! Can I go in there?" I asked.

I went into the caravan. It was very dark inside, and there was a smell of incense. A gypsy woman was sitting at a table. On it was a pack of cards and a crystal ball. She told me to sit down opposite her.

"Let's see your hands, dearie."

She looked at both my palms. She told me I would do well at school and have a successful career. Something disappointing would happen to me, but that would eventually bring me happiness.

This was nice to hear, but it was rather general and not very exciting. I had heard that fortune tellers often predicted amazing details that later actually happened to people.

"Can I ask you just one question?" I said.

"Of course."

"Who will I marry?"

"A bird," she said.

"What?"

"You will marry a bird."

I was quite shocked. Was she trying to be funny? Or was she crazy? I quickly paid her and left the caravan.

On the way home I told my parents what the gypsy woman had said.

"It's wrong to say that sort of thing to a child," said my mother, angrily, "it's stupid and frightening."

"Those people will say just anything to impress you," said my father. "It's a lot of nonsense anyhow. All they really want is your money."

Back at school I was foolish enough to tell one of the girls about it it.

"How absurd to marry a bird!" she quipped.

She told everyone.

"Lucy says she's going to marry a bird!"

All that week people flapped their arms and went "tweet-tweet" whenever they saw me.

***

When I left school I studied accountancy. I passed all the exams and became a chartered accountant. I got a job in a firm in Bristol. I had left home by now, and shared a flat in Clifton with a girl called Daphne. She was nice, but could be a bit odd at times.

Most of my friends were from Bristol, but I had a few in London too. At weekends we often went to nightclubs and parties. But there was one special event I had heard of, but not yet been to. It was the annual Grand Gala Ball, held in London in the autumn, at a big hotel in Mayfair. This was a charity ball, and was attended by many professional people. Some of my friends were going to be there, and we had got together and booked a table. I bought myself a ticket for the ball. It was quite expensive, but I knew I would have a good time there.

There was another reason for going to the Grand Gala Ball. There would be a fellow called Robin Foxley-Williams on our table. I had only met him a couple of times, but we had got on quite well together. He was handsome and amusing. His parents had a large house in Chelsea and an estate in Hampshire. They ran an important business in the City which Robin would be taking over when his father retired. He was a real catch!

But there was competition. I knew that a girl called Jean Marshall was after him. She had long blonde hair and was extremely pretty, and would also be on our table. I realized that to have any chance with Robin, simply being charming and amusing would not be enough. I would have to look devastatingly attractive.

It took me some time to choose my outfit for the ball. I am quite tall, and have dark brown hair. I wanted to look and feel beautiful, sophisticated and elegant. I finally settled on an evening two-piece, a top and long skirt.

I bought the top in London, from a shop in Bond Street. It had a boat neck and long sleeves, and was made of delicate black silk covered with sequins. I had a pair of silver sandals, and planned to wear a pearl necklace and a gold bracelet as jewellery. And carry a velvet evening bag.

I decided to have the skirt specially made. I found an Indian fabric shop in Gloucester, and looked at a whole range of cloth. Then one particular roll caught my eye. The material was a thick luxurious silk, in a subtle blue-grey colour. When it moved its folds caught the light and shone with a deep lustre. I chose it immediately.

The skirt was to be full length and very wide, so I needed metres of material. An old Indian lady took out two rolls.

"Ah! You have chosen what we call 'the Brides' Silk'," she said. "All the girls in Gujarat wear it when they hope to get married."

I smiled.

"And, if you are not already married, this silk will find you a husband too! May I ask, is this for a special occasion?"

"Yes," I said, "it's for a grand ball in London. I've already got a top, and this is for a long evening skirt to wear with it."

"Then the skirt will bring you good fortune," said the

woman.

She unrolled the material, measured it out, and cut it. Then she folded it and packed it carefully for me.

A dressmaker called Mrs Perkins lived near our flat, and I got her to make up the skirt.

At the final fitting I tried it on and looked at myself in the mirror. It hung perfectly, and flowed beautifully when I moved.

I turned quickly and it swirled out around my ankles. And when I walked it swept along the ground with a swish and a rustling of silk. Sheer heaven!

Mrs Perkins hung it in a garment bag.

"I hope you enjoy wearing it," she said, "but a word of warning. This skirt is fully lined, but the silk material will crease easily. Avoid sitting in it for long periods unnecessarily, such as when travelling. Also it will 'seat' and lose its shape. Best keep it on a hanger!"

When I got back to the flat I put on the whole outfit to show Daphne.

"Wow! You look fantastic!" she said.

I realized I would have to spend the night of the ball in London. So I found a reasonably priced hotel not too far from where it was being held, and booked a room there. I planned to drive down from Bristol in the afternoon, park at the hotel, and check in. Then I would have a bath, change into my evening clothes, and go on to the ball by taxi. After staying the night at the hotel, I would drive back home the next morning.

All this, of course, had involved me in a lot of expense. But I felt it was worth it. And I deserved it too! I had not gone on holiday that year, and had worked throughout the summer. I had carefully saved up for the Grand Gala Ball, and looked forward to it eagerly.

When the day finally arrived, I had my hair done at lunchtime, planning to leave Bristol in the afternoon. But, due to an unexpected crisis at work, I set out for London nearly four hours late. I now realized that, in order to get to the ball in time, I would have to drive there straight from home, without first stopping at the hotel. I rang them and said that I would now be checking in well after midnight. They said that was OK, there was always someone at the desk.

I packed very lightly. I just had my nightie and a change of underwear, tightly rolled up and crammed into my handbag, together with my hairbrush, makeup, and toilet bag. I had a short faux fur coat with me (more of a jacket, really), and I put that on the back seat of the car. I decided to change at home in Clifton and drive to London in my evening outfit. Except that I wore my trainers for driving, keeping my silver sandals in a plastic bag. I sat at the wheel in my sequined top and a very short nylon petticoat. I carefully hung up my long skirt over the back of the front passenger seat, as I did not wish to crease it on the journey.

On arrival in London I would now park as near as possible to the ball's venue. Then apply some more makeup, put on my sandals, skirt and coat, and take a taxi the rest of the way.

As I drove down the motorway I saw illuminated signs saying: SLOW DOWN – STRONG WINDS. And on the radio I heard that the Severn Bridge had been closed to high-sided vehicles.

I noticed I was running low on petrol, so I pulled in at a service station. It was past Reading and on the outskirts of London. I put on my coat and filled up the car. I just had time for a quick cup of coffee before continuing the journey, so I drove away from the pumps towards an area marked: 'Customer Parking'. The tarmac was uneven and I had to avoid several large oily-looking puddles before reaching the parking spaces. As there had been many police warnings about thefts at service stations, I took everything out of the car before locking it. I walked rather awkwardly towards the café, holding my coat together with one hand, and my handbag and evening bag in the other, with my long skirt over my arm. It was very windy indeed.

I had almost reached the café when a huge gust of wind caught my skirt. Before I could tighten my grip it billowed out and sailed away over the parking area. Just then a lorry drove past. The skirt landed flat across its windscreen, and then, as the lorry braked, slid down its front and disappeared under the wheels.

I ran towards it like a crazy demented animal. The lorry had now stopped, and was reversing. It was one of those big articulated things. Several sets of wheels had gone over my skirt. It was lying all crushed and sodden, right in the middle of one of the puddles!

The driver jumped down from the cab.

"YOU ABSOLUTE BLOODY IDIOT!" I screamed, "YOU'VE JUST RUINED MY SKIRT!"

I bent down and picked it up. Although it was now getting dark, you could clearly see black tyre marks and patches of oil and mud all over it. It was ripped in many places too.

"I'm really sorry, Miss," said the driver, "there was nothing I could do. I couldn't stop in time."

I held up the skirt for him to see. Oily water dripped from it.

"Just look what's happened to my skirt!" I cried, "I'm meant to be wearing it for a ball tonight! But now…"

I burst into tears. The driver just stood there awkwardly.

"Is there anything I can do?" he asked.

"No, nothing," I said, "it's too late now. Please go away."

"Are you sure?" he asked.

"Yes. Just go away! GO AWAY!"

He hesitated for a moment, then took a card out of his pocket and gave it to me.

"These are our company's contact details. Once again, I'm really sorry about this."

He climbed back into the cab and drove off slowly.

I stood there for a moment, stunned. Then went back to my car and sat inside it. I turned on the interior light and looked at the skirt. It was completely ruined. I was in total despair. Then I had an idea. If I was quick enough I might just be able to wash out the stains.

I locked everything else in the car and ran to the café with the skirt. There was a row of washbasins in the ladies toilets. I filled one of them with hot soapy water and soaked the skirt in it. Then I scrubbed desperately for well over half an hour. But that only made it worse. The oil stains spread out over most of the skirt in a dirty cloud. It was now covered with brown smudges and thick black tyre marks. It was hopeless!

An old woman was standing at a nearby washbasin. She came over to me.

"You seem to be in trouble," she said.

"I'm trying to get the marks off this skirt," I told her.

"Let me see the garment. I used to be a dry cleaner."

I handed her the skirt. She examined it thoroughly.

"That's diesel oil. Worst thing of all. No amount of dry cleaning will dislodge those stains. And look! It's ripped all over!"

She shook her head.

"Such a beautiful long skirt! What a dreadful shame!"

She gave it back to me.

"Going to a ball then?" she asked.

"I *was* going to a ball, but I can't now," I replied, "my skirt's ruined."

"What a pity. You look so lovely."

I just wished she'd leave me alone.

"Got a nice top to go with it?" she asked.

"Yes, but it's not much use on its own, is it?" I said

bitterly.

"Could I see it? Slip your coat off for a moment. It's a lovely coat."

"I can't," I said, holding the coat together.

"Why not?"

"Why do you think?" I asked.

"Oh, of course!" said the woman. "You've nothing on underneath!"

"Actually I have," I said angrily, "well, sort of."

"Sorry for asking," she said, "I didn't realize. But I do hope you enjoy the ball. You'll look gorgeous!"

I really lost my temper then.

"I just told you," I said furiously, "I can't go to the ball!"

"Why not?"

"Because I haven't got a skirt!" I shouted.

Some other women in there were listening to us.

"You can have mine, dear," said the old woman.

She pulled open her coat, revealing a bright red tartan miniskirt.

It was trimmed with black leather, and had four thick brass zips down the front.

"No thank you!" I said.

And I stormed out of the toilets, dragging my skirt behind me.

I've noticed that often when one's in trouble, some mad old person appears on the scene trying to help. But they actually get in the way and make things worse.

Back at the car I put the limp oily rag that had once been

a beautiful long skirt into a plastic bag, and threw it into the boot. Then I sat in the front seat and wept. What was I to do?

One option was to drive back to Bristol and get hold of another outfit. But I didn't possess an evening dress, and had nothing suitable to wear with my top, as all my skirts were mini. I could try to borrow Daphne's long dress, but I probably wouldn't fit into it as she was several sizes smaller than me. I'd have no time to go round asking my other friends. Anyhow the idea was not feasible. It was now nine o'clock and I was almost in London. To go to Bristol and back, with time to park and get the new clothes, would take around five hours. The ball would be over by then.

If only some fairy godmother would appear and bring me a spare evening skirt!

I could, of course, still go to the ball. But while the other women would be wearing long, floor-sweeping gowns, I would be in an evening top and just a tiny slip. My fur coat, ending six inches above the knee, barely covered that. People would be constantly asking me why I kept my coat on all the time, and I'd be too embarrassed to answer. And whenever I danced I'd have to hold it together. I would feel self-conscious and ridiculous in this short coat and my knee-high stockings!

No – going to the ball now was out of the question. But before starting back for home I rang the hotel to cancel my reservation.

"This is Lucy Morton," I said, "I had a room booked for

tonight, but I won't be able to come after all. There's been an incident."

"You've had an accident? Are you all right?" asked the man at the hotel, anxiously.

"Oh no – nothing like that," I said, "it's just that something has prevented me from attending my function in London."

I didn't want to be too specific.

"We operate a strict cancellation policy," he said firmly, "and require at least 24 hours' notice, otherwise the full amount is chargeable."

"Can't you make an exception," I pleaded, "just this once?"

"No, madam, I'm afraid we cannot. Otherwise we would be doing the same for everyone who cancelled late."

"Could I speak to someone else?" I asked angrily.

"I'll put you through to the Head Manager," he said.

A woman answered. I told her everything in detail, expecting her to be more sympathetic.

"Something like that happened to me once," she said.

"I was on a train in Italy by myself, with no luggage. I was wearing a brand new suit with a pleated skirt. I had hung that up on a coat hook behind my seat, to stop it from creasing, and had the jacket over my legs. I fell asleep. My skirt was stolen and I was left with nothing to wear."

"Gosh!" I said.

"It's dreadful to wake up alone in a foreign country and find yourself without a skirt," she said, "and in public!

You feel vulnerable and humiliated. Every woman will understand."

I was now sure she would let me off paying for the room.

"But I'm really sorry, I can't refund you your money. You see, it's company policy."

I switched off my phone. For a moment I toyed with the idea of driving into London and staying at the hotel, just to get my money's worth. But what would be the point? I could hardly spend the whole evening sitting around in the hotel lounge in my coat! So I'd have to stay alone in my room with nothing to do except watch TV, while everyone else was having a great time at the ball!

I knew I had no choice, and began the long haul back to Bristol. To add insult to injury, I had to drive further towards London before I reached the next motorway exit allowing me to turn back in the opposite direction.

During the journey I had ample time to contemplate the disaster. My long skirt had been wrecked, and with it, the whole evening. That gust of wind had blown away any chance of fun, glamour or romance! I turned on some music to distract myself.

When I got back to Clifton I found no one else in the flat. I hung up my coat, but didn't feel like going to bed. So I stayed in my top and watched TV in the sitting room. I was at a loose end and felt angry and restless. And all this time I could have been having fun at the ball!

After a while I went into the kitchen to make myself something to eat. Then I heard the front door opening and

Daphne came in. She saw me standing there and burst out laughing.

"Oh Lucy! You look hilarious! But I don't understand... aren't you at the ball?"

"Do I look as if I am?" I snapped. "Do you seriously think I would go to a grand ball in a flimsy little thing like this?"

I angrily flicked the hem of my petticoat.

"Well, I see you're wearing the top half of your evening outfit," she said, "but where's your long skirt? It must be hanging up somewhere."

"No, it's screwed up in a plastic bag in the boot of my car," I answered.

"Why?"

"Something happened to my skirt on the way to London," I said mournfully, "and it was completely ruined. I had nothing to wear with my top. So I never even went to the ball."

"What appalling bad luck!" said Daphne, horrified, "I don't know what to say."

She knew how upset and disappointed I was, and did her best to console me.

"And I never had a chance to wear it," I said, bitterly.

Then I burst into tears.

Next morning we looked at the skirt closely. It was totally beyond repair - to take it to the dry cleaners would have been a complete waste of time. Daphne found a bit of material that had escaped damage, and planned to make a cushion out of it. She likes sewing.

"Actually it's all right until 25 centimetres down from the waistband," she said, "you could cut off all the ruined part and still have a skirt, but it would be a micro-mini one!"

"Daphne! Sometimes you can be so tactless!" I said angrily.

That was it, then! There was nothing more to be done. I tried to put it all out of my mind, get on with my life, and concentrate on my work. Autumn was a busy time for us, as our clients' tax returns all had to be in by the end of the year (31st of January at the latest). During that period I didn't go to London once, and actually only made one trip away (to Birmingham). Then there was Christmas, which I spent with my parents, as usual.

***

Next year, just before Easter, I was reading the newspaper when something caught my eye.

FORTHCOMING MARRIAGES

The engagement is announced between Robin, only son of Mr and Mrs Charles Foxley-Williams, of London, and Jean, elder daughter of Colonel and Mrs Andrew Marshall, of Newbury, Berkshire.

So she had got him! I was not surprised, as, after all, she'd had no competition from me on the night of the ball.

A month later an envelope with a thick square card in it arrived in the post. At first I thought it was an advertisement, or about some private view at an art gallery.

No, it was an invitation to the Foxley-Williams wedding, to be held in a church in London.

I was about to tear it up and throw it in the bin, when Daphne stopped me.

"You've got to go!" she insisted.

"I wouldn't dream of it!"

"You're just bitter, aren't you?" she said, taunting me.

"Wouldn't you be, in my place?"

"I suppose so," she said, "but remember – there'll be a lot of people there. And I bet Robin's got a brother or two!"

"No. He's an only child," I said.

"But there'll be other eligible young men there. And there's always the Best Man! You can't afford not to go."

She finally persuaded me to accept the wedding invitation, saying that I should swallow my pride and be a bit more strategic in my attitude. The outfit I chose was a light blue silk dress and jacket, and a dark blue wide-brimmed hat. I thought I looked pretty good.

I went to London by train and took a taxi to the church. It was a very grand affair. All the men were in morning coats, and the women wore really elegant hats and dresses. There were flowers everywhere. The bride looked like a princess in her beautiful white dress. She was attended by a page boy and six bridesmaids.

And the groom was so handsome!

At the reception we all lined up to congratulate the newlyweds. Robin gave me a nice smile, but in Jean's I saw a look of triumph.

There might well have been some 'eligible young men' at the reception, but I didn't meet any. All I got was a really boring chap who kept on pestering me for my phone number; I found it hard to shake him off. I ended up getting rather drunk on the champagne.

Some of the guests had also been to the Grand Gala Ball last autumn, and they asked me why I hadn't shown up. I was evasive, and merely said that something had happened on the way to it.

"What a shame!" said one rather pompous man, "I'm sure you would have looked marvellous. Belle of the Ball!"

One of them, called Barbara, was an old friend from school. I hadn't seen her for a long time, and she lived in London now. She kept on pressing me for details. So I described my evening outfit, adding that I had travelled very light on that occasion. I told her what had happened at the M4 service station.

"So when my skirt was destroyed, I was left with nothing to wear. I had my black sequined top, and then absolutely nothing else, apart from a slip. You can't go to a ball like that!"

"You poor darling!" she cried, "you missed a great party. But Lucy! Why on earth didn't you ring me up and come along to my house? You and I are the same dress size. Remember? I would have lent you my long velvet skirt."

"I don't have your telephone number," I replied.

***

"Tickets please!"

I was sitting in the train on the way back to Bristol, and the ticket inspector was passing through the carriage.

"All tickets please... thank you very much...tickets please ...thank you, change at Swindon."

When he got to my seat I just couldn't find my ticket. I desperately rummaged through my handbag. Panic! He waited patiently. Then I took out my wallet and opened it. The ticket was in one corner of it, and I handed it to the inspector with relief. When I put it back in the wallet I noticed a business card hidden under some others I had accumulated. On it was printed:

J.H. BRANDON LOGISTICS

John Bird

It was the card the lorry driver had given me after driving over my long skirt! I had been so frantic then that I must have put it in my wallet and forgotten about it.

During the rest of the train journey I wondered why he had given it to me. So I could complain to his company, and perhaps claim some sort of compensation? After all, I had lost my skirt and my evening at the ball. And there was the hotel room too. Apart from the grief, it had all cost me a lot of money.

Next day I phoned the number on the card.

"J.H. Brandon Logistics, good morning," said a woman's voice.

"Er...could I speak to Mr Bird?" I asked nervously.

"May I have your name, please?"

"Lucy Morton."

"Could you tell me what it's in relation to?"

"Some damage that occurred a few months ago," I replied.

"John's driving at the moment," said the woman, "I'll put you through to Mr Richards."

There was a click, and then a man spoke.

"Do you think you could come over to our yard, Miss Morton? Then we can discuss it all."

I went to Keynsham the next day. There were a lot of lorries there, some parked, others moving around the yard. I was shown into an office, where a middle-aged man was sitting at a desk.

"Please sit down," he said, "we were expecting you to contact us, and were surprised not to have heard from you earlier."

"I've just been extremely busy," I said.

"John told me all about it," said Mr Richards, "a most unfortunate occurrence! He was very sorry to see you in such distress!"

"Er...I was wondering if there would be any chance of compensation," I ventured.

"We cannot accept liability," he said, "but we could always make an insurance claim. As a transport company we are covered for all kinds of risks, such as damage to third parties' property."

"So what do you think can be done?" I asked.

"We'll put in a claim on your behalf. But first you will have to supply full details of everything."

"I'll try my best," I said.

"We'll have to get John's story too," said Mr Richards, "and hopefully both your accounts will be enough to convince the insurance company."

"Well, thank you," I said.

"Perhaps you could give us your address, email and telephone number, so that we can complete the claim form when we' ve got all the details."

I gave him one of my firm's cards, and wrote down my own phone number on the back. Then I thanked him again, and left the office.

A week later I received an email from John Bird, J.H. Brandon Logistics, asking me to come back to their yard. I made an appointment for the following day.

When I came into the office the lorry driver was in there waiting for me. He looked younger than I had remembered.

"First I'd like to say how sorry I am about it all," he said.

"So am I," said I, rather frostily.

"It must have been an awful experience."

"Yes," I said, "I was going to a ball I'd been really looking forward to. Then this happened, and I couldn't go any more."

"I quite understand," he said, "I would have felt the same way if I'd been you."

Something about him made me rather like him.

"Look," I said, "if I was at all rude at the time, I must apologise. But I was so desperate then."

"I'm not surprised," he said, "and once again, I'm so sorry it happened. But perhaps we should get on with the insurance details."

He opened a file and produced the claim form. We filled in the value of the damaged goods (i.e. my long skirt), the price of the ticket to the ball, the hotel cost, and my petrol for the trip, based on mileage. I wrote a brief account of what had happened, with its exact time, date and location, accompanied by a simple sketch.

Mr Bird said that, in giving his own account of the incident, he would also have to provide a record of his whole journey, during which he had stopped at that service station. The lorry's tachograph would be read. This recorded everything: speed, distance travelled, time spent driving, rest breaks, etc.

"Well, that's about all for now," he said, "thanks for coming in."

Ten days later I got a phone call from him. Unfortunately the insurance company had requested documentary evidence to support the claim. They wanted invoices for the skirt, the ticket to the ball, and the hotel bill.

For most of that I could show proof by providing a photocopy of my credit card statement, but I had paid cash for the skirt. So I had to go back to the Indian fabric shop in Gloucester to get a receipt.

"How much you want me to put?" asked the owner.

"I think it was six hundred pounds," I answered.

Mrs Perkins was also very helpful.

When I had got all this I rang Mr Bird. He suggested we should meet, not at the yard, but in town, in the lounge of the Cavendish Hotel. It would be more convenient for me.

I arrived at the hotel at noon, as agreed, with all my paperwork.

"Insurers are often difficult like this, Miss Morton," he said.

"You can call me Lucy," I said, "but only if I can call you John!"

"Well, no one really calls me that," he said.

"So what *are* you called?"

"I'm known as 'Custy.' Because of my surname."

"I don't get it," I said.

"Bird's Custard. At school people were always singing: *Cowardy cowardy custard, fell into the mustard*. Then one day someone called me 'Custy', and the name stuck."

We finished filling in the claim form, signed it, and enclosed all the photocopies and receipts in the envelope. It was now ready to be sent off.

"I've taken the liberty of booking a table for lunch here," said Custy.

"That's a bit presumptious, isn't it?" I asked, "how do you know I've got the time?"

"I think you have," he said, smiling.

After two weeks I received a full payment from the insurance company. That was great, but there was something even better – Custy and I started going out together. Six months later we became engaged, and got married the following year.

Custy continued working for J.H. Brandon for a time.

But he had always dreamt of running his own business. With some help from my father and my contacts in the world of finance, we raised enough money for him to start off independently. We now have a fleet of fifteen vehicles, and are hoping to expand further.

We live in a nice house in Clifton, and have three wonderful children. Like all families we have had our share of ups and downs, but I can truly say that if happiness does exist, we seem to have found it.

***

When the children were older I was able to go back to work, to my old job. Most of our clients were from the Bristol area, but we sometimes visited others further afield. One day I had to go to London to help with some auditing. It was in mid July, and I was wearing a lovely new cotton dress and a cashmere cardigan. The client's factory was next to some tower blocks in Croydon.

There was a café nearby, and when I had finished my work I decided to have a cup of coffee there, before going back to Bristol. It was almost empty inside, except for a woman sitting alone in a corner. She was wearing an old grey tracksuit. Surely it couldn't be her! I am naturally shy, but somehow gathered the courage to go up to her.

"Jean? Jean Foxley-Williams?" I asked.

"It's Jean Marshall," she replied, "I've gone back to my maiden name. And you're...Lucy Morton!"

"I'm Lucy Bird now," I said, smiling.

She seemed embarrassed to see me. She didn't look

good, I must admit. Her skin was blotchy and wrinkled, and her hair, though still blonde, was streaked with grey. It was unkempt and sticking together.

I ordered some coffee for us and sat down at her table. She told me about herself. At first their marriage had been wonderful. They were a glamorous couple and in fashionable society. They lived well and entertained lavishly. But then things began to go sour. Robin started wildly overspending and got into financial difficulties. To pay off his debts the London house and country estate were sold. Then he went through all of Jean's own money. He started gambling, took to drink, and was sometimes violent. Finally he went bankrupt, and was sent to prison for fraud.

"I had no option but to divorce Robin," she said, "luckily we never had any children."

She asked me about my life. I said it was OK. After hearing her sad story it felt wrong to talk about my happy marriage, our comfortable home and our lovely children.

"The Council have been very good to me," said Jean, "they found me a studio flat in one of these tower blocks. But it's very small and cramped. So I like to come and sit in here and read the magazines. Then I have a cigarette on the way back."

I looked at my watch.

"I ought to get going now," I said, "have to get back to Bristol."

"Er...just one thing," said Jean, "do you think you could possibly lend me a bit of money? It'll help me get back on my feet again. Say, fifty pounds?"

"Of course," I said.

I opened my handbag. Luckily I had my cheque book with me.

"Actually, could you make it seventy-five?" she asked.

"Sure."

"I'm sorry I had to ask you."

"That's quite all right," I said.

I finished writing out the cheque and handed it to her.

"Lucy – I really appreciate this," said Jean.

She reached across the table and put her hand on mine.

"Make sure you give me your address," she said.

I gave her one of my firm's cards.

"I must get on my way now," I insisted.

I stood up and put my handbag over my shoulder.

"All the best, Lucy," she said, "and thank you."

Three months later I received a note from Jean with a cheque for thirty-five pounds, and a promise to send the rest as soon as she could. But I never heard from her again.

TWENTY-FIVE

Greenlite

"Stop snoring!" said Deborah.

Her husband, Paul, turned over and went back to sleep. The slightest sound or bit of light could wake her up.

Paul had been in the construction business, but was now retired. Deborah was younger than him, and was still working as a school teacher, though in her last year. They lived by themselves. Unlike most people they still had a house, and a garden too. Paul had built it himself when they were first married.

They had two sons. Richard, the elder one, was a doctor and was married with three children. They lived in a very small flat. His wife, Veronica, had several times suggested that her parents-in-law should now move out.

"I just can't cope any more. In our place there's no room to swing a cat! And soon the kids will need their own bedrooms. But you've got this big house all to yourselves!"

Richard had shown his parents some catalogues of retirement homes.

"It's called 'Assisted Living'. You've got everything there: your own flat, a restaurant and social club, and round the clock medical help should you ever need it."

"I am not leaving my home," said Deborah firmly. "And what about my garden?"

She said she would only consider it if something happened to Paul. Then she would go off and live with her sister.

David, their younger son, was an electronics engineer and lived alone. He worked for an organization that built computers and designed the latest software.

It was three in the morning. Deborah couldn't sleep.

"Paul! Your greenlite's keeping me awake!"

He turned over and faced the bedroom wall.

Everyone middle-aged and older had a small light, green, yellow, or red, set permanently in their forehead. It was connected to a miniature computer embedded inside the head, powered by the brain's electrical energy. This was also linked to a heart monitor/pacemaker. The device measured the number of heartbeats and seconds of time elapsed since installation. It had been compulsorily fitted to everyone at the age of fourteen. Headgear could be worn, but the forehead light had to be clearly visible at all times, 24 hours a day, everywhere, even at home. And the police were there to strictly enforce it.

Normally a green light would show on the forehead. But when someone had reached the age of around 65 to 70, the computer, having calculated the allotted number of heartbeats and seconds, would, at a precise moment, switch the greenlite to yellow. And after six months the yellowlite turned to red. This signalled you had one month further to live. During the fourth and final week your redlite would flash on and off. You were then obliged to report to a disposal centre; if you failed to do so, you could be arrested on sight. At the centre your life would be terminated by an administering doctor.

The Greenlite system had become necessary due to the world's ever-increasing population. Fatal diseases had been eradicated, transport was entirely safe, there were no more wars, and hardly any crime.

One night Paul was woken up by Deborah crying.

"What's wrong, love?"

"Oh Paul, take a look at yourself," she sobbed.

He got out of bed, went into the bathroom, and looked in the mirror. His yellowlite was on.

To be told he had only seven months left to live was like being punched in the stomach. After a moment he went back into the bedroom to try to console Deborah.

Having finally managed to get a few hours' sleep Paul woke up next morning to reflect on his new situation. He knew he was old but hadn't expected his yellowlite to come on so soon. He had been born in a remote village in Poland before coming to England, and was unsure of his exact age, as his birth records had been lost in a fire.

People with yellowlites (known as 'Yellites') found that others (with greenlites) treated them quite differently. They would either express their sympathy or, being embarrassed, pretend not to notice. Yellites reacted to their bad news in different ways: some became withdrawn, others were quite open about it, often recalling their own lives and 'the old days'. Many spent their savings on cruises and holidays, to make the most of their last months. All sorts of counsellors and psychiatrists were available, and the Church was there to help. But, whatever, as a Yellite you were a marked man or woman.

"I'm going out for a walk," said Paul.

He wanted to be alone, to clear his head and think about it all.

"No – don't!" said Deborah.

"Why not?"

"I really don't want you to," she said, "and I've rung Richard and David. They're coming round straight away."

When they arrived they said nothing and just hugged their father.

"I'll go and make some coffee," said Deborah.

They were so overcome by emotion they found it hard to talk.

"I don't suppose there's anything we can do?" asked Deborah.

Actually, once your greenlite had changed to yellow there was very little you could do. If you tampered with it the redlite would come on automatically. Crude attempts, such as painting blue ink on the yellowlite to make it green were easily detected. You couldn't leave the country as all ports and airports were watched. And anyhow that was pointless, as the same system was used all over the world.

There were closed circuit television cameras on every street, and in all offices, shops, restaurants, hotels and blocks of flats. And there was the police, both uniformed and plain-clothed. (There was a rumour that the secret police were bald with a blue light on top of their heads, and wore a wig to hide it). They had helicopters, drones and spotter planes. There were CCTV cameras on all country roads, and in fields, woodlands, and on the beach. All public transport had them and they were even fitted to your own car. And if you just hid at home, your neighbours might well call the police, as they had a network of informers to report any behaviour that appeared irregular.

"What about the Quota?" asked David.

"We couldn't possibly afford it," said Deborah with a bitter laugh.

The Government had started a scheme in which billionaires, for a large fee, could have their yellowlites reset to green for a time. Then there were 'Exemptions' for the top politicians, actors, business leaders and scientists. And 'Extensions' for athletes and sportspeople to compensate for their hearts beating faster.

"Well there's still the Lottery!" said David sarcastically.

Lottery winners could also be reset to green.

"One chance in a hundred billion," said Deborah.

"I don't know what to say. I suppose you'll just have to kind of accept it," said Richard.

"Yes," said Paul.

"Dad, I'm really sorry."

Richard kissed his mother, and put on his coat and left. They heard the front door close. After a moment Paul spoke.

"I think I'll go and take that walk now."

"No, Dad, don't go out!" said David, "I've got an idea."

Richard and David were in their late thirties. There were no lights on their foreheads. Those in their age group and younger came under a newer system: WCC (Wireless Cardiac Control). They were known as 'Radioheads'. The computer in your head, by means of a small aerial, was in constant radio contact with a control centre, and this counted the seconds and heartbeats. At times equivalent to the lights changing colour in the earlier system, the control centre would transmit a voice message to a small receiver in your inner ear warning you how long you had left. And if, by the end of your last week, you had still not reported to a disposal centre, a radio signal would be sent to your monitor/pacemaker causing a fatal heart attack.

David said he knew someone in a WCC installation centre. They also repaired forehead lights. He would try to obtain a copy of the light system's wiring diagram, and with his own knowledge of electronics, reset his father's yellowlite back to green.

"You'll have to stay indoors for the time being so that no one sees your yellowlite," he said, "Mum will tell everyone you're ill."

Three days later David was back. He had gained access to the installation centre's secure data and had downloaded the wiring diagram. To reset the light was far easier than he had thought. You simply had to remove it temporarily from the forehead, isolate the anti-tampering device, and enter a new code into the computer down the wire to it from the light socket.

He had persuaded Richard to help him remove Paul's light from his forehead and then refit it. As this involved surgery it needed a doctor. A makeshift operating theatre was set up in the sitting room. Only a local anaesthetic was necessary. After just an hour their father's greenlite was back on.

Paul was now able to get on with his life. But things, however, didn't quite feel the same. He realized how much he had taken life for granted before. He became more pensive. Then one of his friends crossed to yellow; this made him feel guilty. And Deborah was now somehow quieter, sadder and more distant.

One day he went for a long walk. It took him past a church. He heard the singing of hymns. He opened the door. Inside was a sea of red and yellow lights. He stayed for a while. In the sermon the Vicar said one should be thankful for the life one had had, and prepare for the next world. Paul was fully aware that the Church cooperated with the Government, and that many priests were police informers. Then he realized he was the only Greenlite in there. He felt conspicuous and left the church quietly.

About a month later the telephone rang. It was David.

"Can I pop round and see you, Dad?"

"Sure. That would be great."

Deborah opened the door. She knew at once that something was wrong.

David said that he had entered the wrong code into Paul's computer. When it had been installed, years ago, an earlier model was in use. It had then been replaced by a newer series (until superseded by WCC). David had mistakenly used the code for the later computer, and this was not compatible with Paul's anti-tampering device.

"I'm sorry, Dad, but we'll have to take out the computer and completely reprogramme it," he said.

Paul couldn't bear the idea of undergoing the operation all over again.

"Yes, but it seems all right to me. My greenlite's on OK."

"I know that," said David, "and it's been fine up to now. But at any moment a fault could be detected. And that would trigger..."

"I am prepared to take that risk," said Paul.

Deborah began to cry.

But after a time David persuaded his father to go ahead with the repeat procedure. A week later the operating theatre was set up again. David arrived first, and then Richard, bringing Veronica to help out.

This time it took much longer, and a general anaesthetic was needed. They had to make an incision in the skull and remove the computer temporarily. And as they had to disturb a wound that had only recently healed, there was a greater risk of infection.

When the operation was finally over, Paul was left in

the hands of Deborah, who had previously had some nursing experience; she was to care for him when he came out of the anaesthetic. Although it was strictly illegal, his forehead was tightly bandaged. This was to all come off two weeks later.

When it was time, Deborah slowly unwound the bandage from Paul's head. To their horror they saw that his redlite was on! They phoned Richard and David, who came straight away.

After the first shock of seeing it for themselves, it was soon clear that there was nothing more they could do. They would just have to come to terms with it – like any other family.

"And do you know what?" said Paul, "I don't really care anymore."

He now had one month to live. To not only make a profound mental adjustment, but to also put his affairs in order. There was so little time! And Deborah made contact with her sister.

He took to going for long walks in the park or along the river, and avoided busy streets, shops and cafés. Everyone looked away when he passed, even Yellites. He would only see his family and closest friends.

One afternoon Paul found himself back at the church. He went inside. This time he did not feel out of place and stayed until the end of the service.

"And don't forget – the Evening Star Club is meeting in half an hour at the usual place," said the Vicar.

As Paul was leaving, a lady, a Yellite, went up to him at the church door.

"Why not come along? Come and meet some more of us. You are very welcome."

She wouldn't take no for an answer. Paul was ushered along with some other people to a building just down the street. They went through a door and down a passage to a large room at the back. It was nicely furnished, with tables and chairs, and a settee in the corner. At the other end of the room was a bar. Paul sat down at a table. Coffee was served, then a counsellor spoke for a while, with comforting words, for everyone to accept their fate calmly and philosophically.

Afterwards Paul went up to the bar. A tall man with white hair, a Yellite, offered to buy him a drink.

"Haven't seen you before," he said, "is this the first time you've been to one of our meetings?"

"Yes," said Paul.

"They're a great help, you know. We're all in the same boat."

"Except that for some of us it's a bit sooner," said Paul, pointing to his redlite.

"Yes indeed," nodded the man. "By the way, my name is John Harding."

After a while Paul began to relax, and bought the next round of drinks. Harding said that he was an accountant, but his main activity now was gardening, maintaining his property, and the odd game of golf.

"Have you got any children?" asked Paul.

"No, we never had any."

The conversation inevitably turned to what was to happen to all of them soon. Paul said it was unjust and unnatural.

"Yes, it is," agreed Harding.

Paul asked him if there was any way at all it could be avoided.

Harding said nothing for a moment. Then he looked quickly over his shoulder, and said quietly:

"I believe there is a way. But it is very dangerous."

Paul was surprised to hear this. At first Harding was reluctant to talk about it, but was finally persuaded to go into further detail.

"Go to the Galleon – the pub just off the High Street. Ask for Frank. He's often in there."

"I'll go there tomorrow," said Paul.

"Good luck."

"And what about you?" Paul asked.

"There's no point in it for me," said Harding.

"Why?"

"I had to take my wife to the Disposal Centre this morning. I've got nothing left to live for now."

Next day Paul went to the Galleon. It was almost empty.

"What are you having?" asked the girl behind the bar, frostily.

She had long black hair. Paul ordered a beer, then asked her if anyone called Frank ever came in.

"Not to my knowledge," said the girl. "The landlord's back tomorrow. Ask him."

He could sense her hostility. A black curl dropped over her greenlite and she flicked it away. He drank up and left.

He went back the following day, this time much later, in the evening. There were many more people in there now. He asked the landlord, who pointed to a man sitting at a table in the corner.

Frank had grey hair, a beard, and a yellowlite. He wore blue jeans and a jumper. He seemed unwilling to talk, until Paul mentioned Harding.

"Ah yes," he nodded.

Frank suggested they went somewhere more private. There was a restaurant nearby. It had an upstairs room. They sat down and ordered something. They were the only people in there.

After a while Frank became more open. He said he had never been prepared to accept it, and had been 'planning his escape' for years. He and his wife had set up a secret hiding place deep in the country. It had large stocks of everything.

"Enough to last a lifetime," he said proudly, "you name it, we've got it!"

He leant back and folded his arms. It had taken them a long time to find a safe hideout, and then to equip it gradually so as not to attract attention.

Suddenly his manner changed. He looked at Paul straight in the eyes.

"You're not a copper, are you?"

Paul was stunned.

"No - no, I'm not," he stammered.

"I don't suppose you are one," said Frank, looking at him carefully. "Anyhow, they say they're all Radioheads."

He told Paul to meet him outside the Galleon on Sunday morning, at ten o'clock.

By the time he got home it was already late. Deborah had been worried about him, though she knew he went for long walks by himself and was now quite erratic in his behaviour - understandable for someone in his situation. Paul, for his part, had decided not to tell her about the 'escape' he had in mind. She still had some years left as a Greenlite, and it was wrong to expose her to the dangers he would be facing.

On Sunday Paul met Frank outside the pub as arranged. They went straight to the station and got on a train. The journey lasted over an hour. Then they took a bus, getting off forty minutes later at a stop right in the countryside.

"Back of beyond, isn't it?" said Frank.

They walked down a track for about a kilometre, then came to a row of old sheds. Frank undid a padlock on one of them, and shone a torch on a large object inside.

"Good Lord! A petrol car!" said Paul. "Haven't seen one of those for years."

"I was a mechanic, or what was officially known as a 'motor engineer'," said Frank. "This is called an estate car. Very handy for carrying things around in."

They got in and Frank started the engine. The exhaust fumes made Paul's eyes water.

They continued along the track, in the car, for another two kilometres, until they reached a wood. Then Frank drove off into some bushes, stopped, and opened the back. There were two bicycles in there.

"Safest thing to have," he said, "no cameras fitted on these!"

They left the car covered with camouflage netting and pushed the bikes through the wood. When they reached open fields again there was a path, and they rode for a few kilometres until they reached a second wood. They hid the bikes behind some trees and walked through the thick undergrowth. They eventually arrived at a wooden hut carefully concealed with branches, leaves, and bundles of reeds. A grey-haired woman came out to meet them. She was a Yellite.

"This is my wife Angela," said Frank.

The hut was much larger than it appeared from the outside. It had two bedrooms, a living room with kitchen area, a bathroom and a storeroom. Frank and Angela had built it themselves over several years. To explain their frequent absence from home they had needed to invent a variety of reasons, such as holidays and business trips.

"I call it 'Creative Lying'," said Frank.

He showed Paul the storeroom. Inside were shelves stocked with all kinds of provisions: tinned food, sacks of rice, dried fruit, powdered milk, flour and biscuits. There were large containers of mineral water, and wine and beer too. In the corner was a cabinet full of medical supplies. They went into an outhouse, where there was an electric generator and a workshop with a complete set of tools.

"What do you think of these little toys?" asked Frank.

He reached up to a rack and took down a rifle, a shotgun, and a crossbow. Paul noticed that he had a tattoo on his wrist.

"Plenty of birds and rabbits around here," said Frank, "and also deer!"

Once, when he was sitting in a hide, a drone had flown right overhead, and he had been greatly tempted to shoot it down!

"How long have you got left?" asked Frank, in a more serious tone.

"Under two and a half weeks."

As soon as he had seen that his redlite was on, Paul had crossed off each day in his diary.

"Then I reckon your light will start flashing in about ten days' time," said Frank, "you must be back here before that."

It was the 15th of June. Paul got up early while Deborah was still asleep and packed a holdall. When she awoke he told her he was going into hiding. She wept bitterly. Then they kissed each other, and Paul said goodbye and left the house. He went to the railway station.

When he got off the train Frank was waiting for him on the platform. They finally reached the hut in the woods. This time there was another man there, a Redlite. He wore a cloth cap. His name was Jeff. Angela made tea.

Paul soon got used to the routine. There was wood to be cut, the hut to maintain, and all sorts of odd jobs to be done. Sometimes they hunted for game in the woods. There was also a small vegetable patch. Paul enjoyed working in it, though it made him think about Deborah in her garden at home.

In the evenings they would have a drink, then supper, and sometimes watch a film on Frank's old DVD player.

"No television," he said, "too easily traced."

Frank and Angela slept in one bedroom, Paul in the other, and Jeff on a sofa in the living room.

"Why do you always wear that cap?" asked Frank, one day.

"Dunno," answered Jeff, "habit, I suppose. Keeps me head warm!"

"Don't you ever take it off?"

"Well, I don't wear it in the shower!"

They all laughed.

After a few days Paul's redlite began to flash. Frank could sense his anxiety.

"Don't worry about that stupid thing!"

Angela went to the medicine cabinet and put a sticking plaster over Paul's light.

"I reckon we too will be crossing to red any day now," said Frank.

It was now the 24th of June, and the first really hot day of summer. They were all sitting outside the hut. Angela was in a sundress and Frank, for the first time, was wearing a T-shirt. Paul saw that his tattoos ran all the way up his arms.

"Had 'em done when I was in the Navy," said Frank.

He took off the T-shirt. His whole body was covered in tattoos. On the middle of his chest was the face of a blonde woman.

"Amazing what a pretty girl can do for you!" he said.

Angela smiled.

Frank put his finger on his chest and pressed the left eye of the face. His redlite turned to yellow. He pressed the right eye. The light now turned to green.

"They're my Christmas lights! And look!"

He put his hand on his head and lifted off his grey hair. It was a wig. He was bald underneath, and on top of his head was a blue light. Angela did the same. She too was bald with a blue light. And Jeff took off his cap.

Paul was handcuffed and they radioed for a helicopter.

"Did you really think you could beat the system?" asked Frank.

On his arrival at the Disposal Centre they entered in Paul's details at Reception. He was then taken down a corridor into a room and the door closed behind him. He was made to lie on a couch and a nurse gave him a sedative. The room was dimly lit and soft background music was playing. Strangely, he began to feel relaxed – in fact it was a rather pleasant sensation.

The door opened. In walked Richard, in a white coat.

"Dad, I am the Administering Doctor. I was able to get special permission for this."

He went over to a cabinet, took out a small bottle, and filled up a syringe.

"You see, I just had to get the house. For the sake of Veronica and the kids."

He took hold of Paul's arm, found a vein, and dabbed it with some alcohol and cotton wool.

"Now you won't feel a thing," he said as he injected him, "it's completely painless, I can assure you."

Richard drew a chair up to the couch, and sat down next to his father.

"David did manage to reset your yellowlite to green. But I had to get him onto my side, to perform that second operation. In other words, to sabotage everything."

Paul was now drifting away. He hardly cared what his son was saying. Excuses, excuses. Why did he have to go on talking? Couldn't he just let him die in peace?

"So we did a deal, David and I. He's having the ground floor and we're getting the rest of the house."

Paul slipped into oblivion.

"And I'm awfully sorry, Dad."

About the Author

Edward Hulton was born in 1945, and brought up in England and partly in Switzerland. He was educated at Eton, and Christ Church, Oxford, where he read English.

His interest in historic aircraft led to the building of a replica 1900s hang-glider in England, and the restoration of a Sunderland flying boat in the Caribbean, before it was flown to Europe.

He lived in France for fifteen years, in Paris and in the Loire Valley where he had a farm. He then spent many years in Gloucestershire. He now lives in London, and is married with two sons.